Pretty Little Girls
And
Other Men's Wives

Dodie Messer Meeks

Panther  **Creek Press**
Spring, Texas

1

Published by Panther Creek Press
SAN 253-8520
116 Tree Crest, P.B. Box 130233
Panther Creek Station
Spring, TX   77393-0233

Cover photo by Jan Horton
Scanning by Jonina Dickey
Cover design by Adam Murphy
The Woodlands, TX

Manufactured in the United States of America
Printed and bound by Data Duplicators, Inc.
Houston, TX

1 2 3 4 5 6 7 8 9 10

Library of Congress Cataloguing in Publication Data

Meeks, Dodie Messer

    Pretty little girls and other men's wives

    I. Title   II. Fiction

ISBN 0-96718361-6-7

This novel is dedicated to my grandchildren,
Jennifer and RandyThompson, in Dallas,
Kelley Dickey and Taylor Terrell, in Houston, and Marissa
Dickey, in Galveston. May they never meet villains such as
these, and if they do, may they give them short shrift.

The Stranger

A stranger came calling.
Blue lights in his eyes.
His cloak of white velvet
was quilted with lies.
Beaded with teardrops.
Embroidered with cries
as slippery as satin.
Sequined with sighs.

His codpiece and buckles
were fretted with gold.
His gloves were of eel skin
silver enscrolled
and he danced me and kissed me,
his blue eyes so bold
a fool could see clearly
the glimmer of cold.

A stranger came whistling
with a wild glinting grin
and a curl on his forehead
blacker than sin.
Black Irish he was
the wildest of men.
And he laughed like a pirate.
And I told him come in.

1

Sixteen-year-old Gregory Van Buren trotted across Broadway onto the circular drive figuring he'd climb the drain pipe to the slanted roof of the cupola next to his room and slide in the window like always, but something was going on. He slowed, rounded the oleanders nearest the street, and stopped, tightening up, listening. Cicadas shrilled in the leggy over ripe shrubbery. A siren cried from somewhere down on the Strand.

He heard it again: bursts of static in the clicking cicadas. Greg shambled a couple of steps, his pulse quickening. The insect rustles turned into syllables: "Fifty-six? Fifty-six? M.E. enroute, fifty-six."

Three Galveston police cruisers were up against the wide steps of the veranda, chattering quietly among themselves. Greg sprinted past them, swallowed a nervous belch, stopped to squeegee sweat from his brow. Man. Maybe the mean little drunken bastard woke up. Looked like he was sliding off the edge of the world. But maybe not. Maybe he shook it off.

Think, Greg told himself. He sucked in air, tried to hold it, to catch the crackling words. "Advise, thirteen fifty-four." And, "ten nine, your last. Lieutenant Rowland enroute your location."

Greg started up again, his legs rubbery, made it up the steps to the door, that had a rim of light along its edge. He yanked the door open and almost ran, head down, into a big cop. Greg stuck out a hand.

"Steady, there." The cop's chest felt like metal under the cloth.

Greg backed up, trying for a grin. "What's up?"

"You live here?" The cop ran a finger around the inside of his collar.

"Yes, sir," Greg said. "I'm Greg. Van Buren. What's going on?"

"Van Buren?" The cop had an anxious frown.

"Yeah," Greg said. "Yes, sir." He swallowed. "Please, what's the deal, here?" He introduced himself again, adding, "My mother's here somewhere. Cathy, my mom, will tell you—is she all right?"

The man stepped back and let him come in.

Cathy huddled on the living room sofa. She glanced at Greg and gazed past him, gulping, her fingers clawing at her upper arms. Her hair stuck to her face, the ends of it wet. Greg ran to her and slid down on one knee. He put his hand on her shoulder. "Mom?"

She groped for his hand. "Oh, God. I think he's dead. He's in the garage. He looks pink. How can he look so pink? His heart isn't beating."

Greg tried to get her to look at him. He brought a knuckle up and gently touched the discolored place under her eye. "You want some ice? That's starting to swell." She caught her upper lip in her teeth and shook her head. Her eyes squeezed shut. Damp wisps of hair along her cheek tangled in her wet eyelashes. She kept quaking. She opened her eyes but she still wouldn't look at him.

"He said he had to go somewhere with Cecil. He was in no condition to drive but he said he had to. I couldn't stop him. I tried to."

The cop shifted, glancing at the floor and the wall, looking at Greg, his eyes dark. Looked like he hated this. He walked out to the kitchen, his cop belt clinking, and came trudging back with a glass of water that he offered to Greg. When Greg shook his head, the cop turned to Cathy and stopped, like he couldn't bring himself to offer her the glass. He started to put it down, glanced at the polished surfaces of the coffee table and the inlaid chess table, and awkwardly passed it from one hand to the other.

Greg got up and took it from him and set it on the chess table.

The cop cleared his throat. "The techs are trying. Those guys don't quit. Thing is, your daddy seems to be—"

"He's not my dad," Greg said, louder than he meant to. He took a breath and started over. "Mr. Benjamin is my stepfather."

The cop's chin came up. "That so? Well. The techs are doing their best." After a pause he added, "The lieutenant will be coming in any time now. Lieutenant Rowland. He'll talk to you."

Greg moved to his mom's side again. He had to bring her out of this, get her to quit looking so dazed and crazy. "Hey," he said, keeping his voice down. "Look at me, okay?"

She pulled away, her hands squeezing her arms, moving to a kind of inner tremor. "I couldn't stop him," she said. "I couldn't stop him. He went staggering out to the car."

"Mom? Listen to me. You're going to be all right." He hated how his voice sounded but it seemed to get through to her. She squinted at him.

"I keep hearing noises. Like leaves." She shook her head. "It's like my head is full of leaves." The whites of her eyes shone. "Oh, God, Greggy, now what are we going to do?"

Greg swallowed. He stood up, forcing himself to look around. Not at the cop. At the floor, the pattern of wood in the parquet, the lights flashing across the tall windows between the drapes. The surface of water in the glass on the chess table caught the lights of the chandelier and shimmered, disturbed by the lazy swing of the ceiling fan. The glass had Tod's monogram on it. The cop had gotten one of Tod's gold-rimmed, fancy old fashioned glasses, the sweating glass now making a ring on Tod's ivory and teak chess table. Little big man would have a raving royal fit.

No. He won't. Ever.

That hit him and sank in. The room tilted. Greg pulled his chin in, made himself look down and grab a breath. He got balanced, focused on the chess pieces on the table. Somebody must have bumped into the chess table or maybe the set got left with the king mated. The black king was lying on his side, rolled up against the white queen's knight and a pawn.

Yeah. Check mate.

Greg looked down at the set for a minute before he picked up the pieces and set them in place, thinking queen on her color, white queen on the white, keeping his face turned down, looking away from his mother and the big cop. When it hit him again, the whole thing, his stomach lurched. He was starting to get about halfway sick to his stomach as he realized, really let himself see, how fast everything would be different, how it would be a whole different game from now on.

*****

2

Tod Benjamin happened to be married to Gregory's mom, Cathy, but that didn't make him anybody's father, even if Cathy did meet him at a Parents Without Partners meeting. The way Greg saw it, Parents Without Partners must not screen people.

Old Toddy might have fairly regular features but no way did he remotely resemble Greg's real father, Joe: tall, like Greg, and blonde, a big Dutchman who worked on boats. A cabinet maker.

All Greg could remember of his dad was a time when something went wrong with the car and they ended up waiting around in this field beside a country road. His father put a soup can on a post so they could take turns pitching rocks at it. When Greg's rock knocked the can off, his dad grabbed him up under the arms and tossed him up and swung him around and laughed and called him a Campbell's kid.

Good thing the old man didn't have a fit about the car or spend that whole time yelling at his little kid to shut up and get in the back seat, because that was all that was left of him as far as Greg was concerned. Just that little film clip.

Greg's mom said Greg was in the family station wagon when his father died, but Greg couldn't call that back. His mother told him about it. She'd gone into Kroger's, leaving Greg and his dad in the car. When she came out she got mad because nobody made any attempt to help her get the back door open or get the groceries into the car. The reason nobody helped her was because Greg's dad was dead. There'd been a weak place in an artery, an aneurysm, like a thin place in a balloon, that popped and he died. Twenty-eight years old. Supposed to be in top condition. Died at the wheel of a Chevrolet station wagon parked in a Kroger's parking lot.

Greg was four then; Cathy, twenty-four. She had hair long enough to sit on back then too, but the snaps showed her with it up in a braid on top of her head because Joe, Greg's father, liked it that way. That was the way his mother and his aunts wore their hair, all of them big bosomy women.

His dad's whole name on the death certificate read "Johannes Jan Van Buren" of Holland, Michigan, in Ottawa County.

He played the cello, too. Greg liked thinking about that. Must have been really nice for Cathy. She didn't have such a great life, actually. After his dad died she could hardly talk for a while. Maybe that's when the stuttering started. When Greg caught on to how much it still hurt her to talk about all that he quit asking about it.

Greg met Tod Benjamin pretty near his fifteenth birthday, the first week of one of the hottest Junes in Houston history. Greg came home to find this stranger sitting in his, Greg's, recliner, sweating up a storm. The house Greg and Cathy lived in then had window units rattling away in the living room and bedroom windows but they didn't cool much. The ceiling fan didn't do much, either, just moved the leaves of the schefflera around.

Cathy had a lot of plants in that high-ceilinged room, most of them oversized; two corn plants, yuccas, a couple of scheffeleras about eight feet tall, a wild fig, a whole mess of hanging pots; spider plants, begonias, every ivy known to mankind. A killer asparagus fern spread fourteen feet from ceiling to floor with mean, sharp thorned tendrils that could leave a mark on your face if you got on the wrong side of the thing. All that greenery had to be making the atmosphere pretty healthy but it didn't do a thing about the heat, that day. Little round Tod Benjamin was dissolving.

Greg let himself in, leaned his cello in the corner of the living room and slid an armload of books to the floor. He didn't think he'd been especially quiet but he must have been, because here was this nappy-haired, heavy-eyebrowed pugnacious little guy looking at him, startled, wrinkling up the *Chronicle*. He left a patch of sweat shining on the back of the chair when he leaned forward.

"I sneak up on you?" Greg asked. "Sorry about that."

The little guy grunted. Greg introduced himself. The little guy said his name: Tod Benjamin. Then he sat there with this big sappy smile, sweat glistening in the wrinkles around his eyes, saying nice place you've got here and you must be your pretty mama's pride and joy, son, my, my, and a bunch of garbage like that, embarrassing both of them. The nerd really liked the sound of his own voice.

After he'd had all he could handle of that, Greg excused himself, saying he had to go wash up. He rapped on the door to Cathy's room, went in, and said, "Gee, Mom. Where'd you find the dwarf?"

She was fixing her face. "So how's the science project?"

"I'm thinking of scrapping it and using your friend, a real live--"

"Greg." Cathy blotted her lipstick. "Quit. Now."

"Dwarf," Greg said. "Like, the attack of the munchkins."

"Lay off. You don't get to pick on my date."

He went all over amazement. "That's a date? They come that old?"

She stopped fumbling in the stuff on her vanity to lay a look on him. "He's g-g-gorgeous. Absolutely gorgeous. And he's exactly the right age."

"Gorgeous?" Greg clutched his throat.

"Eyes like Paul Newman. Who happens to be very mature also. And classic features. He's the most gorgeous man I've ever--"

"You're kidding, right?"

"Could be Paul Newman's b-b-brother," Cathy said.

"Are we taking about the same guy here? I mean, have you taken a good long look at this brillo-haired little--"

"His hair is black and will you keep your voice down?"

"Down," he growled. "He looks like a cold germ."

"Could we go into his shortcomings some other--oh I can't believe I said that," she said. "Come on, it's not that funny. Oh, darnmit. Just look at me. My darned hair is too thick, it's so thick, it keeps slipping. He's got to be dying in there." She had about eight combs in her hair but she shoved in another one. "He's not so little. It's just that we're so d-darned b-big."

"Now there is real Cathy logic for you," Greg said. "How about if I find out if Ginger's doing anything tonight? She's pretty short. On the other hand, forget it. My friends draw the line at freaks."

She was holding a bobby pin with her teeth. "Did you make a big thing of looking down on Mr. Benjamin?" she said, around it.

"No, I'll leave that to you. I just dropped to my knees and genuflected so we could look at each other eye-to-eye, because the guy never hoisted his butt out of my chair, if you want to know."

She yanked the little side mirrors of her vanity forward and peered at herself, waving dismissal. "Go give the man a drink."

"In a regular-sized glass?"

He made it out of there before she could wing the brush at him and went into the living room to announce that Cathy said she was almost ready which would have to mean that anybody waiting for her probably would have time to grow moss on his north side.

The man looked like he'd been eavesdropping. He had a kind of a narrow intent look, chin out, which he held, for a minute there, before he got the toothpaste smile back.

"Mom wants me to get you something. How about a Coke?"

Old Toddy wanted scotch, which they didn't have.

"Well, how are you fixed for a drop of gin?" he said. "Not too early in the season for a tonic, is it? Or whatever's cold."

Greg had to move a chair to get to the gin, on the back top shelf of the pantry. While he was dusting it off and getting out a glass, the old guy worked up a regular running monologue, barking and grunting and whispering all by himself, pacing around the living room, wanting to know, among other things, all about the chess game underway on the table. "Your dad and mother play chess?"

"Mother plays at it," Greg said. "She's got four good openers." The top of the gin bottle acted like it might be rusted on. "But that game is between me and Virginia Gingold. Ginger. She's pretty good. Beats the computer, sometimes. She's taught me a lot."

"Aha, a girl friend, eh?"

"Not really. A friend who happens to be a girl."

"Don't know as I've ever had one of those," the man said, chuckle, chuckle. "This is a pretty ornate little set. How can you tell which one is the king? Oh, got to be this one. It's the tallest. Chinese, eh? Wonderful what those folks can do with this molded stuff. Looks almost like ivory."

"Well, yeah." Greg got the bottle open. Found a couple of limes. While he was working some juice out of them, he said, "That set is ivory. My dad got it. Came from India."

He broke out some cubes, during which it sounded as if the old guy stayed wound up out there, all by himself. Greg had to lean into the serving window, near the sink, to hear him. He was doing that, twisting his head around so he could see into the front room, meaning to ask the man to repeat something, when he heard a click and there's the little guy holding up the chess king in the flame of his lighter. Flaming away at it. Giving it the old test by fire, there, to check its ivoryness. Flicking his Bic.

Greg bumped his head getting it back into the kitchen.

"So," the guy said, "your dad got this set. He a pretty good player? You say he's in India?"

Greg started to answer that but he got distracted. He was coming into the room with the man's drink and what he walked in on was the guy searing the tip right off a branch of Cathy's biggest hanging plant, her asparagus fern. It didn't look like he was testing his lighter or anything. That lighter had to be a butane pipe lighter. A regular flame-thrower.

The guy looked over at Greg like, well, there's this lighter, see, and burning up a little foliage seems like something to do here.

Greg meant to ignore it but he couldn't. Something about the way the man kept looking him over with his chin up, glancing around, running his tongue over his teeth, making sucking noises like he's trying to reach a verdict and Greg and his chess set and his whole crazy living room with the torn place on the sofa and the rattling air conditioner and maybe the whole house couldn't possibly measure up, really got to him. He heard himself saying, "Gee, you know what? Mom happens to love that chess set and that plant. We've had that particular fern through about five different moves and she makes me hold the thing on my lap every time. Is that something? I swear, she talks to it. Calls it her green baby."

"Hmm," Tod said. "That so, son?" his shiny little blue eyes narrow in his shiny little red face.

Then, weird thing, he got all effusively grateful for the drink. "Well, young fella,"—chuckle, chuckle— "you're a pretty fair bartender. I'll bet you're a champion chess player, too. Your mother tells me you play the cello, that so? Now that's a real nice thing." You had to be sorry for him.

"Pretty unusual instrument. Got a lot of competition?" Chuckle, chuckle. "Guess not. Not too many cello players, eh? Of course, that's got to be anything you can count on to make a living...."

Greg gave up. They sat, not looking at each other. The clock on the wall wheezed along. The ceiling fan droned and whuffed. A beetle got caught trying to fly through a window pane.

Cathy finally came out in a cloud of Christmas present perfume that her boss's wife, Chub, had given her. Like she took a bath in it. With her hair pulled up in back, and little clots on her eyelashes.

Before she and Gorgeous took off, the old doofus managed to disgrace himself one final time by punching at Greg's shoulder and flashing this big man-to-man grin, like they'd established this terrific rapport. "See you later, alligator."

Mom's scanner had to be shot, or some damn thing. Or this jerk had some way to put all shit scanners out of commission. And she wasn't the only one. Her friends developed a blind spot, when she started introducing the old guy around. It made Greg nuts.

Ginger had a theory. "It's some kind of wacky protectiveness. People seem to feel that way about your mom. Protective. She's so soft. And...good. Your mom's a really good person. Maybe her friends are glad to see somebody make a fuss over her. A man, I mean. Like, whether you can see it or not, Tod really is handsome. He's got these Irish eyes and the profile and all. So how often does that happen, that somebody who looks like that makes a big fuss over your mom?"

"What are we talking about, here?" Greg demanded.

"Well, your mother happens to be this really nice person and she's got great coloring—I happen to be partial to red hair—but she isn't exactly very, well, she's not what you could call, you know." She looked uncomfortable. "Well, she isn't."

"'She isn't?' Isn't what?"

"Well, she's not exactly little, for one thing. She's not...you know. She's nice. A nice round motherly mother. Got this nice round look." Ginger twisted her hair. "What my mom calls 'churchy.'"

"Churchy? What the hell is *churchy*? I don't get it." He did, though. "You burn me up." He almost let her have it: So how would you like me to let you in on how everybody goes around saying all kinds of things about your hot mom with that leather and all but he didn't. But then he looked at Ginger and realized that he might as well have. She reddened and gave him a shove. "Watch yourself."

"Why don't you think before you open your big mouth?"

Ginger went wide-eyed. "Face it. I pretty well got a handle on all that. Hey, look. What we've got here is opposite problems, okay? You want to call my mom churchy? Feel free." She put her hand on his. "Relax. How am I supposed to know you want your mom to be this person who lights men's fires? Anyway, she probably can. If she wants to. Takes all the combs out of her hair and all the rest of it. You know." She looked over her shoulder and flipped her hair.

"You know what?" He couldn't help himself. "I can see why your mom slaps you. It's not just the drinking. You're such a pain in the—"

"Yeah. Right." She went pale beneath her freckles and shoved him. "Your big problem—you want to know what your problem is? You're jealous, know that? Of your own mom. Is that sick, or what? Get a grip."

Greg headed for the door. "I'm outa here."

"Hey, I happened to be trying to spare your feelings, friend, but that has got to be the truth. Your mom's built like a cello. A big cello," Ginger yelled at him. "If you want to know."

"That would be the bass, right?"

"Yeah, right. You pedantic poop."

Greg smiled and saluted and got out of there.

Not that he and Ginger didn't end up yelling at each other pretty often, anyway, but what got to him was that this little nappy-haired, not very interesting guy, who didn't even know enough to laugh at Cathy's little jokes or anything else, and who smoked, he even smoked cigars, could turn everybody in sight into eight kinds of giggling idiots. It got tougher and tougher to watch. Kind of made you want to go look for a pod in the back yard or something.

One thing, though: Greg kept feeling like he had no business getting in his mom's way too much. He didn't want to see her heading into a lonely old age. After all, he wouldn't be around too much longer, just a few more years, probably. Then he'd be gone and where would she be? How would a few more years look to somebody already past middle age?

Just the same, he did wish, then and later—oh, emphatically, passionately, later—Greg wished to hell that he'd done something, said something, gotten a Polaroid shot, maybe, of old Toddy flaming that asparagus fern, that first night. Shown her, right off the bat.

What was he supposed to say? "Hey, mom. The guy's a plant abuser."

*****

3

That next Saturday Greg woke up to find Cathy in the living room coo ing into the phone. He yawned, walked over in front of her, stuck his finger down his throat and made retching motions until she went pink and waved him off.

"What's with all the flowers?" Greg said, sniffing. "Smells like a funeral in here."

"I'm on the phone," she hissed. She went back to the phone, with an open-mouthed smile. "Gardenias. Roses. Carnations," she said, into the receiver.

"I think I'm getting asthma if you want to know," Greg said. "Your boyfriend isn't very big on restraint, is he?"

"Yes," Cathy breathed into the phone. "Oh, yes." And, to Greg, "Do you mind?"

Greg got out of there. He went over to Ginger's house. Ginger's place smelled like dog but at least a person could breathe there.

The next day, Sunday, he came home early from walking out of a Kevin Costner movie with Scot and Jen and Randy and thank God he didn't take anybody home with him because when he unlocked the door the house smelled like burned sugar and there's his boom box in the kitchen and there they are in there, Little Big Man and Cathy, slow dancing. With Little Big Man's head on *her* shoulder.

They didn't even quit dancing. Looked like Tod wouldn't let go. "We got to talking about fudge and decided to make some," Cathy said, babble gabble. "My, you're early, didn't you like the movie?"

"Crazy about it," Greg said. "So where's the fudge?"

"It sort of got scorched." She waved at the sink. "I might have ruined another pan." She giggled.

Greg said a hasty excuse me and went to hole up in his room.

When the guy finally went home, Greg came out and tried to get Cathy to promise, solemnly vow that she would not ever, under any circumstances, let Ginger or Scotty or anybody see her boyfriend putting his head on her shoulder because if that happened he would definitely have to leave town. She just smiled so hard her eyes squeezed practically shut.

The Saturday that Greg tore up his hand, the whole house stank like a funeral again. That's what Greg woke up to, the gardenias and Cathy on the phone again, with this big box of Gilbert's Nuts and Fruits in her lap, not making breakfast or anything, just giggling with chocolate smeared on the corner of her mouth.

"You can hardly breathe in here," Greg said. "Can't you stick some of those vases out on the patio?"

Cathy said, "I'll have to let you go, now," into the phone and turned to look at him. "You want oatmeal or eggs?"

"I had in mind some nice candy," he said. "How do you suppose he comes up with these really, really imaginative ideas? I'll bet that's never been done before, has it? I mean, in the history of the world. Man, he has to be the most original, most creative—"

"Oh, put a sock in it," she said happily. "Far as I'm concerned, Tod is an original. Nothing ordinary about him. Besides, have you ever noticed any flowers taking up a lot of space around here much before? And lay off the candy, if you disapprove of it so much."

"I just kind of like being able to breathe, is all," he muttered. "I think the whole situation is making me have, like, terminal asthma." He wheezed. "It really bites."

"I beg your pardon?"

"Sucks, then. It sucks."

"We do not talk that way, Gregory."

"I have been trying to talk to you every way I can think of, Mom, and you are not getting the message. Are you *in* there?" He tried to rap her on the brow but she ducked out of reach.

When she went into the kitchen and started banging pans around, Greg followed her, complaining, "You know what? That, right there, is why all our pans are dented."

"They're dented because they're cheap," she said. "You want bacon? I don't think I do."

He got out the bacon. She put it back. "What?" he said. "I'll fix it."

She pulled out a pan out and put some water in it. "Oatmeal, I think," she said. "Fiber. And get out the eggs."

The egg carton felt really light. "No eggs," he said. "Somebody stuck the empty carton back in the fridge, see what I mean? Nobody's home around here."

She turned off the stove and looked at him with her mouth pulling in at the corners. "Now, you listen to me," she said, the mouth practically disappearing and her eyebrows coming down. "We might be getting into something pretty basic here. No, I mean it, Greg. I have sensed a certain antipathy around here but you don't have to be exactly madly in love with everybody I happen to like. I mean, that is not mandatory. I can't stand some of your friends, as you know. Scotty, for instance. Scotty with the dirty T-shirt and the dirty vest and the dirty tuxedo jacket, sometimes seems unprepossessing. Have I mentioned that?"

He went deliberately round-eyed and let his mouth drop open. "How'd poor old Scot get into this?" She could be so dumb, she made his teeth ache. Scotty happened to have a few problems, true, since his old man was on a respirator and his big brother, the Exterminator, was sort of in charge over at their house, but what did that have to do with anything? But the thing was, with Mom, you couldn't win. She'd come at you from some angle that made sense only to her and end up with the buttonhole mouth thing.

"Are you hungry or not?" she snapped. She dumped oatmeal into boiling water. "I am cooking cereal."

Greg took a deep breath and said the Lord's prayer and about half of the alphabet to himself and decided to try another tack. "So tell me you enjoy riding in the guy's car? The way he guns it and swerves around and honks like a damn madman—"

"Next time, stay home," she said. "He didn't have to invite you along. Big mistake."

"What I'm getting at is how you have to be terrified out of your skull every time you get in his big-assed Caddy," Greg said, trying for patience. "You get about half catatonic with Pat or Chub or Hetty Bach. You're, like, clawing at the overhead half the time. So tell me you aren't terrified with nappy head, just tell me that. Jesus wept."

"Greg. We do not blaspheme."

"But we do correct my language. And we will not listen, right? The man is a creep, Mom. So he likes flowers, big deal. He could be dangerous, and I don't mean just the driving thing. He could turn out to be a serial murderer. He's obviously stunted." He got his voice under control. "You keep saying speeding is immoral."

"Immoral?" Cathy bit her upper lip and quit looking so mad. She looked almost...dreamy.

When Greg snorted, she had the grace to blush. "Oh, honey, let's knock it off. I have several friends who think Tod is perfectly charming. And they think you are entirely too outspoken."

"Hey—! I'm a shrinking violet, I am one of the world's shy people, compared to that—"

"And Tod has not had an accident in years and years."

"Well, how wonderful. Did he like *tell* you that, or what?"

"You don't have any idea how annoying that 'how wonderful,' can be," she said. "*Like.*" She kept deliberately not getting the concept. It drove him nuts.

"It's not just the driving. As we both know, the guy's a maniac but that's not all of what I'm son-o-a-bitching trying to get across here—"

"You. Watch. Your. Mouth." She whirled so fast that her hair whipped across her face. She yanked it back. "That's enough. That's just enough."

And now, of course, she was going into full retreat, marching out of the room, totally beyond reason. He never would be able to make her understand. "Mom? Give me another minute, okay? Because this is pretty basic. If you want to sort of concentrate on the driving thing, let's do that. Basically, for one thing, I don't want you riding around with a maniac who drives like that. Just tell me I'm wrong, there. Tell me you are perfectly happy with that. Just say that much, honestly, and I'll give up."

She sighed, turned around, came back. "Okay, I'm not. Not particularly. But Tod is...he's very skillful. There was a president of the United States who used to drive a Cadillac all over Texas just like that, and nobody called President Johnson a psychopath. Except maybe some Yankee politicians."

"I see. I happen to be totally wrong. The guy is totally charming and he's an excellent driver and everybody loves him. When he's sober." It was a shot in the dark, but it touched a nerve.

"I've had a drink or two with Tod and yes, he is very charming. Very. My gosh, Greg. I know what an alcoholic looks like. This is not the first man I have ever gone out with."

"Yeah, well, I know you're not certifiable but you're either being really thick or there is something else working here that I can't get a grip on," he said. "So explain it to me, okay? I mean, what, exactly, is the big appeal deal?"

"The appeal deal? I happen to like this man and he—" She blushed all the way to her hairline. "—he really likes me, and he knows how to like a person. If it's any of your business. And speaking of business, he happens to be very successful. I realize you think his having prosthetic laboratories is simply hilarious, but somebody has to supply teeth to...to dentists and people. There's a real need. And he, well, Tod is bright, he's funny, he dances beautifully, he's sweet and generous and sweet."

"Sweet?" Greg let his lower jaw fall open. "He's sweet?"

"You're straying off the reservation," she said. "Some things are none of your business." She had her chin out. "And that's that."

She would have walked out of the room then but Greg reached out and grabbed her arm. "Sweetly rich, you mean? Is that it? I mean, because if it is, I don't believe it. Since when is that a big deal? I mean, he's got this big-assed car that nobody but a pimp or a hustler would drive and—"

"Greg. Your language—"

"If that's it, I think that is just disgusting as hell, Mother. I do. Way down deep in his wallet he's a sweet guy, that it? The King of False Teeth? Doesn't *any*thing about that strike you as weird? Don't you keep sort of seeing all these snapping teeth when he puts his head on your shoulder?"

She sat down, deflated but mad, practically shooting sparks. "Oh, if you could see your sneer. Quit. Tod happens to think you may have problems, if you want to know. And he might be right."

"*Moi?*"

"For one thing, he thinks you just might be resentful of anybody who might, well, who might care too much for me."

Greg looked at her.

"Anyone who wants to have any kind of a relationship or whatever," she said.

"Relationship? Is that like he wants to be some kind of relative or something? Well, did you tell him how nuts that is? Because it is." He swallowed. "Problems? I've got problems? Like, he thinks I'm some kind of mama's boy? Because if you're sitting around listening to that, well, yeah, I guess I've got a real problem there because that sounds pretty sick to me. The guy's got to be running out of things to talk about."

"It may not be all that sick." She couldn't look him in the eye. Then she made it worse. "We wouldn't exactly know it, would we? It might even be sort of true. In a way. I've gotten so I depend on you so, and, I don't know."

"So the sicko's got you convinced that I'm a sicko."

"He isn't, you know," she said. "He's a very sweet, gentle, lovable man. And, and lonely. He's lonely, too. Was, I mean. And he happens to be a respectable business man. He's a...a Rotarian."

"A sweet, lovable Rotarian?"

It cracked him up. Her, too. She exploded into frantic giggles. For a minute, he thought she might start crying but she looked up and gasped and lapsed into this helpless fit and all of a sudden Greg couldn't stand it.

"I can't take much more of the guy, Mom. No kidding." There was a loud kind of hiccough in the air between them that turned into a sob and Greg started in shaking and swallowing another sob, practically bawling out loud. If he'd had any warning, he would have run like a rabbit. Gotten as far as the bathroom, at least.

It stopped her in her tracks. She went round-eyed and clapped a hand over her mouth.

He went and got a Kleenex out of the bathroom and blew his nose and washed his face. When he came out he walked past her, brushed her hand off his arm and walked out of the house, leaving her with that worried, shocked Cathy look that she did so well.

With the buttonhole mouth.

Later, walking around outside, he got to where he could let himself sort things out. What it was had to be the idea of the two of them sitting around holding hands and making out and stuff and taking him all apart. Boy. That landed right in the middle of his gut. Partly because it indicated how the guy was moving in, fast. No way to fight it. Just coming right on, moving right in on both of them like some kind of tank plowing across houses and trees and buildings, whatever got in his way.

And Greg had to be the only one could see it. Cathy sure as hell couldn't see anything, dithering around in some kind of fugue, trailing her fingertips across the table, looking at herself in the hall mirror like walking in her sleep.

The thing kept riding around in the back of his head. He'd be trying to think, going over his math or practicing, sawing away at Beethoven, or just sitting around with Scot listening to the Eagles, and there it would be, like a cold damn toothache riding around in the back of his brain.

Boy. Even practicing didn't drown it out.

He'd be working away and flash on what Ginger said one time about how Cathy might look if she took the pins out of her hair and there she'd be, Mom, taking all the pins out of her hair and letting it fall around her shoulders and Tod would be there, Little Big Man, his fingers pawing away at her.

It made like a cramp. Like something tearing loose in his belly.

It couldn't be the money. He knew better than that. That had to be a cheap shot.

What, then? Tod sure as hell couldn't be sexy. Weird little dwarf had wiry black hair growing out of his ears. Had these yellow teeth, from the cigars. Yellow fingers, too.

Try not to think about it, Greg told himself.

Thinking about it and not thinking what he was doing kept wrecking Greg's world, though. Like the Saturday he tore up his hand. He was at the church, Clean Up Day, July 29th, he and Scotty and four other guys, over at Sagemont Presbyterian, on Sabo Road. They were hacking away at bushes and vines, just about through and Greg just finished saying, "Man, this is the hand I really am gonna need for my recital," when a piece of wire flipped up and ripped into the index finger on his left hand.

They had to take him over to Humana, to the ER, to get four stitches. The worst part: anesthetizing it. The whole finger sort of bunched up and went white under the needle. Made all these white wrinkles this needle had to shove through. Scotty went green and teetered out of the room.

Big deal. Greg snickered at him on the way home. But Scotty replayed the whole bit for Cathy and she went white around the gills. And then Scotty said, "Well, I got to go. See you, maestro," and it hit Greg about the recital coming up with those two notes five tones apart in the Debussy. Knocked the air out of him. Man. He had to sit down and think.

Concentrate.

No way could he span those notes with a crazy bandage on his main finger. Those fifths were no cinch even with all his fingers in perfect shape.

Man, Mom freaked. She thought he had to be agonizing about the stitches. Suffering all this agony. Well, it hurt like a son-of-a- gun when the stuff started wearing off.

She doled out the stuff for pain from the doctor and said, "Now, you're not going anywhere and neither am I, son."

So after a while he doped out what he could do about the recital and called Mrs. Baron so she could fix up the program before she took it to the printer. "How about I substitute Hayden for the Debussy?" Old Hayden never was as carried away with impossible fifths.

"Oh, darling, how clever," old Baron goes, but she bawled him out. "Cellists aren't yard men," she said. She didn't care that it happened at a church.

Cathy laughed at his imitation of Mrs. Baron, but she was pretty shook up. That night she canceled dinner with Tod so she could stick around. When it started to get dark, Greg limbered up the hand, some. Did the Hayden for her, running over parts of it, sloppy as hell, but she didn't care. Everything felt like it used to be. While Greg was working over the Hayden and a fairly easy Bach minuet she took time out from what she had going in the kitchen to lean into the living room to listen. "Ach." She pretended to sniffle. "Ach, du! Sudge luffliness. I could yust veep," the way she always did. And Greg rolled his eyes at her and there was even this storm that cut the power for a while, while they were eating their eggs in toast boxes so Cathy got the candles out. The whole thing was like when they used to have trouble with the electric bill sometimes.

It was great. Nobody talked about little big man.

The next night wasn't all that terrific, though. Greg made the mistake of going with Ginger to see Meryl Streep, which he thought was going to be such a good idea since Meryl Streep was one of the women Ginger ought to be influenced by. Terrific poise and all. Since Ginger was driving, maybe he should have been more tactful about the poise thing. Not been so emphatic about how he wanted somebody like Meryl Streep to be the mother of his children. Old Ginger let out all the stops. "Streep-schmeep," she goes. "I'm not gonna mother anybody's children. Especially not anybody who freaks if he thinks Mama might have a boyfriend."

She got so mad she drove straight over to the house and took off while Greg was still saying good night.

Then, when he turned around, there was this weird guy standing out in front of the house like he was maybe trying to see into the front windows. Just standing there, out on the walk, in the dark, the only light being the street light half a block up and a patchy place in the clouds running across the night sky. Greg got practically on top of him before he realized the guy was just going to stand there like some kind of a statue.

Greg walked closer—not too close—took a deep breath and asked the man if he was looking for somebody. The guy jumped, startled, whirled around with his mouth open and stood there, not making a sound. Staring up at Greg with a strand of spittle working its way down his lower lip. He didn't move a muscle.

"You lost or what?" Greg asked. It seemed like somebody had to do something or *say* something.

When the old guy lifted his hands up and made fists it was almost a relief. "Whoa," Greg said, backing up, "I think you've got the wrong house, sir," but the old boy still looked like he might come at him. Greg had time to think jeez, I'm a foot taller than he is and he's old and some kind of a cripple, before the man finally sucked in some air and shut his mouth and backed off. Which was a relief since he had major body odor.

He was halfway down the walk when he turned to point at Greg and croak, "What'd he do?"

"Excuse me?"

"He do that?" He was pointing at Greg's bandaged hand that Greg had forgotten about until he looked down and saw how white the bandage looked. "This, you mean?"

"Yeah. He do that to you?" The guy cleared his throat and spat.

"I tore it on a bush," Greg said. That seemed to do it. The old guy turned away. He went weaving down the walk in a kind of hunching lop-sided shuffle. Greg watched him until he turned at the light and went around the corner.

Cathy was curled up on the sofa, dozing over a book. Greg woke her up. "Now what?" he said. "Have we got some kind of a peeping Tom situation?" and he told her about the old guy out in front, hunkering down and scuttling across the room to demonstrate how the old dude moved, like the hunchback of Notre Dame.

She didn't seem much impressed until Greg thought of something: "You know what? He knows your boyfriend."

"Greg. That's ridiculous."

She wasn't too sure, though. Greg could tell. "Well, be glad he's gone," he whispered. "And try not to wonder whether he'll come back." He rubbed his hands and made Twilight Zone noises. "He looked sooo weird. My heart's slamming around in my chest. One of Tod's buddies." He couldn't stop himself. "I'm serious."

"That is not funny, Gregory."

"I know." He went into the old guy's hoarse wheeze: "'Did Tod do that to you?'" and realized at once that he had gone too far.

Cathy got up and came across the room to look into his face. "He said—he asked you that?"

"That's what the man said," Greg said. "No kidding."

She tipped her head. One eyebrow went up. When she moved closer still and looked deeper into his eyes Greg squirmed. She caught his chin and held on.

"Don't squeeze the Charmin," he yelped.

"And don't you monkey with the truth," she said. "It shows. Something slides behind your eyes."

Greg crossed his eyes and pulled away but she had him and they both knew it. "Yeah, okay, maybe that wasn't exactly what he said. What it was, he wanted to know did *he* do this to me." He held up the bandaged hand. "So who else is the 'he' who's been coming around here lately?"

"Oh, for heaven's sake." She plopped back on the sofa. "Some old drunk can't find his house—every third house here looks alike—and you have to make a federal case of it." Her eyes strayed back to her book.

"Hey, the man of the house is home, now. You can relax." He hadn't exactly gotten through to her but what else was new?

The next day, Monday, with the temperature ninety-nine degrees at six-thirty p.m., the living room AC unit started making a weird clacking noise and stinking like burning rubber and after it was turned off turned out to have a fan blade sticking through the vent.

And that's not the only thing that started to fall apart because right about then is when Cathy did not come home from the office one night. Which never, ever, did Greg's mom not come right home from her office at the institute around six or at least call and check in. She and Greg had a pact about that. Ever since a time when Greg and Ginger and some of the guys went to the Woodlands one afternoon and had a little car trouble, Greg knew never to pull that crap and so did she.

It got dark. He walked around the empty house, practiced, tried to write an outline for a speech about bird watching which he didn't know anything about and didn't want to know anything about, drank three Cokes and got about halfway nervous thinking about the weirdo on the front walk and wondering if the car was okay. He thought about calling Chub or somebody but he didn't want to tie up the phone and, God, it started to get dark out and there was nothing but the answering machine on at the office, of course, and finally, finally, the damn phone rang.

First there was the operator: will he accept a long distance call from a Catherine Van Buren and when Greg said sure, right, you bet, there was Cathy, breathless and giggling, *giggling*, running a bunch of words together: "Oh honey please don't worry and please don't wait up or any-

thing I seem to be"—with this really stupid manic giggle— "I'm fine honest I just seem to be caught up in far-off mystic Galveston-by-the-sea so
do you think you can get yourself a hamburger? Greg, do you think you'll
be all right please don't be mad I'm fine everything's fine honest okay
honey okay?"

Greg said fine, he'd never been better, what did he have to be mad
about, he was nuts about hamburgers, and hung up and picked the receiver back up and socked the living room wall so hard with it that it
smashed through the sheetrock.

*****

4

If Cathy had dreamed Tod Benjamin might come strolling into her very
office on a Monday morning, she might have chosen something more interesting to wear to work, rain or no rain. Her big comfortable brown
cotton skirt and low-heeled loafers were perfectly presentable—nobody
paid much attention to her at the office anyway—but she didn't think Tod's
other women went around in longish skirts that didn't show the dirt and
sensible shoes.

Tod didn't even telephone. He just came walking in. If she hadn't
heard him asking Irene at the front desk where she was, Cathy wouldn't
have had any warning. As it was, she looked around at her little cubbyhole
with her heart going thump-thump, thinking wait, oh, wait, multiple waits,
give me a minute, oh, look at this place, while she trashed a dead ivy and
shoved a tangerine peeling into her top drawer. What was left of the tangerine missed her wastebasket. As she bent to get it and straightened up
again, oh, Lord, there he was, Tod Benjamin, looking amused at how she
couldn't breathe deeply and evenly. Her tongue started sticking to the
roof of her mouth, the way it sometimes would do and she shook her head,
fighting it, saying, "G-g-gracious."

It made him smile. He walked in. Lifted her fingers to his mouth to
kiss. Perched on the edge of her desk, grinning his manic grin, his blue
blue eyes half-closed into pleased crescents. Hot blue, his eyes. Bunsen-
burner blue, fringed with tangled dark lashes. He had on a silky suit, pale
as cream, immaculately cool. "Hi, little darlin'. Keeping busy?"

"N-no. Yes. N-n-not very." Cathy laughed on an indrawn breath. "My b-boss is out of t-town. Anyway, he's very t-tolerant. Well. He'd have to b-be, wouldn't he? Look at this." She looked around. "Oh, d-d-dear, there isn't a chair, is there? Somebody b-borrowed my chair, again. They d-do that all the t-time, well, usually I don't even need a ch-ch—oh, d-d-dear— let me fetch a chair."

"Don't worry about it." He lounged against the wall, looking at her, his eyes smiling into hers. Who could look away from such a bright gaze? After a couple of seconds, he slid sideways, closed the door behind him and moved closer, close enough to touch the perspiration on her upper lip with his forefinger. "Hi," he murmured. "Hi, you."

Oh, Lord.

He laughed. "Have you had lunch? I have to go to Galveston. Thought you might like to sneak away with me. Eat some blue crabs. How do blue crabs sound?"

"I think they're somewhere off the scale where humans can't hear," Cathy said. "But I can t-try." She squinched her eyes and hummed. "Can't reach it. I think it's a kind of scream."

His grin widened. "So let's make some blue crabs scream."

"Lunch? Now? Right now?" She slowed down, got her tongue under control. "Galveston's sixty miles away and it's, why this is the middle of the d-d-day."

"That it is," he said. "That's when people eat lunch. Unless you've got a jealous husband or whatever?"

Cathy took her glasses off and looked at them. They were slightly fogged and all fingerprinted. She breathed on them and wiped them. "Galveston? Oh, I don't see how I can possibly—"

"Aw now," he said, the smile unfazed. He made a small, impatient noise, held his hand out palm up, not entreating, just offering to steady her. "Let's go."

Once she'd given him her hand, Cathy needed steadying. He pulled her around the desk and out into the hall, turned and kissed her quickly, lightly, a cool, smooth-lipped kiss, without loosening the grip on her hand as he led the way to the outer office. Irene looked up, affronted, as they approached her. She started to say something but Tod held his hand out at her, waving her to silence. When Cathy started in with a hesitant excuse about having to run an errand, he waved her to silence, too, smiling all around, at all the girls. Everybody looked at him. He saluted, winked broadly at Irene and quickened their pace. By the time they pushed their way through the heavy outer door to the building and into the blinding sunlight he had Cathy running, laughing breathlessly, trying not to trip.

The effect fell apart, temporarily, when she realized she'd left her purse in her desk. He didn't even want her to go back after it.

"Why do you need a purse?" He looked serious. "I don't carry one."

"It has my house k-k-k—" They both laughed. "All my keys," she said. "This is ridiculous. I'm going back. It has everything I own. My lipstick...."

"That's another thing: lipstick. Listen to the word. Leave your mouth alone. Look at it. It's perfect without a thing. And keys, come on. Won't your son let you in?" But he followed her back inside for the purse anyway. And then there was something of an anticlimax, having to rush back out, smiling and winking at Irene and the others all over again.

When they were back on the street, he looked so disapproving. "Where the hell is your abandon?"

"Abandon?" Cathy slid into the car.

"Oh, yeah." Tod said. "Yeah." He twirled imaginary moustaches. "This thing belong to you?" He tweaked her barrette loose. "Put it in that valuable purse. Or...."

When Cathy hesitated, he tossed the barrette right out the window. "Oh, my hair's so slipsy—" She started to protest and settled back, eyeing him. "Well," she said. "One thing, maybe now the whole darned office will quit calling me The Church Lady."

"Is that what they call you?"

"Sometimes." Cathy wished she hadn't blurted that out. It sounded anything but glamorous. "The mother of one of Greg's friends, Ginger, came by, once, and she called me that and it sort of got picked up. Because I tend to dress, oh, you know. I tend to be c-c-conservative."

What a maddening thing to go into right this minute. She tried to imagine what the stout women in the outer office must look like to somebody like Tod and had to give it up. "They're okay. They don't mean to be mean, but, well, I d-don't go to the Flamingo or Swayzie's or the Pub, you know, stop by after work for a d-drink or whatever, a highball. They tend to get sort of disparaging. They've all known each other forever and I'm new. I've been new for years."

It was important to make him understand. "Not that I disapprove. I b-bet it's like those ads, you know, the laughing people having a perfectly splendid time, drinking up and laughing, the way they do."

He had a way of lifting an eyebrow that made her feel silly. "Ah, yes," he said. "The laughing ladies. With a cigarette in one hand and a drink in the other."

"Yes." She'd given him a wrong impression. "Having such a good time. But I can't do that. For one thing, there's Greg. And for another, my grandfather always thought of bars as those dark places and I...oh, never mind."

"Would you like to have a drink?" The eyebrow was still up.

"Oh, no." She hadn't meant to sound horrified. "In the middle of the day? Unless you really—"

"Oh, I couldn't," he said. "Not in the middle of the day."

His car smelled of leather and wax. Tod drove easily, as if the car were an extension of himself. "Your husband go to those dark places?"

"Joe? Never." My, but he did drive fast. The clock on the dash said twelve-thirty as they topped the highest level of the tangle of freeways at the Loop and headed down Interstate Forty-five. Then they were out of town, the road ahead of them seeming to go liquid between the dead weeds baking in a dull expanse of brown in all directions.

Tod touched a button on the dash and grimaced. "Ninety-four degrees. You cool enough, baby?"

Cathy rubbed her arms. He laughed. "What I'm getting at is, why don't you unsnap that belt and slide over here?"

She did.

He smelled woodsy. Tangy. Like oranges. When he dropped his hand over hers and lifted her fingers to his mouth and kissed them she caught her breath.

He drove too fast, though.

She slid away, found the seat belt and snapped it.

At first she told herself he knew how to handle his car, he seemed so sure. So skillful. But she had to keep telling herself that, and that she was probably just not used to his way of zipping in and out of traffic. It would probably be pretty easy to lose track of how fast you were driving in such a very large car. The hood looked vast. He kept glancing over at her, his hand cupping hers, and she kept trying to relax, wishing he'd watch the road, until he sighed and puffed out his lips. "What?"

"What what?"

"What's the matter?" He sounded concerned. "You look like you're afraid somebody'll see you headed for Galveston with an Irishman. Your husband the jealous type?"

"Joe, jealous? My Joe—oh, dear. I'm a little nervous, I guess." She forced a laugh. "Just sort of vibrating, a little. Just, you know, happy."

She tugged her hand away from his so she could hug herself as they whooshed past a man towing a boat and in their wake heard the bleat of a trucker's horn. Tod obviously was a better driver than she'd ever be and this would be a stupid time to go stupidly neurotic. It was hard not to keep from tensing, though, even after she took off her glasses so she couldn't see much beyond the wide, white, acres of shining hood.

He kept speeding up and braking, swerving in and out of traffic. Everyone else seemed to be creeping, though they weren't of course, they were going eighty miles an hour in the glittering heat, swooping and swishing around, flying by. When the back of a pickup with two scared-looking men in it loomed up in front of them, Tod touched his horn, and moved into a narrow opening between a van with surfboards on its top and a Greyhound bus. The bus sent out a warning blast, its brakes wheezing.

"Those guys think they own the road, " Tod said with a yawn.

Cathy got her glasses out of her purse and sat up straighter. "Do you know what makes the road look wet, like that? That's the sky," she said, and, annoyed at the dry, pedantic sound of her voice, chattered on, "We're driving through the sky. P-p-puddles of sk-sk-sky."

They careened past two huge trucks in a row and she swallowed a squeal. "It's really warm air t-t-trapped b-below cold air, I know that, everybody knows that, but what it's actually doing is reflecting sky, that's what shimmers and makes that mirage sort of—do you know what the word mirage means? It means 'to wonder at'—oh, g-g-gosh, do you have to g-go so fast?"

His mouth dropped open. He looked at her and looked ahead and looked back at her again with his eyebrows all the way up to his hairline. "What was all that again?"

"The mirage part or the too fast p-p-part?"

"Both," he said, and laughed soundlessly. "You're such a character." But they were still going almost ninety miles an hour.

"Oh," Cathy said. "Dear. You drive like a wild ass in the d-d-desert."

"I what? A what?"

"Well, b-b-boar, then. Something wild. Very."

He stopped smiling. Settled back, letting the car decelerate. "Why don't you distract me?" He tapped the lighter, got out a narrow black cigar, bit the end off, spit out the bitten end and lit it before he turned to squint at her through a trail of faint blue smoke. "Hate to let anybody pass me, baby. Kind of a big kid, in that way, I guess."

He chuckled unpleasantly. "I just never can handle being passed up, know what I mean? So. I'll make you a deal. You take my mind off all those silly bastards out there and I'll just automatically have to quit being a boor or a bore or an ass or whatever that is, deal? That's how that goes. Works every time." His arm slid along the back of the seat. "Been meaning to talk to you about that."

Cathy stiffened. "Distract you?"

"Yeah." His mouth was curved, lazily ajar. "You know. Drive me to distraction."

"I don't—I wouldn't—I actually wouldn't have the remotest idea how to go about d-d-doing that," she said. "Would you mind t-t-terribly putting b-both hands on the wheel? I don't drive people to distraction, actually." Her face felt hot. She got her tongue under control and said in her coldest tone, "I wouldn't have any idea where to begin."

"You could start by unfastening that damn seat belt," Tod said. "That's how to handle a boor." His mouth twitched.

"You're making a very bad joke."

There was absolutely nothing to look at, outside, but the endlessly flat, baking fields.

Tod seemed to change his mind. "Jesus," he said. "Hey. Where'd you go? I'm kidding, bad joke, you're right. That's my Bogey imitation. Humphrey Bogart?" He didn't sound sorry. He touched her chin with a finger of the hand with the cigar in it, turning her face toward him. "So it's true about redheads."

"If you're referring to temper, that's a cliche. What's true is that you're an immoral driver." The cigar made her cough.

"I see." His grin was positively evil as he jammed on the accelerator again. "What the hell is an immoral driver?"

"Don't look so proud. It's scarcely a compliment. A maddening driver, actually." She was damned if she'd start sniffling.

He looked startled. "What can I tell you, baby. I'm a maddening guy." But he let the car decelerate. "We'll put it on automatic pilot at fifty-five. That make you feel any better?"

She tried to match his chilly dispassion. "I don't suppose you'd take me back to the office or drop me off, somewhere."

Tod glanced at the ceiling of the car and at the sky outside and said, "You sure that's what you want?" and almost at once swerved to the side of the road. "That's what you want, that's what we'll do."

Cathy's heart started to pound so hard it made her ears ring. He wants me to get out, right now. She fumbled at the inside of the car door, trying to find the handle, tears in her nose and eyes—

—and Tod groaned and chuckled. "Hey. What is all this?"

"You think you're so—you're just—" Cathy said, and he took her chin in his hand and kissed her, tentatively at first, and then thoroughly, gently, smoothing back her hair, holding her face in both his warm hands.

When he let her go, he looked contrite. "I am a boor," he said. "Don't know as anybody ever put it like that but you got it, lady. You got it. Now, you call your husband or your other boyfriends that, they might blow it off, see? But that's what I am. Tough part is I know it." He hesitated and glanced at the cigar. "Speaking of which, you want me to put this out?"

Nobody Cathy knew smoked little long, narrow, black cigars. In Holland, Grandfather sometimes smoked a fat brown cigar and the scent of it got into the drapes but this cigar smelled faintly of buttered rum. She looked at it, wondering if it tasted the way it smelled, and said she didn't think he ought to put it out. "I might learn to join you."

Tod stubbed the cigar out anyway and pulled back onto the road. He drove silently for a while before he leaned toward her and gave her a playful shove. "Easy, baby." When they were seated, he sat almost as tall as she. His hand felt hard. His voice, his open-mouthed, go-to-hell smile, the liquid glint of his eyes, and his purr of amusement made her breathe unevenly.

Cathy settled back with a sigh. "I don't know if this will work at all," she said. "We may be different life forms, or something. Totally alien. I might be a Klingon and you, I don't know."

He nodded and looked rueful. "I'm the Klingon. Your husband from your planet?"

"Joe? Oh, yes. Very Dutch, Joe. Very...puritan. Lowland Dutch, all the way back. Dutch Christian Reformed."

Tod pretended to look startled. "You're not Catholic?"

"Indeed, not. Why?"

"I guess I thought—go on. So, Dutch, eh?"

She couldn't help an apologetic laugh and hurried to explain the puritans, large, clean, wholesome types.

"You know those women who defended their honor with their wooden shoes in the big war? World War II? My relatives. That's what people mean by 'You can't beat the Dutch.' Stubborn, too. We can be mighty stubborn. Good solid people, you know, decent and all that, clean clear through. But difficult. If you're not Dutch...."

"Black Irish," Tod said. He lifted a hand for emphasis. "So, where is he? The Dutch husband. He around here somewhere?"

"I thought you knew," Cathy said. "Didn't I—" Why hadn't she told him from the beginning? Now she was only making it worse.

He looked over at her, frowning, his dark eyebrows shading his eyes. He cleared his throat. "So, you leave him? Why?"

"He left me. He died."

"Oh. I'm sorry. I guess I thought, never mind. Didn't you say—I thought you said—ah, I'm making it worse. Sorry."

He didn't look sorry. He looked confused. Deflated. Then, with a visible effort at cheeriness, he said, carefully, "So. A widow. You been a widow long?"

"Almost ten years. August tenth." Why did he look so strange? So sort of disappointed in her? "Gracious," she said. "Do you happen to have some prejudice against widows?"

He grinned fleetingly. "Not at all. Ah, was it sudden? Because you felt to me—you acted like you're still—well—it's really none of my business, is it?"

She wanted to be his business. "How do I act?"

"Oh, hell, I don't know. I guess I thought you had this husband somewhere. In India." He smiled. "The army. Whatever."

"I'm still grieving, is that it? There's no time limit on that." She was determined not to be defensive. "Maybe it's always there, somewhere." Oh, she didn't want to be boring. He looked so blank.

"Yeah, well, I've been in some grief in my time," he said, swallowing a yawn, making conversation, "but that's a whole different thing, isn't it. Did your Joe have some kind of an accident?"

"A cerebrovascular accident." She took a deep breath.

"And you still have that much trouble talking about it?" He shook his head.

"I could hardly talk at all for a while. When my parents were killed, too. And when my grandfather died."

He squeezed her hand. She wanted to change the subject.

"Haven't you been married?" She let herself gaze at him, at his straight nose, his clean chin line.

He turned to look into her eyes, held a hand out and tipped it. "Not my thing. So far."

"You have the bluest eyes in the world," she said. "Especially when you smile with your eyebrows down, like that. But they're not really blue, you know. I mean, not inherently, like a piece of cloth or a bird's egg or anything of that sort. Do you know what makes blue eyes look the way they do? They actually have less color than brown eyes. The nonpigmented particles scatter light and the reflected rays actually look—" She stopped, finally, and inhaled, and sat in silence, chewing at her lower lip.

He chuckled. "So my eyes are actually inferior."

"Oh, no! Just so...different. Less pigmented."

He nodded, ponderously solemn. She decided to be still.

But something else occurred to her. "My grandmother warned me about The Black Irish. I think that was her only prejudice. 'Little-footed, dancing, devilish men they are,' she used to say, 'and the truth not in 'em.' What size shoes do you wear?"

"Eight."

"And you like to dance."

"Oh, yeah," he said. "Oh, yeah. Believe it."

I wish I could say it like that, Cathy thought. That certainly. Fervently, even. But if a person is clumsy, she's clumsy. And size ten, to boot. But for once, she was able to keep her mouth shut.

Some day I'll make him tell me about his planet, she thought. And I'll tell him about Holland, Michigan, and my dad and mom and grandfather and the house on Twenty-seventh Street with the spirea bushes bending into tunnels of white froth out in front and the maples interlocked over the street. And my dad grading math papers and mother at the typewriter, her hair sliding from under its combs. Both of them preoccupied, soft-voiced, absentminded, but there, always right there. Until, of course, they weren't.

"My folks were killed in an automobile accident and I was reared by my grandfather. Dutch, of course. A wonderful man. Very gentle."

"I'm sure of it."

"That's when I started to stammer," she said. "Which you may have noticed. Sometimes my tongue wants to—it clings to the roof of my mouth. But I don't have to. Unless I'm, you know—stressed. Like on a job interview. Or a d-d-date. And that's as far as I'm going to g-g-go into that."

But she rattled on. "I'm talking far t-t-too much. My world is sort of b-boring, actually. Just, you know, water color lessons and Greg's recitals and like that. He's played since he was little. He learned early. The Suzuki method. Twinkle, Twinkle, Little Star and Mississippi Stop Mississippi Stop, you know."

He clearly didn't. She told herself to be still. And couldn't. He looked so puzzled. "It's a way of learning the cello," she said. "Never mind. T-t-tell me about your world."

"My world?"

"Your universe." That sounded even sillier and made it worse. "In ten words or less."

He shook his head. "Like you said, too far away and too long gone." He fell silent. Drove. Broke the silence with a sigh. "No Mississippi Stop—whatever the hell that is—for this kid." His face brightened. "I try to stay the hell away from Mississippi. And Louisiana."

Cathy loved his laugh. Low and fast, a helpless staccato.

"I sold stuff there, when I was a kid," he said. "Magazine subscriptions. Newspapers, when I got big enough to steal 'em back from the big kids. Cloverine salve, door to door. With holy card bonuses."

"What's a holy card?"

He pulled his mouth down and went round-eyed with feigned shock. "Oh, darlin', what am I going to do with the likes of you? That's a question only a she-devil would ask."

More silence. He seemed disinclined to define holy cards. Cathy envisioned them as like baseball cards, only with saints.

"I'll b-b-bet you were very good at it," she said.

He glanced at her. "You ever have to sell anything door-to-door?"

"Nope," Cathy said. "I don't even know what Cloverine Salve is. No. Wait—! Girl Scout cookies."

"In Holland, Michigan. Right." He lit the cigar again. Smoke curled past his eyes. He squinted at her through tangled lashes. "I said, 'have to.'" He was making fun of her. "There's a difference." He talked around the cigar, taking her hand in his warm hand.

Unpigmented or not, his eyes looked very blue, a hot, bright,glinting blue through the blur of those dark lashes. It was hard to look away. A person would see the world differently through such flaming blue. She was so preoccupied with that, with his eyes and his hands, the dark, curling hair above the knuckles of his fingers entwined with hers, that they drove up and across the long curving bridge of the causeway and into Galveston before she realized it.

"Almost home." Tod looked around and waved a proprietary hand. "How much do you know about my Island?"

"Not much," Cathy admitted. "Just the beach and the Strand, where the gas lights are, the Victorian section where the tourists go. I think it would be lovely to live on an island, though, I've always thought so," she said, looking out over the flat, pale water. It reflected the no-color color of the hot pale sky. "Galveston's a lovely, decadent place. All those wonderful, crumbling, old, wedding cake sorts of houses and the blowzy purple of the oleanders along the streets. I've been in Texas for almost fifteen years and I still marvel at big, generous, blossomy kinds of things, like oleanders and banana blossoms and magnolias—oh, gosh, I think magnolias are somebody's fantasy idea of a made up flower. Even those shiny little red seeds in their velvety cones are unreal."

"I've got some magnolias," Tod said. "Transplanted them. There's a superstition about that, did you know that? They're supposed to be deadly. Transplant a magnolia and somebody dies within the year." He gave that growly chuckle and gazed at her as if he were trying to make up his mind about something. "Wanna see my magnolia trees?"

"Why, well, yes." Cathy hoped she didn't sound as uneasy as she felt. "I'd never heard that about the magnolias, but widows are supposed to be d-deadly, too. You know what Dickens said. 'Be wery c-c-careful of widders, all your life.'"

He didn't want to discuss Dickens. He slowed and turned those blazing eyes full on her. "Decision time. Want to see my magnolias or not?"

"Well, how much t-t-time d-d-do we have? I'm sort of hungry." She tried for a laugh. "Is that anything like 'wanna see my etchings?'"

"You like etchings? Wanna see my etchings, little Dutch girl?"

"At your pad?"

"Yeah, my beach shack. It...needs work. But I'm getting there. You can see what it's going to be, if you look at it right."

He turned the car around, headed back along the oleander lined boulevard the way they'd come. "Ah, yes, the magnolias and oleanders," he said, becoming a sonorous guide: "On your left, we have what the Historical Foundation has designated the Silk Stocking District, a graceful hodgepodge of architecture from the last century, made up of Romanesque, Greek,

Italianate, Renaissance, Revival and Horrible Moderne with sheet rock and aluminum siding all over it. Some of the downtown buildings were undermined by the last couple of hurricanes. They're going to fall right down, one of these days. Slide into piles of brick.

"The next storm'll make for instant urban renewal in this old town. You can hose the mortar out from between the bricks of those old buildings. The mortar runs down like melting snow."

He swerved onto the Seawall. "Over here we have the remains of the B room. The Balinese. Used to be notorious. Friend of mine owned it. This is the place Sheriff Biaggne couldn't raid because he couldn't get in, he said, because he wasn't a member. Roulette, craps, one-armed bandits, the whole bit. Rococo bamboo and gals in sequins and guys in rayon shirts with red and green palm trees eating chicken-fried shrimp."

The Balinese Room didn't look like a room. It looked like a ruin at the end of a long, rickety pier. Cathy lowered the car window and sniffed. "Oh, I do like beaches. I grew up on a beach. Lake Michigan's. This one's so salty and quiet, though. And it has palm trees. It's nice."

"Very nice." He put a finger under her chin. "Peaches. Peaches and cream. Strawberries and peaches and...."

"Quit," Cathy said. "You're making me feel edible."

"Oh, yeah," he said.

"Scaring me, too, a little b-b-bit, if you want to know." She inhaled. "I hate to be a p-p-pain in the neck but don't be scary, can you n-n-not? I guess I am a pain. You know, a prude." She clucked a nervous cluck. "I have mentioned that, haven't I?"

"You have." He lifted an eyebrow. "I think I'll show you my place, just the same, ready or not. Relieve you of the decision."

She was silent, thinking of houses on stilts, those mostly all-bedroom places with aluminum and glass tables and cracked plastic couches and, of course, a metal cot, it being focal, when Tod pulled into a circular drive surrounded by manicured shrubbery in front of a brick mansion with a filigreed Victorian porch.

"Oh, please," she protested and realized, at once, how dumb that sounded—and that Tod wasn't joking—and she clapped her hand over her mouth. Tod had gotten out of the car and trotted all the way around to her side before she let the hand drop and got her tongue under control. "Where are the magnolias?" she squeaked.

"They're here." He stood back, beaming. "In the upstairs. The master bedroom. You can just see some of the foliage from here." He followed her eyes. "You like my faces? At the tops of the pillars, up there. Those were carved by a guy from Florence a hundred years ago." He stood looking down at her, glowing, perspiring, sweetly eager.

When he held out his hand, Cathy took it and pressed down on it, clumsily, clambering free of the car. Then she leaned, even more unbalanced, gaping up at the faces he was pointing to. They ringed the house, each pillar carved into a face in the curve where it joined the eaves. The faces were of cherubim: fat, curly-haired, renaissance angel-baby faces.

"Oh," she said, transfixed, and could say no more. She let go of Tod and clasped her hands over her heart. "I feel like somebody in one of those silly grocery store books." She giggled.

He watched her, biting his lower lip, blinking, bright-eyed and when she swallowed he took her face in his hands and looked at her some more, and kissed her fiercely, not letting her go until he was finished. "You're the lovely wonder," he breathed. "And I'm the one to appreciate you."

"B-but you can't make magnolias g-g-grow ind-d-doors," Cathy stammered finally. "Not even you can d-do that."

That "even you" might have been what sent him into that long staccato chuckle, so low it was almost a growl. He threw back his head and laughed happily, helplessly, until he had to fight for breath.

"Ah, that's where you're wrong, little darlin'," he said, then. "There isn't much I can't put where I will. That's what your grandmother didn't tell you about the Black Irish, isn't it now? The winnin' glad ways of us, and the power. And the dreams we can dream up. Let's go in, darlin'."

He bowed, indicated the door with a flourish. "After you."

*****

5

"**I** transplanted my magnolias," Tod said, as he unlocked the front door. "They were down on the west end, on the wrong side of the vegetation line so I rescued them from being drowned by the Gulf. 'They're for my lady,' I told myself. 'Some lovely lady, with the lovely, long, red hair on her, who might like to have some grand, green, white-flowering magnolia trees.'" He swung open the heavy carved door and stood back, flushed and bright-eyed. "What do you think?" he demanded. "The best place to see those trees is from the balcony off the master bedroom, upstairs." He waggled his eyebrows. "Just kidding, just kidding. Well, come in, come into my house. This is the foyer. Lot of fantastic wood in here."

Cathy sighed, gazing, scarcely listening to his earnest prattling. She swiveled, thrilled into breathlessness, at the sight of lustrous, carved redwood paneling and a grand wide, curving staircase with elaborately carved oaken nymphs holding aloft beribboned, wooden bouquets of lilies and ferns and wide, glossy leaves. Rays of afternoon sun, tinted ruby and blue and gold by faceted panes set in a jeweled window, cascaded over Tod.

He stood grinning in a rhomboid of gold and ruby red and blue light, talking, talking, bouncing on the balls of his feet, saying, "Now *this* is a real picture window, not those glass things. More than a hundred years old. Look at the way those tendrils of vine and the grapes are worked in. Is that craftsmanship?" He laughed. "You want to know how they got the idea? A guy named La Farge, John La Farge. A painter. He liked the way the sunlight came through a tooth powder jar on his window sill."

"Hush, " Cathy breathed. "I can't think. Did you grow up here?"

"Hardly." He was leading her off to the right, into a circular room. "This is the turret. For parties." He chuckled. "Me, born here? Ah, darlin'. I was born in Arkansas, during the Great Depression. Just got this place. Haven't had a chance to furnish it."

The rooms were almost empty. One had a recliner and a television set on a rickety stand. He let go of her hand and walked into the center of that room and flung his arms out. "Plenty of space, eh? I just haven't figured out what to do with it. Been kind of camping out in here." He followed her eyes and scrubbed at his scalp. "To tell you the truth, this damned old mausoleum is eating me alive. It was supposed to be a steal and that's what it does. It's been stealing up on me and from me ever since I got weak-headed enough to buy it. These old houses are like they say about boats; holes to sink money into. Look at these windows, though. Even the plain glass isn't plain. It's like crystal, isn't it, darlin? They put a lot more lead in this glass than we do today. Really gives it a shine. That fan light is real stained glass. And look at this floor."

Cathy knelt and touched wood fitted into patterns, like quilts made of small bits of wood, honey and maple, dark oak and ebony.

"Oh, come on, rosy lady, my peachy rose—" His voice changed as he pulled her along. "This is the back hall and here's the grand kitchen. See that tile? Brought in some wetbacks to do that." When she flinched, he added, "I mean, it's hand made and hand set."

The doors to an empty expanse of dining room slid open and disappeared into paneled walls. "Had a guy in the Valley fix those doors. The panels are hand-carved, too, but they made up some kind of a press for the wainscoting." He tugged her along.

"It would be lovely to hang some copper pans in the kitchen," Cathy said. "Not too many kitchens today have fireplaces."

Tod looked at her. "See? See? Now that's the darling way of you, to be thinking of that kind of thing. Copper pans. This place wants a woman, like you, if I'm not frightening you off."

A circular back stair led upward from a narrow kitchen door. He waved his hands and recited, as he backed up the stair ahead of her: "'If I do but climb the stair to the tower overhead, when the winds are calling there, or the gannets calling out in waste places of the sky, there's so much to think about that I cry...I cry.'"

The wainscoting in the first room at the top of the stair was the color of honey. Cathy ran her hand along it, stroking with the grain, savoring the sweet, dry scent of the wood. Tod walked her past the next room, changed his mind and opened the door. There was a mattress on the floor with sheets and a frayed quilt. It was impossible not to look at it, though Cathy tried.

Tod saw her and lifted his chin defensively. "Well, now you know about me, I guess. Thing is, I haven't decided what I want to put in here."

A pair of French doors opened onto a balcony. Past that was another room and another, four bedrooms, all of them hot and still and dusty, papered in yellowing, torn paper.

"Top floor's too hot this hellish hot day," Tod said, but Cathy went on up the curving stair.

"Oh, window seats," she said, at the end of the hall. "Oh, Tod. This place is wonderful. Full of wonders, end to end." She knelt to touch another length of parqueted floor.

The floors had had to be refinished, he said. "The last owner partitioned this place up into little rooms and put shower stalls in here. They sank a drain here and, I think, over here, somewhere. But the floors survived."

He led her to a freckled full-length mirror. "And what is it you see, darlin'?"

She glanced at herself and tried to turn away but he held her in place, talking, talking, while she perspired in an agony of embarrassment. "Look!" he insisted, and, as she was thinking, ah, yes, the church lady, he began to recite, his eyes half-closed, one hand moving as if he were muting an orchestra: "'Would not painters paint a form of such noble lines....Such a delicate high head, so much sternness and such charm'?"

Cathy pulled away. She looked rumpled and frowsy, her hair sliding frizzing out of its twist, her face moonlike on its too long throat, clumsy and plain and...and *big,* almost a head taller than this antic little man, who insisted on holding her, forcing her to lift her eyes to the brown-flecked glass. "You've come home," he said, rapturously. "Can't you see?"

Cathy closed her eyes. When he wouldn't let go, she opened her eyes and looked into Tod's gleaming, blue, blue eyes. He turned her around and kissed her. His kiss was not tentative. He held her as he wished and kissed her as he wanted to, pressing her back against the mirror, a small, hungry groan in his throat, his hand cupping her breast. When he let her go Cathy groped behind her for balance. Her palm slid on the mirror's surface. He smiled, his teeth white against his lower lip in a fleeting grin. He steadied her until she was balanced again, as balanced as she could be while he stood so close, inhaling her breath, looking, looking into her eyes that could not look away.

He cleared his throat and laughed. "Would you like a cup of tea?"

In the kitchen, he set out a Dresden tea set, with matching cups and saucers from somewhere in the tall dusty cupboards. There were creased pastel linen napkins and a box of Earl Grey tea and when Cathy unfolded a napkin and came upon a small, plastic-threaded price tag— "$4.50 ea."— on its inner corner, she tried to unobtrusively refold it. Tod saw the price tag and his smile faded. "Don't mean a thing," he muttered.

She poured tea, wondering why his having her see that he slept on a mattress on the floor seemed less mood shattering than a silly tag on a napkin. "Of course it doesn't." Trying to put him at ease.

"Don't. Doesn't. If you're gonna correct my grammar, you have your work cut out for you." His smile didn't reach his eyes.

"I wasn't," she said, stammering. "N-not c-consciously, anyway." His eyes slid away from hers. "There's c-certainly nothing the matter with n-nice new napkins," she said.

"Yeah." He looked like a small boy, suddenly gloomily sullen.

"Th-this t-teapot looks like an heirloom," Cathy said.

"Hair what?"

"Heirloom," she repeated. "Oh, dear."

He flicked his fingertips against the Dresden teapot, dismissing it. "Picked this up in an auction barn on Telephone Road. Bought it to impress you, and that's the shining truth. You want a teapot? I guess you've got a few teapots but this one's yours if you want it. No, take it. It's yours. Suits you a hell of a lot better than me." He scowled, his chin on his chest. "Go ahead and take it."

"Indeed not," Cathy said. "It belongs right here, in your lovely house." The "belongs" stuck in her throat; came out "be-be-beelongs" and she went on, hastily. "I d-don't think anybody ever has bought a teapot t-to make an impression on me. They might have, if they'd thought about it, but it never has occurred to anybody." She talked still faster, fighting a silly trill of embarrassment in her voice. "Shades of The Great Gatsby."

"Whose be?"

"Gatsby," she said. "Oh, dear. Never mind."

Tod sighed and held his hands up, his fingers stiffly out, commanding silence. "You don't want the damned teapot?"

"Oh, please," Cathy said. "No. As I said—." He held the teapot at arm's length and let it drop.

Cathy gasped. She couldn't look at the shards of china on the floor or at him. After a moment she said, in a small voice, "I want to go home."

"Jesus," Tod said.

"Profanity," she said, tears in her throat. "How could you?"

"Don't worry about it," he said, stiffly.

"How could you?"

He stamped his feet and came around in front of her, forcing her to look at him, at his mottled face, his eyes glittering. "I don't know," he whispered. "Jesus. Shit." And, in a moment, in a growling rush, "I'm going to level with you, baby. I'm a pretty crude old bastard. I've come a hell of a long way, taught myself plenty. I've earned some dough. And dough makes dough." He waved a hand. "Started out working for one dentist, and now I've got a nice little chain of labs, got the government sucking at me and employees hanging off of me and all kinds of shit but it makes for dough and dough's a great little educator, you know. Don't look at me like that." He repeated himself, "Dough's a great little educator." He laughed. "And dough is a great little deodorant. You ought to see your eyes."

Oh, she thought. You ought to see your eyes.

But he pushed away from the table, got up to walk, to pace, talking, talking: "I don't know doodly squat about architecture or any of that crap. What you do is hire people. That's all. You hire the right people. Maybe that takes talent, I don't know." He stopped at a window, stood talking, like somebody giving an address, the colored light slanting behind his head." You can hire anybody to do just about anything. Why, darlin', there's a guy drives around all over the country just fixing stained glass. That's all he does. All over the country. Makes his living doing that."

Cathy stood up, looked around. "Well. How many times have I said 'lovely' this afternoon? You should be very proud—"

"Believe it, darlin', I am." He stopped. Then, with some difficulty, moving his hands uneasily, he added, "I spent a hell of a lot of time looking into other people's houses when I was a little kid, know what I mean? Standing out in front of other people's houses. Families sitting around with each other in these places with chandeliers—well, hell, now how would you know about that? Depends on where you're born. Whether you're high born or not."

He got up stood with his hands in his pockets, his back to her. "Delivered papers. Sold magazines. Ran errands for people like you've never met. Chicago gangsters. The only people who had money, during the depression. They came down from Chicago to Hot Springs, Arkansas, to gamble. Thugs and molls and—what I'm getting at is, I've spent a lot of time looking into other peoples' houses." His mouth twisted. "From the outside."

He came back to the table and picked up the cups and saucers. "Ah, I always talk too much."

When he came back and sat down, she touched his hand. "It can be lonely inside a house, if you're an only child."

He raised his eyebrows.

"Besides," she went on, "I was always sort of, oh, c-clumsy and d— d-different; the one with her nose in a book, leaning against the building reading. A head taller than everybody." She hesitated. "Well. Fatter, too. So, see? I think some of what you've been through, the tough part, might have been good for you. It's made you quick and smart and sure of yourself." She thought for a minute. "Gregory calls it *snap*. Gregory greatly admires snap."

"That so?"

"Oh, he does." What could be wrong with having this glowing little man think that Greg admired him? "He always has," she finished. "Admired snap, I mean."

A flush of pink spread across Tod's cheeks. "I'll be damned." He cupped her face with both his hands and kissed her and drew back and laughed at her as the skin of her face warmed beneath his hand. "She blushes, the lady of my delight! Why don't we go down to the Strand and get something to eat?"

Cathy called home but there was no answer so she agreed. Tod took her to the Wentletrap, a marvelous restaurant on the Strand with fresh carnations on the table and the faint, thready, plaintive call of violins in the background. He ordered a shrimp bisque and nutty filet of speckled trout sautéed with capers and croutons and a Caesar salad tossed tableside.

They finished a carafe of wine and strolled along the Strand, hand in hand. He said wistfully, "Someday, when you feel right about it, you'll come back to my house to see my magnolias in the moonlight, with their dinner-plates of dripping, heaven-sent, sweet-smelling bloom," and he stopped so suddenly that a couple behind them almost walked into him. He stood in the middle of the sidewalk and leaned toward her. "We're going back right now," he said, his hand squeezing hers, his gaze boring into hers.

"Gregory!" she said. "What t-t-time is it? Oh, no. I've g-got to get to a t-tele—I've g-got to get home, right away.!" so frantic that Tod said, "Whoa, easy," and handed her his cell phone.

Gregory answered but as she was explaining to him Tod let go of her hand to run ahead of her, leaping into the air and clicking his heels, calling out, exultantly, "How's that for *snap?*"

"Oh," Cathy said, "stop. You look like a cheerleader!"

"And you look like a blushing gentle woman," he said.

As they headed home, Tod drove past the house, all shadowy carved lace behind its drift of oleanders, its cherubim smiling in the fading light of the sun.

Gregory was in front of the TV, so mad at her that he couldn't even talk about it.

Cathy apologized and apologized. But she couldn't explain. No one, certainly not a sixteen-year-old, could understand a man like Tod, who had grown up with gangsters from Chicago, who smoked slim black cigars, who could be liltingly lyrical—"Ah, penny, copper penny, you are looped in the loops of my heart"—as he cupped her to him, his hand sliding over her breast, so sweetly gentle one minute and so angry, angrier than anyone she'd ever known, the very next. With such hot, glittering, piercing pinpoints of fire burning in his blue, blue eyes.

*****

6

He did not call.

By the time Tod hadn't called for fourteen entire days and nights, Cathy got so distracted in painting class that she gave the last of her tube of Cadmium red to the kid at the next easel and spent several minutes trying to find some more red, any red, before she gave up and just stood in front of her stupid overblown painting with her arms folded, staring at the thing. She'd been working for days on a banana blossom; a big, unwieldy thing, purple and orchid, several shades of reds and blues, in a nest of banana leaves, with baby bananas sticking out every which way and what she had wasn't a work of art. It was garbage. It looked as messy as her life.

Chub circulated around the room offering advice, making like a teacher. When she got to Hetty Bach's table, near the front of the room, Chub paused and said, "Oh, nice. More." The kid next to Cathy got a friendly pat.

When Chub got up behind Cathy, she said, "H'm," and stood with her mouth screwed up." After a minute she said, "Well, honey, might be time to start over. If you vomited into the stew, you wouldn't keep seasoning it, would you? What do you say we get another sheet out and try to save some of the white?"

Cathy had to agree but all of a sudden she was looking over at Chub through a haze of tears.

"Gee, whoa," Chub said. "Let's all take a break. Time for milk and cookies." Chub led the way into the cafeteria and got coffee from the machine. "There," she said, "have some nice dishwater."

"I'm being ridiculous," Cathy whimpered.

"I'm so sorry," Chub said

Cathy blew her nose. "I'm dying." She blew her nose some more.

"I'm so sorry." Chub said again, touching Cathy's shoulder.

"Well, I don't even know all that much about him," she said, nasally, fishing around in her purse for more tissues. "Just that he's poetic and great looking and I thought there was some chemistry there and—do I sound like a goofy teenager?"

"People in nursing homes have crushes." Chub sipped her coffee.

"Why is that so not consoling?" Cathy said. She put her face into her hands. "Crush is the word, though we had such a great time and he's got this great house and he's so—so exciting. He's got these Paul Newman eyes and you ought to see the way he is, in that house of his.

"Two weeks. He hasn't called in fourteen days. Unless he's calling tonight, right now, while I'm sitting here keeping you from teaching our class which I have no business doing." She inhaled and went on. "If he calls while I'm not home, I don't have any idea what Greg might say. Greg can't stand him."

Chub looked stricken. "He can't?" Her eyes narrowed. "How'd you meet this Tod?"

"At a Jack in the Box," Cathy mumbled.

"Right," Chub said. "Sorry I asked."

"No. Really." Cathy looked away. "I told Greg we met at Parents Without Partners, but that's a lie. Tod's never been married."

She hesitated. "We met at that four-way stop at the corner of Kingspoint and Fuqua. A pickup truck came through out of turn. I got so nervous I killed the motor in front of this perfectly huge Cadillac Eldorado. A couple of cars went across the intersection and the next thing I knew there was this car door slamming behind me and this darling curly-haired man in an Armani suit, with his tie all jerked loose walked past my car and went out and stood in the middle of the intersection."

She stopped for breath. "He got out in the middle and bowed this exaggerated theatrical bow from the waist—remember Richard Dreyfuss in Rosenkrantz and Guildenstern?—and waved me on through."

They had come to the door of the classroom but Cathy wasn't through. "My hands were so sweaty they slipped around on the wheel. So I drove from there to the Jack in the Box across from that junior high on Fuqua and parked and went inside. And this man came in and stood looking at me. He has the most expressive eyebrows and thick lashes and the bluest eyes. He said he was sorry but there must be some mistake because I seemed to have his table. So I invited him to sit down, of course."

"Of course," Chub said, opening the door to the classroom.

It wasn't possible to talk in class. Cathy spent the next hour redrawing the darned banana blossom and several sizes of palm leaves on a fresh sheet of paper. By the time she got to wetting and dropping some blues into an unfolding purple leaf with a row of embryonic bananas around the crown, she realized she had almost, almost forgotten about how Tod Benjamin hadn't called. For a couple of minutes, anyway. Almost.

At nine o'clock she gathered up her supplies and hurried home.

Greg didn't even look up. He was watching "Law and Order" and crumbling peanut butter and crackers all over the carpet.

"Are you making a nest?" Cathy asked.

He looked around and let his eyes swing back to the set. "Your boyfriend called," he said and immediately waved her into silence so he could hear the babble on the tube.

The scene on the set faded and went antic.

"Talk," Cathy demanded.

He strained toward the television screen. "Said he'd call back."

Cathy moved around in front of him and crouched, weaving between him and the set, "Don't talk with your mouth full. That's it? When? When did he call?"

"Jeez." He craned, breathing peanutty breath on her. "I dunno. About an hour ago."

A baby gurgled and chortled on the television screen. "You are staring at a stupid commercial, Gregory. Are you interested in a Superior Waterbed? Give."

"Talk about your rotten manners," Greg said. He put three greasy crackers in his mouth whole.

She waited, eyes narrowed. "I've had a headache all night and you're not doing a thing for it," she snarled. "So. Tod called. And?"

"Ah, me," Greg said, scuttling sideways. "The three decibel 'and' coming from the incredible shrinking buttonhole mouth."

"Did you explain to him that I was in class? Am I supposed to call him back? I'd hate to have the man think that somebody more than six feet tall isn't bright enough to relay a simple telephone message. What, exactly, did the man *say*?"

Greg got up and leaned against the wall, licking at his finger tips. "I'm not sure you want to know everything the man said," he said. "Mr. Benjamin is what you could call one of your more weird conversationalists." He shambled toward the door.

Cathy walked over to the television and gave a knob a vicious twist.

"Now, that's what's the matter with the channel selector," he said. "That, right there, is totally what happens to be the matter with the channel selector."

Cathy started for him but he was too quick. He wheeled and ducked through the door. "He didn't say much," he said from his bedroom.

"What. Did. He. Say?" Cathy shouted. "Unlock this door. I realize how dreadful it must make you feel to think that someone might make me happy, but—"

"You didn't look all that happy on your way out of here tonight."

Cathy went into her bedroom and slammed the door. She knew there wasn't any Tod Benjamin listed in the phone book but she looked again, anyway, before she gave up and crawled into bed.

She was still awake, trying to find her place in a Larry McMurtry novel, when Greg tapped on the door. "So. How did class go, tonight? Did you get the banana blossom thing down? Are you basically gonna be okay?"

"Go to sleep," Cathy said. "I don't like you any better now than I did twenty minutes ago."

He tapped on the door again and pushed it open. "You want an Oreo or an aspirin or anything?"

"I already took something," Cathy said. "The label says 'Caution, may cause drowsiness.' Go away and let it cause drowsiness."

"Yeah." Greg opened the door wider and stood gazing at her. After a minute or two he began moving back and forth against the door jamb, scratching between his shoulder blades. "Old Benjamin's definitely weird, Mom. I mean it." He thought for a minute. "I'll spare you the details and the language and all, but he sounded pretty smashed. He really has a way of switching into about ten different guys. Maybe he's possessed. You ever notice him twisting his head back to front or anything?"

"Oh, please. It's late. For the record, you're good at switching personalities. When I left for class tonight, you were being halfway human."

"Aw, come on. I gotta keep up my kid image, don't I?" He went padding off to his room.

Tod called. Cathy sat up and hugged herself. Tod called. He'd call again. But he might not. Why should he? He might have been looped in the loops of her hair and all that for a few hours, but he'd looked disappointed when she'd gone into that about being a widow. She must have sounded so stupid and stodgy, with the damned, damnable childhood stammer coming back. That only happened once in a while these days. Only when a person least wanted it.

A man like Tod Benjamin must have an address book full of wet-lipped females like those skinny women on the cover of Cosmopolitan, with their necklines open down to their flat bellies and the aureoles of their nipples showing. He'd want a woman as sexy and impatient as he kept being, with that little growl in his throat, with his hands so quick and hard they felt like they would leave bruises.

He'd called, though.

Cicadas buzzed and racketed in the lull when the air conditioner kicked off. The bed was damp and hot. She sat up and threw her pillows on the floor and stretched out, her face in the crook of her arm. Her arm smelled of baby talcum. That's me, she thought: Ivory soap and baby powder. Damn it, anyway.

*****

7

The next morning Greg got out of the house before Cathy was up. He got over to Scotty's house in time to catch Scot sitting in his bed, pawing at sleep kernels in his eyes, trying to make up his mind about the costume of the day. "The fatigues or the orange stripe? The dragon goes okay with the scrubs, don't you think? But they need a belt over the drawstring."

"Whatever," Greg said.

"You see my World Trade Center memorial cap?" Scotty said, rummaging. He had about eighty-seven caps. He held up a T-shirt with a photograph of women's breasts. "Nah. Definitely not Dobie."

"Decisions, decisions," Greg said. "Let's go." He wanted to talk about little big man and the weird call, but Scot about broke his jaw yawning most of the way to Ginger's house. Then, after they got there, all she wanted to talk about was her mom, the town drunk. So Greg ended up tuning them both out, trying to dope the bit out by himself.

Man called about ten. Greg had felt a little chill even before he picked up the receiver. Then there was this three-pack-a-day voice, old Toddy, growling, "Hope I'm not interrupting anything, son."

"No, sir," Greg said, wishing he'd gone into his answer machine routine but that kind of thing had a way of falling apart. "Mom's at her painting class." He tried to sound busy. "She generally stays late because the teacher is a friend of hers so there's no telling when she'll get home. Sorry."

"That's so? That's a nice thing, isn't it? That she's got a nice hobby."

"Yes, sir." Greg thought how Cathy would love hearing that. He'd have to get the old boy to pull that one on her. Nice hobby. Oh wonderful.

Tod chuckled. "I'll just bet she's a whiz, too. Your mama ever do any sailboats? I bet if she did some one of those gift shops in Kemah might be interested. People pay good money for those."

"You mean with the sunset and a palm tree or two?" Greg fought an ecstatic snicker. "Now, that's a great idea. You need to talk to her about that. Mom's all the time looking for great ideas like that."

There was a pause and he thought he might have overdone it. "Well," he said finally, "I'll tell her you called."

"Uh, Gregory, hold on a sec." The man started in on a bunch of inane bull about homework and how were the music lessons coming. The old guy actually seemed to think Greg wanted to listen to him. "Yes, sir, your mother must really enjoy her art class. Gives her something to do, eh?"

Greg kept trying to cut him off but the old boy kept talking. Greg had time to get a couple of pillows and hold the receiver out so the cord could unwind. When he brought the receiver back to his ear the old boy was still going on, like the Energizer bunny. It was kind of sad, actually. Greg started to get this picture that he really did not want to see, of old Toddy nodding away in some bar and toddling home to sit around in these pajamas that old men wear that gape open at the belly, spilling ashes all over his hairy little paunch, in this empty bedroom in this empty house that Cathy was all the time raving about.

"Harrumph." The old guy cleared his throat in Greg's ear, for about the eleventh time. "I understand you've been giving your mama a hard time about that, son, and I want you to know I'm on your side." Greg quit fooling around with the receiver. "Can't say as I blame you," Tod said.

He paused and Greg, wondering what he'd missed, said he'd try to keep that in mind. Tod said, "Now, I don't want to get in the middle, but I just think you ought to know I'm in your corner on that."

"Yes, sir," Greg said.

Toddy chuckled. "I don't guess your mama's mentioned that, eh? Well, I was a lot younger than you when I got my license."

Greg sat up. "That so?"

"So why don't I pick you up? Got anything lined up after school? I've got a little something up my sleeve. I could come by about four, four-thirty, tomorrow afternoon."

As a matter of fact, Greg had a cello lesson after school, but when he mentioned it, Tod said why didn't he break loose about five or five-thirty.

Greg started to say he didn't know about being late, but Tod ran him down. "Strategy. We're need a little strategy. You open for a driving lesson?" He chuckled. "Just between us. No point making a federal case of it with your mama. I understand that's something of a sore point, am I right?"

"Well, Mom—"

"So why don't we keep this between the two of us? Let me handle your mama on this. Young fella your age ought to be driving."

Unreal. Awesomely unreal.

By the time Cathy came in from her painting class, Greg was mad at himself for listening to the dork long enough so that he felt halfway involved and halfway mad at her for encouraging somebody like him in the first place. But he was curious. Tod might have been drunk. Halfway sounded like he was. He might not even show up.

But, at twenty after five, there he was, in a red jeep instead of his usual big-assed, day-glow, white and gold Eldorado. The man got out and handed Greg the keys. "Wheels," he said. "Young fella like you ought to have wheels, am I right or am I right?"

*****

8

Greg drove. He drove out of the school lot and over to Almeda Mall and around that parking lot and up and down the streets of Kirkmont and Sagemont and Hall Road and Blackhawk, oh, man, Gregory drove that jeep. He knew everything was going to fall apart the minute he got home. Old Tod could sit there with his big, know-it-all grin but no way in hell could he keep things from falling all apart the minute they got back home.

It started to get dark a lot too soon.

On the way to the house, Greg kept looking over at the man, thinking how funny it was to see a guy look so pleased with himself while he kept gnawing on his fingernails. "Man," Greg told him, "thanks. This has been really great. No way is my mom going to let me use your jeep, but thanks."

Tod grinned and shrugged. "It's worth a shot."

Cathy came to the front door with her long-snouted watering can in her hand. When she saw that Tod was with Greg she almost dropped the can. She let the watering can tip down and sprinkle the floor. That led to a lot of kidding around and mopping up and gave Greg a chance to go into the kitchen to get a glass of milk.

The kitchen smelled like tomato sauce and cheese and garlic. There was this brown around the edges, dried up lasagna looked like it had been waiting around for a while. Uh, oh, he thought. But, out in the living room, Tod started in booming about how the three of them ought to go somewhere and get a little bite to eat and when he went back in there, Cathy fluttered around. She couldn't get a whole heck of a lot of conviction into how worried she'd been and how they both had some explaining to do. She kept batting her eyes at old Tod, King of the World, and he kept bellowing how everything was all his fault and he could explain, Ma'am.

Then they went outside and Cathy gathered up her skirts and clambered up into the jeep and looked around like she rode in jeeps all the time. "Why, I didn't know you had one of these, what fun."

Tod drove to Webster, to a crowded Italian restaurant, where he slipped a guy a bill, got a table and started in winking at Greg, recommending some wine like Greg was supposed to know about it. "They use fresh sweet basil and fresh rosemary here," he said.

All while they ate, Tod kept talking, talking, putting his hand out anytime Cathy tried to say anything. After he got past apologizing for making Greg late he swung into high gear: "Been trying to persuade our boy, here, that he ought to have a driver's license. Pretty important thing for a young fella to have a car. He's got to be *responsible*, isn't that the ticket?" Most of his sentences ended up questions.

"Of course I want him to be responsible," she said, but he cut her off.

"That's how I figured you'd see it. He's under a lot of pressure from the other kids. So what we've got to do, we've got to make this young fella see how important it is to be damned careful, right?"

Before Cathy could get a breath or open her mouth, he went on, looking around, big authority. "What we want to do, here, is see to it that this young fella can get around. He's got to be the only kid in his class without wheels, that right, Greg?"

Greg had to wince at that, because he'd already tried that one on her and he knew the answer. But somehow, when Tod was pitching, things came out different. She got to dubiously biting on her lower lip a couple of times. She even tried to interrupt again. "Aren't jeeps sort of d-d-dangerous? I thought they were supposed to be..."

But Tod had the floor: "President Reagan had a jeep." Anytime he needed a breath, he waved her down, with both hands. "Ronnie loved his

Jeep. It's the only vehicle he, himself, personally, owned. Same model we've got here, for our boy. I've got a feeling he'll take good care of it."

"I'm sure he'd take c-c-care of it. That's not the p-point—"

But Tod was saying, "Now that's the way he seems to me. A responsible sort of young fella." He gave her that splayed-fingered peremptory little wave while he grabbed a couple of gulps of wine. "That's the way I see it, too. We've got a very dependable young man, here."

Oh, man, Tod discussed Greg's trustworthy dependability and how he was going to have to drive sooner or later, ready or not, and President Reagan's feelings for his jeep, while she sipped wine and listened, sweat shining on her brow and a faint upside down triangle dampening the front of her blouse, even though the restaurant was plenty cool.

Then, right in front of God and the people at the next table Tod took both of Cathy's hands in his, turned her hands palm up, and *kissed* them.

Cathy shot Greg a look and concentrated on looking at the table cloth, but Tod wouldn't let go of her hands. He held on until things got quiet and he said, "Look at me, my dear."

She gazed into his face, blinked, looked down and said, "Tod."

Tod wouldn't let go, though. He sat there, hanging on to her hands, breathing so you could hear him. "Don't fight me on this," he said, begging but threatening, too. "This is something I want to do. The boy needs this. Believe me, I know what I'm doing."

Jeez, Greg thought: are we still talking about me driving, here?

Cathy started to argue. "I'm sorry. I, I don't see how—"

"Ah, but darlin', you don't understand. That's the thing. I'm going to give the kid the jeep, don't worry about it, we'll handle that, Greg and me, Greg and I," and he drew in a shaky breath. "I'm going to marry you."

When Greg could lift his eyes, the old boy nodded at him, his eyes brimming. "I'm marrying you guys." He chortled and wiped his eyes. "That's what I'm going to do."

Boy. Talk about a bunny caught in the headlights. Cathy shook her head but Tod didn't pay any attention. "Oh, yes," he crowed. "That's what people do, isn't it? That's what people like us do, when they feel like this, isn't it? They get married. Sa-ay, what we need over here is champagne, any champagne in this place?"

He laughed when Cathy pulled away. He had his eyes closed. "What we need is a little wine, over here."

The guys at the next table started clapping and so did a couple of waiters.

"Don't think I haven't been thinking about this, now," Tod said, his handkerchief out, wiping his eyes, blotting his neck. "You want me to go down on one knee?" He bounced out of his chair and slid down next to

Cathy and took her hand. "What do you say? Will you be my wife?"

"I say g-g-get up, this sec—this min-min-minute," Cathy said, laughing but about half crying.

Greg stumbled to his feet and said why didn't they head for home. He helped Tod get up on his feet. Cathy grabbed up her purse, threw down some bills for the check, and they got out of there. But it still wasn't over.

When they got to the parking lot, Tod got between the two of them and grabbed them, hugging Greg around the shoulders, pinning his arms down, half-strangling Cathy, saying, "My little family! Why, you two are the first people I've given a damn in the world about for so damned long I just can't tell you." He got all choked up. "Somebody to love. Now, what else is there? Somebody to love and love me, why, I don't think anybody ever—ah, hell, what's the matter with me, noisy old bastard, got to be embarrassing the hell out of you both."

He let go of them, straightened his tie, put his shoulders back and tossed Greg the keys. "Take the wheel, boy. Show your mama what kind of a driver you are."

*****

9

One of the women in Chub's painting class, Marjorie, sometimes shared a table with Cathy. Marjorie always showed up with a dramatically long, bright, satiny scarf wound around her heavy dark hair and she wore real jewels on both hands even when she was working with acrylics or gesso. The rest of the women in the class marveled that the scarf and all those heavy rings didn't get in her way. Everybody was impressed with the way she looked but they got very tired of Marjorie's endlessly nasal opinions.

"She's as full of bull as a teenager," Chub said once over coffee, and Cathy immediately thought of Greg's friend, Ginger.

"How well do you know your Mister Tod?" Marjorie asked. "Does anybody we know know anything about your beau?"

"That's what Greg's teenage friend says," Cathy admitted. "So annoying. But she's a teenager, after all."

Marjorie sniffed. "Oh, really. Well. Out of the mouths of babes. A person can't be too careful."

That would seem to be Ginger's opinion. When Greg told Ginger about the way Tod had proposed in that Italian restaurant, how carried away he had been, Ginger had sneered, "So, how come?'"

"Hey, Mom: Ginger wonders how come Tod doesn't have anybody to love," Greg reported. "She says we should have come right out and asked the man, 'How come you don't have anybody to love?' I mean, how old is he, anyway? She might have a point."

He couldn't wait to relay that little gem. He was so frustrated about not being able to drive the Jeep. It wasn't enough to be loaned one. Owning it would take insurance and money for gas and maintenance, and she wasn't about to ask Tod for help with any of that, since he seemed unaware of the problem. He probably expected Greg to somehow find a way to take care of that. But he couldn't, unless he got a job, and the kid couldn't get a job without being able to drive so he was in a Catch 22 situation. Meanwhile, the Jeep sat in the garage. One more thing to argue about.

Marjorie flipped her silly scarf over her shoulder. Cathy kept thinking she'd get at least a few splatters on all that flowing silk but she never seemed to, even when she was tossing paint around on other people, busily shaking her brush half a foot above the paper to splatter yellow ochre into the background of the bright green landscape she was working on. "Houston has gotten so dangerous," she whined. "Did you read all that about those ghastly priests in today's *Chronicle*?" Scandals about priests sent Marjorie into raptures. "Arthur and I weren't a bit surprised. We knew it. We just knew it, all the time. Those priests are as bad as the nuns."

When nobody asked her about the nuns, Cathy rather hoped Marjorie might be still for a bit, but Chub chose that moment to come into the room and gently tease Cathy about running away to Galveston. One of the other women said, "I want to see a picture of that gorgeous mansion," and Marjorie said, "What mansion?" and things got entirely out of hand.

The Scarf Head had to have the last word. "You rode off to Galveston with this stranger? How could you do that? I'd no more get in the car like that than fly. You're insane. Didn't you read about those women buried alongside the Gulf freeway? What to you know about your Mister Tod?"

"Just that he's wonderful," Cathy said, and immediately wished she hadn't said that much.

"I'll have my Arthur see what he find out." Marjorie's Arthur was an absolute whiz on the internet. "I mean, if a person can't trust a priest!".

"I doubt my friend's ever been remotely interested in the priesthood," Cathy said, feeling her face grow warm.

"Benjamin? Benjamin Tod? I think my daughter might have said something about him." The Scarf Head looked sly. "My daughter teaches," she said. "You wouldn't believe the things she runs into. Benjamin Tod?"

"If you say it that way you have to insert a comma," Cathy muttered.

"Yes, well, you can't be too careful," Marjorie said. "That's what I always say."

Chub broke in. "Ah, yes, that goes without saying. And I want to be the first to say it."

Marjorie didn't show up for class the next Wednesday night. Everybody painted away in companionable silence, but when Cathy and Chub took a coffee break, Marjorie's scarfy head popped up like a toadstool the minute the two of them got to the cafeteria.

"You look so happy," Chub said, tentatively, as she pulled up a chair and right then, before she or Cathy could say another word, things started to go sour. Something hesitant and careful in the way Chub started shaping her words sent a small sick chill all through Cathy.

"I am happy," she insisted. "Deliriously." She lowered her chin and gazed at Chub. "What?"

"What, what?" Chub said. "There's no what. I want you to be happy." Her eyebrows drew together. "I do."

"I can tell," Cathy said. "Quit doing that with your hands." She took a deep breath. "I wish you could see Greg with that darned Jeep. He's dying to drive it. It's driving him crazy."

Chub's smile looked strained.

"What?" Cathy said.

Chub caught her upper lip beneath her teeth. "I want you to be happy."

"Is that why you're sitting there looking like I just ran over your puppy dog?"

Chub blinked. "Am I?" She blinked again and tried for another smile. "Well, maybe I am. I guess I am. Sorry, love. It's just that, well, hell, how can you do that? How can you let this person, this stranger, really, lend Greggy a car? That's the most manipulative thing."

"Of course it is." Cathy started to get up.

"Wait." Chub deliberately unclasped her hands and put them in her lap. "Sit down. We have to talk. You don't know this man. And this whole thing is so wildly manipulative. Accepting a car."

"It's a loan." Cathy said.

"That's what I mean," Chub said.

"Maybe I like being manipulated," Cathy said. "Maybe no one has ever even thought about wanting to wildly manipulate me. Maybe it's just terrific to have a person like Tod want to—"

"But what about Greg?" Chub interrupted, her voice going querulous. "Look at what you're doing to Gregory."

"Well, he'll have to get some sort of a job, that's all," Cathy said. "That wouldn't be so bad."

Chub looked around. "Okay. Marjorie called me up. Her daughter, the teacher, in Galveston, knows your Tod." She hesitated. "Knows *of*." She kept swallowing. "That's the thing."

Cathy put down her spoon. "Tell me."

"There was this kid, one of her students, who had a crush on a grown man who used to come and pick her up from school."

Cathy could hardly breathe.

"Fourteen," Chub said. "A fourteen-year-old."

"Wait." Cathy cleared her throat. "Wait."

"Oh, God. Don't look like that," Chub said. "I'm just saying. Marjorie says he wasn't arrested because they snapped to what was going on and the girl's parents stepped in, in time. But she wants to talk to you about it. She got so upset at the very name. She says this person seemed so respectable and handsome but older, a business man, in a suit and tie." She stopped. "I hate this. Please don't look like that. I just wish we knew more about Tod." She had her hands on Cathy's. "I'm just saying that none of us knows anything about this man. That's all I'm saying."

Cathy stood up so fast her chair nearly tipped over. She caught it and righted it and reached for her purse. "Let me be sure I've got this straight. Smarmy Marjorie knows about some teen who had a crush on some...some male named Benjamin? Is that what you're getting all weepy about? She couldn't even get Tod's name straight."

"My point is that we don't really know him," Chub said. "It takes time to know someone and this Tod person seems to be moving in on you so fast and we love you, Cathy. That's all."

"We?" Cathy said. "Since when do you pay any attention to the scarf head? You know what I think it is? I think Tod might not quite measure up. He's not quite up to your standards, is that it?" She made a face. "He's not faculty. Well, you know what? Neither am I. Thank God." Her mouth was pulled so tight she could hardly talk. "I don't want to hear any more of this happy little reminiscence. I might ask Tod about it, if I can find some way to work it into the conversation, thank you very much. I might do that but I do not care to go on with this conversation."

"Oh, Cathy." Chub tugged at her frizzy hair. "I'm so sorry. But I had to tell you. And I do think you'd better talk to him. I do."

"Yes." Cathy said. She smoothed her sleeves and looked away. "B-but people sue people, d-don't you k-know? And you can stop p-playing the b-b-big m-mother hen."

Chub nodded, her eyes sorrowing.

Cathy almost added, Not that you would know anything about mothering, but that would have to be the cruelest thing anybody could say to Chub. So Cathy looked into Chub's too bright eyes and tightened her lips. One more word would have them both in tears, right there in the San

Jacinto College cafeteria.

On the morning of the next class night, Chub called to apologize. "Marjorie isn't sure the man's first name is Tod," she began.

Cathy cut her off, bitterly scornful. "Well, you're a bit late. Tod and I have already discussed your little nastiness. He was appalled." Her voice shook. "I hope I never see him as hurt as that again. Tod is a very sensitive person. I'm afraid I'm going to have to drop the class," she said. "We seem to be awfully busy."

"Ah, honey," Chub said. "Don't do this."

It took some doing and it took some time but Chub sounded so miserable that night, and Chub kept sounding so miserable every time she called, that Cathy finally forgave her. She didn't go back to the painting class. She might have given in to a yen to tie a knot in that damned scarf and throw one end over the exposed pipes in the classroom's ceiling. See if she couldn't turn off Marjorie's nasty, niggling, nasal voice.

*****

10

On the second Saturday in September Tod took Cathy to the Spindletop, because she said she'd never been there and he must have taken that as a hint. It was everything she'd hoped it would be, a glamorously lit restaurant revolving high above the city, with gorgeously dressed women and expensively suited men, quite a few of them Japanese.

As they sat down at their table, Tod grinned. "Are you all right? You look a little pale. Not that it isn't becoming."

"That glass elevator felt like it might swing on up off the building." d.

"Remind me to take you bungee jumping," Tod said.

"Oh, please."

"I mean it." He had an one eyebrow up. "Believe it."

"Well, I'm not about to do any bungee jumping," Cathy said. "I wore braces all the way through high school."

She couldn't remember the last time she'd been in a restaurant with lovely napery and crystal and chandeliers. She grew so preoccupied with the wavering reflections and the play of light across the buildings as they circled around that she had some difficulty focusing on what Tod was saying. He talked nonstop, leaning back expansively pleased.

Now he leaned toward her, tapping his front teeth, his voice an intimate growl: "Speaking of teeth, this is sort of embarrassing but we're going to have to get past a little something here, sooner or later. Some of my teeth are, well, let's just say I lost a couple teeth, a while back. That going to bother you? Knowing that, I mean."

"Oh." Cathy hoped she didn't look flustered. She tried to think of a casual reply. Tod keep holding her eyes with his. She broke the eye contact. There were geometric shapes on his tie.

Tod's hands kept moving and after a moment he reached for her hands, and his smile broadened. "Does bug you some, eh?" He licked his lips. "Don't worry about it. Nobody's ever seen me without 'em or ever will."

"Oh, for heaven's sake," Cathy began. "A lot of people have their teeth capped." But that wasn't what he meant and they both knew it. And now that he mentioned it, she could see that some of his front teeth, on the side, might not be his own. His own teeth had a faint yellow tinge, from the cigars, probably, but his eye teeth were porcelain white.

He endured her gaze. "Happened a long time ago. Don't know why I brought it up. Guess I just wanted to be up front about the thing." He sat back and sighed expansively. "You want to know how it happened?" Cathy shook her head but he started in, rapidly. "There was this accident. A pickup truck slid under an eighteen-wheeler on Allen Parkway, on that chute leads into the freeway? Hell of a thing. The whole front of the truck slid under the trailer and the truck had a little kid trapped in the cab. So. I pulled the door off, me and a couple of other guys. Got the little kid out. It was one of those things, you know. First there's all that noise, the truck goes screaming under there"—He grimaced, remembering—"You never forget that, the noise, I mean, God, there's all that noise, right in front of you on the freeway. And the car's smoking, people are yelling and running around in circles. Nobody's doing anything." He waved his hands and almost dislodged an ashtray. "I guess I got pumped up."

"It sounds positively heroic," Cathy said.

He shrugged. "You don't know what you can do until you have to."

"I'm impressed," Cathy said. "Truly."

"Young and dumb," Tod said. "Burned my hands. I've still got some scars." He held his hands up to show her. Cathy couldn't see any scars. His hands were very masculine, blunt-fingered, dark, with curling dark hair on their backs. "Singed my eyebrows off." He chuckled and lifted an eyebrow. "Grew back, didn't they? Overcompensated, you might say. Well, hell, I guess I'm lucky all it took was a little hair and a couple of front teeth. And, well, I did get a little medal." He chuckled, swallowed a small belch, made a fist to hammer his chest. "Damned medal didn't do doodly toward paying the dentist, but that's the way the ball bounces."

He held a hand up, got the waiter's attention and waved two fingers before he turned to her, smiling, gazing into her eyes with a kind of blue ferocity. "Good. Now, let's see. What else can I say to make you blush?"

"Was all of that just to make me blush?"

"No." He lifted an eyebrow. "Not all of it." He laughed. "But you do. Blush."

"So I'm told." Cathy didn't know where to look. "D-don't."

Tod sighed and shifted in his seat. "Do you always believe everything you're told, kid?" He brought his hand across his mouth and looked pensive. "You want to know what really happened? I broke out my damned front teeth when I fell down some basement steps with an armload of milk bottles when I was six years old."

Cathy swallowed and looked away. Silver clinked on china. A waiter hovered solicitously near Tod and backed away. The pretty lights went on revolving, twinkling on the pretty panes of glass outside the window turning, turning alongside her. I am having a perfectly splendid time, she told herself, I am having a perfectly splendid, exciting time with an exciting man and I am not going to pull a dumb Cathy here and stupidly make a big thing of being teased by a silly little fib. Comforting word. Fib. She was, at once, reassured. Why! How thrilling, actually, to think that she had made a grown man, a successful businessman, sink to such adolescent behavior. She very nearly interrupted him with a prim motherly admonition: you must be careful with the truth, my friend—

—or, equally adolescent, liar, liar—

But Tod's voice was going on and on and now he leaned toward her, slapping his palm to make a point: "My aunt felt pretty bad about the whole thing. No. She didn't. Aunt Beverly never felt bad about things like that, but we're not going to get going on my aunt Beverly, now—you cold, honey? You ought to have a wrap, these places are always chilly— ah, hell, what's the matter with me? What kind of a conversation is this?"

Another round of drinks arrived.

Tod reached across the table and took her hand in his and chafed it lightly, murmuring, "Air conditioning too much for you? Your fingers are cold, little peach."

"I don't much care for my coloring, you know," Cathy said. "I love yours."

He laughed and caught the waiter's eye, pointing to his glass. "We want another one of these."

When Tod's lobster and Cathy's filet came he ordered another martini to go with dinner and everything was wonderfully good. Cathy said she'd never seen such a huge lobster, she didn't know they grew that large, but then they'd finished dinner and the next thing she knew she and Tod were giggling and leaning on each other, leaving the restaurant. She was being led bumbling along a hotel corridor. Because Tod had reserved a room. And he was saying how lovely she was and oops when they bumped into things and Cathy was thinking, foggily, well, now, this is what this feels like. I am going to a hotel room with a man.

"I didn't know you'd arranged this," she said, as he clutched her to him with his right hand and wiggled the key into the door with his left.

"You didn't?" he asked, owlishly. "You want to be carried?"

Hoisted, you mean, she thought, and giggled. "You could try a fireman's carry." He didn't seem to find that as funny as she did. "You're not going to believe this, but I haven't been in many hotels. My grandfather didn't believe in wasting money, and Joe and I didn't either and since then nobody's ever been especially—"

"We don't have to go in," Tod said. "We can spend the night whispering out here in the hall."

"Oh, I think we'd better look at the room, at least," Cathy said, wondering what a room would cost in such a sumptuous hotel. She had terrific misgivings, though. She'd been having unhappy small prickles all along as they stumbled up the corridor but right about then she knew with a lurch of sick certainty that things were going very wrong indeed. "Listen," she said. The word sounded mushy but she had to make Tod pay attention. "I never have had such a lot of martinis at one sitting and, no, I mean this, now, this is important. I never have gone into a hotel room to ah, do this. Like this. To, to you know. Never. In my life. I'm sorry. I really am sorry."

Tod looked disbelieving. "Never?"

She shook her head. "I'm sorry."

"Well, don't be sorry." He didn't believe her. His mouth drew down. A vein pulsed in his temple. "You sure about that?"

Cathy fought the stammer. "Wish...with like this withish a strange man," she said, her voice quavering.

"A strange man?" He looked very annoyed. "When did I get strange? You want to skip it? Why don't we skip it. You don't have to make excuses, baby." He grabbed her arm, turned her about and pushed her toward the door.

"Wait," Cathy said. "I'm having to consider. That's all." She shook him off. "Can't you wait a minute?"

"What for?"

The room was done in shades of blue, with a perfectly huge mirror in a rococo frame over a huge chest of drawers and two perfectly huge beds. Two of them. Acres of bed. Cathy walked all around the blue-covered beds and paused to look at her reflection in the mirror. She looked awful, disheveled and sweaty, mascara rubbed into the wrinkles beneath her eyes. "I look like something out of Bertolt Brecht," she said.

"That so?" Tod sat down on a bed and got up to pace, his face blank.

"Or a TV evangelist, maybe," Cathy said. She giggled. "Oh, I don't blame you for looking bored," she said and paused, dismayed at how slushy she sounded. "I don't blame you a bit. I think you're wonderful. Give me a minute. Maybe I'm, you know, just a little dizzy."

"You aren't going to be sick, are you?" His annoyed tone deepened.

"I don't think so. Would it make you mad if I were?"

"Mad at myself, I guess." He shrugged. "Why do I feel like a white slaver?" He lit a cigar and sat back gazing at it. "Want to try one of these?"

She laughed shakily. "That's all I need."

He got up and walked around. She wished he'd sit down but when he did, his sitting down didn't help. He slumped, his mouth bitterly bracketed, gazing at the carpet . Cathy couldn't think what to say or do.

"You want to come over here?" he asked finally.

There was only the one chair, the one he was in. She approached him hesitantly and, when he reached for her, slid clumsily to the floor facing the wrong way, sitting at his feet with her back against his knees, listening to him breathe. After a few minutes, she got up, leaned down to hug him and lost her balance. He had to hold her off for a long moment so she could get her feet under her. Tod sighed.

"We could try kissing," Cathy said.

He sighed again. When he kissed her, she closed her eyes and remembered to open her mouth a little way. Ecstasy, she told herself. Think ecstasy. But she'd have to really concentrate because Tod would hate any pretense.

It wasn't entirely pretense.

She sank into kissing him but then she started uneasily wondering how her breath might smell and whether he could sense that her right arm seemed to be going numb at the elbow. He always seemed to be able to sense everything. He could tell how wrong things felt. She was sure of it.

He began busily unbuttoning and unzipping, trying to gentle her, to wait her out, his arms growing tight and tighter, my, his arms were like clamps fastening her closer and closer to his hard little chest. At first his firmness seemed a comfort but as he held her increasingly hard and tight she could scarcely inhale and the flesh of her arms gave beneath his fingers. She could feel her flesh bruise as he moved against her, pulsing, his mouth hard, too hard—

—and she fought a wild giggle, improbably caught up in an insane bit of something she'd seen, a film clip of Tony Curtis complaining in some interview that kissing Marilyn Monroe was like kissing Hitler—what a thing to be thinking of—Marilyn Monroe and Hitler—it made her fight a wild burst of hysteria.

His mouth stayed hard on hers, too hard, then sought her, deliberately, his lips shaping hers. He made little growls, kissing her throat, biting little nips, his mouth moving warmly to where his warm fingers moved, cupping her, touching her nipples, making them erect and aching, answering his please, oh, baby, please.

It did not work.

It was terribly important that he not know. She fought his hand away. She didn't want him to touch here—there—and realize how unready she was. She couldn't help it, couldn't help anything. He seemed so busy and she couldn't breathe. She couldn't get away. It felt like being cornered, shoved into a very small thick place with all of him swarming at her.

"What?" he said. She shuddered. Tod rolled over and sat up. "It might help if you put down your purse."

"I'm so sorry." She put her purse down. Tears flooded her eyes and nose, filled her mouth, came bursting out to wash over her cheeks and chin. She blubbered: "Ah hah ah hah ah haaaah."

Tod pulled away, got up and went to the other side of the room. "You can hold onto your purse if it means that much to you," he said, wearily.

After a time, he pulled the curtains at the room's wide window and stood looking out, moving restlessly from one foot to another, impassively discussing the look of the lights in the parking lot outside. He took out a cigar, bit the end off, spat it out, said, "You mind?" and lit it.

When she shook her head, he said, "You know what I think all this is?" His hair stood up, damp and curling. He swiped at it, ran his hand along the back of his neck and drew himself up. "I think you're pretty well convinced that you think you're too good for the old chump, here. Can't say I blame you." He sounded tired. "You couldn't be more right."

She didn't want to start bleating again. "Oh, no. Truly! It isn't you, it's this place. I really can't do this like this in here with all this much bed. I cannot just lie down and do—you know—things. I can't. And that damned print, over there. Look at it. I loathe and despise art deco. Always have. Would you look at the blues? I'm sorry, truly, but it's impossible. It isn't you at all. It's, you know. All this. This whole thing."

She heard herself going on and on, babbling about starving artists and how they ought to just go starve for heavens sakes, starve and shut up about it, since all of them were forever stamping out the same mountains over and over for heaven's sake, all of it calendar art, and who ever painted mountains anymore? Until nothing made the least bit of sense. She had to gave up and go into the chilly immaculate little bathroom to run water in the sink so he couldn't hear her urinate.

After she'd finished, she washed her face; her hideous, blotchy, horrid face, that looked awful.

When she came out of the bathroom, Tod got up and walked to the door so he could open it for her with a little flourish.

They walked down the hall in silence.

Cathy fought tears, remembering how wonderfully excited she'd been just a few hours ago, how Tod had looked to her then and at that first moment, the very first time she'd ever seen him, in that intersection, bowing, so graceful, bowing from the waist, his arms wide, beckoning to her. Well, she told herself, this ought to do it. Now he knows about me. I'm not difficult. I'm impossible.

They waited in silence for the man to bring the car around.

Tod drove too fast, his mouth making chewing motions. They had gotten almost to the turn-off at Fuqua before he asked, not looking at her, "What the hell is art deck?"

"Art deco." She added breathlessly, "That's what it was, the awful picture over the bed. Didn't you find it impossible? Never mind."

"That so? Deck-oh? And what was all that about the artists?" He nodded, concentrating on driving. His mouth widened. "Art deck-oh," he said. "And starving artists." He said it again, his voice going up. His flipped a hand and his shoulders started to shake as he snickered. "Starving artists?" He took a hand from the steering wheel and pounded his knee, peering ahead, glancing at Cathy and snorting and tittering. His chest heaved. He threw back his head and laughed, a high, long, helpless squeal. He laughed until he had to fight for control, gasping for enough air to form words. "It isn't you, oh, it is, it's you, all right. It's you, baby. But it's the situation, too, ah, hell, I'm sorry, I'm sorry, but you're too much." Veins stood out on his brow and temples, his face glistened as he pawed the air, driving with one hand on the wheel, lolling, helplessly trying to make her see how funny the whole thing was, oh, hee, excuse him, she had to excuse him but, but really?

"I'm f-f-f-forty-what?" he gasped, "and I don't know how to get past first base—" and he waved at her, convulsed.

Cathy laughed with him, nervously at first—she did so wish he'd put both hands on the wheel—but agreeing, delighted to agree with him because he was right, of course. It was funny. She was funny. They were funny. They were hilariously funny. No wonder he had to gasp and loll and mop his eyes.

They were driving down toward a deserted stretch of Fuqua before he was able to explain. "It's me, baby. I can't help but crack up at myself. Honest. I wouldn't, why, I would never let myself laugh at you like that, I mean I think this kind of thing is pretty damned important, huh? But, forgive me, it's just so, well, hell. Super lover-boy, big Lothario, here. Haven't learned a damned thing, in how many years? Still getting the pretty lady drunk. Filling her up with booze like a high school freshman, oh, come on, you've got to see how sappy that is. What the hell. Sex is an appetite, like any other. Sometimes you're gonna be hungry and some-times you're not. It's no big deal. You don't have to wear yourself out trying to make the old man happy. You've got to know how crazy I am about you. You want to play hard to get, what the hell. I'm not sixteen, baby, what the hell."

So. He forgave her. Forgave both of them, sputtering that the fiasco had to be his fault. He was the one knew about gin, wasn't he? "You ever work in a bar? Now, I'm the one knows about booze. That's the thing. What do you know about booze? Too much of a lady, sure, I get it." His world was full, he said, of "motel dollies."

He talked on, waving his hands, driving, fast and slow, up and down the Beltway, in and out of subdivisions. He pulled over, finally, behind some trucks in a construction area, where he turned the key and faced her, still earnestly talking because he had so much to tell her, to make her understand. "You're my girl," he said. "My baby." His arm crept around her gently and tightened until he had her close, calling her his porcelain lady that he'd dreamed of, that he had always yearned for, all his life.

That he yearned for. That he wanted. Now.

He kissed her. And kissed her. Drowned her in warm kisses, teasingly and oh, so sweetly, his chocolaty voice saying, over and over, oh, my love, my lovely love, my only love—

—as they came together explosively, hard and fast, yanked together without compromise or thought, slamming and grunting, Cathy squealing rapturous screams and, finally, unable to make one more sound.

"Breathe," Tod said, holding her. "Take a big breath, little one. Come on. Did I—are you all right? I must have—God. Did I hurt you?"

"No. Yes. I don't care," Cathy said. And, wonderingly, "We just had to, didn't we?" She laughed. "I wouldn't have thought that would be physi-cally possible, would you? I mean, with the steering wheel and the gear shift and everything?"

"There isn't anything we can't do," he said, his head on her breast, crooning, "All right, everything's going to be all right, baby, baby, I'm right here." He kissed her fingers, one by one.

She kept reliving that night, sometimes at the most inopportune mo-ments. In the cafeteria. In the office, when she was supposed to be con-centrating. It put exactly the wrong look on her face in front of all kinds of people. "Where'd you go?" the girls at the office would ask and she'd feel her face get warm. Just remembering made her ache. She needed him so.

After that night, they made love almost every time they were together, one way or another. They were forever looking for places where they could be with each other. When they had time, they went to Galveston, to Tod's wonderful house, but other times they made love in the car, against walls, behind shrubbery, in mall parking lots. Finding places where they could be alone, however briefly, became an urgent continual quest. It thrilled Cathy to think of how needful he was, they both were, all the time, dying for a place, any place other than some stupid horrid hotel room. Oh, I hunger and thirst for my lady, Tod would say, his mouth on hers, hands reaching up inside her blouse, under her skirt, hurting her, sometimes—

—until, on a golden October day, the first Tuesday of the month, one dull gray dawn it dawned on Cathy that she should be—

—should have been—at least she ought to have begun—

—menstruating—oh, Lord.

September had passed, the whole entire month had passed.

She'd been on the pill, of course, and the pill was foolproof, of course. Wasn't it? Except, of course, she'd been so busy, and she could be so stupidly absent minded.

*****

11

The kit from the drugstore said she wasn't.

Which she knew, of course. Only she was still late. And the kit might not be foolproof and she had been an absolute fool. Her breasts hurt and she was late and she was never late. She had the pill, of course, but there had been a couple of times…but that kind of thinking had to be crazy. It's premenstrual tension, she reasoned. No. It's being obsessive. Whatever, it's strictly my own business. I can handle this. I'll tell exactly no one. Maybe I'm menopausal. Hah. Maybe I ought to get another kit. Maybe I ought to just say no. I can not live from month to month having nervous breakdowns. So I am not going to keep thinking about it.

I'm going to think about Tod's coming over to enjoy a wonderfully extravagant roast, in our nice clean house tonight. Maybe I can get Greg to play a little Chopin after dinner. Vivaldi. Mozart. Something. Tod's never heard Greg play. He has no idea. It's going to be a lovely evening.

Everything went wrong at the office. On her way home, the oil light came on in the car. She had to go out of her way to get to a Texaco, where she could use the card, to get oil. So she got home late, and Scot, Greg's friend who liked to costume, was there, lolling on the sofa, heavy-lidded and slack jawed, in some green mesh shirt thing and baggy clown britches, everything but the red nose and big shoes. Scot on the sofa and Greg sprawled on the floor. Scot got to his feet and said, "Good evening," intoning, doing his vampire voice.

"Good evening," Cathy said. "How about setting the table for four? You can stay if you help me talk Greg into playing after we eat."

"I don't think so," Greg said.

Cathy thanked him and hurried to the kitchen. She set the oven to preheat, got out the frozen rolls and string beans. When the oven began to smoke, she shoved the roast in to sear. There wasn't time for a shower but she ran upstairs and took one anyway.

The smoke alarm went off just as Tod was coming in the front door. Cathy was on her way down the stairs. "Nice going," Greg screamed, over the alarm. He turned it off as Scotty tossed the roast, what was left of it, into the kitchen sink. "No biggie,' Greg said. "My Mom thinks the smoke alarm is a timer."

"I forgot to turn the oven off," Cathy said. "You're supposed to get the oven hot and turn it off and let the roast cook itself."

"Into a hockey puck," Greg said. He turned off the faucets and held up the roast. It dripped brown rivers down his forearms. "Ashes, ashes," he said, "all fall down."

"Oh, wipe that goofy grin off your goofy face," Cathy said.

"Hello," Tod said. "Hello?"

"I mean it," Cathy said.

Greg's grin widened. "I'm shaking. My shoes are falling off."

"Hello?" Tod said. "Shall I go out and come back in?"

"Good evening." Scot leered and rubbed his hands. "Don't be afraid."

Tod frowned. "What did you say to your mother, young man?"

Greg and Scot and Cathy looked at him.

Tod broke the silence. "What was that about a timer and hockey puck?"

"Hockey puck?" Greg looked deliberately bland. "We frequently have baked hockey puck. It's considered a delicacy around here. It can be done in the microwave but the oven is the method of choice. Adds to the ambience."

Tod scowled. "You going to let this young fella talk to you like that?"

"Well, it is a hockey puck," Cathy said. "Look at it."

"Good evening," Scotty said again. "I'll take mine on the hoof." He and Greg high fived each other.

"Forgot to turn the oven off," Cathy said, distractedly.

"No shize, Sherlock," Greg said. "Any other hot clues?" and Cathy headed for the pantry, wondering what she could do with tuna fish without celery or lettuce, since the lettuce was the wrong kind, leaf lettuce, with carrot slivers, when she realized that Tod was growling again, looming in the doorway.

"You going to let that young whelp talk to you like that?" She turned around. Tod was headed for the front door. "Who needs it? Feels like I'm running a circus with a bunch of clowns. I get enough of this at the lab. You kiddies ever get anywhere near the real world? Either one of you ever try to pull your own weight?"

He looked at Cathy. "See what the market's doing? Turn on the TV."

He tapped Greg on the chest. "You're pretty hot with the smart ass talk, think you're hard to keep up with, well, I'm here to tell you, you get in the habit of shooting off your mouth in the real world, you're gonna end up walking without kneecaps."

Both the boys were staring.

"I don't know what the hell you think you're doing, talking to your mama like that," Tod went on, bright pink streaking his cheeks, his eyes glittering. He stamped one foot and then the other. "Hockey pucks, my ass. Couple of smart ass kids."

"Get a grip," Scotty said, under his breath.

Oh, good heavens, Cathy thought. The stupid kid must think Tod is deaf.

"What's that?" Tod looked around, sputtering. "Plenty of people ready to hold your feet to the fire, in the real world," he went on, getting in deeper, the boys silent, their faces blank.

Tod shifted gears. "You kids gotta learn when to shut up, when to breathe through your noses and keep the traps shut, or sooner or later you gonna run into guys talking about piano wire, you know what I mean?" He puffed, trying for an expansive smile, and held his hand up. "Sooner or later—"

But Scotty interrupted. "Gee, you mean like on the TV?" He smiled, deliberately innocent and Greg chimed in, his hands prayerful.

"Piano wire?" He looked bewildered.

"Ah, hell," Tod said. "You people have your own act going here. You don't need any input. Why don't I run along?" He got as far as the door and turned around. "None of my business, if you want to smart off at your mother." After a long moment he wheeled around and walked over and sat down in the recliner. He picked up the paper.

"All right," Cathy said, talking to herself, mentally discarding the tuna, wondering what else there was in the pantry or freezer.

"You seen the market reports?" Tod asked.

"I just got home," Cathy said.

"We hardly ever worry about the market.," Greg said, and all of a sudden Tod was trying to get out of the recliner when one of his feet slid down in the space in front of foot rest. He twisted and jerked the foot free, squatted down to retrieve his shoe, and, when he came up, walked stiffly as far as the front door and stood glowering, shrugging into his blazer. He took so long that Greg and Scotty had time to stroll off to Greg's room.

Cathy knew she was supposed to try to smooth things over, start telling him that she'd straighten Greg out, but she just couldn't. It had been a long day full of mistakes and accusations at the office and the darned roast was charcoal. Besides, she'd had it with running interference between Tod and Greg. She was tired of promising to straighten Greg out. He wouldn't straighten.

And her son's smart mouth wasn't Tod's business, actually.

"Listen," she blurted, "I don't care to discuss it, okay? But I'm sick and tired of worrying about being pregnant from month to month. I might even be pregnant this minute though I doubt it but that's not the point. I don't know what the point is. Don't say anything, please. Just go. Please. I want you to go. I have to pitch out this roast and do some serious thinking, okay?"

Tod looked at her, his beautiful eyes flaring blue. He stumbled a little, backing away, caught the edge of the door with his shoulder. He reached behind him to open the door and backed through it.

After Cathy slammed the door and ran to the window, he was clumping stiffly down the steps in the slanted rays of sunset. He got into his car and sat there with his head bent for a long couple of minutes before he started the engine, gunned it, and backed out.

Well, that's that, she told herself.

Later, in the shower so she could cry without Greg's hearing, she promised herself she could always find out about getting an abortion, if it came to that, which it wouldn't, since she wasn't ever going to be stupid again.

In the morning, she woke early enough to have time to cry in the shower again and almost didn't hear the telephone. She grabbed a towel and caught the phone before it could wake Greg. It was Tod, sounding gravelly and breathless.

"You asleep? I couldn't sleep. Could you sleep? Hell, I've got to start paying attention to this place. Sometimes I feel like I'm running a regular Barnum and Bailey circus here, with a bunch of clowns. Had a guy plow into a light pole yesterday, that's the kind of people you get to drive these days—listen: I'm not getting fancy with this. What we're going to do, we're getting a license."

Cathy shifted the receiver to her other hand.

"You still there?" Tod sounded more gruff. "Today. What do you say? This morning. Soon as they open the courthouse."

"A license?"

"Yeah. Now, hear me out. I know I'm probably scaring the shit— sorry—scaring you, baby, honey." He chuckled. "I'm scaring the shit out of me, too. Ah, I'm not going to talk that way any more. Gonna clean up my act, you'll see. This is something we have got to do. I could explain all day and all night but the gist of it is this. Some thing, some damned thing, is going to get in our way if we let it. Something or someone is going to move in on us and just, hell, wreck the works. So far, it's pretty cute, the way he acts like some kind of husband, driving you nuts, worrying about you, hell, I can understand that. Kid feels like you belong to him. But he's going to have to back off."

"A license?" Cathy couldn't seem to get her breath.

"Yeah, before we get arrested, the way we've been carrying on. Like a couple of kids. Wish you didn't have such a problem with hotels, but hell, baby, way I see it, I'm going to have to make an honest woman of you." His voice went deeper. "Listen. Nice kid like your boy, his age, he's got to respect his mama. I know I always had that to hang onto. A kid has to know his mother is, you know, what you are. That's important to a kid. Besides, we both know what we're going to do anyway, sooner or later, don't we? Hell of a lot better to make it sooner, know what I mean? Matter of timing. So. I guess this isn't so romantic, just the straight skinny. You looking out the window? See that orange line on the horizon? It's gonna rain but there's the sun out there. A new day. What do you say? Cathy? You with me?"

"Yes," Cathy said nasally. "You think we should get a marriage license. Now?" She stood up. Looked down at the damp place on back of the couch from her wet hair. "Greg's asleep."

Tod laughed. He sounded shaky. "Well, wake him up. You know what time it is?"

"I mean, that's why I sound funny. I'm trying not to wake him."

"Ah, no, that's not why you sound funny, darlin'," Tod said, his voice husky. "You sound funny because you've been crying. That's another thing I want to put a stop to." He waited. Sighed. "I love you."

"I was in the shower."

"That right? See? We get married, I can help you with that, too. You just don't have any idea how handy I can be. Handy as a shirt pocket. I know I'm talking too much, hell's bells, I always talk too much, but I've got to get this thing across. You like my house, don't you? So what good is it empty? Man comes home to an empty house, what is that?"

"I see," Cathy said. Rain ticked against the window and lightning lit the room.

"I don't think you do," he said, his voice going up. Cathy held the phone away from her ear: "—even if you're not so sold on it, thing is, if we keep this up we're going to louse everything up, listen, none of this is the way I thought I would set it up but I'm not in this for all kinds of chills and thrills, why, chills and thrills, that's easy, that's nothing, chills and thrills are a dime a dozen—I mean, compared to what we've got going, why, people go around wasting themselves, tossing away themselves, you don't have any idea what I'm talking about do you?" He sounded as if he might be snickering. "Me, either. Guys like me, we go around spreading ourselves around, wasting ourselves, scratching around for, hell, for nothing. A guy could waste his entire life chasing around after—by God, I'm thirsty for you, I'm hungry for you, for all of you, all the time. I'm damned if we're going to horse around and toss the whole works, when we're so close—listen. Cathy, you ring in my head all day. I can't get anything straightened out around here until I get this squared away. Let's be practical about this—"

"Now, then," Cathy said. "We'll talk about this tonight."

He couldn't slow down. "That car you're driving, that thing's dangerous. I can't have you driving around in a car like that and you're not about to let me help you out in that department. Now, how long do you think that thing's going to run, burning oil like it is? I don't want you worried about things like that. I don't know how you sleep either with that air conditioner rattling away. You got these blue shadows under your eyes." He hesitated. Cathy took a breath to break in, but before she could say anything, he went on, almost shouting, "Wait, wait, now"—she could see him, his hand splayed toward her, jabbing the air, furiously insistent— "I want you to know that I'm making it my business to take care of you. You want some breakfast? Why don't we get some breakfast?"

"It's, my gosh, I've got to get dressed and get to the office."

He laughed. "How long will it take you to jump into your jeans?"

"Wait," Cathy said. "Lunch is better. But I can't go to Galveston. Not today. Come by the office and we'll talk about it."

"The hell with the office," he said, and the receiver hummed in her ear. Good grief, he was on his way.

Greg was up. Cathy wrapped the towel more carefully around herself. The movement yanked the telephone from the table. She giggled, righting it and hanging up the receiver. Rain pounded against the windows. She ran back into the bathroom to rinse the soap out of her hair, got into her robe, walked into the living room toweling her hair and the whole room lit up and all the lights went off as the transformer on the pole across the lawn erupted with a bang. Shoot, Cathy told herself. No hair dryer. She ran to her room and held things up to herself, trying to find something to wear better than her lavender blouse that looked almost like silk—well, maybe it wouldn't in the bright light of day—and a thrift store skirt that was the bottom of somebody's cast-off suit, but it did have a lining and it made her stomach look flat. Sort of.

Greg came out of the bathroom complaining about the dark. "What happened to the candles used to be in the junk drawer?"

"I don't know. How do I know? I threw them away." She ran and got a candle for him, and matches, and handed them around the edge of the door. "There's supposed to be a flashlight in one of the cabinets. Hand me my eye stuff, could you? Better still, how about letting me back in there for a minute?"

"Not a chance," Greg said. "You used up all the hot water."

"I'm sorry." She leaned against the wall next to the bathroom door. "Tod's on his way here. That was him on the phone."

"Wonderful," Greg said.

"I can't find my keys," Cathy said. "Have you got my keys?"

Greg tossed his key ring at her. "Don't lose these, guacamole-for-brains."

Cathy pocketed the keys and went back to her bedroom to stare at herself in the candlelit mirror: Ophelia, she looked like. The mad scene. Or Camille, with the dank hair and the bruised shadows. He'd noticed those shadows. Greenish places under the cheekbones. Purple under the eyes. Ah, Tod, you poor, crazy, lonely, darling man. You deserve better, she thought. You truly do.

She was in the kitchen, putting away the corn flakes Greg had disparaged on his way out of the house, when Tod arrived. "The power's off," she said, flustered, at his ardent kiss. "My hair—I couldn't—and there's no light to, you know. Don't look at me."

He took her hands down and kissed her chin and her cheeks. "Lovely," he said. "Beautiful." He put his face against her breast and groaned. "Can't take much more of this."

Cathy forgot the rain, forgot everything.

Half an hour later they were in the car, surrounded by blinding, pounding rain. Tod scarcely seemed aware of not being able to see, but watching him continue to pass cars made her heart jump.

"Slow down," she said. "Could we pull over? These storms blow over, usually, if you give them a minute."

"Pull over?" He laughed. "The woman's insatiable."

"No, she isn't." She tightened her seat belt. She wished he'd pay more attention to the road and quit turning to look at her. The wipers couldn't begin to keep up. "It's like we're speeding at the bottom of the ocean."

"Are you, my love?" He leaned into the wheel, peering, and turned all the way around to face her. A red light loomed up. They slid to a stop.

Cathy caught her breath. "We haven't known each other very long, actually," she said miserably. "And there are alternatives. To, ah, to almost anything." Her voice went away.

He started up, spun the wheel, drove past a line of cars waiting in line at a construction site so he could swerve onto the feeder leading onto the Gulf Freeway. "Now, that's one hell of a crazy thing to say." He looked at her from under his dark brows. "You don't mean it, though, do you? You didn't get any sleep, last night."

Oh, he drove too fast. He drove far too fast, frowning, talking, talking, impatient at lights looming up through the rain, passing cars, trucks, a Greyhound bus that was throwing up walls of water. "You can tell Patrick you're quitting, darlin'," he was saying. "I'm not getting married so I can go on sitting in an empty house."

The rain didn't let up until they reached the causeway. One second they were driving through a deluge and the next Cathy was watching a little sailboat below them, its white and blue sails heeling over in the choppy waves, in the lee of Tiki Island. Patchy gray clouds scudded across the sky and a rainbow formed straight ahead.

"And aren't we headed for the pot of gold?" Tod said, his eyes pushing up into crescents. "Ah, you don't have to look at me with such anguish, darlin', if you're having such doubts, we can wait, if that's what's called for. We can get the license, though, can't we, now, as long as we're that close?" And he explained that they wouldn't have to actually *use* such a license, once they had it. Plenty of people took out marriage licenses and never got around to using the things. It happened all the time. The thing was, she was to humor him. Kind of like getting a passport. A person never knew when it might come in handy. "All we're doing is picking one up," he said, his hand warm on hers. "The rest is strictly up to you."

He couldn't stop talking. She went up the wide walk to the Galveston County Courthouse with her hand tight in the crook of his arm, watching his mouth, hearing his voice, his staccato chuckle, his guttural persuading. Tod talked while they filled out the forms, chattering to Cathy and to a little woman with frizzy white hair who stole glances at him as she fussily presided behind a splintery wooden counter. He flirted with the woman. "No law says you have to get married just because you fork over the fee, is there?" and the woman said that there wasn't, as far as she knew. "The thing's good for how long? A month or two, is it?"

The clerk smiled at him.

The thought of having Tod's baby didn't seem so awful. She and Tod just might have a perfectly beautiful little blue-eyed baby. A little girl, maybe, with his Irish eyes, his black lashes, his fine straight nose, the sweet curve of his Irish mouth.

"Now, is this so bad?" he asked, tucking her arm in his.

"I loathe making decisions," Cathy said, as they walked back down the echoing hall. "Not being able to make decisions can make a person be a big pain in the neck. Ask Greg."

There was more, but Tod interrupted her, his eyes ecstatic. "Ah, my darlingest girl. I'll make all your decisions. You won't have to decide so much as scrambled or sunny side up, from now on."

The sun was blinding after the dim cool interior of the building. They stood on the courthouse steps hand in hand, like good children emerging into a world clean and new and brilliantly alive. The grass and masses of chrysanthemum and pansies flattened by the storm were lifting up, visibly stretching and shaking off sparkling drops in the shafts of light coming through the shining trees. The green lawn steamed.

Passersby smiled and nodded. "Good morning," Tod said, dipping and bowing. "Good morning to you."

Maybe he really could make all her decisions for her, she thought as he led her to the Cadillac. Maybe Tod could take care of everything. How good. How good to have all that surging vitality, to be so sure.

They ate shrimp and drank wonderful golden wine at the Beachcomber's and had more wine, champagne, back at the house, sitting up cross-legged on Tod's mattress to toast each other and the day. Tod dropped to one knee out on the little balcony of the bedroom, proposing again, because he said he hadn't done that properly. When Cathy suggested that they really ought to be getting back to Houston, Tod put a finger to her lips and silenced her. He traced the shape of her mouth with his finger, kissed her thoroughly and took her back into the bedroom.

They drove home in a golden haze.

Houston was all puddles and downed tree limbs. It had rained all day.

Gregory was waiting, his shirt stuck to his chest, his hair plastered to his brow, lolling on the front stoop with his long legs lying in muddy grass, icily saying, "You mind giving me back my key?"

*****

12

Tod would not shut up. He went on and on, insisting that all they needed was a nice supper somewhere where they could sit and talk things out. "That's the agenda." He rubbed his hands, genially aiming a fist at Greg's shoulder. "Damned few things can't be straightened out by a nice little supper, what do you say, fella?"

Greg gazed at Cathy and at the sky as she stood on the stoop fumbling for the house key, taking things out of her purse and dropping them back in until she was ready to upend the damned thing. She finally found the key and got the door creaking open.

Tod pranced in, chuckling, explaining, cajoling, getting in Greg's way, trying to force an answer out of him. "Now, this whole thing's all my fault. Let's get that straight, right now. I kidnapped your mama, but maybe when we all sit down, you'll understand."

Greg looked coldly blank. "Excuse me."

"Just a minute, here," Tod said, bouncing and socking his fist into his palm. "Hold on, now."

Gregory shot Cathy a black look. "I'm getting the carpet wet."

Tod moved aside. Greg went squishing off to his room.

"Give him a few minutes," Cathy said. Tod looked deflated.

She went to look for a couple of aspirin. Tod said he didn't need an aspirin. He seemed to find it an affront that she did. He sank into the recliner, put his feet up and sat watching her swallow pills and finish off a full glass of water. After what felt like a long silence he said, "You want to see whether junior might be ready to snap out of it?"

She shrugged. "It might be well to give him a little space." She sighed. "I can't believe I went off with his key."

"Oh, let's not go on a guilt trip, here. He's a big boy. He didn't have to sit out in the rain." He reached over and got the Chronicle, slid it from its plastic sleeve and shook it open. "Why don't you go take a look-see? See if he's ready to come out of it." He clipped the end from a cigar and settled back. "Take your time, honey. I'm a genial cuss." He flipped the paper open to the financial pages.

She went into the kitchen and stood with her brow against the cool of the refrigerator. When she went back to the living room, he looked up with a brief wintery smile and went back to the paper. She inhaled deeply and braced herself. "I think the shower is running. This might take a while.

Maybe you'd better give the two of us some time to straighten things out."

"Sure thing." Tod appeared to be engrossed in the financial section. "Damn," he said. "I don't believe this."

"I mean, just the two of us," Cathy said.

Tod looked up with an absent frown. The frown intensified. "Oh. Sorry." He got to his feet and walked to the door. "The two of us? I guess I thought things might be...different, now. Kind of figured that 'the two of us' might mean the two of *us*. My mistake."

"Oh, please." Cathy's head ached. "Don't do this."

"What am I doing?" He hunched unhappily. "I'm doing something? You mind telling me why it's such a mistake for me to want to take a stab at fixing things up?" She couldn't find an answer.

"You know what?" he said. "I lost another five thousand this afternoon. That probably doesn't mean much to those of you got the teat of the State of Texas to suck on, but the rest of us in the real world are having a hell of a rough time. Lost another five K. On top of fourteen K yesterday. The whole damned market is falling apart. The only way to rationalize is to say it's universal and try to hang in there, wait it out, but that's a hell of a lot of money and some of that paper isn't mine. But it's only money, what the hell. I'm trying to rise above it, do the right thing by you, baby, help you straighten up your life. I thought we had a pretty good thing going. Now it looks like you're ready to kick me out so you can sit around and coddle junior? Aw hell. I'm going. I'm going." He got as far as the door. "You mind telling me what's the matter with letting me try to reason with the kid? Might be time to let a man handle him."

"Manhandle?" she said. He stood there looking at her, his chin out, cheeks bright pink. "Manhandle him? Is that what you said?"

"Jesus," he said. "Does Greg bawl in the shower, too?"

After he left, Cathy locked the front door and leaned against it.

Greg wouldn't let her into his room.

"I'm not yelling any more apologies through a door," she said.

After a time she could hear Greg practicing. The cello sounded elegiac. He was working on Bach, maybe. Phrasing it the way people in the funeral business always seemed to. The kid was playing a damned dirge.

"What is that?" she called. "Sounds like a funeral."

"I wish," Greg said, just loud enough for her to hear.

*****

13

The next Saturday, Tod wanted to take Greg and Cathy to brunch at some grand hotel, but when he came to pick them up, he tugged Cathy out to the front walk and said, "Now would you take a look at this golden October day. What we need is a picnic," and the next thing she knew the three of them were running around Randall's, filling a basket with fruit and cheeses and pate and wine and a loaf of warm French bread, with Cathy saying, "Oh, what fun," to Greg, and Greg muttering, "Yeah. Right."

When they were back in the car Greg said, "Is this gonna take long? I got stuff I've got to do. I can't blow the whole morning."

Tod grinned at Cathy and gunned the Cadillac. "Bolivar peninsula. You ever been to the beaches on Bolivar? Couple of things over there I bet you've never seen." He swiveled completely around to look at Greg. "Champagne in one of those bags. You think you could open a bottle of champagne, young fella?"

Cathy did so wish he would keep his eyes on the road. Then she realized what he'd said and said, "Oh, I don't think, I mean, it's not even noon and Greg's never had—" and there was the explosion of the cork and Greg was saying, "Sure, I have," and the next thing she knew they were sipping champagne from Styrofoam cups, inching along in the line at the Bolivar ferry.

The wine was delicious. The ferry creaked gently along through flat glittery water. Tod said, "Welcome to the Richard S. Thornton," and came around to help Cathy out of the car. The three walked to the stern to watch mullet leap and splash. Terns and gulls wheeled behind the boat, crying their cat cries.

"Oh, what a beautiful morning," Tod sang. He didn't sing very well. He didn't seem to know many of the words, but he made up for it, improvising, waving his arms, trying to get her to join him.

After the ferry docked, they drove past Crystal Beach to a secluded area, to unpack the dark slices of delicatessen bread with grapes and pears and three kinds of cheese, all of it so good that they agreed they'd never want to eat cheese or fruit again without a little salty sand in it. They ate and threw their crusts to the gulls and at each other. Tod and Cathy idly made drip castles but Greg built a huge castle with a wall, turrets, bridges, towers and a moat, reinforced with shell and driftwood.

"A golden day," Cathy said, "we're having a perfect, perfect golden day," but even as she said that, she looked up to see a frown flicker across Tod's face.

"I can't stand having a day such as this one come to an end," he said. He looked restive and added, almost begging, in a small voice, "Why can't life be a perpetual picnic?"

"Oh, there's a question for the philosophers." She used an even smaller voice, trying to make a joke of it.

"I want us to get married."

"I want us to be alone to talk about that," she said, trying for a childishly wheedling voice, to match what was beginning to be a little boy's pout on Tod's face.

Tod's mouth pulled down. He looked impatient. "You're a wet blanket," he said, joking but not joking, gazing from beneath his shaggy brows. "Where the hell is your abandon? Why can't we just do it? Elope? Where's that wine? Here, give me that," and, when Cathy shook her head and wouldn't offer her cup, he stalked off down the beach, the bottle swinging at his side.

When he came back and threw the bottle into a refuse barrel, Greg glanced up and went back to his sand castle.

"So. Are we actually engaged, or not?" Tod demanded.

"It might be well if we went home, now," Cathy said.

"Fine." Tod said, his mouth tight. He threw the remains of their lunch into the trash barrel, along with the plastic box of wine glasses, a package of napkins and the plastic cutlery, wasting the lot, and stood slapping sand from his hands. "Let's go."

Cathy rescued the box of cups and was reaching for the package of napkins when he said, again, almost sneering, "Let's go. Feels like we're out of sync here."

As soon as the ferry chugged away from the dock, he got out of the Cadillac and walked away by himself. He turned to look back once before he went to stand at the prow of the boat, his shoulder shielding his face from the spray.

"What a jerk," Greg said. "A total jerk."

"Sad," Cathy said. "He looks so little and sad."

"Oh, what's with you," Greg said. "You telling me you're going to make up?"

That, of course, was exactly what she wanted to do. Sort of. "You can't say he hasn't been generous," Cathy said.

"Whatever," Greg said.

Cathy invoked what used to be one of their codes. "You're not the boss of me."

Greg shrugged. He wasn't having any. He turned away and slid down in the seat as she opened the car door.

Tod stood in silence, gazing at the water, until she reached for his hand. After a while he lifted her hand, kissed it and said, "I'm botching it. I generally do." The salty spray lifted and they turned away. "Figured I'd probably blow it, sooner or later. Pull some crap, excuse me, and blow it."

She winced.

"See?" he said. "You get to know me, that'll pretty much be that." He swayed and closed his eyes. "I oughta jump off of this fucking thing."

Cathy closed her eyes. "Can you not be this way?"

He didn't hear her. He said, his voice so harsh it had to be hurting his throat, "Sure, oh, sure. Lousing things up, making a chump of myself again, why not, that's what the chump does—"

She put her fingers over his mouth. "Hush. Hush, now. That's enough. Do you hear?"

He caught her hand and kissed it and held it to his face.

The ferry thudded along through the water. The salty spray washed up, washed up. When a heavy gust of the salty wet hit them, they backed away, supporting each other.

Somebody yelled and Tod hugged her to him and pointed. Porpoises. "Look at that!" People came running up behind them. The animals dove in and out of the curving wake, whooshing and blowing spray. Tod turned to Cathy with a rueful smile. "Peace?"

"Oh, yes," Cathy said.

Greg appeared to have been dozing in the car. When he sat up, bleary eyed, his hair every which way, Tod grinned. "You see the porpoises? You know, son, if you get out in a small enough boat, one of those little keel boats, say, those things'll come right up alongside and blow their fishy breath right into your face. Whew. You ever take cod liver oil? You talk about halitosis. You do much messing around in boats? We're going to have to get you some kind of a little boat. Every boy ought do some messing around in a boat. I knew a gangster had a little yacht once." He giggled. "That's what we ought to have. A little boat. One of those sail fishes."

Greg shot Cathy a heavy-lidded look. "Excuse me. Got to go to the john."

Tod frowned. "I'm damned if I know what it would take, with that boy," he started, but when Cathy leaned close to brush a lock of damp hair from his brow, he caught her hand and grinned at her. "What we need is a little more bubbly." He eased the cork out of another bottle. It didn't make a sound. He kissed her, poured each of them a foaming cup full and lifted his. "To us."

"To a wonderful picnic," Cathy said. "On a wonderful day."

He swallowed and interrupted. "Life. I want to drink to—no. I want to *make* a wonderful life. For us. I can do it, too." His chin sank to his chest as he swallowed a small belch. "Believe it."

"I do."

His eyes flamed. "The magic words." He took her face in his hands and kissed her. The kiss grew feverish. Cathy was glad Greg wasn't in the back seat. When Tod had finished kissing her, he looked into her, all the way in, his eyes piercing. "Say that again." He let go of her and sat up straight. "By God," he said. He slapped his brow. "By God, lady," and he hurried out of the car and came around to open the door on her side and tug at her, crowing. He kept tugging at her, running along the slick metal deck, sliding against automobiles, laughing. He didn't slow down even when she slipped. He yanked her to her feet and ran, pulling her along, hurting her hand, impatiently insisting she hurry. He led her to a ladder with steel rungs that led up to the ferry's wheel house. The metal door at the top had a sign on it: "No admittance. Employees only." When she refused to climb the ladder, he told her not to go away. He climbed the ladder, wrestled the door open and went in.

Cathy waited. After a few minutes Tod came out and came down the rungs, the back of his neck very red. "Silly bastard won't go along with it," he said. "I told him we've got a license, hell, I've got the damned license in the glove compartment of the car, and he can marry people, he's a captain. He's probably married all kinds of people." He frowned at her. "Maybe if you asked him."

"Let's go back to the car," Cathy said. "I think I'm a little tiddley."

"He's a captain." Tod was breathing heavily, his lower lip out. "I pay taxes. The guy works for us. He can't tell us what he will or won't do. What do you say? You want to talk to him?"

When Cathy said she didn't want to talk to the captain, Tod said he didn't want to come back to the car with her. She didn't realize she was weeping until she'd gotten back to the car.

Greg was looking around uneasily. "You okay? We're about ready to dock. Where the hell's your boyfriend?"

"Tod is talking with the captain," she stammered. "He'll be here in a minute."

The ferry bumped and bounced to a stop. The attendants lowered the ramp and opened the chains so the first row of cars could drive off. "Well, we'll have to get out of here one way or another," Greg said. "You got the key?"

Tod came stamping back, white-faced, breathing hard.

They were on the causeway before anybody said much of anything, then Tod said, "I'm going to report that silly bastard. Find out where his boss is and get him fired the hell out of there." He swerved in and out of traffic.

By the time they were almost to League City, Cathy ventured, "I've never seen porpoises close, like that."

"I'd like to feed that jackass to the fishes," Tod said. But he was ready to be placated. He reached for her hand. "Don't look so miserable. I just wanted something different. The kind of thing you might want to remember. How many people you know can say they were married by a ferry boat captain? Thing is, you want to *be* married, all right. You just don't want to go through the rigmarole of getting there. That's probably true of most people." He warmed to the subject. "A Justice of the Peace can do it, but there's nothing unique about that. There's one in Bacliff runs a liquor store."

"A liquor store," Greg said. "Wonderful."

"What's that, young fella?" Tod leaned back to peer into the rear view mirror. "Didn't quite catch that." But he had.

They swerved past a truck and a bus and Cathy said, "Oh, please, do we have to go so fast?"

Tod yanked the wheel a half turn and the car swung onto the feeder. "That better? We can make this last just as long as we..." and he stopped talking and straightened, his mouth widening into a smile. "Forest Park East," he said. "Now, there's a little chapel over there. I bet they do weddings. I got a buddy in charge of one of those crews knocks on doors peddling cemetery lots, what's his name, Cary. Cary Winn. Cary says they do weddings at the park all the time. Why don't we have a look-see?" He glanced into the rear view mirror, grinning. "What do you say, son?"

Cathy didn't have to look around. She could feel Greg's eyes. "That's quite enough," she said, a shake in her voice.

Tod pulled over and stopped. "What do you say?" He breathed audibly. "Well?"

"How's that sound to you, Mom?" Greg said. "Okay if I open another bottle of the bubbly?"

"Why don't you just do that, son." Tod started up and drove to the next underpass; spun the car around in a U-turn beneath the freeway, careened past several cars on the feeder on the other side.

"Please," Cathy said. "Please."

"I'm always careful," Tod said. "Pass that bottle to your mama, why don't you?"

Cathy waved away the bottle in Greg's hand and massaged her temples. "Where, I mean where are we going?"

"Going to the chapel," Tod sang. "Going to get married," giving the last word four syllables. "Going to the cha-ha-haple, going to get ma-ha-

harried." He kept singing until he swerved to a stop inside the gates and parked in front of what did appear to be a chapel. Then he turned to Greg and took the champagne from him. "No more jerking old Toddy around," he said, after a long swallow. "The kid seems to know what you want. God knows, I don't."

"I want to go home," Cathy said. She took the bottle and made herself swallow and swallow again.

"No more laughing at the chump," Tod said. "Hell, no." His voice shook. "I'm giving you and the boy, here, a choice. One choice. Once. This is it. Your turn, Greg. Here. Hey, give that back to your momma. Now, listen: either we get married or we don't. Make up your mind."

"Way to go," Greg said. "Don't let her jerk you around, Tod." He hiccupped.

"I don't think you want to marry anybody," Cathy said, fighting a small delirious hiccup of her own. "This is just your way of...of being horrible so you can scare me off, after all the things you keep t-talking ab-bout." She stopped, swallowing tears, fighting off crying because if she knew anything, she knew she mustn't keep crying. She might begin to retch. When she looked over at the heavy door to the chapel, the horizon tilted and swung.

"Air." She clambered out of the car, slammed the door, marched up the little walk and gazed at a bed of chrysanthemums.

By the time Tod caught up with her, she had things under control. She looked back at Greg, standing next to the car, watching her. "Well?" She folded her arms, her chin up. "Are you coming?"

There weren't any gardenias but the little chapel smelled strongly of gardenias. The late afternoon sun poured benevolently through stained glass. There was, incredibly enough, somebody canoodling away on a pipe organ. She inhaled the strong artificial gardenia scent. She was listening to the organ, trying to identify the piece that the organist was playing, trying not to hear Gregory's insistent whispering, "Mom. Mom? You know these guys? What the hell's going on? You know what's going down here?"

Tod was talking to a couple of men who seemed to be friends of his. He and the men kept slapping each other on the back.

"We're going to have a house," she whispered. "Great big. It's so beautiful. A house in Galveston. There's a music room."

"The guy's a freak," Greg said. "He freaked, back there. Didn't you see?" Greg had the hiccups, but he wouldn't stop. He sounded so frantic that Cathy couldn't think of a way to get through to him.

"He's really not like that. Well, not all the time. We hurt his feelings. On the boat, I mean. The captain or whatever hurt his feelings. Tod is really very—oh, this isn't the time to go into it. He can be dear. All he wants, really, is to have us all be happy. You'll see. Let him think he's in charge, for heaven's sake, if it matters so much. Why do you have to keep baiting him and—" She hushed, because Tod was back, smiling uncertainly, introducing his friend.

The friend didn't seem to think there was anything the least unusual in a person's inquiring about a wedding in a funeral chapel. "Happens all the time," he said, nodding.

Tod peeled bills off the wad in his pocket, folded them and handed them over. "All the time," the man said, goggle-eyed.

Cathy was beginning to wish she had not swallowed so much of the very acidic wine when the other men arrived, one of them, Tod said, an old friend, who just happened to own a liquor store, and who just happened to be a Jay Pea.

Cathy ran that back through her head and stiffened. "Jay Pea?"

"Justice of the Peace, little lady," the man said, squeezing her hand. She could feel the knuckles give as he squeezed. "Toddy here tells me you folks got all your ducks in a row."

"D-d-ducks?" Why should they be discussing ducks?

The man moved away, slowly, as if under water, and came back, languidly close, to murmur something unintelligible and go wading off again. Tod's mouth widened into a goofy grin. Everybody kept talking at once until they went, suddenly, very quiet and she looked up to see the J. P.'s fat arms overlapping the edge of a podium. He peered over his glasses to read words and waited, suggesting she respond. He nodded. Cathy smiled. The man nodded again and looked peculiar, his face screwed up, whispering, "I do."

Tod nudged her.

"I see," Cathy said, realizing why the Justice of the Peace looked so peculiar: He had two different colored eyes, one blue one and one brown. He kept talking and nodding, a huge, doggy-faced, jowly man, while Cathy tried, dreamily, to not keep gazing into those eyes. When he leaned close to prompt her, repeating whatever he'd just said, he smelled of something peculiar, but totally inappropriate. She couldn't think what it was. And then she could: popcorn.

The brown-blue-eyed man smelled like the lobby of a cinema.

She was trying to recall what breed of dog it was that had different colored eyes, when the man said, "Do you?"

"Oh," Cathy said, "I do."

The man nodded, pleased. Greg hiccupped.

Light rain began to patter on the window as the man read rapidly.

Leopard cow dogs, she thought, and gave a small shuddery giggle, not certain that she hadn't said it out loud. Leopard cow dogs like the neighbor's dog, that they named Evil Eyed Fleagle. It kept getting lost and being called all over the neighborhood. The silly animal went through the broken slats in the fence. The J.P. had eyes like Evil Eyed Fleagle's.

"You may kiss the bride," the man said. Cathy lifted her hand, intending to shake Tod's hand. She didn't want Tod to get all feverish in front of Greg and the strangers but Tod pushed her hand aside, grabbed her close and kissed her hard. One of the men began counting. "Fourteen, fifteen, sixteen." He chuckled, and one of the men said, "Now there's a man knows how to kiss his bride."

The Justice of the Peace gave Greg a playful shove and whispered something to him. Greg winced and moved away.

Cathy looked at the motes drifting in the colored shafts of light shining through the windows, and gazed around at the strangers, thinking dispassionately that Tod ought not to keep insisting on giving everybody money. "Greatest thing," he kept saying, deliriously overriding objections, shouting, "No, no, by damn, greatest thing, you know, greatest day of a man's life."

Greg looked greenish. That made Cathy realize that she was going to be sick very soon. She asked if there mightn't be a ladies' room and the big man with the peculiar eyes said he'd help her. He half carried her, being entirely too helpful with his surprisingly hard fat arm all the way around her up under both her arms, and as they hurried to the ladies' room she realized why he smelled of popcorn. He had a partly filled bag in his jacket pocket.

She just made it to the toilet in time.

After she had washed her face she leaned against the cool tile wall of the little room, tears dripping down her cheeks and chin, crying for Greg and crying for herself, mad at herself for being so clumsy and stupid and silly, standing around crying her heart out, when she knew everything was going to be all right.

Everything's going to be all right, she told herself, as she put on more lipstick. Everything is going to be all right. I wonder if he'll let me drive us home.

*****

14

"**B**oy, Chub and Pat're going to be mad," Greg said from the back seat.

Cathy wanted to console him but she could hardly breathe because of the way they were hissing through the rain in the heavy traffic on the Gulf Freeway. "Oh, wait till they see our house," she said, distractedly. "There's a music room."

It was raining torrents and Tod was so noisy that Greg might not have heard her. Tod kept singing, "Happy days are here again," adding verses that he kept making up as he went along.

When Cathy turned around to look at Greg, she saw him slump down and close his eyes.

Tod sang and talked and talked, swerving to pass cars and trucks, the Cadillac throwing up waves of water. Cathy tried not to watch.

"I'll call Chub the minute we get home," she said.

"Our home, you mean?" Greg yelled. He sounded shrill, tremulous. "Mom? Because I've got things to do."

"Our home," Tod sang. "Our home." He tried to pull Cathy against him but she shrank away as they sizzled by a van.

"Five o'clock traffic," she said. "Oh, this rain. It's like being under an ocean. Do you have to pass every single car, love? Can't you let some of these people just—"

"Ah, no," Tod caroled. "Not this day." His voice burbled in his throat. "That I cannot. Not us. Not today. Hey—" He swiveled in his seat, turned all the way around to face Gregory—"You want to drive, son? This baby practically drives itself." He pushed a button. His window went down. He leaned, cupped his mouth, yelled into a gust of rain: "World, world, I cannot get thee close enough. Got me a lady, oh, she is my love. And already she's making noises just like a wife."

"Tod—!"

"That I am," he yelled. "Tod, here. World, world, world, see my bride, with her wild red hair blowing?"

Cathy fumbled at the buttons in the panel on the door on her side. All the windows slid down and up, maddeningly, up and down, as she squealed, "Please."

Tod leaned back, grinning at her, and all the windows slid shut. "Now what is it that you don't want everybody to know? Ah, woman, is there no pleasing you? Are you determined to sit all the way over there, with that infernal belt buckled around your lovely middle?"

"Where are we going?" Greg yelled. "Mom?"

"Home," Tod shouted. "I'm taking my little family home."

"Dickinson city limits," Greg said. "Mom? Are we going to Galveston? We're passing Dickinson." He grabbed Cathy's shoulder. "Mother? I've got to get home."

"That's where we're headed for sure," Tod said. "And tomorrow, why, tomorrow we'll go off on a grand honeymoon. I'm the happiest man alive, the happiest man God in his heaven ever made." He sniffed and blinked, wiped at his eyes with the palm and the back of his hand. "Every man should feel like this, that's what I wish, that every man, everywhere, should know the grand feel of such a grand day."

She slid her hand down alongside the seat so she could reach around into the back. She groped for Greg's hand and found it but he pulled away and when she got her fingers around his ankle he twisted it away too.

"Tod, you're not thinking straight," she said. "Wouldn't it be well to make some arrangements? Oh, please do look at the road, you're not being very—"

"Arrangements?"

"For Greg. I think he'd just as soon not be with us tonight?"

Tod slapped his brow. "Ah, hell, good hell, now, what's the matter with me? Delirious, is what I am. Gregory, my boy, you're going to have to forgive the old man. Not myself. Of course it's home you'll be wanting to be now, home in your old place. For now. For tonight, at least."

Cathy had an idea. "Why don't we call Chub and Patrick? See if they're home. They might want Greg to stay with them. How does that sound, honey?"

"Come on," Greg said. "Since when do I need to be baby sat?"

"Let's just go see what they say."

"West University Place it is," Tod said.

"They're gonna be hacked," Greg said, bitterly pleased. "Isn't it illegal to drive on the shoulder?"

Fortunately, Pat and Chub were both at home when Cathy called, and they agreed at once that Greg should stay with them.

It had quit raining by the time they pulled up at Pat and Chub's. The minute they got out of the car, Tod signaled for silence, pushed past Cathy to stand in front of Patrick, drew his shoulders back and said, making an announcement of it: "You just happen to be looking at a married couple, here, my man."

"Well, well," Patrick said. His smile didn't reach his eyes. He laughed uneasily. "Well, well, well." He shook Tod's hand, shook Greg's hand, kissed Cathy, walked them up the walk to the house and turned to shake Greg's hand again. "Well, son. Well, well."

Chub came out of her garage studio wiping her hands on a paint rag. When Patrick said, a subdued warning in his eyes, "We seem to be, ah, celebrating, here, honey. Got a couple of newlyweds here," Chub wiped her hands and wiped her hands.

She finally said, falsely cheery, "Well, why. Why, congratulations," as she led the way into the house.

Cathy hadn't expected their announcement to come as great glad tidings of joy, exactly, but she felt a flicker of resentment. Chub didn't have to look tearful. "Would anybody mind terribly if I go to the bathroom?" Cathy asked. "I seem to be full of champagne and swimming in all this celebratory love."

When she came out of the bathroom, the Gallaghers were in the kitchen, ostensibly putting on a pot of coffee. Tod was pacing around in the den. He looked around, his mouth puckering in distaste. "You can always tell when people have cats."

The big, sunny, many-windowed room was cluttered, full of plants, baskets and assorted cushions and pillows. Patrick's guitar and a zither stood in a corner. Smoky, a mewling Siamese, prowled along the mantel, stepping in and out to avoid a collection of dusty, blue and green, antique bottles. The table next to the sofa was covered with magazines. Tod had to move a book and several magazines to sit down next to Chub's desk in the corner, with its glasses and bowls full of drawing pencils—HB sixes, most of them—and sticks of charcoal and what looked like the remains of a still life: three dried lemons and a withered apple.

"Don't you love all the plants?" Cathy didn't know why she felt she had to defend the place. "Smoky and Tiger were abused or abandoned and Pat and Chub love them dearly."

The Gallagher's cocker spaniel was sniffing at Tod's ankles. "Good doggie," Tod said, crossing his legs. "Go away, doggie. Does he always growl like that? Can't see keeping animals in a house. Matter of fact, I can't see keeping any animal anywhere, unless it's to eat." He laughed uneasily, shoved at the dog with his shoe and Cathy said, "Here, Tiger. Sit."

"I'm sitting," Tod said. "Hey, there. Come over here. You seem a little distant." The champagne was wearing off, leaving a pinch of pain behind her eyes.

Tod's voice stayed carefully conciliatory but his eyes were darkening as he eyed the dog, shivering now, growling insistently, until Chub bustled in, saying, "Tiger, shut up. Pat, get that ravening beast out of here. So. Are you two going off somewhere exotic? We'd love to have Greg. He's the only one who can get the edger started. The guy who does the lawn thinks we need a new one. Oh, I can't bear to think of your taking my yard man and his cello off to live in Galveston."

"Thanks," Cathy said. "Oh gosh. Thanks." She looked up to see Greg in the doorway.

"I thought you'd be upset," he said to Chub.

Chub didn't say anything. She looked at Greg and Greg shot his mother a bitter, victorious look.

"You're giving me a headache," Cathy said.

Tod flashed Patrick a man-to-man grin as he came back into the room. "We need to straighten out something," Tod said. "Tell your boss, here, that you're no longer a working gal, honey. You are officially resigned, as of now. I didn't get married to come home to an empty house. So. No more working gal. Now, that doesn't exactly go against the grain, does it?" He aimed a forefinger at Greg as if were a gun. "You've got a full time mother, son."

"Lovely." Cathy fought a stammer. "I'm not sure this is the way I wanted to resign. You sound sort of 'Me, Tarzan. You, Jane.'"

"And you don't sound all that sure," Patrick murmured as he walked around turning on lamps.

"Maybe I'm not," Cathy said, thinking, oh, Tod doesn't want to hear that, but Tod ignored her. He kept laughing and stretching his neck and moving around, touching things.

Cathy had a roaring headache all the way to Galveston. It started as they swerved onto the Southwest Freeway and got worse as they crossed the causeway. By the time they reached the house, she wanted only to get out and lie down and have Tod quit purring and hugging at her. But when they pulled up in front of the house, he stiffened in his seat, his voice suddenly irritated, demanding, "What the hell is that?"

Cathy couldn't see what he was talking about until he'd come to a full stop. He sat with the motor idling, staring at a battered white car parked across the street from their driveway entrance.

"Maybe some youngster's bought a jalopy," she said, wondering how Tod could switch moods so fast. "Should we care?"

"The thing's an eyesore," he snapped.

"It's somebody else's eyesore," Cathy said. "Can't we just pull in? I'd like to get out of this car."

But he sat there, eyes narrowed, perversely peevish, squinting at some neighbor's vintage car until she said, "Could we go in?"

The house smelled of damp wood. "Every spring when we opened the cottage we used to find nests with baby mice in them in the bureau drawers," Cathy said and when Tod looked annoyed, added, "I can't imagine what made me think of that."

"Probably that clunker out in front," he said.

Cathy wondered if she could find something stronger than aspirin in one of his medicine cabinets. He kept talking, following her around as she searched. "What do we care if some neighbor has some old kick-the-can car," she said.

"Damned thing's an eyesore," Tod said.

"Well, my head *hurts*."

"Hell of a way to start a honeymoon," Tod grumbled. "A bride with a headache," and Cathy lost all patience.

"If you can't smell this place you might want to consider giving up those cigars."

"That so?" Tod's voice went up. "Anything else you'd like to get off your chest?"

"Oh, please," Cathy said.

He pranced in a little circle and came back. "What happened to the bashful, timid, stammering lady, eh? Where'd she go? Huh?"

She lumbered up to the master suite with the mattress on the floor. The bathroom adjacent to it had a drop hook so she could lock the door and fall to her knees in front of the stained commode.

During the night she woke up a half-dozen times to be sick. Finally she took a blanket and curled up on the cold, cracked, blue and white, dirt-edged tile of the bathroom floor, trying not to see the paint curls on the claw footed tub and the rust stains on the base of the toilet. Tod woke up a couple of times but he seemed accustomed to his mattress. When Cathy walked around she could hear him snoring three rooms away. She couldn't think how she could not have known that he snored such big, ratchety, catchy snores. They sounded as though they were rending his throat.

The last time she crept out of the chilly bathroom, weak and penitent, she stood gazing down at her shuddering little bridegroom. His dark mouth kept gaping open and snapping shut, the snores pulling his lower lip in and out and distending his nostrils. The sheet had pulled away from a corner of the mattress.

We're going to buy a bed tomorrow morning, she promised herself. And some sort of armoire, so we can hang our clothes.

She tiptoed across the room to where four of Tod's shirts hung from hangers on a hook. She eased one shirt from its hanger and put it on. The house kept swaying in gusts of wind. Tod had told her it would do that, that it was built like a ship, meant to give, so it could bend in a storm, creaking and groaning. The tall dark panes of the uncurtained windows bowed, glimmering and shuddering as rain sheeted down the panes. These strong torrents ought to be some color, she thought; a hectic red or purple, a purple storm she was in the midst of, a purple autumnal storm, laced with flames of lightning, shaking with melodramatic rolls of a kettle drum.

During a lull in the rain she watched that stupid old wreck of a car that Tod had gotten so upset about begin to move, adrift in the water swirling down the street. That's why those curbs are so high, she thought. The street is a regular river. The car moved more purposefully, emitting a drift of steam or smoke as it drove away, throwing a wake down the street.

She went and got Tod's jacket to cover herself and crept, shivering, to curl up on the wide window seat. It seemed very like being in a boat. She was too chilly to sleep, too aware of Tod's mutters and snorting gasps—his breath stopped from time to time and started up again with a sharp rasping noise—but she must have drifted off, because she opened her eyes in blinding sunlight. Leaves shone through the filigreed rail of the balcony. Slick tattered leaves and broken bits of stem and bark littered the white paint. The sky gleamed, pure azure, beyond the dark polished green of Tod's beloved magnolias. My magnolias, now, she thought. In my house.

Tod stood with his arms folded at his chest, leaning against the rail of the balcony, his blue eyes rapt, gazing in at her. He'd been waiting for her to wake, he said, as he came in. He must have been to a bakery. A silver tray on the floor beside the window seat had breakfast plates, napkins, coffee, a loaf of French bread. "Marmalade or strawberry jam?" He put a napkin over his arm with a flourish. "I've been meaning to get a nice little wrought iron table and chairs for this balcony. Would you like that? If that's what you'd like, we'll do it." His eyes shone. "Whatever madam desires."

When Cathy sat up and stretched and pushed back her hair, Tod blinked and grinned and grew even more rapt. A tear ran down the furrow beside his mouth. "Ah, my dearest lovely," he said. "You look...you look just the way I've always wanted you to. I can't believe you're here. Did I make you up?"

The tear reached the stubble on his chin and hung there, glistening. Cathy wished he would wipe it away. "Did I dream you?" He looked into her eyes and looked, his eyes brimming. "I didn't know being too happy could be so hard," he said, mopping his face with the napkin.

Cathy disentangled herself from his jacket. She opened her arms and he came to her, ardent burrowing. "Don't," she said. "Don't cry. I'm here. I'm right here."

"Where you belong," he said. "Where you belong."

As they breakfasted he told her they had reservations at the Pavillon, in New Orleans. That was all the warning she had.

A string ensemble was playing as Tod led her into the lobby of the hotel. He turned and said, only half teasing, "Are we going to be all right? This is a hotel, but I don't know what hell else we can——"

"It's lovely," Cathy said. "Don't be a goose. I've never seen so many chandeliers." The chandeliers shimmered. A violin cried, tremulous, delicate, sweet. There was the faint scent of roasting meats from a kitchen not too near. And the scent of Tod's recently extinguished cigar. "It smells like Sunday dinner, in Holland, Michigan," she said. "That might be my Dutch uncles, on the strings, tuning up. Oh, Tod."

"Aw," he said. "Aw," growling, pleased.

In their room, as he waited for the obsequious bellman to close the door and leave, he said, again almost teasing: "We're not going to run into any art deck here, are we?" Cathy couldn't answer. His eyes glowed, looking into hers, looking into hers, as he took her hands and kissed her fingertips one by one, murmuring, as only Tod could, "She is my lady, oh, she is my love."

He touched her and bathed her, his hands moving to all the places that he made ache for his touch. He crooned and murmured, his voice warm on her skin, warmer than the towel that covered and uncovered her breasts, that he called beautiful, so beautiful, as he touched, barely touched them and left them to come back more insistently. He held and caressed and gazed at her, naked and cool in the moonlight. "Come out in the silver," he said, drawing her with him out on the little balcony to be bathed in moonlight. He looked and looked into her eyes, smiling, so gentle, such a gentle, graceful man, looking far into her, laughing a little and looking away, drawing away, breathlessly leading her out onto the little balcony and asking that she look, making her look at herself, look at the two of them together in the pale diffused magic of the deliciously damp Louisiana night.

"Ah, now," he said, "this is what I want, most of all, just to look at you. I'll never have enough of it."

She shivered, grew tremulous, letting him do that, letting him lead her back into the room and the bed, letting him draw back to gaze and murmur before he kissed her, kissed her toes, the calves of her legs, his face burrowing into her thighs before he drew away to murmur and purr, making her lift to him, thrilled, head to toe. "Beautiful, beautiful, oh," he said, his voice thick in his throat.

Every time they awoke he gathered her close, making her quiver with need. She salivated, holding him, clutching at him with all of herself, arms, legs, mouth, oh, yes, her mouth open, oh, she ached for him, she was dying for him and he wanted her so, yes, yes, he wanted her yes he did but not yet, not yet, he whispered holding back, stroking and whispering and tasting, calling her his kitten, his delicate lady, his baby, his delicious baby who begged for him. His kitten that he would have, yes, his little Dutch girl that he'd eat alive, this little love. And wasn't she crying for him? But he wouldn't enter her, he wanted to look. To hold her and move against her until it became a torment. She gathered up, everything inside twisted and gathered up, fiercely, deliciously tight until she came—

—crying out that she couldn't—

—oh, please, she couldn't, she could not wait—

—but that was all right, that was what he wanted, baby, baby, let it come, catching at her flailing hands, holding her fingers in his mouth, telling her to breathe, oh, my love, breathe, take a breath now—! because that was only the beginning and now they were to begin again.

And they did.

He held her and brought the fever back, made her half sick with wanting him, kissing her breasts and her knees, the palms of her hands, finding places that she didn't know were to be kissed, over and over until she cried out, heard herself crying his name like an incantation, Tod, please, without breath enough and when it lifted and tightened in her again he did enter her slowly, and then hard, yes, as fiercely as she wanted, fast and hard to that need and inside was the bunching up, the knot that drew tight, tighter until it burst and he was groaning, his face above her, dripping, his eyes and teeth gleaming, shining in that silvery light and even at that moment, during the crest of that lifting moment, he stayed in control, catching his breath to hush her. "My angel, love. Breathe, my lovely love" until they grew more calm, he almost laughing, nestling his wet face between her breasts, moving against her to bring her face against his breast, muffling her against his hot skin, pretending to reprimand. "There might be other people in this hotel." And in a little while, he was blowing gently on her brow, cooling her face, kissing her and making her laugh at him, at herself, promising, teasing, assuring her the next time would be better, much better, only she would have to promise him to be "more quiet, a little more subdued."

And the next time was. Better.

"No wonder people keep making such a big fuss over sex," Cathy said in the morning, and was, immediately, embarrassed at Tod's explosive roar of merriment. He laughed, tried not to laugh, attempted an apology and exploded, helplessly, tearfully, as she sat up and tucked her feet under her. His shoulders shook. He doubled over, helplessly pawing the air, his face so pink it was Cathy's turn to tell him to breathe. That sent him off again.

He finally subsided. "Yes," mocking her. "No wonder."

He rolled over and slept. She couldn't sleep. She was too aware of him to sink into oblivion. She watched him breathe, seeing the small cup of moisture in the center of his upper lip, the indentation at his collar bone, the dark epaulets of hair curling on his shoulders, the crisp whorls of hair on his chest. He had unusual feet, the toes very nearly webbed. The membranes between his big toes and next ones were attached almost all the way to the knuckles.

When she did doze, she woke to see him gazing at her, rapt and smiling. "My retroactive virgin," he said.

I want you, she thought and he smiled lazily and caught at her hair, pulling her head back so he could smile into her eyes as he drew imaginary sustenance from her breasts, demanding in his growly voice, "What was all that about the queen of the passive resisters?"

There were knocks on the door and trays were left, with champagne and fresh peaches. Croissants and beignets. Bacon and shirred eggs and tiny pots of jam. They ate ravenously, fed each other, made love on the sticky sheets.

When Cathy finally murmured something about how they were, indeed, in a fairly famous place, the French Quarter, after all, and it might be something of a shame not to go out walking at some point, he smiled. Later, he said. When he breathed against her, temporarily sated, wondering if she thought they ought to go swimming, the hotel had a heated pool, she said she was too heated.

Eventually, the telephone on the floor next to the bed made a small sound, the beginning of a ring. Tod answered it and looked annoyed. "Damned crazy female on the switchboard," he said. He looked so different, so suddenly, that Cathy's stomach lurched but he smiled and said, "Let's go down to the pool."

Tod dove into the pool, swam the length of it rapidly and came back underwater. He surfaced, snorted, and dove back under again. Cathy watched him, amazed. She hadn't been allowed to swim. "My cousins all swam," she explained, "but the lake always frightened my grandfather." Having water splashed against her face, even playfully, made her anxious. Tod didn't seem to understand. He offered to hold her and she knew that she was perfectly safe in the clean, tile-edged, faintly blue hotel pool but she wanted to get out.

Tod cupped his hands over hers, forcing her to move her arms. She tried, but when he insisted she stay near him in water up to her chin while he dove and snorted, sleek and wet as a seal, tossing his wet head, flicking water into her eyes, Cathy kept hoping he wouldn't notice how she clung to the edges. When he swam underwater to the other end, she went puffing up the slippery rungs of a metal ladder, annoyed at herself. He surfaced and she said, trying too hard to sound casual, "I think I'll play spectator for a spell. Isn't swimming one of the spectator sports? I love watching you." Tod splashed. When he swam to her end and turned around, she groped behind her for a towel—he splashed, a lot—and was startled to feel a pair of sandals with feet in them. She looked up, startled, and apologized as a chubby man backed away.

"I'm so darned near sighted," the man said. He dropped to the wet concrete a couple of feet away. "Always wanted to learn swim like that. If you grow up in Midland, you don't learn to do that unless you've got a pool."

She glanced down, wishing her suit were more modest.

The man had a pinkish, round, freckled face and two rings of belly but his smile was timidly ingratiating. He, too, felt a little uneasy in the water, he confessed. "No fins on me," he said. "But you have to wish you could do that." He watched Tod.

She started to agree but "wish" started to come out "w-w-w-wish" so she gave up and sat in silence, wishing she had a towel or something to cover the white tops of her thighs, even though the man was watching Tod with a vague smile nestled in a double chin.

Tod lifted his head from the water, climbed out of the pool at the middle ladder, trotted over to them and stood looking down, dripping, moving from foot to foot. "You coming back in?" Before she could answer, the chubby stranger stuck his hand out.

Tod knocked the hand aside. "You drunk?" he said, his lips tight against his teeth.

The man scrambled clumsily to his knees. He got up on one leg. Tod kicked him in the knee. The man fell heavily to his knees, and, with a little grunting squeal, fell into the pool.

Cathy scrambled to her feet.

Tod dove in. The man flailed away from him, fought his way frantically up the ladder, got to his feet and hopped limping away.

Tod came out of the pool. "Friend of yours?" His mouth twisted. He stood clenching and unclenching his fists, the muscles alongside his jaw working. She thought, wildly, that he might be going to kick her, too.

"What is this?" she stammered. "You're sc-sc-scaring me."

Tod stared at her for as long as it took to draw the first half of a deep breath that broke in the middle before he turned away. He walked rigidly away from her across the tiled floor and through the aqua archway to the carpeted hotel corridor. Cathy watched his shiny back, her heart thumping and squeezing. After a couple of minutes she scrambled to her feet.

He reached the door to their room and was wrestling with the velcroed pocket at the waist of his swimming trunks, trying to get the key out, by the time she caught up with him. The key was almost too large for the pocket. "You're going to rip that," she said. His head swung around to glare at her so menacingly that she stepped back, reaching for his arm. He wrenched away from her hand. She stumbled against the wall, cracking her head, her tongue between her teeth for a brief agonizing second.

"Leave me the fuck alone."

She went through the room to the bathroom to rinse her mouth. After she came out, Tod went into the bathroom and urinated noisily without closing the door.

She was on a chair, too wretched to care that her damp bathing suit must be making a spreading wet place on the velour, hugging her knees, too miserable to move or think or try to say anything, when Tod came back into the room and pulled his suit off. He yanked on his trousers, saying, coldly, throwing the words into the room like a hand full of gravel, "I'm taking a hike."

As he went out, he jerked on the door, trying to make it slam. The door wouldn't be slammed. It made a scruffy sound against the carpet and, finally, clicked closed.

*****

15

When Tod came back he looked subdued, but he seemed determined to act as though nothing had happened. He stood around asking, "You want to go for a walk?" in an overly polite voice, glancing at Cathy and looking past her. When she shook her head, he busied himself reaching for a cigar.

"Please," Cathy said, hating the way she sounded. "We have to talk. There's something basically—"

"Oh, basically what?" He made a fist and looked at her with distant appraisal. "You're really hipped on that word. I'm a simple kind of guy. Figured you might have doped that out by now. Or is that what's so goddam basic all of a sudden?"

He shielded the cigar, lit it, went over to the window and gazed out. "You want to take a walk or not? We're in the French Quarter, after all."

Cathy shook her head, her throat aching. "N-no."

"All right," he said. "Fine. If that's what you want. Foul up the works. You want to scuttle the whole damned honeymoon? Up to you, baby."

She sat on the bed and scooted up to the headboard so she could brace herself and sit hugging her knees. "I don't understand."

"That right?" He started to the door and came back, demanding wearily, "You feel like talking now? You sure you wouldn't rather be talking to that big slob at the pool out there?" He drew a ragged breath. "Who wouldn't feel like shit? That slob moving in on you and you sitting there smiling off into the distance and me playing the chump, jumping through the hoop for the two of you to giggle at the chump, what the hell did you think I was gonna do?"

"That is so crazy."

He blew a smoke ring. "Crazy?" He wouldn't look at her. His eyes glared, red-rimmed, maybe from the chlorine in the pool, or maybe he had been crying—could he have been?—but they looked so awful. So bloodshot and threatening. Her heart pumped heavily, hurting in her chest. He kept moving around, pounding his fist into his hand, stepping up and down, ranting around the cigar clamped in his teeth. "So don't say you didn't give him the glad eye. I was there, baby. I saw it. Gave this nobody the big come-on. You think I didn't see you?"

"Oh, Tod."

"You sure as hell weren't giving him the brush, were you? And don't act like you don't know how to give the brush, baby, you're an expert. Hell, I ought to know. Or am I the only one turns you off? Some schlump comes out of nowhere and you can't wait to give him the glad eye, that it? That it?" He stepped against the wastebasket and gave it a kick. "So what all did he say? Your buddy moving in on our honeymoon—yukking about the big show-off chump in the pool, right?"

He had his elbows together, his hands flapping, imitating a seal. "He tell you to toss a fish? I'm your goddam husband for Christ's sake." He was in front of her, his face close to hers. "You sit around letting some drunk bastard hooraw me? You sure he wasn't somebody you know? One of those faculty profs sucks on the teat of the State? That's what you really want, isn't it? A hotshot professor. But you hadda settle for the chump."

Some part of him had to know that he wasn't making sense. She could see it in his face, hear it in his voice. He just couldn't seem to stop. She realized, suddenly knew, that he had to be helped to stop. "Tod." She stood up and lifted a hand, her fingers outspread. "That is enough."

It didn't even slow him down. He went on growling, demanding to know what they had said, she and her fat buddy, what had they found so damned funny. That's all he wanted to know. What had they been saying about the old chump. He kept spitting that word. "Chump," he said, "chump." Did she think he was a chump.

When he began to run down, Cathy ignored the way he held his hands out, motioning her into silence, and broke in to protest. "Tod, enough."

This time he stopped and looked at her.

"Listen to me. A poor, timid, fat man sat down for a second. If he seemed to be laughing it might have been in embarrassment because he was clumsy."

"Embarrassment?" Tod went from a little scream to a whisper, his head jutting, bouncing, his hands shaking. "That what you call it? Embarrassment? I call that being on the make, baby."

"You have to stop this," Cathy said, tearfully. "He was embarrassed and you're crazy."

"Crazy?" The word choked him. "That what you think you're stuck with? The crazy clown, the chump, oh, I can see, I get it now. That's the bit. It's embarrassing as hell the way you're stuck with this joke you're ashamed of, splashing around in the goddam—"

"You hurt him." The words seemed to echo in the room.

She stiffened, thinking yes, that's it and suddenly she wasn't as frightened. She was wondering, oddly detached, watching this pacing man who kept punching his fist into his palm, snorting, almost sobbing, now.

He neared her and turned on his heel, his eyes darting, unfocused, trying to make her realize his misery, trying to force her to know that he had to accuse her, "because you're supposed to be my wife, now, God damn it, don't you have any idea how to act like a married woman?"

He glared. "This is supposed to be our goddammed honeymoon. You have any idea how much this place costs? This is supposed to be it, the real big goddam deal. You got some half-cocked idea you can take me, think again. I don't go for divorce, that's not how I was brought up, to crap all over people or let them crap all over me." And she began to know that she'd have to find some way to help him. He couldn't tell her what it was. He didn't know. It wasn't something that might be explained.

She got up and moved over to stand in front of him and said, her finger at her lips, "That's enough." Her voice, her hands, her eyes said the rest. "Enough." She opened her arms.

He walked into her arms. They held each other, swaying, until he let her go and went over to the bed and sat down with his head in his hands.

"I am your wife," Cathy told him. "I'm right here. And it's going to be all right. But now you must stop this."

He inhaled, his breath catching. His mouth opened. Cathy lifted an admonishing finger. "Hush."

He fell back on the bed with the kind of wrenching sigh that sleepers sometimes give. "Jesus," he said. "Jesus." He lifted his hands. "I don't know."

She lay beside him. He curled into her, his head on her breast.

They made love. After a time they dressed and went out to find a wonderful restaurant somewhere in the French Quarter.

They ate. They talked of many things. Tod talked into the night. Neither of them mentioned the man at the swimming pool.

Every argument doesn't have to be totally resolved, Cathy told herself. None of us is without some sort of sickness.

That night, as Tod slept, she reasoned that he might have felt threatened in some way she would never understand. Maybe he'd overheard the freckled man laughing and misunderstood. Maybe she had seemed to be derisive. If he'd overheard her giggle, he might have leapt to that conclusion. She tried to remember what the man had said. She couldn't remember what he looked like, other than the way the fat on his chest made him seem slightly effeminate. She might have been pitying and tried too hard to mask it, and seemed to Tod to be...trying to be charming. Or charmed.

She'd always been so clumsy.

Or maybe, just maybe, that might be what people meant when they said someone was "insanely jealous." That word, "jealous" was so often preceded by "insanely" it had become a cliché and clichés were clichés because they were so very often true. Her new husband might just happen to be truly insanely jealous. It made her sit up straight on the bed, thinking. Nobody'd ever been the least bit jealous or even very possessive of her, that she could recall. A man on his honeymoon ought to have some right to be jealous, if any man, anywhere, ever were to have that right. She lay back and drifted off to sleep with Tod's hand cupping her breast.

The next day they walked, ate prawns and gumbo, drank wine, took wine back to the room and, some time during the night, made love, slowly and sweetly. Cathy held Tod to her, crooned to him, quietly explored and knew him. The lovemaking was less tempestuous but it was good.

Afterwards Tod had a cigar and fetched a bottle of wine to the bed, contentedly lazy. "You look so young," he said, "for somebody with such a great big kid. Greg's practically a man, you know that? Jesus, the things I was into by the time I was his age. My mother was younger than Greg when I was born. I never knew her." He had been reared by his father's mother and his father's sister, Aunt Beverly. "Fundamentalists. Church of the Nazarene. My mother had to get out of my grandmother's house." He hesitated. "Oh, what the hell. My mother, my mom, all I know is she was arrested once for lewd dancing. In New Orleans—! Is that a riot? I wasn't supposed to know about that, but I heard, all right." He snickered. "That really turned Aunt Bev inside out. Didn't take much. She and old granny were big on sin. Everybody was, in Nacogdoches. They still are."

"Nacogdoches?" Cathy squinted at him, confused. "I thought you said you grew up in Arkansas?"

"Arkansas," Tod said. "Oh, well, yeah. There, too. We started out in Arkansas and then, well, let's see, how old was I? Doesn't matter. We ended up in this big old house on a hill in Nacogdoches. Nacog-no-where. My mother's father, my granddaddy, was a self-appointed self-anointed preacher but he got TB. My old man drove into town with a vaudeville show. He got my mother pregnant and drove away. Black Irish. So you can see why I got the strap. They tried to beat the Black Irish out of me."

He didn't want to talk about it, he said, but he got out of bed and kept pacing and talking. "Nacogdoches is a pretty old town, but our house was one of those old places kids like to say is haunted. Big old ramshackle place, bougainvillea and honeysuckle and a wraparound veranda. It's kinda pretty, I'll take you there some day. But my aunt and my granny couldn't keep the place up. So. That's how it was. My aunt Beverly and Granny and me. Ah, they weren't so bad. Got stuck with me and I was a rotten little kid. That leather strop of Aunt Beverly's might have been the only thing that kept me out of jail. It's a tough world. That's the thing you and Greg don't get. The sooner a kid learns that, the better off he is. Listen, my aunt and granny might have been tough but their system beat hell out of all this permissive psychology bullshit. Aunt Beverly did the best she knew and I tell you what, she did a pretty fair job of it." He laughed. "Last time I ran away, they bent my spoon and threw away my plate."

He seemed to expect her to smile. She tried.

He looked annoyed. "It's called discipline," he said.

"Punishment isn't discipline. Punishment is punishment."

"Discipline," Tod said, smiling but irritated, his eyes taking on a perplexed glint. "I'm on solid ground there, lady. I figured you for one of those, though, right off."

"One of those?"

"You know. Not much respect for discipline around your place."

"Discipline," Cathy said, "is how music is learned. Discipline is control. It's all kinds of things, none of which have the least thing to do with punishment."

"Whoa." He waved both hands, interrupting, "You're getting the wrong idea, here. Aunt Beverly was made of stainless steel and my granny never gave an inch. She had arthritis so bad when she cracked those knuckles they sounded like castanets, but she cracked 'em. She'd stand out in that yard cracking those knuckles, never gave an inch. And she'd whale the daylights out of me if I pulled some of the crap that those kids pull at your house. Maybe she didn't know much about kids but, hey, she put some steel in this one, didn't she?" He nodded. "Damn straight. You want to know something? You're headed down the garden path when it comes to the fine points of raising a boy. Boys aren't like women like you think. I'll tell you what: you never ought to let that kid talk back to you like he does. That's one thing I learned real quick long before I got to be anywhere near as tall as Greg. Drives me up the wall to hear the way he talks to you."

You never will be anywhere near as tall as Greg, Cathy thought. She turned away. "My son and I have no trouble communicating."

"You believe that?" Tod got up, lit a cigar, waved the match around and broke it in half, making a little ceremony of it. He exhaled and peered at her through the smoke. "Well, if that's how you see it," he drawled. "But he'd better not communicate with you like that a whole hell of a lot in front of me. I'd like to make that much clear right now."

"Just what do you have in mind?" Cathy asked.

The telephone rang. Cathy was nearest so she picked it up and answered. The line was for silent so long that she repeated herself and almost hung up before a woman asked, "Are you Toddy's latest, honey?"

"I beg your pardon?" Cathy said.

The woman laughed. The laugh turned into a cough. "That's what I said, darlin'," the woman said, coughing harder. "Toddy's latest." She stopped coughing and said, "You tell Toddy that Lynn's waiting for him."

*****

16

"**I** was going to tell you about Lynn," Tod said. He tried to draw Cathy down next to him on the sofa but she pulled away. She sat across the room, on the other side of the bed, hands covering her ears. She could not go away, could not walk out of the room, the way he had one. She ended up at the head of the bed, her arms around her knees, her ears ringing.

When he came over and tried to take her hands, she said, "Don't say say anything. Don't touch me."

"Cathy, listen."

"You're touching me," she said. "Don't."

"I won't," Tod said. "Just listen. May I talk? Will you listen?" He sighed. "You have to understand." He hunched and straightened and clasped his hands, reaching for words. "Lynn was, like, well, she was my wife, yes. Do you want a drink? Tell you what. I could use a drink. Why don't we go somewhere and have a drink?"

Cathy swhispered, "Your wife?" She pressed her hands to her eyes, briefly. "You lied to me." She couldn't look at him.

"Ah, hell," he said. "In another life. A lifetime ago. When I was a just a kid. We were both kids. I was going to tell you but things moved along so fast with us and, I don't know. Are you going to be able to handle this?"

It sounded like such a strange word. Handle. Cathy looked at her hands, thinking, wife. Your wife. And did you tell this wife, this Lynn, that she was your lady, oh, she was your love? Did you quote Yeats? Did you kiss her and kiss her and kiss her until she forgot to breathe and then tell her to breathe? It was hard to breathe.

He wanted to gather her up.

"Don't touch me," she said. "When? When did you intend to tell me about your wife?"

"I don't know." He sounded hoarse. "When I thought I could, I guess."

"How could you?" she whispered. "How could you keep lying? Don't touch me. You're touching me. I said do not touch me."

"Don't keep saying that," he said. "Aw."

The word sounded strange to her. "Aw." He has his own language, she thought, distractedly. He says "handle." And "Aw." Staring at me with his wrinkled red face.

He kept talking. "Aw, come on, honey, this is nothing to get so wrought up over. It's something that happened a long time ago. Doesn't have anything to do with us. You've been married. See?" He was beginning to sound accusatory: "You had a marriage. I had a marriage. I guess I just didn't feel like talking about mine. Does that make any kind of sense? So now you know. That's pretty much that." He gazed at her in silence and when she couldn't respond, an angry flush streaked his cheeks. "Maybe that's how you separate the broads from the ladies. There isn't much a lady can't handle."

That word again. "Handle?" Cathy said. She pushed his hand away. She didn't want to punish him. She just wanted to have her ears stop ringing. To be able to understand, somehow, enough so that she could get rid of the lump in her throat and be sure she wasn't going to burst into tears, because if she started to cry she would cry until she retched. "Lynn."

"That was her name."

"Was?"

"She's gone," he said, wearily. "Lynn is dead."

"Why would someone say Lynn is waiting for you?" She took a deep breath. "No. If you get up and walk away I can't—I will not stay in this room. Don't keep looking at the door. I have to understand. That woman said to tell you that Lynn is waiting for you. Why is Lynn waiting?"

He sighed and sat down. "This is ridiculous. Okay. Maybe some hysterical female isn't so happy about breaking up with me, or some damned thing, I don't know. How do I know? Does anybody know what makes women do anything? Let's see if we can get past this. Lynn was a nice girl and she died. She's dead. I'm damned if I know who that was on the phone but Lynn died years ago."

He got up and walked over to the sofa and shoved a pillow behind his head. "I was going to tell you about her." He lit a cigar and went on, his eyes narrowed against the smoke. "I was seventeen, but Lynn didn't know that, and neither did her mama and daddy. She was almost twenty-one, but she was a young twenty-one. I was a lot older than she was, if you know what I mean. Lynn was just a nice big kid. A little bit heavy. Not fat. Not at first, anyway. But she came of pretty stout folks and she put on some weight. Not that I minded." He rubbed his face. "Look. Lynn was a big blonde. Her mother was a big blonde. Norwegian. American but she had that look, you know. Norwegian. The mother liked to cook. Lynn liked to eat, liked to dance, liked to...everything. A big blonde." He sighed. He smiled but when he looked at Cathy's face he stopped smiling and got up and tried to put his arms around her. "Honey, I'm sorry, but it was a such a long time ago."

"You're touching me." She pulled her arm away and chafed it.

He went back to the sofa. "You have to understand how hard up I was all the time, in those days." He glanced down at himself with a rueful laugh. "Thinking with the little head. Damned thing was driving me crazy. Even having my jeans rub against it drove me wild. Whatever I had to do, I had to take care of it first." He gazed at the ceiling. "That kind of thing can screw up your life. Tell you what: I don't think monkeys are funny when they play with themselves in front of God and everybody at the zoo like they do. I know just how the poor little bastards feel." He ran his hand over his mouth and chin. "I was a damned maniac. And right about then I met these good people, Lynn's mom and her daddy, a real sweet guy, the only daddy I've ever known. My best friend, for a while there, Lynn's daddy. Sweet guy." His voice grew husky.

"See, Lynn's people took me in. In Nacogdoches, the mothers of the other kids used to make me get off the porch. I never was good enough. I don't know what it was. Maybe it was my aunt Beverly or my granny, supposed to be some kind of a witch. And I got in a little trouble, now and then, I admit it. But then I met Lynn and here was this family. Lynn's mother had this herb garden. First herb garden I ever saw. Lynn's dad was a mailman. The guy could fix anything. Lynn's mother was a big German woman, kind of the way Lynn was headed, I guess."

He wanted to stop. Cathy just looked at him.

"Am I ever going to be able to touch you again?" He clasped his hands and stood up, his head swaying side to side, wearily sad.

"I don't know," Cathy said. She truly didn't.

Tod began to pace. "Lynn's mother, I don't know, she was great. Lynn's mother taught Lynn how to make bread in these crockery bowls? Onion bread, cheese bread, nut bread. I was hungry all the time, back then. What the hell, I didn't give a damn about a little, you know, weight problem, in a woman. More of her to love." He rubbed his hands. "I think people who like to eat like to...everything. And people who don't like to eat don't give a damn about much of anything, way I see it."

So. Lynn, Cathy gradually came to realize, was Lynn, with a mother who took in a boy who was desperate for mothering, a hungry youngster. And this Lynn liked to do everything. She was, as they say, a lot of woman. She taught Tod how to love and be loved, and something about life.

"Ah, darlin'," Tod said, "Lynn could dance. She danced from the top of her head to the bottom of her feet. Used to scare me sometimes. I used to get scared I'd have to kill some son of a bitch some day. You should have seen the way those guys circled around."

But somehow things didn't work out.

"I went to work in this drugstore and there wasn't enough money and I don't know. She got so she wanted a divorce." He looked around, apologetic about talking too much, nervously afraid to stop talking, asking her if she was getting to where she understood. "Hell, baby, all this was a long time ago." He shrugged. "We were so poor. We lived with Lynn's parents and then we had two rooms up over Haley's Drugs. I had a job there. After a while, I guess, you know, there were differences."

He sighed. "There were some little girls kind of started hanging around after school."

"Little girls?"

Tod looked sheepish. "Well, hell, baby. I literally worked in a candy store and I was just a kid."

"I see," Cathy said. She was beginning to see.

He shrugged and went on. "So, I got a job in Florida and Lynn met Gus. Gus Merriam. He's okay. Good old boy. Lynn met Gus and then she got sick and she's dead. You know what? Let's get off of this. This is a hell of a thing. I mean, this is our honeymoon. Why don't we go out and find some new place to eat, maybe hear some music? Be a crime not to hear some jazz in New Orleans."

"But that woman said she's waiting for you," Cathy said.

"No. She isn't. I don't know who that was but it couldn't be anybody knows anything about Lynn. Lynn is dead. She died in Seabrook years ago. Jumped out of a window. It wasn't that high a building but she landed in water." He shook his head. "Terrible thing. Just about killed Gus."

"She jumped?"

Tod sat up and stretched. "Hell, do you see why I didn't want to go into this right off the bat? Are you going to let a lot of ancient history get in the way of what we've got going here? I guess Lynn couldn't handle being sick. I don't know. She had a little weight problem by then and maybe she and Gus weren't getting along. Are we ever going to get past this?" He moved toward Cathy to gather her to him and stopped.

"Don't," she said. "Touch me."

"Not ever?"

"I don't know."

During the night he tried to kiss her but she couldn't respond.

Their flight back to Houston was delayed. They landed at Intercontinental at two a.m. in a dripping fog. Tod couldn't find the card to claim the car. Neither of them could remember which lot they'd left it in. Cathy had been in such a daze when they had come through the airport, she had been so wildly happy in that former life, that she hadn't made any attempt to pay any attention to anything. Everybody they ran into at the airport at that hour of the morning, the woman at the information counter, the porter, the woman who drove the electric go-cart, everybody spoke Vietnamese or Spanish or Polish or Russian or some unidentifiable mideastern dialect. They were driven from parking lot to parking lot, craning at parked cars looming up in the fog. It seemed a bizarre but somehow appropriate ending—Tod called it a reality check—to their honeymoon.

"Are we in America here, or what," Tod complained. "Where did these people come from?"

After they had gotten home and were settled on Tod's mattress, Cathy kept thinking about the woman's voice on the telephone and Tod's endless explaining. There seemed to be something vaguely wrong with some things he had said about his grandmother and aunt in Nacogdoches, even before the phone call. Hadn't he said it was his father's father who had been the preacher? But it couldn't have been. His father had come through town, the Irish vaudevillian. He had taken advantage of Tod's teenaged mother, the dancer. The lewd dancer.

Cathy couldn't sleep. I am going to, as he puts it, handle this. Get past it, she told herself. I am not going to go into shock over something that happened years ago, not going to have a nervous breakdown over some stupid woman's voice on a telephone. I am going to sleep. Not sleeping can make everything seem dreadful and messy and impossible.

Once, one awful night before she had been able to afford a phone even, when Greg was little, he woke with a fever. Cathy couldn't find the thermometer. She rocked him and rocked him. He cried and cried. When he finally went to sleep he was so hot she didn't put him down but held him to her, scared and shaking, thinking what a rotten mother she was to not even have a telephone or know where the thermometer was, how she was so stupid that her baby might die because she couldn't take care of him by herself. In the morning Greg slid down from her lap and said he was hungry. He didn't want to be kept home from kindergarten.

Cathy took him to a sympathetic neighbor to watch and went to the office all puffy eyed and her dear good boss, Patrick, brought two cups of coffee and sat down to discuss the dangers of not getting enough sleep. "All two a.m. thoughts are black liars," Patrick said, that morning. "Believe it, Chicken Little. All two a.m. thoughts are the blackest of liars."

A person ought to keep that in mind, Cathy thought, especially if she's really cramping and doesn't have a hot water bottle or any Midol. In the morning, menstruating or not, she'd have to go out and buy a decent bed. Two beds. One for Greg. And she'd have to, oh, Lord, pack every thing she and Greg might want to keep, so they could move to Galveston, to this wonderful old house where Greg could enroll in a new school and begin a new life. Oh, let it be a wonderful school, she thought, letting the thought become a prayer, oh, Lord, with a wonderful orchestra, please.

And help me to forget all about some silly woman's voice on a telephone. Help me to be understanding and tolerant and wise.

*****

17

"You're supposed to be packing your things," Cathy told Gregory.

"Quit bugging me." Greg kept standing around eating crackers, alternately being sarcastic and cajoling, insisting Chub and Patrick wanted him to stay with them until the end of the semester. "Or I could stay at Scotty's. Why can't I stay at his house?"

"Because you'd start wearing green mesh jerseys or opera capes or some darned thing. Besides, Tod says he'll pay you to do the yard in Galveston and that will give you gas money for the Jeep. Don't you think it'll be fun to have a Jeep and live on an island?"

"Why are you packing all the books?" Greg tapped the ash from an imaginary cigar and lowered his voice: "'Haven't you read all these books, baby? You gonna read all these books all over again?'" He waggled his eyebrows. "'You want some nice new books? We'll go get you some nice new books, baby.' Boy, the man's a real biblipole, isn't he?"

"That's 'bibliophile,'" she snapped. "The pole one means dealer."

"That's what I mean," Greg said. "The man's a real dealer."

"Go pack," Cathy said.

Greg sneered. "You're gonna keep that crummy quilt?"

Cathy had her quilt folded and ready for the box but it did look sadly frayed and tattered. "It was my grandmother's, in Holland."

"I know that," Greg said. "I was just asking."

"Unhand my aluminum tray. Go pack. I have to make decisions here."

Greg dropped the aluminum tray into the trash. "You haven't made a conscious decision in years, Mother."

Cathy was glad Tod wasn't around to pick up on that. He came at noon, though, and Greg managed to precipitate a minor skirmish then, even though Tod came in with two big delicatessen bags full of pastrami sandwiches and salads and lovely big pickles.

She fished the tray out of the trash and held it up for him to see. "This may be the last tangible sign of my son's affection," she said, unswaddling it. "See how the 'love you mom' runs uphill? Greg made this in shop in junior high. He had to work fast and keep covering it with his arm. See?" She hugged the tray to her breast before she tucked it into a box. "He used to be this sunshiny little boy, believe it or not."

Tod had a blob of baked clay with a small handprint in his hand. "He do this, too?"

Cathy nodded. "One of a kind."

"Yeah," Greg said from the doorway where he had suddenly appeared. He rubbed his shoulders against the woodwork. "A naked singularity."

Tod's eyes narrowed. "A naked what?"

Greg shrugged, but Cathy explained, hastily, "It's a cosmic term." She shot Greg a look. "Don't be difficult."

"Moi?" Greg said, all injured innocence.

"It's something that happens," she explained to Tod.

Tod looked wary. "That so? We talking in code?"

Greg smirked. "A naked singularity happens just once," he said. "It's a cosmic term."

Cathy busied herself wrapping plates in newspaper.

"So it can't be traced," Greg went on. "Pow. Physicists are crazy about naked singularities."

Tod wiped at his mouth. "So it's one of those things," he said.

"Nope," Greg said. "It's a one time thing. You ever watch Nova? With the black holes and all?"

"Black holes?" Tod chewed his lower lip. "I don't see where we're going with this."

"Black holes don't have any hair," Greg said.

"He's being pedantic," Cathy said. "Don't be a pedantic poop," she said, to Greg.

Tod ran his tongue over his front teeth. "This the way you and your mother like to talk?"

We're going to go from crisis to crisis, Cathy thought. "Let's eat," she told the two of them. And they had lunch.

The moving men came early in the afternoon. Cathy and Greg's furniture looked pretty awful in the new house but Tod insisted it would do, until they chose something more permanent. He said that Cathy and Greg needed some of their own things so they could feel at home in the new house, even if the things were a rump sprung sofa and two battered old chairs, which looked ridiculous in the cavernous living room.

The only thing they owned that looked as though it might belong in the Galveston house was Greg's cello, with its stand and metronome.

"Play," Cathy said. "I'll bet the acoustics in here will blow you out of your socks." Rays of sunlight sifted through the glittering windows, bathing the instrument in glowing light. Greg sat down and straddled his cello. "I could do with a little Vivaldi," she said. "Do the autumnal one."

Greg played.

"Ach," Cathy said. "Sudge luffliness." The acoustics were splendid. The music seemed to sing in and around the house as beautifully as the light shone through the stained glass windows. How could this be more perfect, she was thinking, when Chub and Patrick rang the front doorbell. They said they knew they had the right house when they heard the cello from the front sidewalk.

"Moving day. Are we a darned nuisance?" Chub asked. "Could you use some help?"

"You talk about timing," Cathy said. "Come in, come and see this house. Gregory is in the music room."

"But of course," Chub said. "The music room." She hugged Cathy. "Oh, all those wonderful little faces out in front—! And look at the wooden flowers."

When they got upstairs, Chub kissed Greg and told him not to stop. "This is all this house needs, isn't it? Greggy and his marvelous music."

Cathy showed them all through the house. "I feel like a Gothic heroine," she said, the back of her hand at her brow. "Our furniture looks awful but we're going to do something about that, right away."

"You look like a Gothic heroine," Chub said. "Let's eat."

They ate. Patrick and Chub helped put the dishes away, climbing up and down stepstools and ladders to load plates and cups in the awful tall, moss green cabinets in the kitchen. When they had finished and were ready to go, Patrick said, "Moving can be traumatic, Chicken Little. You might want to take it easy."

"Oh, I won't try to do everything all at once," Cathy said.

His eyes showed concern. "You going to be all right?"

Chub poked him with a wifely elbow. "Get a grip. Look at this place. Of course she's going to be all right," but she was too hearty and Patrick's smile faded.

He looked at Cathy, his face furrowed. "Keep in close touch, okay?"

Cathy crossed her heart. "Hope to die."

After Chub and Patrick left, Greg quit playing. The house felt very quiet. Cathy roamed around, thinking how perfectly awful her old velour sofa with its frayed arms and her tired chairs looked, wondering what Greg's new school would be like.

She found Greg in his room, eyeing a wall, his beloved star chart poster still in its tube on his new bedspread on his new bed, that he'd picked out, that he now didn't seem especially pleased with. "I don't know where to hang anything," he said. "Not that it makes any difference since nobody's going to see it."

"Oh, honey. Scotty and Ginger will be down. You'll see." She knew better than to say he would meet people. He didn't want to hear about meeting new people.

He held the poster up to the wall. "We got any thumbtacks?"

"Maybe we ought to get some of your posters framed and see about some way of hanging them without damaging these walls."

"Oh, right. The walls." Greg looked disconsolate. "This place is going to be a real pain."

You ought to try cooking in that kitchen, Cathy thought. "I think the Victorians must have been crazy about ladders," she said, looking around. "The rooms are sure tall."

"So if we hate it enough do you think we could move back home?"

"Oh, honey," Cathy said. "Don't say that."

"He basically can't stand me, you know," Greg said. "If you're so crazy about this house and living here, I guess I can handle Galveston, but me and him, that's not going to change, Mom. It's not. Why couldn't he be, like, ninety-nine with one foot in the grave, and you could get him to put you in his will or whatever? Like that stripper, you know, married the old millionaire and he kicked off. How old is he, anyway?"

"Oh, Greg," Cathy said. "That's dreadfully unfunny."

"I know," Greg said. "But a guy can't help dreaming."

The misery in his face made her ache. I have made the most terrible mistake of my life, she thought, but that night, the night of their moving day, Tod bundled her into the Cadillac and drove all the way from the east end of the Island to the end of the sea wall at the west end. The moonlight made a glittering path on the Gulf and there were stars, stars all across the night sky, some of them falling, magically coursing through the dark sky. Cathy hadn't seen stars for the longest time, in Houston. There never were any visible from any window of their Houston place Tod drove right out onto the sand and parked. Then he kissed her soundly and, when she shivered, said, "Are you chilly?"

"A little," Cathy admitted.

He got out of the car, opened the trunk, and came back with her frazzled old quilt. "Here," he said, tucking it around her knees. "Some people don't know beans about what to keep and what to throw away."

Cathy couldn't answer.

Tod came around and got back in and snuggled close. "You need a caretaker," he said, gruffly. He put his head on her shoulder. "And I'm it."

The next day Cathy went to enroll Greg at school. The principal was tiny but she looked like a no-nonsense sort of person, with frizzly gray hair and bluish pouches under her eyes. She summoned a youngster to show Gregory around while Cathy filled out forms. When Cathy said she was particularly interested in the music department the woman sounded as tired as she looked. "Your orchestra," Cathy said.

"We used to have an orchestra," the principal said.

"Used t-t-to?" Cathy's tongue got stuck. She shook her head, fighting the stammer. "You mean there's n-no orchestra? Th-th-the only high s-s-s-school in t-t-this t-town has no orchestra?"

"Sorry," the principal said. Musical instruments take funding, she said, enunciating precisely.

Greg was deliberately dispassionate about it. "I can't believe there's no orchestra," Cathy stammered, on the way to the car.

"Believe it," Gregory said. That was all he said, all the way home.

She followed him into the kitchen, got out the milk and handed it to him, wanting to sit down with him and talk about it. He wasn't having any talk. He drank the rest of the milk left in the container and leaned against the refrigerator and gazed at the kitchen ceiling.

"I'm just shattered," Cathy said. "I can't see how the only high school in a town of almost seventy thousand people can not have any orchestra."

The mottled color beneath his skin was the only indication that Greg was even listening.

"I should have checked," she went on. "Oh, honey, I'm so sorry. Do you know how sorry I am? Greg? Look at me. I could just—I don't know. This is all my fault, isn't it? It's all my fault. Please say something. I feel like this is all my doing."

Greg moved past her into the living room. He sprawled on the floor and picked up a magazine. "It's a thought, Mother. It's a thought, isn't it?"

*****

18

"**N**o problem," Tod said. "We'll let the boy take the Jeep to Houston to do his thing with the cello. Damned shame there isn't any orchestra but our boy can rise above that, can't he?"

The look on Cathy's face stopped him. "I don't want him careening up and down the freeway," she said. "We've been over that."

"I could stay at Scotty's," Greg said. "Scotty's got a garage apartment that they don't even need and he says I can stay there. I wanted to move in over there in the first place."

"Now hold on," Tod said.

"As if anybody around here gives a shit what I want," Greg said. He tipped back in his chair and, when it slid, stood up and righted it.

"What was that I heard?" Tod said.

"Some things are better left unsaid," Greg said, "and I want to be the first to say them. What I said was—"

"Oh, stop," Cathy said.

"Nobody's going to talk that way to my wife," Tod said.

Cathy said, "Oh, please," and Greg said he was getting as bored with the cello as he was with the conversation and went stalking off to his room.

Tod stubbed out his cigar in the remains of his apple tart and went off to work.

Greg came back downstairs as soon as he left. "What was that I heard?" he asked, doing Tod's imitating Tod's brusque, irritated growl. "If he heard, what's the point?"

"I don't know as there is one," Cathy said, miserably. "It makes me sick to hear you say you're bored with your cello. You take that back."

Greg shrugged.

When Cathy looked back at that moment of that autumn day she realized that was when Greg began to change, when he seemed to ... lose focus. He went languid and distant. He didn't complain about school but it didn't seem to matter, terribly, whether he went there. He got harder and harder to wake up. That was the scariest thing. All through the years, back in Houston, Greg had been an early riser. Cathy used to complain about it. "He comes up like a helicopter," she'd say. "How can anybody be so darned eager to face every day?" She'd come yawning out of her room to find her son, damp from the shower, whistling, shining comb marks in his hair, going over and over the stacks of homework he'd done and redone the night before until he thought it was perfect. By the time he'd give up and go to his beloved cello to work out his frustration, there'd be a welter of crumpled paper in and around the wastebasket but his homework would be as flawless as he could get it.

"I'm not all that much brighter than the rest of the kids," he would tell her. "It's just staying on top."

That's how things used to be. In Houston.

Now Greg would not wake up and sometimes he wouldn't get out of bed when he was awake. He'd lie there with his eyes open and refuse to get dressed. It wasn't that he turned in too late. The big kid couldn't seem to stay awake through the ten o'clock news but Cathy simply could not get him going of a morning. She bought an alarm clock and put it in a metal dish pan next to his bed. It made a horrific noise. He ignored it. When she shook him awake he rolled away. When she stormed at him, "You're too big to lift," he would pull a pillow over his head.

Greg didn't even want to go with them to darling Patrick's birthday party on the seventeenth. He said he had other plans.

"What other plans?"

"Hanging out," he said. "With some guys."

"Who are some guys?"

Greg looked away. "Don't worry about it."

That's what Tod kept saying. Cathy got tired of being told not to worry about things. She and Tod left Greg home and drove to Houston early the night of Patrick's birthday, so they could stop off somewhere and pick up a birthday gift. Tod parked at Almeda Mall and said he'd wait for her on a bench outside Foley's. She didn't see anything to buy, and when she went to look for Tod, he'd left the bench. She hurried all through the store and finally spotted him, roaming around in the ladies' lingerie department, of all things. He looked as though he actually might be enjoying himself but he jumped, startled, when she touched him on the arm.

"What have we here?" he said, looking around at rows of skimpy teddies on padded satin, drifting peignoirs, nightgowns of liquid silk.

"You want some of these?" He roamed from rack to rack, stopping to hold a crimson satin teddy beneath Cathy's chin, draping a blue satin robe over her shoulder. "You like this?"

"No," Cathy said.

"Ah, you're right," he said. "Not your thing." He strayed to another rack. "Beads." He held up a peignoir with smocking and rows of seed pearls. "How about this?"

"Oh, please," Cathy said. "You've seen my gowns."

"Um," he said. "That I have."

He waggled his eyebrows. "These are slinky. Ah. Look at this."

"I have night gowns," Cathy said.

"But I didn't pick 'em out," Tod said. He grinned at her. "From now on, I pick. You wear. That goes for everything."

He bought four white cotton nightgowns with tiny tucking on the bodices and lace-edged long sleeves. She felt they were wildly extravagantly expensive but Tod beamed. "They're pure and lovely, for my pure and lovely lady. Let's tuck these in the trunk."

When they got back inside the mall Cathy said, absently, "I think Chub chooses Pat's clothes," and Tod stopped walking so suddenly that he was run into by a couple with a stroller.

"She does what?" He feigned horror. "That's completely bass awkward. A woman never ought to do that. Pat should pick out Chub's clothes." He slid an arm around her. "That's what we'll do. I'm going to enjoy dressing you." He frowned. "As soon as the cash flow loosens up, that is. Damned market."

They found an eel-skin wallet for Patrick and separated again, to go to the toilet this time, agreeing to meet in the food court.

Tod took so long that Cathy roamed from the food court to an adjacent booth with a display of rings. An Indian saleslady held a ring out toward her, saying, "Doesn't it look real?" Cathy slipped the ring on and turned to see Tod, frowning up at her, his mouth twisting derisively. "What are you doing with that?"

"It's less than twenty dollars," the clerk said.

"That's obvious," Tod said.

Cathy took the ring off, handed it back to the saleslady and had to hurry to catch up with her bustling husband. "Crap," he said. "I hate crap." And I hate that word, Cathy thought, but Tod hadn't finished. "You want a ring? I'll get you a ring." She wasn't sure she'd heard him right. "Corrigan's is over here," he said. He bowed, touched his brow in a small salute, tucked Cathy's arm in his and led her into Corrigan's jewelry store.

"I like that emerald in the window," he said to the man who greeted them. "Let's have a look at that."

The ring slipped on easily. The man said that the huge green stone, marquis cut, was a Columbian emerald. "This ballerina setting is unique. Eight faceted baguette diamonds. Remarkably well done, don't you think?"

The heavy stone shimmered on Cathy's hand. She looked and looked at it, hearing the clerk go on and on, saying such depth of color, so unlike most of the stones mined recently, most of them pale or flawed. This one, it seemed, was flawless.

Tod watched her, expansively genial, the creases at the corners of his eyes deepening at her hesitant smile.

"Oh, I don't think," Cathy said, but he lifted a finger.

"I do." He picked up her hand and kissed it. "I do. I do. With this ring I thee wed," he said.

They ate, Cathy gazing at her hand in a daze and Tod smiling, smiling into her eyes. They almost forgot to go back and pick up Pat's gift wrapped birthday present.

All during Pat's birthday party people seemed to keep noticing the ring, possibly because Cathy kept noticing it. And later, on the way to the car, Tod said, "I didn't see any emeralds on any of those faculty wife types, did you?"

They were so happy that night, that they didn't even get too upset when they got out to the car to find the trunk lid ajar and the Foley's bag with Cathy's expensive night gowns gone.

Tod insinuated it must have been one of Pat's guests. "I'm not as impressed as you are with all those boys sucking on the teat of the State," he said. "Bunch of arrogant bastards."

She wondered why he always had to make "faculty" sound vaguely dirty. "Please don't drive so fast," she said.

Tod sighed. "Yes, wife." But he didn't slow down. Then, as they reached home and slowed to pull into the circular drive in front, an elderly neighbor with a dog on a leash came toddling over, beckoning as though he had some portentous announcement. Tod stopped and opened the window on his side of the car.

"You being taken for a walk?" he said, nodding at the dog.

"Lizzy's a light sleeper," the neighbor answered. He peered into the car with the anxiously earnest look of a man who couldn't quite catch what was being said. "I guess I'm a light sleeper, too." He extended his hand and Tod shook it. "Lou," the old man said. "Lou Johnson. My son just bought the place on the corner. I've been thinking that we ought to have a neighborhood watch." He leaned closer and confided: "You people notice that white Buick keeps parking up the street, here?"

"White Buick?" Tod sat back and gazed through the windshield, deliberately genial. "That so?"

"Big old ugly car," the man said. "Has to belong to somebody around here. Comes around and parks here all the time, especially at night. You just missed it. Pulled away as you drove up."

Tod yawned. The dog tugged at the leash. The man said goodnight and went his way.

Cathy wondered whether any of Greg's new friends might know something about a an old white Buick. She went to his room, tapped lightly on his door, and went in. Greg was asleep, the ceiling fan turning gently, the tall windows opened to the cool breeze. She stood and looked out the window at the street, inhaling, thinking that the soft, cottony wind somehow made her think of beach fires and boats; it smelled faintly of burned rope.

The master bedroom was moon lit. Tod made her stop and observe the light coming through the windows before he turned on the rosy lamps Cathy had found to go with the new nightstands and the king sized bed. At first he had pretended to not like the bed. He had gone into an act," You will write, won't you?" but then he'd bounced on it like a little boy and pronounced it perfect.

As Cathy pulled her dress over her head the emerald in her new ring caught the edge of a seam. When she disentangled it from the fabric, she lifted it over her head and it got caught in her hair. Tod moved to help her but he couldn't bear to tug at her hair the way she did. He made a small mournful sound and stood clear, slapping at his thighs, murmuring at her, as she worked the dress up and off and got the ring free of her hair. When she stepped out of her half slip, he bent quickly to gather it up. She watched, embarrassed, as he buried his face in the slip.

When she took off her panties he groaned and moved close, tumescent, one hand at the back of her brassiere and the other cupping her close. "Pears," he said. "Peaches and pears. Yum. Little firm cherries." He smacked his lips. "They even taste like cherries."

Later, as he moved against her, murmuring rapturously, patiently trying to make her gather herself into a seething tight knot beneath him, patiently waiting her out, wanting her skin to warm beneath his hands, Cathy kept feeling the edge of her ring.

"Going to eat you alive, little Dutch girl," he said, as she tried to turn the ring around so it wouldn't cut into her fingers.

It wasn't just the ring that was so distracting, She realized later, in the dark, with Tod snoring beside her. She pulled away to her side of the bed, thinking about the neighbor with his dog, out in front. Outside, the long leaves of the banana palms nearest the balcony moved, sending flickering shadows across the ceiling that, unaccountably, reminded her of that crazy telephone call, that honeymoon night, the woman on the phone sounding so...disembodied. So demented. And the man on the front walk that night, back at the old house, that Greg insisted said that he knew Tod. What had Greg said? "He asked if your boyfriend did this." Talking about his bandaged hand.

How poor they were, back then. At times she still felt that pinch.

Money could be so worrisome. Tod seemed to have such peculiar feelings about it. He could be madly spontaneously generous. Making the man take her ring right out of the window of Corrigan's, for goodness' sakes. Her beautiful emerald. So big she kept feeling it. The weight of it on her finger was making her wakeful.

But he had a way of looking at the leftovers from a meal and insisting, falsely exuberant, "Now that looks like the makings of a pretty good lunch to me. How about you, Greg? No point in throwing away money buying cafeteria food when we've got all this good stuff left."

Oh, how Greg loved to imitate the way Tod sounded. "The guy's about as tight-fisted as they come, Mom."

But it wasn't that Tod was tight-fisted, exactly. Just...somewhat peculiar. He wouldn't let her keep her checking account or join him in his. "Confuses the issue," he said. He loathed credit cards. Why should he pay some bank to dole out money to his wife when he enjoyed doing that? All she needed to do was ask.

He made her cut her VISA card in half and, when she asked for his, to pay for a table cloth from Penney's, he explained that plastic was, essentially, for business expenses only.

"You've always worked for the State, baby," he said. "You and that boss of yours on the faculty never have had to find out what it's like in the real world. You need a little cash, you come to me."

That's why he'd married her, he said. To take care of her. And it was lovely, wasn't it? Being taken care of?

*****

19

The second week of November Cathy unpacked her cookbooks for Thanksgiving; *The Joy of Cooking*, *The Herb and Spice Cookbook*, her funny old, *I Hate To Cook Cookbook*. There were two full boxes, including a stained and tattered paperback entitled simply *The Best Cookbook in the World* which it wasn't, but it did have some terrific desserts. She dumped the lot out on the floor of the garage and lugged her favorites into the terrible old mildewed kitchen with its tall narrow cupboards and its horrid old black monster of a stove. The stove had been converted to gas from coal in one of its lives but it was still tricky. The oven door didn't always stay shut by itself.

Cathy leafed through her favorite feast recipes, musing over toasted wild rice stuffing; green peppercorn gravy, eggplant provençal, crème brûlée, wondering about doing cream puffs. She was still at it when Greg came in. She looked up. "Do you think we ought to have something sort of exotic for Thanksgiving? Goose, maybe? How about Beef Wellington? I did that, once."

Greg looked wary. "What's beef worthington?"

"Wellington. Wrapped up in a shiny puff pastry. They have it at Kroger's. The pastry, I mean. Frozen. You liked it at the Burgess's dinner party, that time."

Greg shrugged. "What's the matter with turkey?"

That's what Tod said. He hadn't had a roasted turkey in years, he said. "Isn't that one thing this old cook stove will do?"

When she came in and unloaded all the groceries on the day before Thanksgiving, Tod clutched his throat, feigning alarm. "Did you lose all control, woman? This ought to last us the winter, right?" But he helped her put things away, apologetic about the way it took a step stool and a small ladder to get to most of the shelves.

When Cathy leaned from three steps above him to kiss his brow, he worked his way closer and slid a hand up her leg. She laughed. "Why don't you go out and look for a dining room table for our grand dining room? We need a round oaken table with lots of leaves, don't you think? An antique."

Tod withdrew his hand, muttering about having to watch his cash flow, which ought to improve after the first of the year. "We're gonna have to watch it," he said.

"Then let go of my leg," she said. "You're unbalancing me and hospitals are expensive."

Tod seemed forever so eager to keep nuzzling at her. He stayed so constantly flushed and sweaty and ready to fondle and knead her breasts, to push up against her in the kitchen, in the dining room, the living room, the vegetable aisle of Kroger's, where he insisted nobody noticed or cared. But people did so notice. They looked over and looked away, embarrassed. Toddy's insistent and everlasting preoccupation with sex was beginning to be something she wished she could help him get under control. It was tiresome to have him shiny-eyed, waggling up to pant in her ear or against her neck. "Let me, honey, c'mon, what's the matter?"

In the kitchen on Thanksgiving morning it was all she could do to keep from flapping her apron at him. "You're as bad as a dog we once had. He used to rub up against my leg like that. Quit."

Tod leered and ran his tongue along his lower lip. "Make me."

Cathy looked at him. "We had to get rid of that dog. Quit."

But he wouldn't. As she gazed up at the embossed ceiling and let herself be kissed she realized a part of what was troubling her. "You never seem to come up with poetry anymore," she said.

He mumbled against her throat. She drew away. "I'm serious."

"Sure you are," he said, irritated. "This is basic, right? Another one of your basic things?" He dragged the step stool across the uneven floor and climbed up to sit looking down at her from beneath his dark eyebrows.

"What happened to the coppery pennies in my hair and all that?" she said. "And...and the shepherdess of sheep?"

"You want poetry? I'll give you poetry." But he didn't. He climbed down from the stool and stood in front of the sink. "You can be the most irritating damned woman. Maybe it's this kitchen."

"No," Cathy said. "It's that you're different. I just realized how very different you've become. You don't sound at all the same."

"As what?" He walked in a little circle. "What's the bit, here? You mean the way I was when we were getting acquainted?"

"You're...I don't know."

"Crude, that it?" His mouth pulled down. "I told you I was—"

"No, no," she said, wishing she'd been silent. "I miss it. Having you the way you were. Quoting all those lovely bits. The poetry. The Irish poems. You seemed to know such a lot of poems."

"Baby, baby," he said, smiling again. "Doesn't everybody do that? You want a poetic lady, you come at her with poetry. The show closes, you move on." He stretched his arms over his head and moved his head around, up and down, to one side and the other, stretching and easing the muscles in his neck. "You know what I mean." His eyes were darkening but she couldn't seem to stop herself.

"I thought you loved Yeats," she said.

He looked derisive. "*You* love Yeats."

"I do," she said, forlornly. "I do."

"See?"

She didn't want to see. "And you don't?" she whispered. "That was all an act? A kind of fakery?"

"Not exactly." He couldn't meet her eyes. "Guess we ought to do something about this kitchen," he said, brusquely, pacing around. "I don't see how you turn out the things you do, baby." He sighed. "Fakery. God. What a thing to say. People make an impression, don't they?"

I'm making too much of this, she thought. "Like Irene, pretending to be crazy about football," she said.

"Something like that," Tod said. "Did she land the guy?"

"Land?" She swallowed, suddenly so despairing she was afraid she might begin to weep. She went to the sink, found a clean cloth and wiped her eyes.

When she turned around, Tod looked at her with deep hurt. "Sorry to be such a disappointment, kid." He stamped his feet, one foot and then the other, and walked out of the kitchen.

The turkey took eight hours to roast. It was nearly four o'clock before everything was ready and they could sit down at the sheet covered kitchen table in the dining room, with lit candles spilling translucent wax down the heavy silver candlestick holders that Chub and Patrick had given them as wedding gifts. Gregory had chosen the blessing. "I will wash my hands in innocency, O, Lord: and so will I go to Thine altar; that I may shew the voice of Thanksgiving: and tell of all Thy wondrous works."

Tod bowed his head but his eyes stayed quizzical under the tangle of his dark brows. "Shew?"

"Shew." Greg looked sly. "That's what it says. Want to see? And that part about innocency, too."

"Innocency." Tod carved the turkey, flourishing an electric carving knife, a halo lambent around his head in the rays of the afternoon sunlight through the stained glass window in the hall. "Well, let's hear it for innocency." He proposed a toast. "To my little family," he quavered. "To togetherness. And fine family feeling." He smiled. "Fine family feeling." Suddenly the smile wavered and he was wiping his eyes with a napkin, fighting for composure. His hand shook a little as he took a sip of wine. "I want us to be a family. That's all I want. And that's what this is all about, isn't it?" He put the glass down unsteadily, knocking the base of it against the edge of his plate. As if in response to the small chime of crystal against china, the kitchen telephone rang.

Greg got up but Tod waved him back to his seat. "I'll get it."

The minute his stepfather left the room, Greg arranged his face into a beatific smile and lifted his glass. "Let's hear it for Alexander what's his name," he said. "For keeping us from throwing up."

"Graham Bell," Cathy said, distractedly. "It's Alexander Graham Bell. Please hush. Do you want him to hear you?"

"Isn't he dead?" Greg batted his eyes.

Tod was too busy yelling into the phone to hear much of anything. "Who the hell is this?" he shouted. "The hell you trying to pull...damned outrage..what? Son of a bitching son of a bitch."

When he came back in to the dining room, he walked heavily to his chair and stood frowning at his plate.

Cathy cleared her throat and peeked at Gregory.

Tod held his hand up, yanked his chair out and sat down. After a minute, he mopped his brow. "Damn it," he said. "I'm going to have to run upstairs for a minute. You two go ahead." He gazed at the table absently, shot Cathy and Greg an unseeing look, hurried from the room and went stamping up the back stairs.

"Well, well, well." Greg spooned creamed onions onto his plate and into his mouth. "A little attack of telephone indigestion?"

"Don't talk with your mouth full," Cathy said.

Greg swallowed and inhaled happily. "Kinda makes you wish little big man wasn't such a tightwad, doesn't it? Because if he didn't have such a fit at the idea of giving the telephone company an extra nickel we could have caller I.D.," he said. "Maybe even an answering machine."

"Pass the salad," Cathy said.

After a very long while, Tod returned. "Business," he said. "Don't worry about it. Doesn't mean a thing. I got this big damn Cajun silent partner forgets he's supposed to be silent." He spat out a laugh. "Keeps threatening to kill me. Cecil. Talked me into partnership insurance." He shot Greg a look. "Pretty funny, eh?"

Gregory's face went very blank.

Tod filled his plate and looked around. "Where were we? Conversation wise, I mean."

"I think we were discussing fine family feelings," Greg said.

Tod shot him another look. Greg let a smile widen his mouth and as if he figured he had gotten away with it. She knew what he was thinking: Tod loved that expression. "Now isn't this a fine family feeling thing?" he would say at the dinner table, his face in shiny red creases, his little hands clapping, until she could tell that Greg could hardly stand to be in the room with him.

On the Saturday after Thanksgiving Tod toddled in with a large white dress box balanced on his tummy, his vest unbuttoned and the rosy glow of the setting sun bouncing off of his cheeks and chins. He looked like one of Santa's elves, Greg said later. All he needed was a little talcum powder in the hair and a cottony beard.

Greg had gotten a fire going in the fireplace and Cathy'd fixed some eggnog and the whole scene was enough to send the old boy into happy spasms. "Now this is the high point of my day," he said. "Coming home to my little family. Don't you want to know what's in the box?" He winked at Greg. Greg apparently thought better about about winking back.

"Got your mama a little November present," little big man said. Cathy opened the box and took out a kind of a stretchy green dress covered in little shiny fish scales. This is definitely not a Cathy kind of a dress, she thought. She tried not to look embarrassed as she got the thing out of the tissue paper. By the time she got a good look at it, she couldn't meet Greg's eyes. She could tell he was having trouble enough tamping down a hooraw or two.

She said in a small voice, "Oh, dear, it isn't anywhere near Christmas yet," but Tod stood around rubbing his hands, his face all joyous crinkles, his eyes in happy little crescents.

He said, "Come on, baby, let's see how it looks," going on and on about how they were going to have Christmas all the time in their happy house.

Cathy held the dress up under her chin. It shimmered and twinkled. "Where would a person wear a thing like this?"

"Never mind where," Greg muttered, but she hoped Tod didn't hear. "The big question would have to be why."

She really was doing a pretty fair job of acting as if she loved it. "Gracious," she twittered. "Gracious."

"Oh, gracious, that's my lady, lady gracious," Tod said, dancing around, balancing himself on the balls of his feet, punching at Greg's shoulder. "I know of a few places. We can go to one tonight, Lady Gracious."

The redder his face got, the paler she looked. She murmured something about how she didn't think the dress would fit. Looked like it would have to be too small here and there.

"But it's made to give, here and there." Tod slid his hands under her elbows and propelled her toward the stairs. "Go on up and put it on."

The thing fit, but the way she looked in it was totally bizarre. Like a big green chandelier. Like she ought to have tap shoes on, or a big feather in her hair. Happy Halloween. When she came down, Greg took one look and had to leave the room.

Which was a mistake.

If he'd stuck it out, he could have given them the old, "aw shucks, that's okay, I'd just as soon stay home, folks, honest," and he might not have had to go along with Tod and Cathy to Houston that night. Of course he would have missed the fireworks.

Because a half hour later Cathy came knocking on the door of his room, wearing the wretched dress. Greg told her to come on in. She moved some of his clothes off of a chair, and sat down to announce, all out of breath, "We're all going to this absolutely marvelous place for dinner."

"Uh uh," Greg said. "Negative."

"Tod is so darned eager and anxious to get the least little bit of approval," she said.

Greg hesitated. "Okay," he said. "I'll start radiating approval." He showed her his teeth.

"Greg? I'm trying to talk to you."

"I noticed," Greg said.

"Well, you seem to be having all this trouble with math, all of a sudden, and I'm told Mr. Dickey's an excellent teacher but you know what? Tod's very good at math, too. He taught himself calculus by mail. So maybe he could help you with your geometry."

"Gee. Do you think?" Greg batted his eyes at her. "That is so sweet." As yet she didn't know that his trouble with math had more to do with not showing up for Mr. Dickey's class which happened to be the last class of the day.

"Tell me something," he said. "Doesn't that dress hurt? To sit on, I mean? Because all those little sharp things look like they might hurt." He squeezed his eyes shut and made a face indicating great pain. "They're reflecting streams of light into my eyes, too. I was sort of dozing off in here. Do they make those things out of the same stuff as bike reflectors?"

"Sequins," Cathy said. "Lout. Undoze and get under the shower." She stood up so he could follow orders.

"Under the shower?" Greg asked. "Say. Do you know the difference between a sailor and a shower?"

She sat down again and looked at him. Sighing.

He charged on. "Well, then, don't get under a shower," he said, "until I explain it to you."

She finished the punch line with him, sighed and stood up again. "Come on. Tod particularly wants you to see this place. He says you'll love it. He's making reservations for the three of us, la Tour d'Argent, it means the Silver Tower—"

"Two," Greg said. He held up two fingers "Tell him, reservations for two of you." He sprawled on his bed and closed his eyes.

"Three," Cathy said, lapsing into her hissy motherly voice with her mouth shrinking in.

"Ah," he said. "See the lady without any lips. Step right up."

"You. Step. Right. Up. Now. This restaurant happens to be on the other side of Houston so I would appreciate it very much if you could be ready as quickly as possible. Do you mind telling me why there's a dirty sock draped across your lamp shade?"

Greg got up and took the sock off the lamp shade and went into the bathroom to drop it into the hamper. "I don't know," he said.

"You're big enough to find the hamper," Cathy said.

"Hey. Relax," Greg said. "Look. I'm putting my socks in the hamper. I am taking the hamper downstairs."

The garage was full of boxes, some of them stacked so haphazardly they looked somewhat menacing. "What's with all the boxes?" Greg said.

Cathy ground her teeth. "You're the one who insisted we move *ev-ery*thing we own. We may never figure out what to do with all this mess."

"We?" Greg said. "Hey. I don't know why I even brought it up. We?"

"We?" Tod had found them. "What are we doing in the garage?"

"We're looking for my...my socks," Greg said. "Black ones, so I can get dressed up." That didn't make sense but it bought him a little time.

Cathy sighed. Greg got dressed.

What with the sparks in Tod's eyes and the sparkles from the new dress and the general snap, crackle and pop of static electricity in the atmosphere around the place, Greg caved in.

Who could figure the little creep out anyway? All the way to Houston Greg tried, sliding around in the back seat, trying not to notice the way the geezer drove. But never mind. Maybe he could call Ginger or Scot from the restaurant. It would be cool to talk to Ginger. Probably give the old boy apoplexy, tho'. For somebody who liked to give away emerald rings and fish scale dresses, old balloon pants turned into a raving maniac about your more basic normal charges, like the phone bill. Every month when the phone bill came, he about burst into tears. "What are all these seven one three and two eight one Houston calls? Here's one for three and a half dollars—and five. Five dollars." It sent him right off the visible spectrum, even after he and his mom explained that what Tod was yelling about happened to be Ginger's number and Scotty's, maybe, a couple of times.

Tod sat around shaking his head and making speeches. "You know how many words there are in Genesis?"

Greg loved that one. "No. How many words are there in Genesis?"

He didn't know. "The point is, you can tell the whole damned story of creation in a couple of minutes. That's the point. So what's with these fifteen, twenty, thirty minute phone calls?"

Crazy-crazy. Of course, he didn't have to make sense, did he? It was his house, after all. His car, too. That he drove to beat hell.

Greg probably couldn't have handled a whole evening with the jerk if he hadn't had a little loosener-upper before they got underway. All the way into Houston and through downtown Tod stayed close to eighty, even on the Pierce Elevated and in some subdivision when they got lost. He kept grasshoppering in and out, hitting his horn anytime anybody didn't fall back fast enough to let him in. He had this terrific technique of closing in on the car ahead, fast, with his hands crossed over the steering wheel so he could uncross them while he spun the wheel. Real flashy.

When they passed a U-Haul by making a road through some gravel at a construction site and knocked out a couple of cones and went over a curb, Greg leaned into the front seat to ask, "You okay with this, Mom?" interrupting one of Tod's monologues, something about how he was getting bids on burglar bars for the house because he was so concerned with his family's safety.

"What?" Tod exploded. "What's that?" He whirled around—man, Greg really wished he'd keep his eyes on the road—he swiveled completely around and smiled real big. "Something bothering you, son?"

"Not me," Greg said.

Mom didn't say one word. Probably couldn't get her breath.

La Tour d'Argent wasn't what he thought it would be, from the name. It was a big log cabin built on different levels and different kinds of animal's heads and huge trophy fish on the walls.

"You figure it's safe?" Greg had to ask when they sat down. "We could get chomped by that moose."

"That's an elk. We'll have to go elk hunting some time, son."

Mom wasn't so impressed by the animal heads and fish, but she was dazzled by the art. "Museum quality," she said. The head waiter liked that.

Tod acted as if he and the waiter were old buddies, making a big point of mentioning that Cathy was his bride. The Maitre d' kept glancing at her with this tremendous approval even if she did have on the dress of a thousand lights.

Tod ordered for himself and Mom, going into a big song and dance about some dish made out of bone marrow. Greg made a face and got a sirloin, medium well.

While they were sitting around pulling artichoke leaves through their front teeth, the waiter suggested some dessert, cherries jubilee. Another waiter a couple of tables over ignited a platter that sent up bright blue flames at the same time. And another table was getting flaming cherries, too. Flames all over the place.

While Tod was talking to the waiter about the dessert is when Greg glanced over at the swinging door to the kitchen and did a double-take. A slouching old guy standing in the lighted doorway was sort of looking over, trying to see into the room. Greg swallowed and the hair prickled the back of his scalp. That's the guy who was on our front walk that day, he thought.

The kitchen had several rows of fluorescent lights and the guy in the doorway was just a dark shape, a silhouette, but Greg was pretty sure. The man kept getting in the way of the waiters with their trays, standing there with his hand up over his eyes, trying to peer in their direction. Something about the way he slumps, man, that's got to be him, Greg thought. Looked just the way the old guy had held himself out on the front walk that night.

No way could a bum like that get into a place like this, though. Although he wasn't in, exactly. The waiters kept coming around him a little off balance.

Then, in a far corner, another bowl full of something was lit up and— brrraap—and this loud smoke alarm revved up. Maybe all those little blue and yellow fires in one room was too much or the kitchen had something hot going on.

"Wild," Greg said, "Oh, man, *wild*." The alarm screamed like a son of a gun. "Maybe the sprinkler system'll kick on."

But something even more bizarre happened. The lady harpist at the end of the room kept on playing. Through the bedlam she kept plucking away at the strings—everybody skate—you had to hand it to her. She leaned into her instrument, and then rocked back and forth, her straps sliding down her shoulders and her hair popping combs, working up a sweat with a gypsy folk dance. Or Liszt, maybe, the one where Franz popped the piano wire.

Greg caught his mom's eye and she looked away quickly before she laughed. After a minute she lifted her hands and started clapping and pretty soon the whole room began applauding.

When Greg remembered to look for the man in the kitchen doorway, he wasn't there. He wasn't anywhere in the room either, although, when he looked around, the room didn't look all that cozy anymore. Maybe it was the animal heads. Like the moose's head. Somebody had to shoot that moose and cut the head off. And tear out the brains and eyes. Stick in plastic teeth. Shove cotton or sawdust or whatever into the neck. Poke in those big glass eyes.

That night Greg had a nightmare, probably because of all those dead beasts's heads hanging around on the walls of that joint. That and the wine that Tod thought had to be such a big deal. He wasn't used to wine.

He dreamed he was in some kind of trouble, wading through tall grasses that he could hardly fight his way through. They kept coming alive, weaving around his legs like snakes, tripping him, keeping him from getting anywhere but he had to run.

He woke up in such a sweat that he had to sneak out to the back yard and light up some of the maryjane these guys at school had—a pretty risky thing to do that close to the house—to zone out. It wasn't real good dope. These guys at Ball High said they found it washed up in these bales on West Beach. That's why it was so cheap. They found the stuff and dried it so they could sell it. They knew where Greg could get some better stuff, they said. As soon as he could afford it.

*****

20

The first week of December, Cathy sloshed two coats of Hunter's Green deck paint all over the back porch and steps and bought a ladder so tall that it kept getting away from her and swinging all over the kitchen every time she moved it. The wobbly thing was tall enough so that she could reach the top shelves, though. She gave the insides of the tall crazy cupboards in the kitchen two coats of a high gloss paint such a bright yellow that it lit up the room every time anyone opened the cupboard doors. When she got through, the cupboard's lemony insides made such a startling contrast to the rest of the kitchen dungeon that, though she showed them her handiwork at different times, both her men went into the same pretending-to-be-struck blind routine the minute they saw them. "Do you think they're too much?" she asked.

"What makes you think that?" Greg asked, groping for a wall with his arm around his face.

"Well, they look terribly clean," she said, defensively. "And they'll wipe clean, too, now."

On the fifteenth, she made Christmas cards. They didn't need many. Some for the Dutch aunts and uncles in Holland and a few for Tod's employees—though he said all they wanted was checks—and some poinsettias and trees for Irene and the staff back in Ethics and Humanities in Houston. And, of course, a big one for Chub and darling Patrick, whom she felt terrible about, since she'd totally given up driving back for her watercolor classes and hadn't even so much as called Chub in weeks.

She did the cards in something of a hurry, tearing old watercolors into collage paper and gluing in some gold and silver joss squares from a Chinese grocery for some of them and doing some simple ones, holly and poinsettias and Christmas trees, with Chinese brushes. She did the whole batch at once, late one night, humming to herself while Tod watched, all thrilled and bemused. He didn't know she could do that, he kept saying, his hands prayerfully under his chin as he gazed across the kitchen table at all this activity. After she'd finished and spread the cards to dry he paced up and down, slapping the sides of his legs, carried away with how wonderful the little pictures were, insisting they were far too good to send. "These ought to be framed," he said. "Get 'em matted and framed. These are *art*. Hell, we can buy cards to mail."

She mailed them.

Tod was too easily impressed. She'd made the mistake of showing him some of her class projects and old watercolors and he'd had a fit. The adulation ought to have been flattering but all it did was make her uneasy. About him. She had to tamp down a small nagging sense of disdain every time he got so carried away.

The minute the cards were finished, he smoothed her hair back so he could kiss her on the neck and slid his hands around her to cup her breasts. Cathy remarked, absentmindedly, that she hadn't meant to keep him up so late and he did have to get up early, didn't he? Which made him cranky but he got the message. When they got into bed he moved to his own side and let her sleep, saying, huffily, that he supposed she needed her sleep so she could sing.

Cathy sang. A lot. Off tune and quavering, but she sang, crooning carols as she balanced paint and teetered on the ladder in the green kitchen and Gershwin tunes as she dust mopped the empty living room. She explored the acoustics in the foyer and the front hall with sappy Doris Day ditties—"Que Sera, Sera" and the one where the trolley goes ding—and sometimes swung into rounds all by herself, in an incessant quavering wail. "Christmas time is coming," she yodeled, "the goose is getting fat. Won't you please put a penny in the old man's hat" until Greg couldn't stand it another minute and came to stand in front of her with his eyebrows going vertically, beseechingly vertical and his hands clawing at his hair.

"Go make some real music then," she pleaded. He wouldn't.
She did long so for the sound of his cello. He had to be missing it, too, but he'd gotten stubborn about not touching it anymore.

Maybe if I don't nag he'll go back to it, she told herself. Greg's cello had been a part of their lives for so long, so strongly sweet, a sweet presence they both needed. Even when he practiced with his door closed in the old house, she could feel the sound of him vibrate along the floor. It resonated through her after he'd stopped and warmed her with anticipation when he was on his way home.

"Not hearing it hurts my heart," she told him. "I miss it so. And you do, too. You're hurting both of us."

Which was the idea, of course, and she knew it. He'd begun by punishing her for moving him to this town, for marrying Tod, for packing him off to a school where there was no orchestra, no Mrs. Baron—oh, lucky Mrs. Baron, her house forever alive with the sound of strings—and now it was a battle of wills. He just got mad when she brought it up. "It's completely boring," he said.

"Boring? Last year the Bach suites—?"

Greg looked away. "That was last year. This year we've got all this fine family feeling: you, me, and the king of false teeth, with his busy labs turning out all those choppers."

A few days before Christmas Cathy made small elegant cookies of almond paste, butter, sugar and flour. She shaped them with her hands; green peas nestled in open pods; strawberries dusted with red sugar; little bananas freckled with cinnamon; small, pale, bifurcated, blushing peaches; fat little pears with clove stems; tender, pale, green leaves with pinkish veins and edges pressed out with a serrated grapefruit knife. Tod had a fit over them. "They're much too pretty to eat," he said, glaring at Greg for tossing three and four at a time into his mouth.

Greg yawned. "Mom goes ape with marzipan cookies at Christmas. It's my job to dispose of 'em. Got to keep up my kid image. See how many she's got? Kind of scary isn't it? Like she's going back to Play-Doh."

"You have to talk to your mother like that?"

"I beg your pardon?"

"Oh, why do you make those words sound so hateful?" Cathy asked. And Greg stood and gazed at her as she thought, for the umpteenth time, oh, why can't they be kind to each other for few minutes now and then? "We have such a Christmasy house," she said. "Can't we at least pretend to be glad?"

"Maybe it's the turpentine smell," Greg said.

"Well, doesn't turpentine come from pine trees?" Cathy said.

Greg shook his head. "That's a real Cathy thought, right there."

"And what was that?" Tod asked. "What did you say?" as Greg stalked off to his room.

Tod didn't want a Christmas tree. "Damned things are a fire hazard." And he didn't want to "drag in the neighbors."

Cathy wouldn't even have known about the Christmas pageant at Ball High School if she hadn't overheard Greg on the phone, talking about tickets. When he hung up she said, working at being cheerful, "Tod and I don't have anything to do this Saturday night."

"Okay," Greg said. "But I'm going with some guys."

So Greg went to his school with two of his peers—scruffy ones, two big kids, as hairy and unwashed as if they'd stepped right out of the sixties, she thought—and left his parents to attend the big high school function of the season by themselves.

It turned out to be a not very good pageant. The auditorium was so chilly that Cathy was shivering by the time it was over. She and Tod were shuffling along, trying to get to the door, when a skinny teenaged girl shouldered her way through the crowd and pushed in front of Tod and stood still. Tod pulled his head back.

"You bastard," the girl said. She tried to hit him in the face. He threw up an arm and ducked. The girl kept hissing, her mouth wide, her wild eyes gleaming in a face wet with tears, a pale, crazy, sick person. She made Cathy think of a cornered possum, all that hissing. Tod couldn't get away. He fended her off with both arms but there was no stopping her. The girl punched and pummeled, "Bastard, bastard," clawing at the sleeve of his jacket until a man shouldered his way through the crowd and tugged her away.

"I'll get you!" she shouted past the man as he dragged her off.

"Come on, now. Come on, this isn't any way to be," the man said. There was more, but Cathy couldn't catch it. He looked old; his face furrowed and closed and opened like an accordion.

Tod ran. He let go of Cathy's hand, ducked and hunched and shoved his way ahead along the crowded aisle to the front door.

The accordion-faced man had the hissing girl muffled against his chest as he stared after Tod, turned an unseeing look on Cathy and pushed his way up the aisle, against the crowd, holding and hustling the girl through a door at the left of the stage.

Breathing hard, Cathy made her way to the front of the school and hurried down the steps, looking for Tod in the thinning crowd under the street lights in front of the school. She crossed an expanse of wet grass and broken concrete, stumbling at first as she picked her way, trying to remember where they'd parked. For a brief maddening minute she had no earthly idea where they had left the car. When she found it she thought it was empty until she got close enough to see Tod huddled behind the wheel with an unlit cigar clamped in his teeth.

He leaned across the seat to open the door and beckoned her in, muttering, "Hurry up. Now wasn't that a hell of a thing?"

After they'd rounded the corner and were moving up Forty-first street, he shoved the lighter in on the dash and lit the cigar. "You know who that kid might be? That might be Dixie's girl," he said. "I ever tell you about Dixie?" He glanced at Cathy and looked away. "Damned if I know what the kid's problem is, though."

"Dixie?" She wished he'd pay attention to his driving. He'd run past two stop signs without so much as a glance right or left.

"Woman I knew once." He laughed shakily. "Long time ago."

"And she has a daughter?" Cathy said. "Please slow down. We're almost home, we can talk when we get there."

"I don't know anything about any daughter," Tod said. "I'm just going by what that guy said while he was trying to get her off of me. Didn't he call her 'little Dixie.'"

Cathy hadn't heard that. "Everything happened so fast," she said. "Why is she so angry?"

Tod snorted. "Hell if I know. Because I broke it off with her mama, maybe? But I don't know anything about any 'little' Dixie. Maybe it's a coincidence. The name, I mean."

He kept trying to get the lighter to function, shoving it in and fooling with his already lit cigar. The third time he popped the thing in and reached for it when it popped right back out, Cathy took it away from him saying, "You don't need this."

"Damn straight," Tod said.

"This Dixie. Was she very—was it a very long time ago?" Her voice sounded silly. She cleared her throat and repeated herself.

The car purred as they waited for a light to change. "You really want to go into all that?" Tod turned on the heater. She shivered.

"I guess that might be your privilege if that's what you really want. We can dig into my past some more. Might be one of your basic things to do. A little something to add to the Christmas festivities," he said. "God, I love women."

"No," Cathy said. "I mean, no. I don't know if I want to hear about Dixie."

"Let me know when you change your mind on that." He wanted to elaborate. He sounded aggrieved. "No point in making a big damned dramatic thing of it." He inhaled deeply. "Thing is, she's quite a woman, Dixie. Or she used to be. Ran a little bar. She's got a good heart. This is back when I was batching it, of course, keeping up the Lothario image, you know. Had to do the Lothario thing."

Maybe he's more shaken up than he wants me to know, she thought. He can't very well say, oh, I was so scared. But then he chuckled, and she felt a bracing surge.

"I know how you love women," she snapped. "We have gone into that a time or two."

"What's that?"

"You've told me about the Lothario bit," she said. "Repeatedly. In front of my son. In bed, a few times. In the yard. At the table. I do not care to discuss your Lothario stage any further."

Tod took the cigar out. He opened his mouth and closed it. When he opened his mouth again he growled, "Like I said, let me know if you change your mind on that."

They were on Broadway, passing the cemetery. Cathy glanced over at all the sleeping dead and flashed on a sing-song rhyme Gregory and his friends used to annoy her with when they were grade schoolers and she had to drive them past Forest Park on the way to Cub Scouts. "Who takes the next breath/Is the one who faces death," the kids would chant and she'd look around to see a back seat full of red-faced, bug-eyed, little boys clutching their throats, flapping their grubby little hands at her to go, hurry, get past the place with the tall iron gates so they could inhale great hoarse breaths and fall all over each other, panting and gasping.

As they reached the corner of the cemetery, she filled her lungs and held her breath. The car drifted along Broadway. She counted to herself. Forty-third street...Fortieth. The end of the cemetery. When they passed the corner of the fence she inhaled deeply.

Tod's head was pulled down into the collar of his jacket. He drove the rest of the way in silence.

After they got home he walked all around, peering through the front and back windows, checking the locks. "Going to have to get some bars around this place," he grumbled. "I hate to be the first place on the block with burglar bars but this town is getting to be as bad as the rest of the country. Bunch of dopers and psychos running around this town now."

That night, lying very still on her side of the bed, Cathy thought about the way the girl had looked. Deranged. Furious. If that man hadn't gotten to her she'd have scratched Tod's eyes.

I should have let him talk about her, she thought, wearily. Let, hell. I should have made him explain. There was something hugely satisfying about turning him off, though. He seemed to enjoy his endless explanations. Who wouldn't be tired of his fumbling, chattering, endlessly messy reminiscing? I've heard all I want about sweet, fat, adoring Lynn, and comes now another one. Spare me.

Swallowing her curiosity gave her a scratchy feeling in the back of her throat. It started to hurt that night. The next morning she had a low grade fever and then a genuine hundred-and-two degree fever and she could hardly get out a whisper.

On Christmas Day in the morning she woke up hot and cold and aching in every cell.

Tod and Greg opened their gifts in the bedroom while she lolled against a heap of pillows, warning them to keep away, not letting Tod so much as kiss the hot skin of her hands, even after he'd opened his hardware store gifts. They were sort of strange but they were what he'd said he wanted, a six-drawer tool center with screwdrivers and hammers and sanders and vises and all manner of things that Cathy had no idea about—she suspected Tod hadn't, either—but the man at Ace's Hardware had seemed to think they were wonderful. Just the sort of thing a new homeowner ought to find glorious, the man said.

Tod found them glorious. He thanked her tearfully. Which was touching, she thought, since they were bought with his money.

Gregory wasn't tearfully grateful for a handsome pair of slacks and a black-faced watch with all manner of functions, ostensibly from Tod, which she'd picked out, and shirts and socks and underwear from Cathy. He didn't even open the Dobosh torte, just pocketed the twenty dollar bill tucked in its silvery bow. He said a mannerly thank you but what Greg was, mostly, was drowsy.

So was Cathy. Tod gave her a beautiful watch. It had little diamonds all around a narrow oval face. Cathy blew him kisses for it and went to sleep.

In the afternoon, Tod baked the roast she'd planned to fix for dinner. It smelled salty and terribly nauseatingly meaty, for hours.

The next day, a blustery Thursday, Tod took her to see some doctor a woman in his office recommended. He examined her, insisted on blood and urine samples, said she looked anemic and the flu was probably viral. Prescribed bed rest. Fluids. Aspirin.

On New Year's Eve and New Year's Day and the day after, the fever worsened. Cathy said not to worry, nobody her age died of flu and she'd always been anemic, not to worry about that either but Tod wouldn't even leave her to go to work. He worried and fussed, swabbing her brow, changing the sheets, trying to get her to swallow soup. If she didn't swallow soup he thought she ought to be in a hospital.

Greg came and went, solicitously demanding assurance at intervals. "You gonna be okay, Mom?"

Some time before dawn on January the third Cathy got up to go to the toilet and looked at herself, really stood still in front of the bathroom mirror and took a long look at her pallid, quaking, rheumy-eyed self and decided she looked pretty scary. She went back to bed to lie there, ruminating about how obituaries sometimes read, "after a short illness." When it began to get light she curled up to Tod's back and slept.

Woke up damp and weak and glad to be alive.

Tod had rigged up a bird feeder on a pulley between one of the magnolia trees and the bedroom balcony. A red bird sat on it, darting and eating, twitching its tail in dappled winter sunlight.

Tod brought her tea. She could have wept over the good scent of it.

"We have to find an old Christmas tree," she said. "For Chub and Pat's party, remember? On the sixth. Next Monday night."

"You think you'll be well enough for a beach party?" Tod asked. "Who gives a party on the beach in January, anyway? For that matter, who gives a party on a Monday night?"

"Someone wanting to celebrate Twelfth Night," Cathy said.

"Twelfth night? on the sixth?" He was so happy to see her sitting up and smiling at him that he looked giddy. "I don't get it."

"Twelve days after Christmas," Cathy said. "It has to do with Epiphany and the Magi. Christ's appearance to the gentiles. It's an ancient rite, though

I'm not sure if the medievalists burned old Christmas trees out on a beach. And yes, I'll be all well by Monday. I'm practically all well right now," she said and thought, how can he not know about Epiphany and dismissed the thought as he asked wouldn't it be damp and chilly, out on the beach?

"Being sick is all in a person's head," Cathy said. "I'm well. It'll be great. You'll see. The trees will make a big hot fire. I wish we had one to contribute."

"You want a tree or two, I'll get them for you," he said. "They're everywhere. All over every curb in town. And if you really want to go to this shindig, we'll go."

Cathy threw her arms around him. He nuzzled her throat, sighing.

"Go," she said. "Find some discarded Christmas trees. I'm dying to see Chub."

*****

21

The map Chub sent with her rhapsodic invitation—"Come ye, come ye, to a grand Twelfth Night festival on Dia de los Reyes"—directed Tod and Cathy to a tall A-frame Chub and Patrick had rented in Palm Beach, way out on the west end of the Island.

"Darlings!" Chub shouted, as they stepped out of the car, so gaily shrill that Tod muttered, "Your faculty friends must be a couple of drinks up on us."

"Cathy and Tod, everybody," Chub said. "Come and meet our host, Dr. Crowder."

Dr. Crowder moved toward them, his big shoulders rounded and his big head far forward. Tod sized up the pedantic, diffident, tall man's slouch and the mumble-rumbling voice and made a small sniggery sound under his breath.

Cathy sighed. "We don't have to stay long."

"Damn straight," Tod said, working his face into a smile. "So," he said to the tall man, "this place yours?" He stamped the sand from his shoes as they reached the upper landing at the front of the house. "Nice."

The cottage, on weathered stilts, had rusty screens. It leaned slightly.

Tod never would understand cottages, Cathy knew. He called them farm houses without farms.

Milton Crowder looked down with a lopsided smile.

"What do you teach?" Tod asked.

"I'm, ah, a bug man," Milton said.

"So. A bug man, eh? No harm in that." Tod looked as though he thought he might have sounded patronizing. He shook Milton's hand too heartily, adding, "Bugs have to be about the only things holding this Island together, right? Cockroaches and termites, yes, sir. Know much about termites?" He chuckled.

Milton Crowder blinked in some confusion. "Well, I'm more interested in, ah, different kinds of bugs."

"That so?"

"Yes. Um." The big man turned to throw someone across the room a get-me-out-of-this look. "Beetles," Milton added. He lifted a hand, and let it drop, and looked away.

Cathy said, "You're an entomologist?"

A woman came across the room to tuck her arm in Milton's, saying, "Dr. Miltie's the one who has my daughter giving mosquitoes enemas."

"Oh." Tod looked restive.

"She does it well," Milton said.

"Vector studies," Milton said, apologetically. He looked away.

Tod's smile looked pained. "Made an ass of myself, I guess," he said, stiffly. "That's pretty much what I do. Excuse us. The wife says she has a headache. Don't know how long we can hang around too much noise out here." People were whooping and dragging trees over to a huge stack near the water's edge. "Looks like you've got more trees than you can do with," Tod said. "I don't see our boy here anywhere. He's in a rented U-Haul, gathering up some more. So is there much call for giving mosquitoes enemas?"

"Our Milton was in Newsweek, last week," the woman said.

"That so?" Tod said.

"Indeed," she said. "And he's done such marvelous things with his former frat house that it made House Beautiful last Christmas."

Tod looked away. "That so?"

"And Milton was one of the earliest researchers to work on the pine beetle," she said.

"Enough, already." Milton said, his cheeks mottling. When he started to speak, Cathy realized that he, too, had to fight a stammer. He spoke carefully, working his tongue around his words. "There's a bar, of sorts. Up in the kitchen."

Tod smacked his palms. "Now you're talking." He took Cathy's arm. "Good meeting you," he said. Milton and the woman walked with Tod and Cathy to the house, the woman asking, did they know how many acres of trees a pine beetle can kill in three days?

Cathy hugged Tod's arm to her side. "A drink sounds marvelous," she said. "I think Tod has something he'd like to contribute to the bar."

"Matter of fact," Tod growled, "we just happen to have some good stuff from Jamaica if you people happen to like rum."

"Milton knows how many," the woman said, her voice girlish. "Acres and acres."

Milton looked at Cathy, lifted his shoulders and let them drop.

Then, as if in answer to Cathy's silent but fervent request to the Almighty, Greg and his friends came, in the rented truck, followed by a little wreck of a blue car. But her relief was short lived. The U-Haul had great rooster tails of dusty sand all along its sides.

"Damned kids," Tod said. "Been high-tailing up and down the beach. Look at that thing." He started for the boys but Cathy tugged at him.

"Look at the trees they got. Why don't you bring in the rum?"

Tod went to the car and came lurching back up the steps with two jugs of rum and a shopping bag with quantities of real butter, brown sugar and cinnamon sticks, exclaiming that he didn't want any help. He aproned himself with a towel and took over the kitchen, melting butter, stirring steamy, richly scented, sweet brew. "Hot buttered rum," he announced. "Wait." He ran to the fireplace, heated the poker, ran back to the stove to plunge the red poker theatrically into the pot.

People applauded and crowded around.

"Fireplace poker as magic wand," Crowder murmured. "Splendid."

"I think he got the idea from Julia Child," Cathy said.

"Does your husband like being spectacular?" a man asked, focusing on Cathy, as bright-eyed and inquisitive as a nosy child.

"I didn't catch your name," she said. He said his name but she still didn't catch it. The noise level in the room kept going up.

When she turned away, smiling uncertainly, Milton said, in her ear, "That's the detective who caught the thief who robbed that credit union that was on the news a couple of weeks ago. Did you see it?"

The man kept looking at her, pleasant enough but unsmilingly earnest. He probably doesn't know that he's almost rude, Cathy thought. "I'm afraid I don't know about any credit union case," she said, practically shouting. "Was he a Galvestonian?"

The man smiled and shook his head.

"No," Milton said. "They caught him in Friendswood."

After a bit Cathy came upon a quieter place to sit, in a window seat, near the man Milton had pointed out. "I don't know as I've ever met a detective," she said, glancing around, wondering where Greg and the boys might be, or Tod. She saw them out on the sand, a tall boy, the one with long hair, Shep, and Gregory, shouting, lifting trees from the truck to a boy who seemed to have trouble handling them. She turned from gazing out the window to find that the detective had gotten called away by someone in the crowd. The big room resounded with the glad cries of people coming in out of the damp chill to the warm scent of Tod's butter and rum and the scent of baking meats.

The A-frame was one of a row of weekend cottages, one long room, almost the size of the sitting room at home, with worn wicker couches and chintz on the chairs and heaps of floor cushions. Tod had gotten crowded out of the wee kitchen behind a formica-topped breakfast bar and was talking to a woman with a white streak in her hair who was arranging delicatessen platters. Cathy went over to help. The woman said wasn't Tod's rum marvelous and Cathy's marzipan cookies were museum quality only they were too pretty to eat.

Milton sidled up to confess that his contribution was the only thing he knew how to cook, an entire roast tenderloin. "You just get the oven as hot as it will get and put it in and turn the oven off"—with a couple of loaves of French bread and his specialty: sour cream horseradish sauce. "I know how to stir in horseradish."

The woman with the white streak, who said her name was Gloria, talked while she and Cathy spread things out on the bar and the cottage's butcher block table, but it was too noisy to catch half of what she was saying. When Cathy turned around she caught Milton Crowder timidly sampling some of her pate with his finger.

He stuck the finger in his mouth with such a guilty grin that she had to laugh. "It *is* to eat," she said.

"Um, yes," Milton said. "But no one else seems to be dipping in, just yet. Certainly not bare-handed."

"Well, possibly everyone is wanting to burn up some pine beetles first," Cathy said. "Does fire discourage your beetles? It has a way of discouraging most the-things." She bit her lip. "To belabor the obvious. I'm n-not at all g-good at p-party chatter."

"Nor am I," he said.

"Yes. But that's because you know so much," she said. She hesitated, stricken. "What a thing to s-say."

His mouth twitched.

"K-k-keeping silent c-can be a science and an art," Cathy went on. "M-maybe that's what my tongue's t-trying to tell me."

The big man put a hand beneath her elbow and steered her away from the window seat to a corner where there were several big cushions. Cathy looked around for Tod but he was nowhere to be seen. She slipped off her shoes and slid down, cross-legged. "So. How did you fight the beetle?" she asked.

"Would that it were so simple," Milton said.

She smiled. He looked so...helpless. "Um," Milton said," they're persistent. A veritable plague. Nobody has the real answer but we've done a bit of work with pheromones."

"Beetle pheromones," Cathy said. "Seductive." She wondered where Tod was.

Milton's voice went on and on, pleasantly sonorous; he truly did seem quite taken with his beetles. "If we take a forested area they've already devastated, and we introduce the enticement, the female pheromone, they can be attracted into a mass suicidal plunge. The...ah, the female pheromone, is virtually irresistible. Then, of course, if the periphery of the area is sprayed with the male pheromone it discourages their leaving. The male pheromone is what tells the entire crowd that an area's overpopulated, you see. This makes a most effectively discouraging barrier."

Such a nice man. Going on and on. In such a nice warm furry voice, a voice as gentle as an afghan.

A burst of laughter startled her awake. "I'm a notorious bore," Milton said.

"Oh, no," she stammered. He was, of course. But so *nice*. "It's just that I seem to be so sort of cozy. Maybe it's the rum." She smacked her lips. "I am sorry. You have a lovely voice. Rather like a cello. And your beetle *is* interesting. It's, um, dramatic. Poignant, actually. I mean, he does just as he's supposed to, exactly the right thing, absolutely tickety-poo and then, well, it turns out he must die because of it. Seems unfair, isn't it? I can't imagine where my husband has g-g-gotten to."

"Why don't we go and look for him?" The man's smile was as gentle as his voice.

"Let's not," Cathy said. "So, once the beetles have come rushing into this lean and hungry site, they're sexily trapped, right?"

"Trap themselves, so to speak." His eyes were earnest.

"And they all starve to death and fall right off of the trees?"

He nodded." Starved to death. Or bored to death."

"And the trees are saved," Cathy said. "Are there tons of terrible parasites we need to be aware of that might go after our oaks and magnolias?"

"Probably," Milton said. "Be glad some parasites are specie specific. Unlike acid rain. I could probably put you into a regular stupor."

Cathy laughed. "You over estimate yourself. You know what? You sound rather like my grandfather." What a stupid thing to say. "We, he and I, used to take what he called nature walks, in the woods near our cottage in Macatawa Park. There's a vine covered bridge, a nice dappled tunnel, leads to the beach. He had the loveliest chocolatey voice."

"I know Macatawa," Milton said, surprised. "Lake Michigan. Yes. The tunnel. My family had one of those places cantilevered up the side of one of Macatawa's hills. We summered there. A lot of Chicagoans did. Long before your time, I should think."

Oh, someone who knew about Lake Macatawa! Cathy hadn't talked about Grandfather Tein and the maples around the cottage in a very long time. "He wanted to be a forester," she said.

It turned out that Milton Crowder had started out wanting to be a forester. He didn't have a stammer when he talked about that.

When someone said the boys with that rented truck were taking off, Cathy looked up at the salt-stained windows and realized, shocked, that they'd become dark. She felt a stab of familiar misery, knowing how Tod would have to be sick with rage at her spending so much time with –but he wasn't. Tod was out on the cottage's steps, entertaining a youngster with a braid down her back, demonstrating how to tie the stem of a maraschino cherry into a single knot with his tongue. "No hands," he lisped. He poked his tongue out at Cathy with the stem curled on it like an insect's leg. "Where have you been?"

"Where have you?" Her voice was a shade too cheery, she thinking that he didn't look ready to explode, but it could be so hard to tell.

"She's been learning about pine beetles," Milton Crowder said, shambling up behind her.

Tod took the silly stem looped into a knot from his tongue. "Want to see how I can swallow a goldfish?" he asked.

"Eew. Gross," the girl said.

Tod's face gleamed at the girl, but he looked somewhat apprehensive as he peered up at Cathy. "You see the way those boys took off?" He patted the youngster on the shoulder, dismissing her, and the youngster pouted for a second, smiled brilliantly, helped herself to half a dozen maraschino cherries, strolled into the crowd and came back at once with the tall woman, Gloria, in tow. The one with the blaze of white in her hair.

"The boys will be all right," Cathy said, distractedly.

"It's the truck I'm worried about," Tod said.

"Try not to think about it," Gloria said. "Teenagers. I have four. They ganged up on me. Twins, in my old age." She didn't look anywhere near any old age, Cathy interposed, but the woman groaned. "Want some advice? Don't do twins. That's what did this." She touched her white streak. "Teenagers."

Or Clairol platinum, Cathy thought, though it might be natural. People were forever asking Cathy what she used to keep her hair so coppery.

"Have you met our handsome detective?" Gloria asked. "He's the one who caught that man who stole a million dollars from that credit union. Isn't he cute? That's what I call 'clean cut.'"

"Dick Tracy," Tod said. "Let's go back in."

When they came into the house the detective was silhouetted at a window, as if to demonstrate his Dick Tracy profile. He did have a hatchet nose and a squared off chin but when he turned to smile at Cathy and Tod, the smile faded.

"Catching that fellow must have taken a lot of doing," Milton said. "A lot of whatchamacallit. Surveillance."

"Sifted through a lot of garbage," the detective said and suddenly Cathy did know what they were talking about; she'd scanned newspaper's coverage. "The Chronicle didn't say how you were tipped off," she said.

There was a lull in the noise level and she repeated the question. The detective shrugged. "I got curious. I get curious about situations. Someone pays cash for a house, say. Or if they hang out with interesting people."

Cathy gave him what she hoped was an inquisitive look.

He shook his head. "It's mostly waiting around," he said. "Sifting through garbage. That kind of thing. This particular guy was spending a lot of money and he didn't have any income that we could figure out. He looked and acted like a criminal but we had to figure out the crime. It took a while. And then, after we had it figured out, he came in by himself. He had some noisy neighbors he wanted to file a complaint on so we invited him in. When he came in, we introduced him to the F.B.I. End of story."

"Maybe the neighbors were all jolly from drinking quantities of rum," Cathy said. "Everybody here but you is drinking quantities of rum."

He laughed and steered her toward the door. The beach was quieter than the house, but she and the detective discovered some small children burning holes in their clothes with sparklers. The pretty youngster who'd been watching Tod do the maraschino stem stunt was ostensibly taking care of them but she seemed somewhat careless.

"You're not being very vigilant," Cathy said.

"Well, I never did have hot buttered rum before," the girl said, giggling, as Cathy eased the burning wire of a burned-out sparkler from a small boy's hand. You don't look old enough to be having it now, Cathy thought, but she didn't say that because the girl's mother, Gloria, loomed up behind her.

"Your husband is sooo cool," the girl said. "Does he always give people good stuff?"

"Oh, dear," Gloria said. "I don't think we could make ourselves heard in the house." She gazed at her pretty teenager. "This is Ellen. Ellen, dear, don't ever tell a woman her husband is so anything."

Cathy laughed. "Well. Tod's pretty cool. And you're very pretty. And, yes, my husband likes to give good stuff to people." She held up her hand to flash her emerald ring.

"I think my poppet is referring to maraschino cherries," Gloria said.

"I am not," the girl said.

Gloria turned to Cathy and shrugged. "Fourteen. Look at this child. Can you believe it? Go put on a sweatshirt or something. Aren't you cold? Cover up that chest." She sighed a motherly sigh. "All this happened within about the last half hour or so. The boobies, the hips, the whole bit. I can hardly stand it."

"Mo-ther!" the girl squealed.

"They go from cherub to nymphet in the wink of an eye," her mother said. "I can tell you about every single hair in this white streak, give you dates, days, hours, name the places—do you have children?"

"I have a son," Cathy said. "Haven't seen much of him this evening. He and my cool husband keep getting lost."

It had gotten very dark very suddenly. She roamed around, looking for Greg and Shep, wondering if Tod might be looking for her, making himself sick. The entire beach front was enveloped in the kind of inky black that swallows light. The lemony circle of light shed by a vapor light on a pole in front of the cottage wavered through droplets of mist, scarcely able to reach the periphery of the heap of trees at the water's edge.

Cathy moved from group to group, in growing unease. She was still looking, beginning to be almost frightened, when Milton called out that it was time to ignite the trees. Everybody gathered in a ragged semi-circle to gaze at the dark mound of trees. The Gulf lapped and washed up on the sand. Milton called out in what he said he hoped was a Druid-like voice that they should all be reverently silent. An offshore breeze rustled through the heaped trees. A small child demanded to know, in a clear, piping voice, why she was being squeezed, and a man said, "Stay back here with Daddy," as Milton leaped up onto an upended barrel to toss a burning taper onto the pile. The trees breathed out one big breath. Milton jumped down and backed away. And the entire heap of greenery exploded, imploded, whooshed into rushing, wheezing, hot, white, bright, soaring flame.

The mother of the Devereaux twins screamed in delighted terror. "Wow, they go up like firecrackers. See if I ever put one of those things in my living room again."

"Hotter than Dutch love," Cathy giggled, but stopped, the giggle caught in her throat. If she hadn't been looking around for Tod or the boys, she wouldn't have seen it. Someone—a kind of a skinny apparition—was standing alone, out on a small dune on the far side of the vegetation line.

"You all right?" a voice near her asked. It was the detective, he of the chiseled profile. She menat to say she was, but she got a foot caught in a beach vine trying to back away from the sudden heat. When she stumbled against him, fighting for a footing in the soft sand, he offered her his arm.

"Now I am," she said, accepting his help. "Thank you."

"You're quite welcome. I know your husband, you know," he added.

"Do you? What threw me off is that there seems to be somebody out there," Cathy said, shielding her eyes to peer. "Over there. Just at the edge of the light. Possibly one of the kids, but you'd think they'd—well, it looks like she's gone. Maybe it was somebody from one of the other cottages, come to see what all the commotion's about. She looked so eerie."

She shivered. She wouldn't even have seen the lonely figure if it hadn't been for the sudden brightness as the trees exploded. Whoever it was must have been taken by surprise by the surge of light. That's what it looked like, standing out there, like she was startled, her draped arms akimbo, a swirling wraith, before she ducked away.

The moon shone suddenly, bathing the sand and water with a bright silvery glow that made everything, grasses, sand, the rows of cottages, stand out in startling clarity. Masses of stars bloomed in the sky. When Cathy looked into the detective's face, so close to hers, he seemed to be eyeing her in a way that made her self conscious.

She let go of his arm. "So was everybody terribly grateful after you caught the thief?" she asked.

The man sighed. "There was a reward. It's kind of a long story. I felt like the money ought to go to the department. They pay me, after all, but giving it to the department led to a big political fuss. Some folks didn't think the department needed the money." He looked even more earnest. Everything seemed to be important, to this earnest intense person. "The city council got in on it. Money leads to trouble," he said.

"My husband says it's a great little deodorant," Cathy said.

"Does he?" The detective paused. He looked so unsmilingly stern that Cathy wished he'd move along and find somebody else to stare and gaze at with his sharp eyes. He cleared his throat. "Some people want to use the reward for a park. Give it his name. The thief's." His eyes went to dark slits and he jutted his chin. "Guess that's the way most people are. Don't give a damn."

Cathy hadn't been paying very close attention. She'd been looking around, wondering where Tod might have gotten to, again.

The man waited, his eyes boring into hers. Something about a park, she thought, he'd just said something about some park. And she was expected to have an opinion. "It might be lovely to have a park named after you, I should think," she said. "Do you have any children?"

"They want to name the park for the criminal," the detective said.

bitterly. He looked annoyed at her inattentiveness. "Guy steals a million dollars and people want to name a park for him. The man's a lousy criminal." He followed her up the steps and back into the noisy warm room.

"And he didn't even have a Bonnie," Cathy said, possibly too merrily. The man looked at her. "You know. Bonnie and Clyde? Folk heroes?"

"You think they're heroes?" the man said, not smiling. "How do you feel about sex offenders?"

Strange man. Cathy knew she must be looking blank as blank, but he had such an unpleasant way of cutting off his words. She cast about and remembered a joke. "I guess ten percent of 'em give the other ninety percent a bad name?" The man gave her a wan smile. He got it, but he was not amused. He shrugged.

Someone had to say something. After a minute, she ventured. "Were Bonnie and Clyde, you know, troubled, that way too? They must've been very troubled." She hated fighting the stammer.

Just then she looked up to see Tod sitting on the cottage steps, his face turned toward them, watching. She couldn't help a fluttery sigh of apprehension. "Oh, There's my wonderful husband. He's wearing the smile he smiles when he wants to go home. His 'me, Tarzan. You, Jane,' smile." She knew she sounded fatuous.

The detective's mouth wrinkled into a sardonic grin. "Whatever floats your boat, lady," he said, and turned his back and went stalking awkwardly off across the sand. It took her breath away.

But when she looked around Tod was smiling at her, his head back, an open-mouth grin of startled approval wreathing his face.

He did want to call it a night. All of a sudden everybody seemed to be leaving, all thanking Milton effusively, everybody hugging everybody, promising to get in touch with everybody *very* soon and then they were in the car, driving up the dark beach road with Cathy wondering if Tod felt as drifty and off balance as she did when the car skidded on a soft place. "Are you okay to drive?"

Of course he was, he said, crossly. "You have a good time talking to Sherlock all evening?"

"Oh, Tod," she said.

"Looked like you weren't paying much attention," he said. "Falling asleep in one guy's face and I don't know what you said to Dick Tracy but he sure got a sour look on his puss, baby."

"I know," Cathy cooed, "I spent most of the party watching you charm the socks off everybody." That seemed to do it. He yawned and, thank you God, smiled into the night and drove them home without another word.

After they got to the house, Cathy ran quickly up to Greg's room while Tod locked up. Greg wasn't in his room. His absence set off all sorts of alarms. Woke her wide awake.

"I think I'll read for a while," she said. Tod grunted sleepily and let her go off to the little blue room she'd begun to think of as her own, with her narrow bed, cozy as a quilted cocoon, with all her plump cushions and books and her good old afghan.

She couldn't concentrate on her book. McMurtry's cowboys seemed galaxies distant. When she turned out the light and counted breaths it felt as though her eyes stayed wide open, staring beneath the lids. She was still awake, stewing about Greggy, trying to convince herself that he'd come waltzing in any minute, trying not to be completely silly, when the phone shrilled in the other bedroom.

*****

22

Cathy couldn't reach the phone before it woke Tod, who picked it up.

Five minutes to five, the bedside clock said. Four minutes to five. Click. Three minutes to five, while Tod said, "Yeah?" and listened, maddeningly silent, his face perfectly blank. "Talk," he said. "Can't you talk to the old man, here?" He looked at Cathy. "It's your boy."

"Give me the phone," Cathy said, pulling it from his hand. "If you please."

"—so the U-Haul truck is totaled," Greg was saying, "and we're at John Sealy. They're gonna set Shep's ankle, I guess it's broken. But other than that everything's okay."

"Okay?" Cathy echoed, weakly. "You're okay? Are you sure?"

"Yeah, no kidding," he said. "Listen. The only thing, the guy here needs you to sign some paperwork. The resident doctor, like."

"I'm on my way," she said.

"Well, don't freak or anything, okay? This is no big deal. I mean, it is. The U-haul is a big deal. But that's it. I'm not hurt or anything and Shep's going to be okay. No kidding."

No kidding.

The phone buzzed in her ear. "They're at John Sealy." She ran to the bathroom, then ran back into the bedroom and hopped on one foot and the other, yanking on her jeans, bumping into Tod who kept getting in her way. "One of the boys has a broken leg."

"Wait," Tod said. "Wait a minute."

"His ankle," Cathy said. "They're setting it. Can we discuss this another time? They're not hurt. Other than that. Something's happened to the truck." Oh, he really is not hurt. Let him not be hurt. Oh, was he lying about that? "They're not hurt," she said. "Except for the ankle."

"Right," Tod said. "Easy, babe."

She slammed a drawer with the heel of her hand.

"Easy," Tod said.

"I have to go," Cathy said. "Sounds like rain. Is it raining? At least they're not seriously hurt, or he wouldn't have sounded so—what are you doing?"

He was sitting up in bed, scrubbing at his head, watching her, not getting dressed, just sitting there. "Staying out of your way. You're dangerous. The kid tell you the whole story? He get a ticket or anybody get arrested?"

"What are you babbling about?" Cathy demanded. "We can talk when we get back."

"Totaled," Tod said. "He says the truck is totaled. Well, that's what insurance is for. Will you hold on, a minute?"

Cathy got her purse under her arm and made it down the stairs before he'd gotten off the bed. She snatched up the garage opener and car keys and was opening the garage door before he made it into the kitchen, mumbling, "Now, hold on a minute."

"Yes, well, I'm in a very large hurry, Tod."

"I noticed. Is that the way that's supposed to be buttoned?"

Cathy unbuttoned and redid her blouse as he followed her, complaining, begging her to sit down, couldn't she sit down, please, and listen for a minute?

"We can talk when we get back," Cathy said, enunciating carefully into his silly blank face, as she pushed past him. "Unless you want to get into the car now, right this second, if you please."

He didn't please. Not in his pajamas.

He wanted to prance and shout. "Hell, you mind if I get my shoes?" He got in her way, dancing with indignation. "You had plenty of time to talk all night to anybody wanted to give you the glad eye at that faculty party, didn't you?" He got in her way, panting. "Plenty of talk going on there, huh? Plenty of wiggle waggle and talky talk for Uncle Miltie and that Dick. You got an eye for the po-lice, now? Just hold on a minute."

I'm going to slap him, she thought. "Get out of my way."

"Oh, I guess I know better than to ask for a whole hell of a lot of consideration around here," Tod yipped, "not with Greggy-boy calling for his mommy. He's in a waiting room. That's what they call 'em. Waiting rooms. Places where people wait. Those kids are not going anywhere. You hold on, now."

There was more, but she couldn't hear it. He'd gone stamping out of the kitchen and up the back stairs, talking to himself.

She got the car out of the garage and around the drive all right, but it slid and went up and over a boggy place in the lawn when she tried to turn out onto the slick rain wet street.

How stupidly vacant Tod had looked, gnawing at his fingernails, raving about people talking to each other at the party. That's why it's called the Green Eyed Monster, she thought. That's the look. Stupidly, monstrously stupid. But no time. No time now to think about that. She had to concentrate on turning off of Eighth Street to the emergency room. Surely they must be in the E Room. And surely it was around behind the hospital, somewhere. Oughtn't an E room be easy to find? Greg wasn't hurt. He'd said so. Twice.

Her stomach wrenched. That's what he would say, of course. Besides, people could be injured severely and not be aware of it. She should have asked if a doctor had examined him. That's why she had to hurry, to be sure that no one assumed anything, that he wasn't walking around bleeding inside or with a concussion or—

What, exactly, had he said? Other than "no kidding." In that falsely reassuring slightly goofy way that boys sound when there's something terribly wrong, lying to her in that helium voice. His voice had sounded exactly the way it did when he fell out of the tree house at the Messers' that time, in Heritage Cove. Scared silly. Chattering about how he didn't feel great but not to worry, he'd just slid out of an oak tree. And all that night Cathy had done what the doctor said, made him wake up so she could shine the penlight into his eyes every half hour—well, the doctor'd said every hour but she hadn't been able to wait that long—checking to see if he had a concussion. Always so stoic, even when he was little.

People who worked in hospitals were supposed to know about such things, but they were busy. Busy or not, surely they'd know better than to let a youngster sit around in an emergency room or roam up and down the corridors and babble on the phone if he had a concussion. Wouldn't they?

Not if they knew it.

They didn't know about Sylvia's boy, that awful time. He'd been sent straight to an E room after his motorcycle hit that wall and everybody was so busy with the other boy that they let Sylvia's boy go home. Sent him home. "Treated and released," the paper said, the next day and everybody was so relieved but by then, it was all over. First Sylvia called early that morning, just sick with relief, so glad that the damned motorcycle was gone, and her Ricky home, in bed, and the other boy was going to be fine too, in Southeast Memorial, in good condition. Then when she went to call him for breakfast, Ricky's eyes were wide open. The pupils of his eyes were black all the way to the edges of the irises.

Sylvia walked right out into the street and down Tenth Street, making such terrible noises that everybody had come out to see what was the matter, oh, Lord, oh, God....

Cathy parked and ran.

Her boots sounded clattery in the tiled hall. She needed to get the heels fixed.

She heard Gregory's high helpless giggle in a little waiting room. When she got there, he and a burly policeman looked up with the canted smiles of men caught in the middle of whatever it is that men find to laugh at whenever there's an emergency. They looked so companionable they sent a dizzying wash of relief all through her. Greg jumped up and introduced her to the man, an officer Patrick Flanders. "This is my mom, Cathy Van Duren."

"Benjamin," Cathy corrected him. "Catherine Benjamin-how-do-you-do-has-anyone-looked at-you? I mean a physician?" She shook the policeman's hand. "Have they checked for a concussion? How do you know you don't have a concussion?"

"I'm all right," Greg said. He was the greenish color of the hospital wall behind him. His mouth was hideously swollen and bruised and there was something the matter with the way he held it. "I'm fine, no kidding," he said, slurking, and then he added, even faster, so fast that it got garbled, "We sort of hydroplaned on this loose gravel, and we sort of slid into the street sign at Tenth, and went over the seawall. It's a real mess, Mom."

"Let me see," she said. "Take your hand away from that mouth. Have they checked your eyes? Sometimes when people—"

"They checked."

The policeman kept grinning. "You know what your boy said? I watched these kids climb out of that thing, and I said, 'Well, well, you gentlemen have an accident?' and your boy looked up and said, 'No, thanks. Just had one.'"

The man looked at Cathy and the grin faded. "He's, ah, he might be pretty shocky, ma'am. I'd take it easy on him. They gave him something so they could put in those stitches."

Cathy's hand went to her throat. "Stitches?"

"Just my lip," Greg said.

"Show me." Cathy said. "Now."

"It's my mouth, mom." It came out mouf. "Boy. I thought there was this big piece torn right out of my gum," he slurked, "but it turned out to be just sort of shoved up and folded under. This guy who sewed it up says he doesn't think I did anything too bad to my teeth or anything but I ought to maybe see a dentist."

By the time a subdued Shep was finally wheeled in, in a wheelchair, in torn jeans with one leg straight out in front of him in a cast, the windows were turning gray with rainy dawn light. Shep mumbled a greeting. A metal barrette held his dirty blonde hair back in a frowzy ponytail. His hair, the color of his eyebrows and his long-lashed pale eyes, framed a long face, the mouth coarse over braces. From the bridge of his nose on up he was almost pretty, Cathy thought. The slack-jawed mouth didn't seem to fit his face..

When a weary physician came into the room to discuss Shep's ankle, and have her sign forms, Cathy stopped him before he began to talk. "Only this one is mine," she said, indicating Greg. "The one you've just patched up there is a friend." The three adults looked at Shep. "Have you called your parents?"

Shep squirmed. "We had a little trouble reaching my mom. My dad's out of town. I'm okay, ma'am. Or I will be, if you'll give me a lift home."

The doctor looked alert. "Hope we've got all the paperwork straight here."

"Yeah, yeah," Shep said. "Like, about the insurance? I'm over eighteen and I signed everything and all. We're covered." He shifted uneasily. "My old man works here in the medical complex."

"Shep's not dying to wake up his mom or anything," Greg said. "She gets real upset."

The inference was rather flattering, but Cathy frowned.

"Are you certain you don't want to call your mother?"

Shep shuddered.

She had to drive the length of the seawall to take Shep home. An early morning downpour lashed the angry Gulf up and over the boulevard. Palm fronds slithered across small lakes in the wet pavement. Rain blew across the windshield in solid washes too heavy for the Cadillac's stuttering wipers. "I never can figure out where I am in this dreadful automobile even when the sun is shining," Cathy said. "It's like driving a small town. I hate this thing."

Shep and Greg rode in silence.

"I'm sure you don't want to hear my diatribe about Cadillacs," Cathy said. "Which of you wants to go first? I'm dying to hear about your adventure."

Silence.

"Did you know that most rainwater is in the sky for about three weeks before it falls?" she heard herself say, and, for some reason, Shep and Greg giggled, and all three of them chortled until Greg got the hiccups.

"Man," he said, "it felt like we were in the sky for about three weeks before we came down. Then it got real noisy. You wouldn't believe how noisy it got."

"That truck came down," Shep said. "Hit the rocks like a yo-yo."

"Yeah, you know, like in the movies," Greg said. For the rest of the trip the boys relived the accident. By the time they reached Shep's neighborhood, they were interrupting each other, almost relishing the whole thing. Shep did not want Cathy to come with him to the door of his house, a perfectly beautiful two-story house in Havre La Fitte. He clambered out, hastily insisting no one was home, and went lurching up a flagstone walk.

"We can't go off and leave him on crutches like this," she said.

The house had an unlit, lonely look. It was nicely landscaped but it was one of those places with swimming pools facing a man- made lake cut into an island in the back. And it looked somehow deserted.

"Trust me," Greg said. "He doesn't want you to come with him. He'll handle his mom."

Cathy drove slowly back up Broadway while Greg went on and on about the accident. Shep was at the wheel. It sounded like he'd been behaving like an absolute damned fool, speeding and slamming on the truck's brakes, skirling along a deserted section of the beach. "So when we got up on the seawall, I took over," Greg said. "So I got up near Tenth and there wasn't anybody else around so I guess I had to get a little nuts, too. I sort of stomped on the accelerator and the thing swung around, hit this patch of gravel, and there was the street sign and bam, we nailed the pole and rode the fence, and sailed right on over."

"You've got a lot of explaining to do," Cathy said.

Tod did get a more complete explanation, after they got home. The next morning, at breakfast, he listened with a blank face, without uttering a syllable, lifting his hand, palm out, like a traffic cop, each time Cathy tried to interject a question. After Greg had gone through the whole thing again and again, Tod looked at him with his face blank and his eyes the color of dirty cement.

Tod finished his eggs and toast. He touched his mouth with his napkin, and stood up. "I'm selling the jeep. No point in letting the moron wreck it, too." He looked at Greg and inhaled as if he were being made to smell something disgusting.

As if Gregory stank.

After Tod left, Greg went into the bathroom, locked the door and cried.

Tod took care of everything. He called his attorney, filed the insurance claims, paid the hospital, the doctor and, eventually, the dentist.

When Greg tried to thank him, his nose wrinkled and his eyes went that chilling, blank, heavy gray.

Greg never did explain why Shep had been so reluctant to call his mother that day, except to say, "Shep's parents are sort of strange." He didn't want to talk about Shep. Or anything. He refused to go to the doctor to have the stitches taken out. The darned kid took those stitches out by himself, using Cathy's eyebrow tweezers and her manicure scissors. He didn't even sterilize them.

His mouth healed.

By the time Greg's mouth had healed, Tod had gotten to where he could look in Greg's direction without that bitter pinched look. Sometimes. Well. Greg made it easy. He kept out of the way.

They didn't even share meals any more. Greg took to eating on his way out the door—he seemed always to be on his way out—hurriedly gulping food from his hands, helping himself from whatever he found on the stove or in the refrigerator, leaning above the counter or the sink to chew and swallow, preoccupied and distant, almost furtive.

She should have put her foot down when that first started happening.

She did, in a way. When she told Tod that she did so wish that the three of them could sit down to eat together of an evening, he looked at her with icy distant appraisal and said, "Isn't that all I've ever wanted?"

When she told Gregory how it put a lump in her throat to see him wolf down his food and ease out the back door whenever Tod's car pulled up into the circular drive out in front, Greg didn't even look in her direction. "Seems simpler," he said. "Doesn't it?"

After everything blew up, though, Cathy wished she had put her foot down. Made both of them sit down and listen to her, early on, before things got so crazy.

*****

23

On the first Saturday night in February, the telephone woke them at ten minutes past three. This time the phone was on Cathy's side of the bed. Tod sat up and watched her pick up the receiver. It was Greg. Again.

"I don't know how to tell you this," he said. "Please don't freak out because it isn't as bad as it sounds, Mom, but I'm in jail, okay?"

The receiver hummed. "Jail." Her heart pounded. "*Jail?*"

"Let me talk to him," Tod said. "Give me the phone."

"I'm on my way, " Cathy said. It was like a broken record, this whole scene. "Downtown? Galveston jail? I'm getting dressed."

Tod took the receiver from her, listening, watching her yank her clothes on. After he'd hung up, he came over to Cathy, wanting to hold her. He kept getting in her way, wanting her to sit down so he could hold her hands and talk to her. "Jail means lawyer, baby," he said. "First things first." When she pushed him away, he yawned, and went shambling down the stairs, muttering coffee, coffee.

Cathy didn't want coffee.

"Let's be sensible, here," Tod said, as she clattered down the stairs. "We've got a few minutes. The kid isn't going anywhere. What we've got to do is—"

"Keys," Cathy said. "Car." She held her hand up the way he always did to hush her, her fingers splayed out, motioning him into silence, but when he stopped talking and gazed at her she didn't have anything to say. She rushed to the kitchen door and ran out to the garage. As she backed the car and started around the drive, Tod came out, waving both hands. She rolled down a window.

"Sure is nice to be invited," he said.

"Go back in the house," she said and closed the window. He seemed to be talking, waving his arms, as she neared the street side of the circle. He had on his green and yellow pajamas, a pair she hadn't had a chance to hem up. The too-long legs hung in rumpled folds. He looked like a child in hand-me-downs, standing in the driveway, talking, yelling at her now, as she adjusted the seat and the car mirrors and drove down the street.

As she turned off Broadway, wishing the tires wouldn't keep squealing, a siren sighed and yelped behind her. She pulled over. "Good morning, ma'am," a patrolman said, peering into the car. "May I see your license please? You didn't see that light?"

"No," Cathy said.

"Afraid I'm going to have to write you up," the officer said.

"Yes, yes," Cathy said. "If you will, please. I'm in a huge hurry." She handed the policeman her driver's license and scrabbled in the glove compartment for the insurance card. When she didn't find it, she pulled everything out of the compartment all over the front seat, a clutter of papers, yellowed receipts, a telephone bill, a receipt from Foley's. She found the insurance card and handed it to the man.

While the policeman went back to his car to do whatever it was he had to do, Cathy distractedly shuffled through the papers, thinking they ought to be thrown away. The policeman kept talking away on his radio in his car, back there behind her.

Cathy flattened out the receipt from Foley's. Those silly nightgowns that had gotten stolen from the trunk were on it. Almost a couple of hundred dollars' worth. A hundred and eighty-eight dollars. What a ridiculous amount of money for nighties. Stolen, that night. But here was the silly receipt. How did the receipt get into the glove compartment? But, oh, so what, so what? because now the policeman had come back to stand beside her, nodding and solemn, telling her she could go, suggesting that she drive carefully. She drove the rest of the way with exaggerated caution.

There were three women and a scruffy looking old man in the brightly lit reception area of the jail. The scruffy man slept with his head cradled in his arms, his shoulders heaving with stentorian snores. Two of the women, elderly and black, sat rigidly upright, their hands on the purses held on their laps. The third, a large pale woman with wide, slightly protuberant eyes, got up as Cathy came in. The belt of a long sweater coat trailed on the floor until she noticed it, wound it around one hand and offered the other, her left hand, to Cathy as she introduced herself. "Melva," she said. "Shep's mother. You must be Catherine. Isn't this something?"

Cathy sat down, biting her lip. Melva seemed to know what the boys were charged with, but Cathy was almost afraid to ask.

Melva pawed through her purse and poked at her hair. "My husband's in Chicago. At a seminar. I don't have any idea what to do, do you?"

That's when Cathy realized that she probably should have waited for Tod. The two women looked at each other and looked around. There was a police officer behind a glass window set in a wall but he seemed preoccupied A telephone hung on the wall next to his window. After a minute Melva went over to peer in the window and stood there tucking long strands of gray hair up under her knitted cap.

The man at the desk looked impassive. After a couple of seconds he pointed to the phone on the wall and mimed putting it to his ear. Melva picked the phone up, listened and beckoned to Cathy.

The man sounded tinny: "Mr. Benjamin called." Cathy nodded. "Your husband?" Cathy nodded. "He says he has everything wired. Mr. Arnold— your lawyer?—your attorney is on his way." Cathy expelled a breath of relief. The man added something about "going for pre-trial release" which might take a while. He suggested she take a seat.

"May we see the boys?" she asked. The officer said he'd ask the sergeant and went back to his switchboard.

Cathy finally worked up the courage to ask Melva as she sat down next to her, "What are they supposed to have done?"

Melva looked tearful. "Shep said something about a stolen motorcycle." Cathy couldn't close her mouth.

Melva sniffed and said, around a Kleenex, "We've never permitted any of the kids to go anywhere near motorcycles. The people in the Closed Head Injuries unit have such horror stories. Franklin is in Physiology."

Cathy had to stifle a nervous snicker. "A *motor*cycle? My son is a cellist." Melva nodded but she looked confused. "Gregory's never had any desire whatsoever to have anything to do with a motorcycle," Cathy said. "There must be some mistake."

"Do you live in that huge apartment complex on the east end?" Melva asked.

"We do not," Cathy said.

The man dozing on the bench slid feet first to the floor. This seemed to exasperate the man behind the window. He came through a buzzing barred door, shook the sleeping man and told him he had to leave. The man stood up and peered around. He looked clownish. He went lurching out the door.

"I'd like to avoid having to tell Franklin about this," Melva said in a quavering voice. "You might as well know, Franklin and I have decided that it might be just as well if our boys didn't see so much of each other. Franklin's already had a long talk with Shep. It just doesn't seem that Gregory and Shep are a very good combination." Her bulging eyes glistened. "Shep was doing so well," she said, "before."

The eyes must be a thyroid condition, Cathy thought. "I can't recall ever having been told that my son is a bad influence."

"Oh, I'm not saying that it's all Greg's doing," Melva said. "It's just that what one doesn't think of the other does. And then there's the marijuana. Franklin has been very understanding." She snapped and unsnapped the catch on her purse.

"Marijuana?" Cathy said, her blood rising. "I don't think so."

Melva tucked a long hank of hair up under the cap. "I hate to be the one to tell you," she said.

The pre-trial release man and Tod's disgruntled attorney didn't arrive until full daylight. The attorney, Mr. Arnold, tall, lean and exasperated, had on a terrible tie, with yellow smiley faces. He had on a good suit but the tie was so bizarre that Cathy felt a hard lump of anxiety form in her chest. Mr. Arnold walked in, gazed down at Cathy and Melva and stood shaking his head, sympathy in his eyes and the lines of his furrowed face. Cathy didn't catch the other man's name. The two men introduced themselves and went to the telephone on the wall. They were immediately allowed to go in to see the boys.

"I hope we can keep this from Franklin," Melva said. "We don't even know anyone who's ever been, you know, arrested." Her eyes swam with tears. "Franklin's first wife is a married to a Presbyterian minister and his children win debates and..and scholarships."

Cathy opened her arms, all animosity forgotten. "There, there," she murmured, as Melva sniffled against her. "Now, then. There, there."

"They sit around thinking up ways to kill them, you know," Melva said. 'Their stepfathers. It's a joke but not a joke." She drew back and honked into a Kleenex. "I'm sure you've heard them. It's so sad."

"I haven't heard them do that," Cathy said.

"Well, they do," Melva said. "All the time. It gives me the creeps." She looked at Cathy and looked away. "I think Gregory started it."

The metal door clanged open then, and Gregory and Shep, or Carleton Vincent Peabody the Third, came walking out, feverishly bright-eyed and disheveled. Shep thanked Cathy and bent to hug his mother.

Greg's long arms went around Cathy. "I'm really sorry, no kidding."

On the way home, it was all Cathy could do to keep the car on the road while Greg explained. And explained. He and Shep had stopped at a convenience store and persuaded a couple of girls to buy beer for them.

"Beer?"

"Well, yeah."

Cathy decided not to interrupt again.

The girls flirtatiously invited the boys to an apartment.

"An apartment? How old were these—"

"Mom. It's okay. Anyway, they gave us a wrong address."

The boys realized that they had been given a phony address. Shep got out to try to find the girls' apartment.

Greg followed him, trying to persuade him that the girls didn't want to be found. "When Shep has a couple of beers, he can get pretty hot. He started running all over the place, yelling for these chicks to come out." That's when they saw the motorcycle. "A hog," Greg said. "A big one. Parked out in front of this apartment in front of the pool." He hesitated. "I backed Shep's truck up and shoved it in."

"In?"

"A pool. It was next to this pool. The fence was down."

"Wait," Cathy said. "Why?"

"I don't know." Greg paused, remembering. "I just—I don't know. It made a hell of a splash."

The motorcycle's owner heard the splash. The motorcycle's owner, a large, muscled-up guy wearing ragged jockey shorts, appeared to be, Gregory said, "one tattooed, big-armed, bad ass."

His appearance so terrified Shep that he leaped into his truck and told Greg to "burn rubber." The motorcycle's owner ran alongside the truck, jerked open the door and yanked the boys out onto the parking lot. Which explained the abrasions on Greg's arms and face.

The boys scrambled through shrubbery, over and around garbage cans, up and down stairs behind buildings and, at one point, tried to scale a chain link fence, before a patrol car came screaming up, one of the tenants of the place having telephoned the authorities at the motorcycle owner's first outraged bellow.

"No way can I ever make you know the things that guy said he was going to do to us," Greg said. The boys were delighted to be arrested. "The cops laughed all the way up Broadway."

Cathy bit her tongue. He was so blasé. Jail. Underage beer-drinking. Wanton destruction of property. How was she to deal with this?

After they got home, Greg caught Cathy up in a fierce rib-cracking hug out in front of the house, just as Tod came out. Cathy saw Tod, but it felt so good to feel Greggy close and safe, with his long skinny arms around her that she didn't want anything to get in the way of it.

Tod stood staring at them for what felt like a long time before he turned on his heel and went back into the house.

"He's going to kill me," Greg said.

The next morning, after they'd had breakfast and Greg had gone over the episode again for Tod, Cathy began to think that if it had happened to someone else, it might be almost funny in a dreadful sort of way. The motorcycle owner, in ragged underwear, had roses tattooed on his biceps, Greg reported. "Big purple roses." Tod didn't see anything funny about any of it.

Tod left most of his breakfast. He got up, kissed Cathy's cheek, looked at Greg and walked, stiff legged, out to the garage. As Greg sat staring at his plate Cathy thought, unreasonably, of Shep's mother's confession: "They keep thinking up ways to kill them, you know."

Tod's attorney seemed even more disenchanted than Tod, at the hearing, in April, than he had that awful morning at the county jail. A tall, gaunt, aging man with skin the color of a dehydrated lemon and cigarette stains on fingers and his long teeth, he stood in the corridor outside the Justice of the Peace's chamber, wearily saying that Mr. Benjamin had assured him that this would be the last of this sort of thing. Mr. Arnold sighed. And sighed. He said he was not a criminal attorney. He did not choose to deal with adolescent miscreants.

Gregory and Shep—a newly shorn, scrubbed Shep in a navy blazer like Greg's, with a buttoned down shirt and navy tie, looking very Carleton V. Peabody the Third—stood terribly erect, their trousers rippling on their skinny legs, hanging on the attorney's every nuance, bright-eyed, sweat shining on their brows.

"I do not offer gratuitous advice," Mr. Arnold said, his long fingers moving languidly, his yellowish eyes coldly appraising. "There is one thing

I should like to make plain, however. When I was your age, marijuana was readily accessible in certain neighborhoods. No law specifically prohibited its use. Gin, however, was forbidden." He paused long enough to drag on a cigarette and throw it away. "Gentlemen. Keep this in mind. I did not drink gin."

Cathy protested that her son didn't know the least thing about marijuana so there really was no point in discussing that. The attorney turned his sorrowing eyes in her direction. She hushed, thinking it was a good thing the Justice of the Peace didn't look as dyspeptic as Tod's lawyer.

They got a merry little JP, a regular round Santa Claus who made Cathy think of those weighted dolls that roll around and right themselves. The roly poly Justice of the Peace noted, with a benevolent chuckle, that restitution had been made. He dismissed the charges.

The bored attorney did not share the boys rapturous relief. He made everybody stand and listen to him when they got out in front of the courthouse. "You have been rightly accused of criminal mischief," he said. "Although we've avoided a trial, the authorities tend to keep track of these things. Texas is particularly nasty about habitual offenses. Do we understand each other?"

"I do not understand all this talk of marijuana," Cathy said. "My son is not a drug addict."

The lawyer ignored her. He looked at Greg until Gregory looked up and met his eyes. "Do we understand each other, son?" the lawyer asked.

"Yes, sir," Greg said. "Absolutely."

*****

24

Greg had to pay for the lawyer and the motorcycle, so that summer, his sixteenth summer, Tod helped him to get a hardship license so he could make deliveries for the laboratories. It wasn't a bad job, Tod said, but it involved a lot of driving, a lot of hours. "Might help the kid can grow up," Tod said. "High time. Time he got off your back. And mine."

Greg wanted Tod to get off his back, but it wasn't that easy.

One Saturday afternoon while Cathy was splattering away at the dishes, Tod came into the kitchen and said, "Got to do something about that sink. It's pretty bad, isn't it, baby," as he tried to tuck a couple of twenty dollar bills into her blouse. When Cathy remonstrated he laughed and stuck the bills under the little smiley-faced magnet on the door of the refrigerator. "Going to be plenty more where that came from." He grabbed her and kissed her, and went whistling out of the room as Greg came in.

Greg barely waited for him to clear the door before he said, growling, "Plenty more where that came from, baby." He opened the refrigerator.

"Don't drink straight from the carton," Cathy said.

Greg closed the refrigerator. "He keeps track of the toilet paper," he said. "You ever heard lecture seventeen about how I'm using too much toilet paper? He stands outside the bathroom and listens to the toilet paper roller. 'Say, now. It doesn't take half a roll of toilet paper to do the job, does it, son?' He ought to be able to pick up some kind of an award with that little gem. That one and how much shampoo does it take to get hair clean." He swallowed milk.

"He's having to do a lot of adjusting," Cathy said. She leaned against the sink and looked around at the kitchen.

Greg followed her gaze. "That stove's got to be an antique. Maybe you could sell it and get a real one. The floor, too. Got to be a big market for cracked linoleum and nice deep double sinks," Greg said. "Even if they are stained and rough in places."

"We probably could learn to be more frugal."

"Well, I wish he'd go frugal himself," Greg said.

"I admit he's different," Cathy said, "but—" and the kitchen suddenly went so quiet that a wall creaked. A branch clicked against a windowpane. Like the ticking of a bomb, she thought. She turned to put a skillet into the sink and stood looking down at it, shaking, her hands shaking, because Tod was in the doorway, rocking from his heels to his toes, his eyes the flat unreflecting color of slate.

"Different?" he said. "Different."

"That's not what I—"

His mouth smiled. "Different."

Cathy started to explain but he waved his hand at her, demanding silence. "I guess I knew that," he said, slowly. "No fighting a thing like that, is there? If you're different."

He walked over to stand in front of Gregory. "Hell's bells," he said. "So. The old chump can go fuck himself, that it?" Greg looked blank.

"I know I'm different," Tod said. "I'm the chump, right? Chief chump, that it? The chump who pays the fucking goddam bills, though, don't you forget that, sonny boy. I might be different, but I'd sure as hell hate to be the little twerp comes crying to Mommy every time he falls into a pile of crap he can't wiggle out of." He pushed his face close to Gregory's.

Greg said, under his breath, "Jump back," but he was the one backing away, bumping into a chair as Tod moved closer.

"Naw, son, why don't you jump?" Tod demanded. "This is my place. Anybody going do any jumping around here, it better be you, get that?"

"Oh, please," Cathy cried. "You don't understand. We weren't actually saying that you—"

Tod held up a hand, commanding silence. "I heard what you said," he growled. "The old man may be a chump but he isn't deaf."

Greg was wedged between the refrigerator and an open cupboard door. "I've been thinking about jumping the hell out," he said.

"That so?" Tod asked. "That so?" He jabbed at Greg with his finger-tips. Greg ducked and tried to shove past him. The door made an ominous creaking noise. "I'm talking to you," Tod yelled. "You got something to say? Get out of here, Cathy. I might have to hurt this little—"

"Mom?" Greg had his arms up around his head.

Tod jabbed his fingertips into the boy's forearms and shoved at his chest. Cathy tugged at Tod's shoulder with one hand and pushed in front of him to close the cupboard door, afraid it would break. As she leaned in, Tod drew his hand back and swiped it across Greg's forearm. When it came back, Tod's hand came back in a hard loud slap on Cathy's face.

There was an instant of shocked silence.

Then they went into a rhubarb, all around the kitchen, the three of them talking at once, Tod screaming had he hurt her? oh God he must have hurt her oh hell how could he have hurt her he must have hurt her, and Greg shouting of course he had of course he hurt her, the little prick, look at his goddam hand print on her goddam face, with Cathy trying to make herself heard, saying they didn't talk like that and oh please please couldn't everybody just sit down for a minute, saying nobody was hurt.

But she was.

She'd bitten her tongue. It was bleeding. She ran into the bathroom and when she looked up at the mirror, Tod's hand print was on her cheek, livid, a four fingered print, until it faded into an angry welt.

Tod stamped up the stairs and down, teary with remorse. He slumped in a chair, disconsolately repeating how sorry he was until Cathy told him to go, he was going to be late.

"Your client must be wondering what's happened to you," she said. "Look. I'll live. It doesn't matter. Really. It was an accident."

He finally went shambling out to the garage, wan and shaken, saying they could iron all this out when they were thinking straight.

Greg didn't care to discuss it. His "Do Not Disturb" sign swung from his bedroom door knob. He didn't have a lock on this door, though, so Cathy went in. The room was a shambles. Greg was sifting and sorting through things. He glanced at her and said, "No."

"No what?"

"No talking, okay?" He mimicked Tod's splay fingered signal for silence. "No. Talking."

"All that about jumping back and jumping, you have to admit you both sounded pretty ridiculous. Tod didn't mean to get so carried away. He left here practically in tears. What are you looking for?" She made a place to sit amid a jumble of clothes on the bed. "What's all this?"

"I'm trying to figure out what to take," Greg said. "Shep's dad is out of town. He always is. He's in England, this time. So it'll be okay. Shep's mom says I can stay there for a while. She doesn't think we'll be a bad influence on each other." That's not the way I heard it, she thought.

"They've got plenty of room. They've got a couple of rooms up over their garage."

"Sounds hot," Cathy said. "Do you really think you'd rather have a room over a garage than this?" She glanced around the room.

Greg looked at her. "What do you think?"

"Oh, honey, listen. Please. You have problems, I have problems. Tod has all kinds of dreadful problems. They keep him awake at night."

"No shit, Sherlock."

She winced. "You look so hurt. But he is, too. He is. Truly."

"Man's all torn up," Greg said. "Sorry about that." He hauled out a box full of music and stood looking at it. "You think you might want to put some of this stuff in the attic, for now?" He scrubbed at his head and nodded toward his cello, in its case, leaning in the corner of the room. "I'll be back for it. And some of the rest of this. Yeah, I know. Little big man is all torn up. Getting to where he can hardly manage the old straight edge, anymore. He cut himself, this morning; you see the toilet paper on his face, there, at breakfast? I was gonna say something about that, about wasting all that toilet tissue but I figured what the hell. It's his house. You mind moving over?"

Cathy's throat ached. "This is just punishing me."

He kept pushing things around; socks, shorts, hangers, paperback books. A box of paper clips had spilled out onto a pillow. She scooped them up, put them back, walked over to put them on his desk. "I'm the one who got smacked and I didn't even do anything."

"You don't get it." He stood up, stretched and yawned. "Maybe you can start sleeping in here, instead of on that window seat or in that room with the broken screens in it. Be my guest."

She didn't realize he'd been that observant.

He looked triumphant. "How come you don't want to sleep with the man? You can't stand him, Mom. Face it."

She could feel herself blush. "I just happen to like the window seat. It's cozy. And Tod is so hot, he's almost feverish. Besides, I like to read, at night. It's a habit I got into. Before."

"Yeah. Before." Greg upended the drawers from his dresser onto the mess on the bed. His socks went every which way, all over the floor. He gave a pair of jockey shorts a sideways kick and, when he caught them, stuck his finger through a thin place. "I don't have a whole hell of a lot of Fruit of the Loom any more, do I? Guess that's part of the austerity program around here, right? How much does it cost? Holey underwear."

Cathy sighed. "You just keep poking at him, Greg. You know you do. Making fun of him the way you do. He was bound to catch you. I wouldn't let Tod make fun of you. You have to learn to give a little. Remember Katie? My roommate I told you about, who always used to get so mad if anybody tried to talk to her before her morning coffee? Terrible tempered Katie? There are a lot of people like that. Besides, he's paid so much—"

Greg stopped rummaging to look at her. "He hates having me here."

"Son, if I really believed that, do you think I could live with him?"

He was in the closet hauling a suitcase down from the top shelf. "You're not," he grunted, "living with him. You're so freaking strange I feel sorry for you. Not sorry enough to stick around and watch, but sorry." He grabbed a pair of trousers from a hanger and looked at them and rolled them up.

"You're ruining those," Cathy said. "Here. Let me. Good thing Tod gave them to you. Guess you'll need them to wear to go job hunting."

He tossed the britches into the closet and picked up a shaving kit. Which used to be Tod's. He held it up. "T.U.B.," he read, tossing it after the pants. "Tod Ulrich Benjamin. Is everything the guy ever owned monogrammed or what?"

"That other suitcase is ours," Cathy said. "Well. Mine. Used to be. Part of my old set."

"Used to be? How wonderful." Greg dumped everything out in a heap and yanked a pillow out of its case so he could shove things into it. Cathy giggled unhappily and said, wildly shrill, "That's monogrammed too. Look at it. It's white on white so you can hardly see it but that's because I had it done at Foley's and...and there it is. See?"

"Crap." Greg looked around, fuming. "Don't we have any stuff left? Did you pitch everything out or what?" He had to stop to blow his nose. He opened the pillowcase and started cramming things into it. "I'll get this back to you, Mrs. Benjamin. Try not to lose any sleep over it."

Cathy cleared a place on the bed and sat with her arms around her knees, gently bumping the back of her head against the headboard, trying to think. Greg emptied the bottom drawer of his desk into the waste basket. The basket overflowed. He stood looking down at it, exhaling.

"Okay," Cathy said. "Hold on for a couple of minutes. How about if I come along with you?"

"You're not invited. They've only got just so much space. Anyway, it's not your style."

"Oh, quit it," she said. "You're not going anywhere." She reached for his arm. He shrugged away, shoved past her and stamped out of the room with his bulging pillowcase on his shoulder.

Cathy followed him out into the hall and down the stairs saying, "Honey, honey, now then, we really have to think about this, will you please let's try to think honey," until he whirled around and bumped into her, so mad he practically spitting.

"That's what you do, isn't it, Mother? You think and think and you never really *do*. You never do anything about anything because you're so frigging busy thinking. When you finally do decide to do something you wreck the freaking world, going totally on feel.' His eyes were blazing.

"Well, you go ahead. You just sit around here and think your butt off. It's a little late isn't it? I mean, doesn't it look like it's a little late? You get to borrow little big man's pimp-mobile now, right? No more worrying about the little light on the dash with the little oil can, right? How's the oil pressure in the Caddy, Mother? Giving you any trouble?"

He kept talking so fast and moving so fast that he ran out of breath and inspiration, and stood choking at the bottom of the stairs. After a long minute he finally got a deep breath, and stood looking down at her, his face solemn. "Listen to me, Mother. Mom. If I stay here, I'm gonna have to kill him. I'll be a murderer. Your son the murderer. I mean it. I'll be in Huntsville with a needle in my arm."

"You don't mean that," Cathy said, her heart squeezing. She tried for a smile, a steady voice. "And you don't mean that about cars. I don't care about cars. When do you think I started caring about cars? You're not making sense. Neither of us is. Come on into the kitchen, can't you? You still have to eat, no matter how mad you—oh, never mind, I won't make you eat—okay—just come on in and sit down, can't you do that, please?"

He hesitated, his head down, and she got an idea. "Tod is so needful. He's like all those people you keep feeling so terrible about, honey. If you could only see it. He's—it's like your blind man, remember? in the park? With the newspapers on the bench? The bag lady, the one you saw jump right into the dumpster? People like that drive you crazy, you know they do. Oh, I don't mean he's poor but he's—it's the same—if you'd let yourself really look at him. He's so desperate. Starved. All he really wants is to have us be his family. How many times have you heard him say that?"

Maybe she was making ground. She went on. "That's all he wants. He's never had a home. Never. It's no wonder he doesn't know how to behave. And oh, honey, he's just eaten alive with jealousy. He sees the way we love each other and he can hardly stand it, it makes him sick—"

"That's what he had to horn in on," Greg said. "No. You look. You know what he fell for? He fell for you because what he wants is somebody who belongs to somebody else. Somebody he can take away from somebody." He swallowed, fighting tears. "He says so himself. He brags about it, all the time." He lapsed into Tod's hoarse whisper: "'Always did go for those pretty little girls and other men's wives, son.'"

"No," Cathy said.

"Oh, yeah," Greg said. "You just don't listen."

Cathy grabbed for him and he backed away, dashing tears from his eyes. "Pitiful, my ass," he said. "It's freaking amazing how some people can't help themselves and how nobody else gets to pull that crap."

"Yes," Cathy said. "You may be right. Please sit down. Just for a second. Yes. Some of us pity and some of us are pitiful, yes, that's how..."

"And they deserve it and they get to use it," Greg shouted.

Neither of them was making sense but Cathy was getting somewhere, she knew it, if she could just keep talking, keep him talking. Shouting, even. Greg sagged against a wall, looking past her, more and more weary, saying, "Hell, Mom. The man stays crazy. We don't have anything to do with that."

"My gosh, my gosh, we have to be rational," she said, maybe to convince herself.

"Now there is some real logic. Right there is where you win yourself the international free-fall extemporaneous debate trophy, right there, with your house of mirrors mind, get out of my way, hey, don't come at me to think. Today I think. Yesterday I thought." His voice was rising. "Many times I fucking have thought and if I try to do any more thinking I am going to ram my head through this wall." He drew back his fist and slammed it into the solid redwood of the vestibule. The wall shuddered and made a sharp explosive sound but it didn't break.

He's broken his hand, she thought.

That's what it looked like. He went white, dropped the pillowcase, bent double and came up cradling his hand to his breast.

Cathy, choking, tried to get him to let her see, demanding that he show her his fingers, could he move his fingers, please, God, had he broken all his beautiful long fingers? But he shoved her away and ran into the lavatory saying awful things through his teeth.

She could hear him through the door, sobbing, "Don't tell me I'll be sorry when you're dead because yeah, sure, I'll be sorry when you're dead, but if I stick around here I'm gonna kill the little prick bastard."

When he quit sobbing she tapped on the door and said please, please let her see. His hand had to be hurting terribly.

"Hell, no," he said. "Hell, no. Leave me alone."

She sat down on the bottom step of the stairs, gazing at the silly pillowcase, telling herself she had to figure out something, she had to think. Do something. Fast. There had to be some way to hold him back. Just keep him around long enough so they could both think straight. He might need a doctor for that hand.

The lumpy pillowcase with his socks and underwear leaned against the wall. She grabbed it up and, hugging it close, went running through the house, clattering out the kitchen to the screened back porch where there was no place to hide the darned thing. When she threw herself against the screen she tripped over the riser while she was trying to get the latch open with her elbow. The door sprang open. The fat pillowcase leaped from her arms to fly up, a springy bird shedding feathers of socks, Fruit of the Loom T-shirts, jockey shorts in shades of white, handkerchiefs, pastel nylon briefs. A polished windbreaker whispered and slid along the wet green grass of the yard. A burgundy nylon pajama top embraced an Esquire magazine and held it riffling in the breeze. Wee silvery gum wrappers twinkled, punctuation points in an almost lovely fluttery kind of composition, an art form spreading the length of the lawn as she stood and stared, bemused and blinking, in the sudden dazzling light of the sun.

But...no. No time. No time. She didn't have time to stand gawking, no, she had to get back into the house.

She slammed the door and leaned against it, panting, before she ran clumsily back to stand outside the bathroom door, wringing her hands. She didn't know what else to do.

Greg came out of the bathroom with a washcloth around his hand. He had washed his face and made damp comb marks in his hair. His face shone, the color mottled beneath the skin of his smooth cheeks. "Don't worry about me, Mom," he said. "I'll be okay. No kidding."

She followed him into the living room. "I'll try not to," she said, collapsing onto the couch, hoping he would follow. But he stood several paces away, out of reach.

She fished a Kleenex from under a sofa cushion. "You still have to eat something."

"I'll let you know what's happening," he said. "And, hey, sorry about the language. Everything'll be okay. A lot better, in fact. For everybody." He tried to smile. "You don't want me to kill him, right?"

"No, no," she said, distractedly. "That would never do."

"You want to wait around for that partner of his to do it, right?"

"Oh, Greg," she said. "You're making such a terrible mistake."

"Don't think so," he said. He kept looking around until he finally had to ask. "Where's my stuff?"

Cathy got up and went into the kitchen. "I'm putting on the kettle. Tea will only take a minute."

"What did you do with my stuff?"

"Or some soup, maybe? Soup only takes a second. It would be silly for you to—"

He got in her way. "Mom. This is past funny. What's the deal with my clothes?" He circled the kitchen, went into the dining room, started for the front door and came back. "I guess I can get along without clothes if I have to," he said. They played who will look away first for a couple of minutes until Cathy broke. She shot an involuntary glance toward the back porch and watched, her stomach sinking, as Greg grunted, walked over to the window and stood looking out.

He did not open the kitchen door. Just stood at the window, saying, "Huh," and something unintelligible that culminated in a long low whistle.

Cathy came away from the stove and stood next to him, looking up into his dear wounded face. "Honey? Do you—"

"Look," he said. He gripped her shoulders and turned her to face the window. "Look at that," he said. "Finders keepers."

A small scurrying figure was running around the back yard, cramming things into a pillowcase, stopping to glare dementedly up at the window and scurrying again, frantic with haste.

Greg started for the door and changed his mind. "I guess that's that," he said, in a cracked voice. "She's got to be half-way dangerous."

The woman did look feral. Glittery-eyed. She got the pillowcase crammed into the basket of her ancient, rattling, rusty bike and pedaled away as they watched.

The blue windbreaker flapped loose and came sailing back to lodge against a tree. Greg loped out half-heartedly and gathered it up.

He stood out in the yard for a few minutes before he came back in.

That settles it, Cathy thought. He can't go anywhere without underwear, can he?

"Be realistic," she said. For some reason, she focused on his wrist bones, so prominent and yet somehow vulnerable-looking on those arms grown long so quickly. She swallowed past a large goose egg in her throat.

"I am," he said. He walked to the door.

The teakettle whistled. She turned it off, shouted for Greg to wait and dumped things into a bag: Ramen noodles, little boxes of Fruit Loops, Jello Instant Pudding. Because he was leaving, he really was, she couldn't stop him. It was all she could do to run up close enough behind him out on the walk and get his attention so she could make him take the grocery bag.

The bag said "Randall's." Greg walked on down the street with it cradled in his arms for a way before he hoisted it to his right shoulder. Cathy stood out by the front door, watching him, her chest hurting. He turned and waved at her as he walked past the oleanders at the curve of the drive. He looked pleasantly preoccupied, as if he had somewhere to go.

*****

25

Cathy walked around crying. Upstairs, into Greg's empty room, down to the kitchen, back to the front door, out to the street. Back to the house. She kept seeing Greg's tired face, the bruised circles under his eyes, his weary resignation. There was no point in trying to talk him into coming back to live in this house.

After a while she made a pot of tea and sat watching lemon juice bleach its way down into a cup of hot tea. That made her cry harder. It brought back how Tod had made tea for her, how he'd stood around spouting poetry the first time he'd brought her into this house.

She was crying in the kitchen when Tod got home.

He peered at her and patted and looked scared until she'd explained. Then he harumphed. "Where do you think he went?"

"To the Shepherds'," she said.

And where might he find these Shepherds?

"Under the 'M's in my big address book," Cathy said.

When Tod looked confused she explained. "For Melva. But I think maybe we ought to let him have a little time there. He's m-m-miserable here. I said everything I could think of to him." She blew her nose. No need to mention Melva's doubts about the boys' friendship.

Tod rumbled and bumbled, patting at her, assuring her that he could handle this. He gave her his monogrammed handkerchief, poured her a glass of wine and suggested she take a lovely bubble bath. "Use some of that stuff I got you, get all comfy, have a little glass of this and relax. I'll go pick up the kid and we'll all go somewhere nice for dinner. That sound like a good idea?"

Cathy said it didn't, but that didn't stop him. He bustled out the door.

She was lying in a steamy haze, trying not to imagine the confrontation at the Shepherds', when she heard the front door open and close. Tod came stamping up the stairs, stamp, stamp stamp, and stood outside the bathroom door, wheezing. Alone.

"Come in. What did he say? Was Melva there?" Cathy got out of the tub and wrapped her hair in a towel.

"The kid isn't there," Tod said." Neither one of those damned kids is. Melva is in a state, too. That woman is a walking nervous breakdown."

Cathy sat down, hard, on the edge of the tub." Tell me," she said.

"Don't look like that," he said. "They're big kids. They'll be all right. Hell's bells." He walked around harumphing, making little growly laughs. "They left a note. Said they wanted to hit the road. Now, hold on a minute, it's not the end of the world. I had some of the best times of my life on the road. Every kid can use a little of that. I'm not worried about that, not for a minute. It's you I'm worried about. Come on in here and lie down."

Cathy didn't want to lie down. She wanted to pace. She wanted Tod to be still. "Did Melva call the police?"

"Oh, yeah. First thing. They—now don't you go to pieces on me here— you have to wait a couple days, big kids like that, the police see this thing the way I do, kiddo, couple of big kids like that. They'll come home when they get hungry enough."

Cathy dialed Melva's number. Got a busy signal. Got dressed. Got the busy signal again. Decided to drive over there. Went out to the garage to discover that Tod had left the car parked out in front. And that there was something the matter with the car. The Cadillac looked strange.

Because its tires were all flat. Tod's car had four flat tires. The rubber looked...puddly. Cathy leaned against the silly car, crying, until Tod led her back into the house.

After he called Triple A and raved about vandalism for what felt like a very long time, she took the phone away from him to call Melva again. This time, Melva answered but she didn't want to talk. She wanted to curl up and be miserable, she said. "Misery doesn't either love company."

The idea that someone would slash his tires made Tod stamp and curse. And shut up. Finally.

While the men from the garage were changing the tires of the Cadillac, Cathy finished another glass of wine. "It can't have been easy to make those tires so very flat," she mused. "It must have taken something very sharp." She had a thought." Maybe you should have bars put all around the drive. Good heavens, I've just invented the fence. Maybe what you really need is a wall. With shards of broken glass on the top of it. That's what we could do, Tod. Have a nice thick wall built around the entire

yard. But then people would think it was to keep us in, wouldn't they?"
His looking so uneasy helped, somehow. It felt...vaguely satisfying.

When Greg and Shep had been gone for a week, Cathy stopped taking showers. She didn't feel like it, when she wasn't getting dressed anyway. She stopped going downstairs.

A week and a day after the kids disappeared, Tod got desperate enough to call Chub. She came right over with an overnight case, three palettes, a heavy duty carrier and a box of Arches 22 by 30 inch hundred and forty pound cold press water color paper so heavy that she needed help getting it into the house. She came into the bedroom saying, "Don't cry, oh, that's silly, isn't it? Go ahead and cry. I'll sit right here and bawl along with you." And she did.

Wonderful Chub. She shopped for groceries amd went into that awful kitchen and cooked wonderful soups with wine and parsley and garlic; salad with goat cheese; fruit with almonds and raspberries in sour cream. She brought trays upstairs at first, until Cathy decided to come down.

Chub suggested Tod leave them alone. He did.

When she let him join them, she made Tod quit talking, talking all the time. She called darling Patrick and got him to recommend a physician in Galveston and drove Cathy over to see him. There were marvelous collages and etchings on the walls. Chub stood over the doctor with her eyebrows pulled down and her hands doubled into fists until he wrote some prescriptions she knew about. The doctor gave Cathy one prescription so she could sleep and another one for some wee three-cornered pills that made her feel very loose in the elbows and lackadaisical about painting, which she did, with Chub, every day, lackadaisical or not.

Chub had her splatter paint all over paper and stand back and squint until she saw which shapes to play with. "Negative painting," she called it. "Paint everything that's not a bit important and see what jumps out, darling. You can do that. The kiddies do that."

After a while some of the paintings looked like paintings. "Darker, darker," Chub said, her eyes half closed. "Whoops. We've got a composition!" And "There! Do you see it? A focal point! Right there," until Cathy saw whatever it was, or pretended to, through a series of halfway interesting efforts. The three cornered pills helped. They made her slightly dizzy but they also made everything so warm and foggy that she didn't even worry about Chub's driving. When Chub drove over a curb when they were turning off of Eighth on their way back from the doctor's office one Tuesday, Cathy just bumped along thinking, my, what a nice curb. What a nice stop sign. Interesting shape.

Chub did have to go home now and then, but mostly she stayed, ate and slept and crooned and hugged Cathy and stayed, until she absolutely had to leave. Then Tod hired Marie, who wasn't Chub but she was big and warm and chocolate-voiced and liquid-eyed and Marie crooned, too.

Marie called Cathy "little one," which didn't strike either of them as funny until Cathy got to thinking about it and realized that Marie was only about five feet tall, herself.

The last Saturday in September was the day they heard about the boys. A physician in a clinic in Baton Rouge called to say could someone please come and get two sick young men because Shep and Greg had been traveling with some hobos in a box car who gave them something called "canned heat" to drink.

The tramps seemed to know how to handle the stuff, Greg said, but this canned heat wasn't meant to be swallowed. It was meant to fuel camp stoves. The boys drank very little of it. Very little was enough to make them violently sick. "Everything keeps coming up," he said.

Greg stayed greenish, wan and chastened for several days. He slept. He drank Ensure. Finally he started thinking about school again.

Marie had two people to take care of, though Cathy quit taking the three cornered pills and began feeling more like herself the minute Greg was back in his room. Someday he would tell her where he had been, how he survived.

The day that Chub and darling Patrick came to celebrate Greg's homecoming, Marie barbecued a whole turkey but that night she said she was moving on, to help a lady who needed help. "Now that you're all well," she told Cathy.

Greg couldn't eat turkey. All he could do was sip a little Ensure, some stuff like baby formula, and watered chicken broth.

Tod kept wanting to make toasts that night. He kept making all sorts of wild vows and promises to anybody who'd listen. He made all sorts of plans, too, mostly talking to himself.

Cathy thought all Tod's talk about taking Gregory on an alligator hunt had to be just some of his usual blather, a bit exaggerated to impress Chub and Pat and, maybe, Greg, too. It made Greg grin.

The opening of the alligator hunting season coincided with Gregory's announcement that he was completely well, though, and Tod brought the idea up again. Tod got a little drunk and announced, all jovial and hearty, "You see the supper that kid put away tonight? Nothing the matter with our boy now, is there?"

He pinned Greg against the dining room wall, smiling ferociously, reaching up to clap him on the shoulder, demanding to know what Greg knew about alligators. Not much? Well, he'd fix that, he said. He'd rented a boat and hired a man. He and his buddy, Cecil, had everything all set, by damn, open season and everything all set, "What we're going to do, we're going to hunt us some 'gators, yes, sirree, sir."

Cathy's misgivings just made Greg laconic. "Oh, why not," he said. "As Tod keeps reminding us, he's picking up the tab. An alligator hunt might be sort of like a nature walk, don't you think?"

*****

26

They started out for Lake Livingston at four a.m., Tod drinking boiler-makers and this friend of his passing Buds behind to Greg before break-fast. Boy, Mom would love this, Greg thought, two for the driver and one for me, but he took a cold one anyway and that's the way it started out, Greg, Tod and a big guy Tod kept calling Bubba, cruising through Houston and up Highway 59, in the dark. Tod kept trying to slap the big guy on the back, like he was this buddy, his business partner or whatever. A big guy; some kind of a big alligator expert, in jeans and a leather vest over a big belly, the partner didn't act like he much liked little big man. In fact, a couple of times when Toddy landed a light punch on his arm the guy shot him a bored look without moving his eyelids. Greg knew the feeling.

Tod said Greg had to ride in the back seat because he needed a whole seat to accommodate his feet." You ever see such shoes on a human be-ing?" he chortled. "Now this kid has to have half of his leg turned under for foot. What size are those things?"

Thirteen, Greg told him.

Tod didn't exactly drive the Caddy. More like, he lolled behind the wheel with what he said was a little old eye opener in his left hand and his usual stogie smoldering away in his right, with one wrist draped over the wheel, one foot up on the hump and the other keeping time with the ste-reo. With the cruise control set somewhere around ninety, it felt like. Ev-ery once in a while some fool wouldn't get out of the way quick enough and they'd close in and flash the brights and hit the horn and the way would clear so they could keep on a-rollin' without his having to take his foot off the hump to tap at the brake. Little big man really loved that horn.

Greg decided to concentrate on the alligator man. He didn't smell bad or anything but he looked like a street person except he had what must be a real leather vest. The network of creases on the back of his neck looked like you could grow seeds in them and he kept this dirty felt hat about as big as a Texas Ranger's on like it was glued to his head. When Tod said Greg's name and Greg said, "How do you do," the big guy rolled a toothpick around in the corner of his mouth and got sharp eyed.

"You're not from around here, are ya?"

"Sure," Greg said." Well, I wasn't born here but my folks chose Texas while I was practically still an infant."

"Greggy and my lovely wife are from Holland, Michigan," Tod said. "You know. Holland?" While Tod laughed at that all by his lonesome self, the alligator man sort of lifted an eyebrow at Greg and Greg started to feel like the guy might be a lot more human than he looked.

"Name's Cecil," he said, turning around to stick his hand over the seat. He pronounced it "See-sill," and added that he'd answer to "Sees," explaining, "Now ain't that some kind of a Cajun name? Reckon my Coonass daddy was good and drunk. Cecil Beaugarden. Reckon de Beaugarden happen' when somebody call my grandaddy dat for he got tired trying to spell bigger name on de payroll."

When Greg grinned and nodded, Cecil dropped the accent and grinned back at him. "I'm like you," he said. "Lived most all my life in and around Houston." He stayed turned around in his seat for a couple of minutes before his smile broadened and he turned back to face Tod, saying, "Well, now, if this nice bashful boy looks anything like his mama, I begin to think you got yourself married to quality, for once."

Then he shut up and Toddy took over, for miles. And miles. When they passed the Dairy Queen outside Shepherd, the alligator man and Tod started horsing around, Tod in his hoarse voice and the alligator man in his deep rumble. They seemed to have some kind of a private joke going about what they called "D.Q. cuties." Cecil seemed to find D.Q. cuties just...indescribable. Talking about them reduced him to gnawing on his knuckle and mopping at his brow. "Oh, those little old gals don't know what they doin' to me," he complained.

"The hell they don't," Tod said, snickering, taking both hands off the wheel so he could shake out his fingers. "My, my, my. Mercy."

Greg was wondering if the old boys could actually be talking about certain specific Queen waitresses and how old could they be, or DQ cuties in general, when Cecil explained. "Met these li'l old gals selling sun tan lotion on East Beach," he said. "This is before your daddy got married, you understand. Between marriages, right, Tod? And what they's doin', these little old gals's selling sun tan lotion."

"Not the lotion," Tod said."Exactly."

"Not the lotion," Cecil amended. "They's selling putting on the lotion. At a dollar a rub." Remembering made the creases on the back of his neck go more red. "Can you beat that?"

"Not with a stick," Tod said.

"Just little old gals," Cecil said. "Like it says in the song, 'don't send me any women over twenty-two.' Just these big-eyed, little-bottomed gals, cute as a button, in them thong things they wear now. Just...just...whooie!" It made him take off his hat and mop the top of his shiny pink head. He swiveled around and looked at Greg but Greg couldn't look back. He stared at the flat dark landscape through the mist of his own reflection on the inside of the car window.

"All this was a long time ago, before I even met your mama," Tod said. "Let's get off the subject. We're going to be getting to the beginning of the Big Thicket out here pretty soon now. Yep. The beginning of the untrammeled wilderness. That's why I brought along the thirty-thirty." He nudged Cecil. "You might want to keep an eye out for bear."

"Bear?" Greg never had heard of any bears in Texas.

"Naw," Cecil said. "That little old rifle's only good for one thing, this trip. Shootin' fish in a barrel."

Cecil really liked that expression, "Shootin' fish in a barrel." He repeated it under his breath a couple of times while they were loading up the flat-bottomed aluminum boat and getting it slid down into the water and again, to himself, when they were getting underway. Once they were in the boat, though, Cecil poled around branches and trash, Greg began to see that there was something really neat about the way he handled the boat, gentling it, talking to it, touching it the way a man touches something he likes. "Just gonna go out in my john boat, shootin' fish in a barrel," he said, "ah, hum," in this crooning bass.

Thing was, it was *dark*, damp and dark, with singing mosquitoes and billions of gnats and every kind of noise from bugs and crickets and grunting frogs. One low bellow that sounded like a bull, Cecil said was a bull all right, a big bull alligator. Greg's shirt started sticking to him right away.

It was still dark when Cecil turned off the motor and let the boat drift up to a line dragged taut out into the water from a pole embedded in the clay of an overhanging bank. "Somethin' on here," he said.

Greg couldn't see what he did but there was a plashy sound and a disturbance on the dark patchy reflecting surface of the water. "Sank," Cecil said. "They'll do that."

"Let's see it," Tod said. "Come on. Let me have that line. Let's have a look at it."

"Why don't you light yourself another one of them cigars and have another Bud?" Cecil said, with a yawn.

"The hell with that," Tod started, a little squeak in his voice. "The hell with that noise."

But Cecil poled the boat on down stream, grunting patiently. "You know batter's that, my man. He's got them foot-long claws so grabbed into some mess of root down there we couldn't prize 'em out with a chain hoist. Besides, ain't but just so many permits."

"Ah, crap," Tod yipped. "You see anybody else around here? You see anybody standing around talkin' about permits? You're the only one talking about permits. Get this thing over to the bank and let's go for it. Let's get out right now and do it to it."

Greg didn't say anything and he didn't think Tod could see him but the old boy's radar must have picked up on how nervous he was. He couldn't help wondering what the hell "Let's get out right now" might mean because it didn't sound good. It sounded like it might be time for someone to climb out of the boat, didn't it? Get out and do it to it—do what to what?—do something out on that swampy bank, maybe? Or in the water? But that would have to be stupid. Nobody had on waders or anything. This seat, Greg thought, is the closest I ever want to get to real live pond slime.

Maybe he was breathing funny. He could feel Tod looking at him." You got some kind of a problem?"

"No, sir." Greg hoped he sounded polite.

Maybe not.

"Because if you've got a problem—"

"Settle down," Cecil said. "You gettin' your skivvies in a twist and they's a bottle float on that trotline and he ain't goin' nowhar. We'll make the rounds and get ourselves back here when it's right."

Greg could see the float he referred to, a plastic milk bottle, tethered and bobbing up and down in lazy circles on the moonlit surface of the water. Cecil saw him leaning forward to see it and volunteered, "Got to mark the place, see? Like on a trotline."

Greg didn't know what a trotline was but this didn't seem the moment to go into that. Tod sounded upset. He stayed seated but he wanted Cecil to know that he thought old Cecil had to be way out of line. "Four hundred and fifty bucks for this little expedition," he grumbled. There was more but it got swallowed along with swallows of beer as he went on. Greg could feel him sticking a hand out at Cecil with the fingers splayed straight out in that endearing way he had, to ward off any interruption.

"Hell of a note," he whined. "Hell of a note."

The more squeaky little big man got, the more calm Cecil sounded. He just poled and sat back, ruminating, like a big old lab, letting Tod snip and snap at him. During a pause while Tod was swallowing or opening another beer or whatever, Cecil said slowly, like read my lips, "Now, Toddy, you know better than that. Ain't nobody around here going poaching."

"Shit," Tod began but Cecil went on, explaining to Greg.

"Against the law to bag 'gators before daylight. We got us a permit but shoot, if they was to let up on that daylight thing, anybody could bag thirty, forty of these suckers a night right in this slue."

"That many?" Greg asked.

"Oh, yeah," Cecil said. "Look around."

It was too dark to see much, but when Cecil pointed Greg could make out small protuberances along the surface of the water, some not too far from the boat. The little bumps glinted. Eyes. All those things were little glittering medallion eyes looking back at him over the water's surface.

"Poaching," Tod yipped. "Four hundred and fifty smackers and the man talks about poaching. "What the crap is that all about?"

Flat freaking amazing, Greg thought. Four hundred and fifty dollars.

"Don't mean a thing to a rich man," Cecil said. "Man makes false teeth for half the dentists in—"

"Prosthetics," Tod said. "I make prosthetics."

"That's what I said," Cecil said. "Choppers, right?"

"Up yours," Tod said.

"Man hates to be reminded how he makes choppers," Cecil said. "Hey, it beat going down the row with a hoe for all dem peas. Man learns a trade in the pea patch and it makes him a rich man, he ought to be real glad he's not back in that pea patch with all the rest of the—"

"And you got a big mouth," Tod said. "You gonna quit shittin' me?"

"Nobody shittin' nobody," Cecil said, his voice soft and low. "You don't want to be reminded of the pea patch, you want to keep yourself loose and cool, friend."

Greg couldn't blame him. Tod was, more and more, beginning to sound like one of those noisy, yappy, busy-mouthed, little terriers that can't shut up and that, if you so much as turn and look at them, will fall over themselves yelping and piddling and scrabbling in circles trying to get some kind of a toe hold with their tickety, scrabbledy, little toenails.

Cecil hummed to himself, guiding the boat along the bank.

Greg tripped out, thinking of the things he could do with four hundred and fifty bucks. That had to be about what his first cello cost, half a lifetime ago, before he got long armed enough to play his dad's. It took Cathy years to pay that thing off. A person could get a used Selmer Four Sax for that kind of dough; replace the one Ginger had, that she dented, that she kept getting so mad. A person could get a root canal.

He could hear Mom on that, the root canal thing, back when it was just the two of them, when they were so hard up. "I am so sick of being poor," she said. "Where is it written that I should have to go without sleep and work two jobs so I can pay somebody to hurt me?" Poor Mom. Came home in a cold sweat that day. Sat around talking through her numb mouth.

"Now I know what a hooked fish has to feel like. No wonder they put up a fight," she said.

*****

27

Daylight came suddenly. The sun shot a red rim around the horizon and the whole sky lit up from east to west, igniting the edges of the pine and scrub and pin oaks and a lot of cypress around them on the shore.

Cecil asked Tod, "Got that rifle handy? I might try to grunt this one back up." He took the long stick he had been using to pole the boat along in both hands, shoved it deep into the water, leaned out to it, got it between his teeth and coughed and grunted.

Weird, Greg thought, plenty weird, sending those deep grunts down into the water, like talking to the lake, talking to the clay under there, to the animals, some kind of Dr. Doolittle routine. He had time to yawn nervously and blink all around before an alligator surfaced, surprisingly close to his end of the boat, a long, black, mossy looking log at the end of the line, not so much being pulled as floating toward them, moving lazily just below the surface.

Tod sputtered and stood up.

"Hold it," Cecil said.

Tod fired.

Cecil poled, putting his back into it, shoving hard, moving them away from the thrashing churning thing in the water, saying, calmly, "Jumped the gun. Well, dispatch him, friend."

The second shot splattered alligator brain and meat onto the side of the boat.

The alligator twisted and thrashed, throwing itself, stretching and doubling in on itself, stretching out again. It wouldn't stop. It went on forever, writhing, stretching out, contracting, while Tod stared, shouting, so excited he was sending out little sparkles of spit, yelling, "Dispatched him, didn't I? Yeah. Dispatched that sucker, whoo, Excedrin headache number three, dispatched him. How big do you think, Sees? How big's this one?"

"Six," Cecil said. "Seven, maybe. A grandpaw."

Greg didn't want to watch the thing but it was impossible not to. It took forever. He kept not looking at it and looking back, wishing to hell it would quit, give up and sink, wishing he never had drunk any of Tod's Bud, promising he never would do that again, never would so much as smell beer again, he'd only drink clean healthy water, milk and stuff, when he realized that what Cecil was saying, under his breath, was, "Easy, son. Dat 'gator, he don't feel a 'ting. He's doin' dem convulsions jus' like a big old dyin' chicken. You know how a chicken does? Floppin' around with a wrung neck? Gator's like dat. Gator don' die unless'n you chop clean t'rew de spine. Sometime not even den. See? Kindly like a big old floppin' chicken, you know?"

Greg didn't, but he nodded, grateful for the empathy. Cecil sounded nice, unruffled."Jus' a big old ham actor, him, don't feel nothing. No t'ing. No more." But he didn't take his eyes from the churning, splashing mess.

When it was over he asked Tod, "You want him?"

"For the hide?" Greg asked, wondering if the thing would have to be skinned.

It wouldn't. "Nyah," Tod said. "Too much trouble. And 'gators stink. Takes a Cajun to handle that." He laughed. "Stink worse than a dead Cajun. Nah. He's all yours if you want him, Sees. Let's tow bait."

Cecil started the motor and piloted them into another cove with what he said were alligator slides along a muddy red clay bank. He took a gory mass the size of a man's head that Greg really didn't want to know what it was out of a Hefty Steelsak, fastened it to a hook bigger than the head of a clothes hanger and wove and tied it into place with heavy twine.

Tod kept talking. "You got to brace yourself," he instructed. "Keep the bait up. Just kind of dandle it above the water. We're not out for hatchlings."

Balancing the bait looked like pretty heavy duty for somebody Tod's size, Greg thought, watching the way he fought the rod, grimacing, handicapped without his hands to talk with. "These suckers come right up out of the drink," Tod said. "You can keep the bait a foot up and they'll come all the way—here. You want to try it?"

No. Greg almost said it before he caught himself. No, thanks. But Tod's face started to get that cunning stupid leer that would mean big trouble. Greg moved away from him and asked, like he thought he might be being kidded, "Hatchlings?"

"That's what I said," Tod said. He snorted. "Cute little baby 'gators. They stink, too. Here, you want a turn at this or not?"

No way could Greg say, "Or not." He thought about it for a couple of seconds and took the damned pole. The bait dripped, out there. He had to ask. "What is that, anyway?"

"Dead babies," Tod said. "Right, Sees?"

Cecil busied himself at the cooler.

Tod snorted. "Any kind of dead baby will do. Cats, dogs, puppies. Puppies are the best. You have to go to the pound to get these strays."

"Hog liver," Cecil said, with a snort. "You want another beer?"

"Okay," Greg said. "Hog liver, huh? That...that's kind of what I figured." He accepted the beer and downed it quickly so he could keep holding the pole. It was kind of hard to manage the heavy pole. Took both hands. Even braced against the seat, it was clumsily heavy. "You figure something will come up? I mean, out of the water, like?"

"That's, like, the idea," Tod said, biting the end off of a cigar. "That stuff is pretty ripe. It's the stink does it. Though a 'gator'll go after about anything. I've seen 'gators could swallow a calf and never blink. They'll grab anything, haul it down and shove it under something to rot. That's what they do. They like things ripe but they'll go after anything. Dogs, hogs, cranes. They love cranes. And skinny legged kids with big feet. We have people get killed by 'gators every season."

Greg hung onto the pole, keeping the bait near the surface, watching the flat, reflecting, scummy water, while they cruised slowly, sometimes silently, with Cecil poling, all along the edges of the lake. Every once in a while Tod would stand up and pee. He was, as Cecil put it, giving beer hell. Greg had downed too many beers. As the air got more warm, the motion of the boat, or something, sort of made him not feel all that great about having any more. Tod kept offering him another, not all that off-handedly, until he felt compelled to make excuses: "I guess I'm not that much of a beer drinker," he said. "Especially, you know, so early. Maybe my little go 'round with that canned heat stuff tore up my stomach so bad that it's shot my stomach."

Cecil grunted an approving grunt but Tod's head swayed side to side. "No drinking companions around here, I don't guess," he complained. "Cecil's afraid of the water, for one thing. He hardly will join a man in a beer in the boat."

"I drink what I want when I want," Cecil said, with a sideways look at Greg. "This my shootin' fish in a barrel boat. Tod forgets dat. Tod forgets who de boss man in de boat, eh? But den—" His voice changed. "— Toddy likes to live dangerous. He surely does."

Greg let the bait dip and touch the water's surface for a second then and almost lost the pole. The bait didn't flip or move around. It dove. Down. The pole slid in his hands. The hook flashed in the sunlight.

Came up clean.

"He's quick," Cecil sympathized. "Maybe he wants to see do we got some more of dat?"

"Noah, let's don't keep futzing around in the same places." Tod swiveled restlessly. "You know any better spots? Let's check the rest of the lines."

They rounded a bend and Cecil poled the boat past a stand of Cypress, gold against the sky, and tall grasses, gray and flat, with a salty piney scent, along the bank. One of the lines there pulled straight out from the bank into a tangle of Cypress root.

Cecil suggested they be patient. "He's on his way up, dis one," he said. "Once that hook is set, he don' got much choice no more. He don't know what it is, but I guarantee dis one he got to be hurting."

Greg's stomach lifted and sank. His throat filled with a hot, beery, sour sensation.

He's got to be hurting.

He realized what that gleaming hook reminded him of: a time when he was five or six and he had tried to jump from the garage roof to a shed where there were hooks lined up for a clothes line. He'd swung out and reached up and caught one of those mean steel hooks in the palm of his left hand and yanked back on it as he fell. The mark from the row of stitches was still there in his palm. He looked at it, remembering how he'd bawled, how everybody had to hold him down so they could clean it up and work on it, and then, trying not to think about that, he realized something else: he did, too, know a little something about alligators. From that same summer. When he was five.

At the zoo when he was five, a goofy, foggy, little kid in a crowd of people all bending down trying to get him to see something, yes, he could see them, couldn't he? Right there, in that clump of grass, see? But he couldn't, for the longest time, all he could see was rocks and shadows until he grabbed Cathy's hand and said why didn't they go back to the monkey house but then there they were, the alligators. One big one, a scaly log on legs came out, trundling along surprisingly fast and another one turned in on it. Their mouths opened. They both had their mouths open. They flipped, rolled together, big tails slamming around, thrashing, until the biggest one snapped. His jaws slammed shut like a car door with the other 'gator's leg caught, flattened in that long snout of a mouth.

And they stayed like that. They just lay like that, absolutely still.

Greg's mom grabbed him up and hurried away with him. He tried to get down. He had to see what was happening back there but she hung on to him, walked away with him kicking at her because he had to see what was going on back there. He couldn't believe it. He couldn't believe that his mother would just walk away and leave those big animals like that. He tried to make her understand that they couldn't do that but she didn't want to talk about it, not then, not ever.

Cecil poled until they got right up to the bank. Then he led them up to some rocks so Tod could get positioned before the alligator came up. As it came, Cecil pulled on the rope. Tod got over next to him and stood there with his knees flexed and the rifle up at his shoulder, aimed at the place where the rope met the water, grinning, showing all his teeth, even some with gold tops on them in the back of his mouth.

Cecil glanced at Greg and rolled his eyes. He didn't let up on the rope but he started grunting, like half singing to himself, ruminating, quietly, "Toddy my boy, oh, Toddy, my boy, we shootin' fish in a barrel, my boy. Jambalaya, crawfish pie...."

This time, when the head broke the surface and the gun went off, Greg was ready. He had his fingers in his ears, looking away, watching some kind of a crane walking along, balancing on long, bright pink legs. Tod looked up and caught him like that, squinting and holding his ears, while the echoes of the blast faded and the dying animal moiled and thrashed in its endless throes.

So many expressions crossed Tod's face so fast that Greg thought, for a couple of seconds, that he might be kidding around. He looked amazed and drunk and cunning as hell and, finally, disgusted.

Well, Greg told himself, that's what I get for turning into the wimp of the universe.

But what got to him, what really got to him, was the stupidly gleeful look on the old boy's face, even while he let himself look about half sick with disgust. Like he got a some kind of a kick out of being disgusted. Opening up his nostrils and the whole bit.

The next kill wasn't as big as the first. It was lying up on the bank, sunning. Cecil brought the boat in as close as he could with the motor running and the thing never moved. Greg was sort of hoping it might be dead but it wasn't. Cecil poled the boat closer and closer. "He ain't in any hurry," he said. "He got fifty years or so, way he sees it."

That one was an easier shot, but he died just as hard.

Cecil said to watch the tail. The tail was the dangerous part, he said. "Lot of hell in that tail. It's pure muscle."

"Kind of like them little DQ Cuties," Tod said. He slid down on one knee while the animal writhed and splashed. After he got his legs under him he went over and sank down in the back of the boat, about half asleep, not even noticing when they went through a cloud of gnats or answering when Cecil looked at him and suggested it might not be a bad idea to go somewhere dry and get something to eat.

One of the times when he didn't get an answer, Cecil turned to Greg. "Well, boy. Now you been on a 'gator hunt. What you t'ink? What do you say we get on back?"

"Yes, sir," Greg said.

"So, what do you think?" Cecil asked again. Greg was so glad to be heading back and so warmed by the friendly low voice that he let down his guard. He just said the first thing that came to mind.

"Well, sir, if you don't have any use for them as trophies or, like, the skins or whatever, it's kind of like what you keep saying, isn't it? Like shooting fish in a barrel?"

Cecil lifted his big shoulders and let them drop. His face creased in a sad old smile. "You got it," he said.

He was still smiling when Tod came roaring up out of his stupor. "What did he say? What was that, kid?" He spat over the side of boat.

Cecil started the motor but Tod yelled over it, "Now what the hell is that supposed to mean, huh? Shootin' fish in a—"

"That's what Cecil says," he stammered. "I'm just agreeing with him."

"Hell, man," Cecil said. "Sit down. Be yourself."

Oh, don't be yourself, Greg thought, but Tod was going to be himself, anyone could see that, Tod was off and running, hands waving, yelling about why was the damned boat turning around? He didn't recall suggesting that they turn around and what the hell was all that about shooting fish in a barrel, smart ass kid. Cecil and Greg couldn't even look at each other.

Right then, Greg realized something. Cecil couldn't stand Toddy because he was on to him. Because what Tod was, was like a reptile, one of those little lizards that change into whatever color they're sitting on. When Tod was around Cecil, he tried too hard to sound like Cecil. When he was around Cathy, he got all precise and careful. He even aped the stammer sometimes, not knowing he was doing it. Whoever he was around, that's who Tod sounded like. And he made a really stupid Cajun. Somebody like Cecil wouldn't even let somebody like Tod hold the door for him, if the old boy didn't pick up the tab, and all. Maybe not even then.

All he is is some kind of an actor, Greg thought. A not very good actor who can't turn himself off, can't even shut up when it's falling apart.

"A real smart ass," Tod said, louder. "What we've got here is a real smart kid."

Cecil watched the water and the trees.

"Smart talks his mama all the time," Tod yelled." Real, real smart. Like you wouldn't believe." He leaned all the way forward with his chest on his knees so he could punch Greg on the arm. "Real funny."

Greg swallowed hard and tried to lean away. He rubbed his arm.

"Hey, Sees, you ever smart talk your mama?"

Cecil acted like couldn't hear it as long as he could but when he decided it wouldn't let up, he said no, hell, no, he knew better than to smart mouth his mama, like he hoped that would shut little big man up. "Me? My mama get my attention with a two by four, I tried dat." He gave Tod a friendly slap on the shoulder that sat him back down. "Hell, man, you ever meet my mama? She wear high heels and a low neckline. My mama'd tow me behind the boat for bait."

Tod wasn't satisfied with that. He got into a half crouch and pounded at Greg to make his point. "Makes me hot ever' time I think about it," he squealed." You wouldn't believe it. I can hardly believe it myself."

"Aw, Tod."

"No, I'm serious. You want to know what he calls her? He calls his mama 'shot, dumb and no good.' She tells me about this. 'Shot, dumb and no good.' You believe that? She told me about that right in front of him. He's sitting there smiling like a damn' ape. More'n once I heard about it."

He probably had, Greg thought, wildly. That whole thing was one of Cathy's pet routines from 'way back when Greg was in the Little League. It had gotten embarrassing but he couldn't get her to see. She'd go into it every once in a while, even now, he could hear her: "Oh, he was so proud, my baby, trying so hard. He hit this ball with all his might, all the way up into the sky. Up, up, it went. And down it came—we're all screaming like crazy—down it came, plop, into Sue Ellen's little boy's glove, but I couldn't stop screaming. Well, I was surrounded. Because I was on the wrong side of the bleachers because I'd run over to talk to Sue Ellen for a minute. Boy. Greggy was so ticked. He stood glaring at me out of this sweaty little face. He wouldn't even get into the car when it was time to leave. He just walked away. Walked all the way home. That night, when I went to tuck him in he said, 'Mom, you're shot, dumb and no good.'"

Not that that was the kind of thing Tod would ever understand.

"Listen," Greg shouted, trying to explain. "That's a family joke, something that happened a long time ago and Mom just—"

"Mom just what?" Tod couldn't sit still.

"She comes up with it any time she wants to make a point about how unathletic she is. Well, and I am, I guess. And about how she, well, about not getting the concept. Being shot, dumb and—that's what we call it."

"The way I see it is, it's a lot of shit," Tod said. "And no kid lives in my house is gonna put that shit over on his mama if I can help it." He'd gotten to where he could get in a barrage of punches at Greg's upper arm.

Greg figured the man had to hate being ignored but he couldn't think of anything he could do.

*****

28

He didn't even dare look over at Cecil. He was huddled down staring at the tops of his knees when the boat lurched and he saw Tod's shadow come across and there he was, Tod, crouched, practically spitting in his ear and on the back of his neck, halfway standing up in the boat.

"Easy, Toddy," Cecil said.

"Don't easy me," Tod said. Greg got his arms up around his head. He glanced over his shoulder, wondering where the rifle was, wondering what he could do, when Cecil turned off the motor and said, in the sudden quiet, "Easy, man." He hunkered up closer and added, "Now, boys. Maybe you ain't used to being around boats, much, Greg, but nobody gets stupid in my boat, understand?" He had gotten in front of Tod's face. All Tod could see was Cecil's back and the back of his head and there's Cecil, giving Greg a big stage wink, saying, like he didn't know any better, "You better watch yourself, sonny." Then he turned around and drawled, "You, too, my man. Sit you'se'f down."

Greg glanced up to see Tod relax. Sort of.

He let out his breath in relief. Big mistake. Tod drew back and aimed a wobbly punch at him. It glanced off his shoulder. Greg grabbed both sides of the boat and ducked.

Cecil heaved a big tired sigh. "Sit, goddam it," he said, biting it off. "Sit your ass down." Tod looked up. They locked eyes. Greg thought, for about ten hammers of his heart, that the big man was going to grab a hand full of that happy hair and belt old Toddy right into the swamp.

What he did was put his big palm flat on top of Tod's head and shove. "Sit," he said. "And stay."

Like saying it to a dog.

Tod stayed, sullen and red-eyed, until he collapsed into a snoring doze while Cecil was bringing the boat all the way up to its shed. Tod slumped into a heap and snored away while Cecil and Greg got him out of the boat and put the boat up and emptied the water out of the ice chest. When they were ready to get back into the car, Cecil sort of propped the little guy up against the car so he could ease the keys out of his pocket.

"Tell you what," he crooned, "I guarantee you want to get some shut eye, don't you want to? Get yourself a little shut eye, let old Cecil take you on home. Later on, you get to feelin' better, you can take the wheel."

Tod sank down into a heap on the back seat and snored.

"You know how to do the Macarena?" Cecil asked Greg, out of the side of his mouth.

"The dance?" Greg said. "Why?"

"Well, you wanna see the DWI Macarena?" Cecil grinned, slapped his hands on his arms, his shoulders, the back of his neck, stuck his hands together out behind him, leaned his brow against the car and spread his legs. "Dat's de one whar you get de pretty handcuffs," he said. "You don' wan' dat, I guarantee."

That was pretty much the last of the Cajun accent. As they were easing out onto the road and he was resetting the cruise control, he glanced over at Greg and asked, "You all right?"

"Yes, sir," Greg said. "Now I am."

"Yeah," Cecil said. He glanced into the back seat. "Likes to live dangerously, your stepdaddy," he said. "He surely does."

"Yes, sir," Greg said.

That's about all anybody said until they got all the way past Shepherd, where Cecil said why didn't they get a cup of coffee at the Dairy Queen.

Greg didn't feel that wonderful, physically, and Cecil didn't seem to be all that talkative basically, once you got him out of his boat but Greg said okay, why not, thinking maybe old Cecil wanted a chance to flirt with one of those DQ Cuties that he and Tod had sounded so thrilled about. They left old Toddy snoring away in the back seat.

They were the only customers in the place. The girl who took their order—just two coffees—looked something like Meg Ryan, a real pretty girl with a big smile, but she didn't smile like she knew Cecil or anything and Cecil hardly even smiled back at her. When she went behind the counter at the other end of the room and started talking on a telephone back there, Cecil sat and looked at Greg. Like he had something to say. But he didn't say anything. For a long time.

Just sat there looking at Greg. Greg didn't want to look back, especially; it was kind of embarrassing the way the old boy looked under the fluorescent lights with the bright sun coming in the window. He had this rheumy-eyed look and these saggy, sad, wrinkled lines down his dark face with the stubble. After a couple of minutes Greg got uncomfortable and said, "What?"

"He's a pain in the ass, eh?" Cecil said. He sighed. "My partner."

"Yeah," Greg said, and did a double take. "Your partner? You're one of Tod's partners?"

Cecil shrugged. "Only one, far as I know." His laugh kind of hissed; came out through his teeth. "What you call silent. Man's got a chunk of my money in that chopper factory."

"But...." Greg was really confused. "How come? I mean, why?"

Cecil's eyebrows went up. "Why not?"

"I didn't think you two were, well. Such big buddies."

Cecil ran his tongue over his teeth. "Been real lucrative. Up until lately. Choppers is what you call a high profit item. So far, anyways."

Their coffee came. Greg put in his two creamers and both of Cecil's when he pushed them over to him and a couple of sugar cubes. The coffee was hot. He sipped at it anyway, trying to get over being so surprised. "So you're the partner he keeps saying is going to kill him for the insurance." His voice squeaked and he swallowed and brought it back down. "So why didn't you let him? You know, back there when he was horsing around? He could've fallen out of the boat. He almost did."

Cecil smiled. "My boat. Now, wouldn't that be a hell of a thing."

Greg smiled back, getting more nervous. "Besides, I was there."

Cecil shook his head. "Yeah." He grinned.

Greg thought for a minute. "You'd be the first one they'd look for?"

Cecil nodded. "And you'd come next, eh?" His coffee had to be boiling—Greg's was, even with all the cream—but he swallowed it in a couple of gulps. "Nope," he said. "That's not how it goes. Not like dat, eh?" He had a real cold smile. His eyes stayed half shut. "You know that Frankie Sinatra song? How he does it his way?"

Greg nodded.

"That's what Toddy goin' to have to do," Cecil said. "Do it his way. One of dese days. No?"

"Are you—is this like some kind of a plan we're talking about here?" Greg wondered if the older man could see how hard his heart was hammering away in his cheste. "Because I don't know if I could actually—"

Cecil smiled and Greg shut up. Swallowed and shut up.

"Oh, yeah, you could, son." Cecil looked like he knew everything. A lot more than he wanted to. The lines around his mouth sank in like furrowed granite. "You don't want to be thinkin' along those lines. That's the kind of thing gets you the pea patch." He wiped his mouth and slid out of the booth. "Let's go."

Outside, in the parking lot, he stopped for a second, still smiling that bored tired smile but sounding more friendly. "Man likes to live dangerously," he said. He shook his head. "Surely does, eh?"

Like Greg knew what that meant. Like it was some kind of message.

The rest of the way to Houston they moved right along, Greg not feeling terrific and old Tod snoring away in the back seat. Cecil didn't tailgate or anything. He just sort of let the Caddy go with the flow up 59 and around the 610 loop to the Gulf freeway. Cecil said he had a friend worked all his life on the Gulf freeway from the time he was a kid. His whole working life, he said, and the crazy freeway still under construction. "You got to keep an eye out, on this thing," he said.

He was one hell of a driver. Good thing. Outside of LaMarque when they were doing eighty or so a tanker skidded sideways into a concrete support practically right in front of them. Cecil didn't even grunt or sit up straight. He stayed totally relaxed. Wheeled them gently on around and past and back into their lane like it was nothing.

He never did touch that damn horn.

*****

29

Cathy came running out of the house and there was Gregory climbing out of the car to bow from the waist and point, with a sardonic little flourish, a twirl of his fingers, at Tod, a snarfling burbling mess in the back seat, smelling faintly of vomit. Dead drunk.

Greg and that big animal of a person that Tod kept calling his good buddy had to carry her drunken husband up the stairs and dump him into his bed. And after that, after that terrible man went away, Greg didn't even want to talk to her.

"Was it...awful?" she asked.

"Was what awful?" He made the word sound silly.

"Greg. Greggy. Come on."

"Piece of cake," he said. "Naw. Shootin' fish in a barrel, actually." He closed his eyes. "That's what Tod's partner calls it."

"His partner?"

"Yeah," Greg opened his eyes and looked at her. He yawned. "Tod's business partner. Good old Sees. You didn't know?"

"Oh, surely not."

"Oh, surely. Ask Tod," Greg said. "If and when he wakes up." He yawned again. "Good old Cecil. Good old Cecil has plans for our boy." He snickered. "You don't want to know."

"That...that lumbering lout?" Cathy said, astonished.

"He's not so bad," Greg said.

"What do you mean, plans?" Cathy demanded.

"Like I said, you don't want to know," Greg said. "Neither do I." He waved her off and went shambling toward the stairs. "He as good as told me that," he said. "That I don't want to know. I think he's going to figure out some way to have the old boy do himself in. Any time now. Fine with me. How about you?"

Cathy paced in circles. Tried to read. Tried to get to sleep, but she couldn't. She kept seeing Greg's pale tired face. Bruised circles under his eyes. His weary exasperation: "You don't want to know." A young old man, now. Shutting her out. Again.

The next morning Tod got up and silently stole off to work.

And Greg refused to get out of bed. Again. Cathy went in to look at him and went and cried in the shower until the water ran cold. Then she toweled off, yanked on her jeans, found an old cardigan and walked to the beach. The silent chill made her glad of the sweater.

A leggy kid rode up on a blue bike, pedaling slowly on the packed sand along the water's edge, the wind lifting his hair. As he came abreast of her he stopped and got off to pick up the bike and carry it up to the seawall. He smiled at her. He looked carefree, his head back, smiling easily. So...red-cheeked. Why aren't you in school? Cathy wondered. Can't your mother make you get dressed and go to school?

Do you have a drunken stepfather and a big stupid dull mother so greedy for a house and car and husband—any man—anything in pants— that she'll do anything, put up with anything, just to keep on keeping on?

She walked along the water's edge, stepping sideways to avoid tarry detritus and sargassum weed, looking for shark's teeth and the great heart shells that the Gulf sometimes gives up in the winter. The Gulf washed up, washed up, gray and calm, the no-color color of the sky. Long, crestless waves pulled slowly, quietly back, mounded and waited before they flattened, moving up in dimpling ripples on the reflecting sand.

A small yellow Tonka truck lay on a partially submerged log. Abandoned by someone's big-headed, skinny-necked, little boy. He'd probably mourn the loss of it. Greg used to love his Tonkas.

What a serious, good, little kid he was. Incapable of subterfuge. No. That wasn't quite true. There had been a time when he'd lied. About peeking at the Christmas presents on the closet shelf. And she'd overreacted preaching at him far too long. He'd been too young to know why she'd gone off the deep end, so disturbed about seeing his eyes slide away from hers that it frightened her to see him but she couldn't bear being lied to. Not by Greg. "You are damaging yourself," she'd told him. "You'll wreck yourself, doing that. You can't lie and still be all right. Lying is—like breaking some fundamental law, like the law of gravity. You just break yourself against it." He'd sat and listened, round-eyed, worried, his head tilted, too heavy for its slender stem. A dear little towheaded copy of his dad, with his dad's heavy pale eyebrows over his dad's gray blue eyes.

Now he lied to her all the time and she pretended not to notice. Everybody lied to her.

Walking helped.

Greg was still asleep when she got home.

What she ought to do, she knew, was put together a resume. Get the Houston paper. Check the classifieds. Call darling Patrick and Chub. See about finding a job, a new place to live, begin, somehow. Alone. Again.

Just thinking about it made her weary. And old and sick with sorrow.

She went to the garage and started her car, meaning to go to Randall's for some detergent, but for a couple of minutes she just sat thinking how a person wasn't supposed to ever sit like that, with the motor running and the doors closed. Though maybe the stacked-up boxes and mess in this garage would absorb some of the fumes. Carbon dioxide, or whatever.

She wondered how long it would take.

Whether Greg would be the one to find her.

She climbed out of the car. Went back into the kitchen. Got the garage door opener and drove around the driveway and out into the street. She passed Randall's and was all the way up the Seawall to Wal-Mart before she realized what she really wanted.

Everybody in Wal-Mart—all the people in the smocks with the tags that meant they worked there—seemed preoccupied with unloading or counting. "Do you have any black hats?" she asked a man who was unloading celery. He looked over his shoulder and raised his eyebrows.

"Never mind," she said, suddenly aware of how stupid that sounded. Wal-Mart did have hats, though. A chubby woman in Women's Wear helped her find them. She picked out a ridiculous black hat, black felt, with a scratchy black veil and a cock feather. Just the thing. And a black suit. Polyester, but almost a hundred dollars. At Wal-Mart, for heaven's sakes. A hundred and four dollars with the hat.

"Could you put both of these somewhere? Under the counter or in back or something?" Cathy didn't have a hundred dollars. "I'll come back for them. I...I seem to have the wrong purse."

The woman looked dubious. "You be coming right back?"

"I don't know, I don't know," Cathy muttered, suddenly so embarrassed that she was afraid she might burst into tears.

"Aw," the woman said. "Is this, like, for a funeral?"

"Yes," Cathy whispered, nodding, but the woman still couldn't put the dress and hat under the counter or whatever.

On the way back to the house she tried to justify spending that much money on a suit and hat, in case she really did decide to go back and get them. Just to herself, of course. She wouldn't even discuss it with Tod.

Maybe she could use the suit to go job hunting. The thought of job hunting made her feel sick and hollow. The look of the classifieds. "Apt. Locator. Payment upon move in." "Topnotch Telemarketer. Evening shift avail." "Subscription Sales Crew Mgrs."

She stood outside the house for a couple of minutes, looking up at the pillared front, the cherubic carved faces antic in twinkling shafts of sunlight. Her house. Where she belonged, now.

How often have I seen Tod drunk, anyway? she thought and immediately could hear herself telling someone, a lawyer maybe or a judge: "My husband drinks too much and he has all these foes that seem so desperate because he's such a...he has a dreadful past...." Past. The key word. Past.

Except...except for that little girl. Gloria's little girl.

Okay. Sick, then. He's sick. Do people abandon people because they're sick? Throw them out and walk away?

She went inside and sat down and tried to make a list, a decision making list, the way she always had to do, to decide anything at all, and wrote, "works hard" and tore up the paper, furious at herself. The whole thing was beginning to feel like those silly letters to Dear Abby: "He wants to be a good husband and father and he's a good provider but he's a terrible person and oh, dear me, I'm so unhappy."

She went up and hurt her hand pounding on Greg's door. "Wake up. Enough of this."

Greg would not open his eyes. He claimed to not have a hangover but when Cathy brought tea and toast into his room he groaned, dashed into the bathroom and made retching noises. After he came out he said please could she be quiet and please could she not open any drapes as he rolled away with a blanket and pillow around his head.

"Every Monday we go through this. Every single Monday. I've lost track of how much school you've missed. Greg, we have to talk."

He didn't think so.

The phone interrupted them. It was Tod, telling her to not leave the house, please, because he'd ordered burglar bars. The men were to install them right away.

"Today? We have to talk about this." Cathy hated the idea of burglar bars. "All over our lovely windows? Oh, please."

"The boys are on the way there. Those are gonna be our safe windows," Tod said. "A lot of weird shit going on, baby. No point in not doing what we have to protect ourselves."

"What sort of weird—oh, Tod, I wish you wouldn't say that word."

"Right," he said. "This outfit gave me a good rate. Man's got a crew he needs to keep busy and he put a pretty sharp point to his pencil. You know what the numbers are now on burglaries in Galveston? Bad news.

Bad news. This outfit does custom work. We'll talk about it tonight."

"N-n-no," Cathy said. "Please." Vehemence brought back the stammer but it didn't matter. She was talking haltingly to a dial tone.

The burglar bar company truck pulled up within the hour. Two men, bearded and pony-tailed, got out and knocked on the door. They had a contract they said. They'd been doing this for twenty years. They didn't have time to spare. They set up shop in the garage and the driveway in front, sawing and welding metal bars. It took them a very long time to encage the massive carved front door. The beautiful old bay windows had to have their metal scrolls cut to size before they could be sunk into holes they would gouge into the solid wood of the inside sills.

Their drilling set Cathy's teeth on edge.

"I'm going to have a terrible time with this," she told one of the men. "I once locked up a whole wall of filing cabinets in an office by leaning back against a lock. It was a little sticking out thing that nobody ever had touched. Nobody had any idea where the key was and the office manager was furious. Some of us just don't get along very well with locks, I guess."

"That so?" the man said amiably. "These things take a key." He went on measuring and drilling and hammering and soldering, scarcely taking time to drink the coffee she made for them.

She sat and watched the men and drank three cups, wondering how Greg could sleep through all that noise, before she decided to run a load of wash. Tod had been campaigning to have Greg wash his own things. She meant to go along with that but it didn't seem to be working very well. He seemed to be getting more and more scuzzy. "Is that clean?" she'd ask and he'd say his T-shirt was the cleanest of the lot and shoot her a look.

She started another pot of coffee and trotted out to load the washer. Her clothes and what was in the hamper didn't make much of a load. Greg's windbreaker was shamefully grimy, she remembered. She went to fetch it.

Greg didn't even hear her knock. He slept, gently drooling, placidly making honking noises, while she searched for the windbreaker which had gotten, for some reason, well to the back of his messy closet. It had to be worked free and there was something the matter with it. The thing felt puffy and crackly. Something in the lining seemed to have gone stiff and crunchy, deteriorated, maybe. Like old foam rubber.

It looked like he'd used it to put out a fire.

Cathy wondered whether it was even worth washing but she gathered it up, telling herself she'd have to ask him about that awful burned rope scent, how in the world did he get his jacket as whiffy as that? Had he been sleeping in a charred hammock?

There were other smelly things in his room, too. Socks and underwear and a couple of shirts and some pretty awful jeans. And more clothes spread all over the room. A full load.

She got the wash started and was back in the kitchen morosely watching the burglar bar men drill holes inside the windows in there, thinking she ought to be out buying a *Chronicle*, when the washing machine went berserk, banging around, out in the garage. The thing was off balance again, hurling itself against the wall.

There was something peculiar floating around in it. Some strange stuff had gotten into the water. It had garbage in it. Saran Wrap and a couple of Ziplock baggies and what looked like trash. The water looked the way the sink looked when the dishwasher drained into the disposal full of garbage. All nasty with weeds, leaves and stems and brownish flotsam circling around and around, too much to drain. Cathy scooped out a palm full and squeezed it, trying to determine what in blazes it could possibly be. She'd wiped it from her hand and was resetting the machine when it hit her. Pot. That had to be pot. Her washing machine was chugging away with a messy mess of marijuana floating and plastic wrap going around and around in it.

She turned the machine off and fished Greg's jacket out. No wonder it had felt so crackly and peculiar. The thing had been a marijuana scarecrow. The stuff looked like herbs. Like sage or tea or...or marijuana.

She yanked the wet load of clothes out of the washer, her heart banging around in her chest, out of balance, while she scooped out most of the mess into a trash bag and reset the washing machine to empty itself.

She went into the kitchen. Walked in circles. Went out to the front lawn. Walked in circles. Walked faster, in bigger circles, telling herself to be calm, remember what the Parent Teacher's group had said about this very situation, what the principal had said, what all those articles in the women's magazines kept saying a person was supposed to do: stay calm. Avoid panic. Keep the lines of communication open.

The washer was empty. She reset it, dumped in the clothes and some more detergent and walked calmly up to Greg's room, breathing deeply and evenly.

He looked so happily stupidly innocent she couldn't stand it. "Wake up, wake up, pot-headed moron," she hissed, trying not to scream at him. "I'm going to call Patrick. You certainly need a psychiatrist. Maybe what you really need is to be clubbed like a bloody baby seal oh, you ought to see what's stuck in a big mess in the washing machine right this minute where in the hell did you get so much of that filthy mess anyway wake up wake up will you wake up?"

Greg sat up, owl-eyed, his hair sticking up in goofy, damp, little tufts, blinking at her. "Baby seal? What big mess? I haven't been anywhere near the washing machine. What's your problem?"

He flopped back down on the pillows with his eyes squeezed shut. She grabbed him by the hair and the arm and shook him, hard. He flopped in her hands for a second before he jerked away and fended her off.

"I could kill you I could just kill you now I know how now I know about you oh sure, a psychiatrist, that's it," she hissed. "Right now, right away, pot head, yes, yes." Afraid the burglar bar men could hear her— they'd gotten quiet out there—she kept screaming softly, shaking him.

"What what what?" Greg yelled back. He got his big bony arms around his head, to bruise her hands against. He was so wobbly-headed, round-eyed, thickly stupid that the silly sight of him put her beside herself, made her stand outside herself, listening to herself choke and stammer.

"Pot pot the washer p-p-put pot in the d-d-d-damned draining cycle." She stopped, panting, and said he had to get dressed, he had to, because they were going to Houston right now, right this minute, because she couldn't handle him, maybe Pat and Chub could do something. "Your little secret is out, mister. Right down the drain."

Ah. He woke wide awake, head to toe. His legs churned beneath the sheet. He came up so fast he nearly bumped her chin with his head. "Hey! Let's give this a minute, Mom. Easy." Then, bearing down, his voice so urgently adult that it silenced her, "Tell me I heard that wrong. The washer? My jacket's in the washer?"

He fell into the closet, scrabbled around, threw things, shoes, pillows, a magazine. Came out wall eyed, tripping, righting himself against her with both hands: "Holy shit. With soap?" His hands lifted in a prayerful steeple. "Not with soap, Mom!"

"Of course with soap," Cathy said. "Well. Detergent."

"All, all of it?" he cried, hoarsely, over his shoulder, running now, thump, thump, nearly bumping into the burglar bar men carrying a metal frame, swerving past them through the kitchen and out to the utility room.

Cathy followed him. They stood and watched the washing machine carry a few brown bits of weed and seeds and stems at the edge of the water that spun into a vortex and were sucked into the drain. Greg slammed the off button with his fist. He leaned against the machine and held his brow, his face contorted. "Oh, most holy holy shit," he breathed.

He stayed like that for so long that Cathy had time to calm down. She said why didn't they go into the house and see what sense might be made of all this. He looked unfocused.

"Greg? Gregory? You're scaring me."

He waved a hand and let it fall.

"I mean it," she said.

"All of it," he said.

"What's that mean?"

"Well, Mother, obviously, I guess what that means is it's gone. And most of it doesn't happen to belong to me."

"How can that be?"

"That can be because most of it belonged to other people," he said, his voice hollow, his face so haggard that, as the implication of that sank in, they changed roles. Now she was frantic. He'd have to take the wheel.

"What other people?" she whispered.

"Some guys," he said, distractedly. "I'm going to have to...I'm gonna have to...I don't know what. Think. I'm gonna have to think. Now."

"Oh, please, talk to me. Tell me about whatever all this is," Cathy said. "Please?"

When they got back to the kitchen one of the burglar bar men asked her opinion of one of the kitchen windows. "Yes yes," Cathy told him. "Excellent splendid. I'm crazy about it."

"What's going on here?" Greg asked but he didn't wait for an answer. He went into his room and closed the door. When Cathy knocked on it he said to let him get dressed.

She got a cup of coffee and waited.

She never did get a satisfactory explanation. The dope wasn't entirely his, he said, when he finally appeared. It was to have been shared. "You don't just go out and buy yourself that kind of stash," he said. It's not like rice or beans."

"No," Cathy said. "It's felonious. What sort of friends can these be?"

A sort she wouldn't understand, he said. Friends. Indeed.

Listening to him, to his creaky voice, watching his eyes slide past her and away, she flashed on a time when he and another boy had hitchhiked to South Padre and then insisted they'd ridden all that way with some "friends." She might never have known that they'd hitchhiked at all but the other boy had tipped her, giggling, "Anybody who gives us a ride is a friend, right?"

"What kind of friends would—"

"Don't worry about it."

"Please don't keep saying that. You frighten me, saying that, looking like that."

"Well, it's my problem, isn't it? I don't want you to feel—"

"Don't tell me how to feel. Nobody can tell anybody how to feel, don't you know that?" She got up and moved to a barred window to watch the men working outside. "My son, the dope dealer."

"No, no, no. Mother. Don't go ape on me, okay? That's all I need." He scrubbed at his scalp and his face, trying to make a smile for her. "Shees. What a way to wake a person up."

Cathy went to him and held him against her. He was Gregory after all, her Greg, with his sleepy cowlicks, yawning nervously, looking at her with a sad, rueful grimace. "We have to talk," Cathy said.

He groaned. "Could I eat something first?"

She left him lying across the bed, went down to the kitchen and busied herself getting out bread, separating slices of bacon, getting eggs out of the refrigerator, breaking them into the sizzle of hot butter, thinking that no matter what happened there was always the need to fix food and the benefice of hot food. Even if someone died. The scent of bacon and coffee. Bread toasting. Maybe throwing in the towel and starting all over again was a terrible idea. She and Greg needed this full pantry, this refrigerator full of good and wholesome sustenance.

This kitchen isn't going to be awful forever, she told herself. It is mine, she thought, hugging herself, my kitchen. And my boy just might need a man around, if only to pay for his messes. Until he grows up.

Greg came down to eat and drink and watch the burglar bar men drill and saw and clank their bars into place. "Unreal. Is this unreal?"

"Just start at the beginning," Cathy said. "I have to know. Not knowing is worse than anything. You have to talk to me, Gregory. You have to."

"Okay," Greg said. "Swell. What'll we talk about. You want to lend me a few hundred dollars?"

She gaped and Greg yawned. "Don't sweat it."

"Is that how much that stuff was worth?"

"Like I said. Don't sweat it." She was dismissed. He chewed and swallowed.

"Are you joking? Because that's a terrible joke, son."

"Yeah," he said. "I'm joking. Sorry. I'm a terrible joker. Wild." He looked around. "Bars, huh? Nice cage we're getting to have here. We going to keep the man in a cage now?"

"Possibly we could ask him to help you—help us—out, again. With whatever you have to—"

Greg put his fork down. "Possibly not," he said, imitating her. "P-p-possibly n-neither of us want to let little big man in on any part of this, d-do we? Think about it." He glared and Cathy retreated.

The men didn't finish with the burglar bars until late afternoon. They gathered up their tools and every bit of their untidiness and went away, leaving bars that cast long shadows on the walls all day and, in some places, at night, even with the muslin and the drapes drawn across the windows. The bars could be unlocked quickly but Cathy wasn't at all sure she wouldn't have trouble with them if she ever needed them open in a hurry. The keys looked small; the kind that would be easily lost.

Tod said he was a belt and suspenders man. He had an alarm system installed, too, right after the bars were in.

Two days after the burglar bars were put in, the Brinks people came and made a sawdusty mess installing wires around windows and over the door. They left a small vanilla box with an eye in it. The light shone clear when the alarm was set and an unwinking red, diabolical as a demon's eye, when the damned silly thing was in need of attention.

The bars didn't look the way Tod thought they would. He kept saying they'd get used to them but every time he came home he'd walk around looking at the shadows on the floors, glancing up from window to window with a restive frown. Sometimes he looked up from the television or from reading as if something made him suddenly aware of them. Cathy'd catch him hunching and unhunching his shoulders, gazing at the play of light through the bars on the floor in front of his recliner. If he noticed her gazing at him, he'd get exasperated and flap a hand at her, as if to say it didn't matter. His fingernails were gnawed to the quick. He kept worrying at them, trying to find new places to chew.

Watching him, Cathy kept hearing Greg's caustic words: "We gonna keep little big man in a cage, now?"

The cage might be my doing, to some extent, she thought. At any rate, Tod seemed to be working hard to pay for it.

Three weeks after the burglar bars and the alarm system were installed Tod came home with the guns; a long heavy rifle; two wicked looking revolvers and a shotgun that he said could blow a man in half.

"You don't even have to aim this baby," he said, hefting it. He wanted to hand it to Cathy but she shook her head and backed away. "Too bad we can't stick a sign on that door or out there somewhere," he muttered. "'Shotgun spoken here.' Get the word out to some of those lowlifes."

"Oh, surely not," Cathy said, her stomach in a knot.

"This one's easy," he said, sighting along the gun, one of his eyes squinted shut. "Just point her in the right direction and pull this. Blam."

"Don't keep pointing it at the refrigerator," she said, trying to be calm. "If you have to shoot something, why don't you aim at our terrible sink?"

When she giggled, Tod laughed, too, a high strained noise, as out of control as her silly neighing. "Even you could use this baby." He looked at her with a lopsided grin. "Not exactly your style, though, is it, my lady?"

Something about the words "style" and "lady" drove her over the edge. Cathy just...lost it. She couldn't stop giggling, her hands over her mouth, flashing—trying not to, but still—back at Wal-Mart's, with the round-faced clerk looking at that black hat: "This, like, for a funeral?" And her own voice answering distantly yes, yes.

The next day she went back to Wal-Mart and bought the suit and hat.

*****

30

The first of March dawned gray and swollen, the sky over the house a big belly of canvas ready to rupture and pour out dark water. The weatherman on the television warned of "baseball-sized hail" in a storm moving in from the north. Tornados had been sighted. Texas had more tornados in any of the states, Tod had once told her. "And that's not just because it's so big. It's because it's so quick, changeable." Tod could be like that. So strange. At times, he'd be so close, so starved for her, that he'd be almost scary, crowding her, feverishly demanding. Then, without warning, he could get so mad over something like the price of a telephone call to Houston that he'd seethe like a crazy July storm. The lightning was always there in him, she thought, a kind of rage, coiled and ready to spring.

Once when Greg had wandered into the master bath looking for an aspirin after Tod had gotten into bed and had seen Tod's partial plate soaking in a glass of water, his stepfather had fumed and cursed. Tod had begun taking his teeth out, at night, these nights. He'd put them in a half glass of water, in the bathroom. Cathy noticed, at first, pretending not to, and then didn't any more, but the idea of Greg's seeing his teeth in a glass, not in his mouth made Tod furious. Why did it have to be such a big thing?

Vanity, Cathy supposed, remembering how vehement he had been, his fierce eyes, swearing that would never happen, "Nobody's ever seen them or ever will," that night in the revolving restaurant. Poor Tod. It shouldn't matter so much. She wanted him to be comfortable, after all.

When the rain came, great waves of it, she felt as though she were in a boat. The whole house rocked.

After the storm, she slept.

She woke to see Tod standing over her, watching her sleep. "I love you," he said, "from your coppery hair to the bottom of your pretty feet."

"They're not," Cathy said.

"Prettier than mine by a damned sight, my webbed feet," he said. He kissed her feet, and he recited a bit of a poem to her about wanting to give her things. "'I will give you brooches and toys for your delight,'" he said, his eyes shining, "'of bird song at morning and star shine at night,' and that's all I remember of that one, but I will, I will give you brooches, to put on your lovely peachy front that belongs to me and I'll rub your peachy back that belongs to me, too, all peachy and delicious. And now you're coming back to my bed," he said. And so she did, and they made love in a variety of gently innovative ways.

"I am married to the sexiest man on earth," Cathy said.

Tod allowed as how she might be right, adding, darkly, that being the sexiest man on earth had gotten him into an unbelievable amount of trouble, in his day. "In the past, that is. I'm what you might call a pretty physical guy," he said. "But only with you, now. Monogamy. That's it, now. Total monogamy, my dear."

Something about the way he kept saying that, his very insistence, made Cathy uneasy. It brought back something Greg said one time when he'd caught his stepfather fibbing. It hadn't been an important fib. Cathy couldn't recall what had made Greg so mad. What she couldn't forget was his voice, saying, "You sure can tell when old Tod's laying one on you, because he looks you right square in the eye every time, doesn't he?"

That afternoon Cathy went hyper-domestic. She washed all their clothes and was scouring the refrigerator when the telephone rang.

She clambered down to answer what sounded, at first, like it might be a wrong number. Some woman identified herself as Gloria. "Gloria Devereaux?" she said, stubbornly insistent, as if Cathy ought to recognize the name. "Isn't this Tod Benjamin's wife? We met at the tree-burning party, at Milton Crowder's, out on the beach? I'm the one with the twins."

"Yes," Cathy said, remembering a tall woman with a distinguished white streak in her dark hair. "With a streak of white in your hair from living with a pair of adolescents."

"It's getting whiter fast." The woman didn't sound at all friendly. "Is Mr. Benjamin there? Or somewhere where I can reach him?"

"Isn't he at the lab?" Cathy asked, wondering if the woman had broken a tooth or something. "Shall I have him call you?"

"I really need to talk to the little bastard before my husband catches up with him. You can tell him we're having him up on charges."

"Up on charges?" Cathy hadn't the least idea what that meant.

"He'll understand. I'm sure this isn't the first time. Tell him my husband's going to kill him. Which is a good idea, but I need my husband and I don't want him to go to jail." The line hummed for several minutes. "Hello? Are you still there?"

"I'm here," Cathy said, and had to repeat herself so the woman could hear her. "What charges? And what isn't the first time?"

"My Ellen," Gloria said. She started making gasping noises. The woman was crying, Cathy realized. "Ellen. You met her."

"But, I don't understand. Your twins are just—"

"Fourteen. Yes. Ellen's fourteen years old. Thirteen at that damned party. When your husband—" The woman couldn't go on.

"I don't understand," Cathy said, but she did, suddenly. Understanding coursed coldly shockingly through her to settle in her stomach in a sick lump. She shivered. "There must be some misunderstanding."

"The hell there is," the woman said. "You know exactly what I'm talking about—"

"Oh, I don't think—" Cathy fought a surge of nausea.

"You want convincing? My fourteen-year-old has been describing your bedroom to her daddy and me," Gloria sobbed. "He gave her a nice white nightgown. And roller skates. Pink roller skates." She choked. "Ellen says there was an aluminum tray under the bed in the bedroom he took her to. The tray has 'Love you, Mom,' on it and there was an apple core on it, a dusty brown apple core—"

"Please," Cathy wept. "Please," scarcely able to hear, now, her ears beginning to fill with a papery sound, a kind of static. "Please."

"He has funny looking feet," Gloria said. "His toes—" and Cathy put the phone down.

She huddled and swayed, sobbing, trying not to sob, trying to stop crying, for a long time.

That's how Tod found her.

When she told him about the call, he looked so disbelieving that she felt a stab of comfort. He came across the room to gather her close, a sob in his voice, "Good God, what a thing," he said. "I don't get it. What am I supposed to have—"

"She said the girl described my tray, that Greg made," Cathy said.

He didn't know what she was talking about. He didn't even remember the twins or their mother. "Let's sort this out," he said. And, after Cathy had become more coherent: "Is the mother you're talking about that shrill dame with the phony gray streak? I remember her now, but I don't think I got anywhere near her little darlings." He snapped his fingers. "The guy that gave that party—what's his name? Milton?—didn't he say the woman with the twins is some kind of a nut case? A pathological liar or whatever?" He smiled a pitying smile and shook his head. "If you ask me, half the people at Miltie's party seemed a little buggy."

Cathy watched her fingers crease and uncrease a place on her skirt. She spoke slowly. "You gave that child one of the nighties you bought me. And pink roller skates. I saw the box. Pink roller skates. No. You aren't going to turn me off. Not this time. She saw my tray, in our bedroom." She hated sniveling but she couldn't seem to stop. "Under my bed. Your bed. Oh, God, my tray that Greg made there's only one tray like that in the whole-wh-whole w-w-w-world." She tried to hit him but he fended her off. She ran up the stairs.

"Didn't you take that tray to that party?" He followed her, talking, talking, insisting that she listen.

He caught up with her to hold her through the worst of a storm of weeping. When she wrenched free of him he stood looking down at her curled up on the bed. "Honey, what did we take to that party, do you remember?" he asked, the voice of reason.

"I don't know. It doesn't matter." She sat up. "She's a child, Tod."

"Sure we did," he said. "We took that tray to that party. Sure." He gazed at her lovingly, patiently. "I don't doubt the young lady or her mother or somebody might have seen that tray, honey. We must have taken it. That's got to be it. Try to remember. Hell, honey, since when do you keep that tray in our bedroom anyway." He shivered and laughed shakily. "I've run into some nut cases in my life but this has got to be the absolute worst. Somebody scaring you like this—the absolute worst, honey."

Cathy couldn't stop crying. "Is that why you bought those skates? To use to seduce some little girl?"

"I told you about those." His face went tight; his mouth pulled down into a bitter, puckered frown. He glared at her, his eyes going flat, glittering with angry disbelief: "I didn't give anybody any nightgown except you and you didn't even want the damned things—good God, Cathy, you don't believe any of this crap?"

"You keep lying." She hated him. "Why do you keep lying? She saw my tray."

He stood up. Tried to hug her to him again. When she shuddered, he let her go and stood in front of her, clenching and unclenching his fists. "I can't believe this. You'd believe some stranger coming around here with some lousy made up—you'd listen to some crazy broad we ran into one time at one drunken party wants to come up with this crap and you, you buy it? By God, anybody came around to me with some goddam rotten story like this about you, I'd kick his ass up between his shoulder blades."

A vein pulsed in his temple. He moved away and came back to look into her eyes, hold her eyes with his, glittering with rage, his fury coiling and uncoiling, making him rant now, wrenching out torrents of words as he paced up and down. "Some kid sneaks in here, comes into my house, supposed to be my castle, isn't a man's house his castle, what the hell, comes around here invading my home supposed to be our home and she comes around with some lousy—" He choked and couldn't go on. He walked into the bathroom and swallowed a glass of water. "And you listen to this? That's what I can't get past. You sit around listening to this crap?" He shook his head, swallowing, fighting tears.

Cathy stretched out on the bed and turned away. "Her husband's looking for you," she said. "Her husband wants to kill you."

Tod laughed hollowly. "Tell him to get in line. No, tell him to wait. Shouldn't take too long. I got a partner just might do the honors. Come to think of it, my partner's got what you might call a vested interest. The man's been paying the premiums on what they call partnership insurance for years now; he keeps betting my life against what we owe. Having him do me in might make sense" and he laughed, chortled, bitterly, as he went on. And on. The words whirled into a furious babble. Cathy tried to tune him out. Some part of her kept hearing him, though, the way she kept hearing the sound of a dried palm frond straying across the corner of the balcony just outside the window. His voice wound around like the motes in the air from the ceiling fan, endlessly spiraling, hoarsely urgent.

That's why they call it "hot air," Cathy thought, dispassionately. He's swimming in hot air.

She went into the bathroom to wipe her face with a wet cloth, came back into the bedroom and sat down on the bed to watch the motes in a slanted ray of light.

"Ah, hell," he said. "This isn't something to monkey around with. You look at me like that, hell, this is something to give Arnold, that's it. Lawyers hear this kind of thing all the time. What I'm worried about is my wife, some psycho calls up and my wife looks at me like all of a sudden I'm a criminal." He kept drinking water, walking back into the bathroom to draw another glass, sputtering and raving. "Got to straighten this thing out. You're always running around saying everything is so basic, right? This has got to be pretty damned basic. Look at me. You think I'm a goddam psychopath? I look to you like somebody goes around scaring little kids? Because if you can believe that, what we're talking about here is some kind of craziness, isn't it? Something calls for a shrink."

"It's a kind of madness, yes."

"So. You ready to believe that about me?" he spat. "There's the difference between us: you get sick, I'm with you. A thousand per cent. And you think I'm sick and what have we got here? I'm not, but that's not the point. Point is, you get sick, in any way, and I'm with you. You hurt your back or your head—" He waved his hands. "—whatever. You're somebody belongs to me. Me, you're ready to—you believe that about me?"

"I don't know," she cried out, finally, meaning she didn't know why she couldn't find it in herself to want to help him, somehow.

Only punish, she thought. I only want to get out and away or punish him. And he's right. He'd never treat me so; there's nothing I could do that would make him as cold as I've become.

She remembered what she'd said to Chub: you don't leave some one just because he's not a nice person.

The next day, Tod came in and sat down and took Cathy's hands in his: "I love you," he said.

Cathy looked at him.

"The Devereaux mess is taken care of," he said. "Turns out this dame has a shrink. You want to talk to her shrink?"

Cathy knew he was lying. She didn't want to talk about it. No, she said, she didn't want to talk to anybody about this. "Are you going to see a psychiatrist?"

"Would that make you happy?"

"Happy?" She shrugged.

"Cost me a little something to get her to see the error of her ways," he said. "But it's worth it. Arnold took care of it. Good man. Good man."

"You paid her off?"

Tod nodded. "She said she didn't want to put her little darling through any more trauma." His mouth twisted. "She can take her little darling to Disneyland, take the whole damned family to Disneyland." He took Cathy's face in his hands. "You want to go to Disneyland?"

Cathy took his hands away from her face.

Time doesn't heal all wounds. It makes some of them fester. It was so crazy: Tod got to where he seemed to expect her to let him forgive her. For not loving him enough. For not wanting to help him? For not feeling the way he would feel, if she were in some awful trouble.

They kept having insane arguments. One awful day Tod fell to the floor, weeping, holding onto her legs, swearing that nothing, no thing anyone could ever say or do would make him turn away from her. "I'm here," she said, dully. "I'm still here" and he stormed, "No you're not."

He grew so...sad. So terribly sad. All the time. It was always there. Cathy'd be doing something, watering a plant or lifting something out of the oven, and she'd turn and catch him eyeing her, chewing his lower lip, his eyes sorrowing with this thing that had come between them. That she let come between them.

That she let fester between them.

She wanted to call Chub. Ask her what women did. What wives were supposed to do. Cathy was ashamed of what was happening, of not knowing what to do, of feeling so desperate, so she didn't call Chub. She did not call Chub then, right then, when she should have.

*****

31

The first time Cathy deliberately listened in on a telephone call was when a man told her to put her "no account low-life husband on the phone" and Tod saw her face and took the phone away from her.

She was still saying, "I beg your pardon?" when Tod eased the phone out of her hand and waved her away. He'd done that before because he was paranoid about having anybody listen in on a business call, of course, but all of a sudden that gesture, that peremptory dismissal, got to her.

Cathy ran upstairs and picked up the extension.

"Two twenty-six," the man said. Cathy recognized Cecil's voice. "Got it for you, all right, but this is gonna cost you. We understand each other?"

"Yeah, yeah," Tod said.

"Seventy-six Buick. Owned by Augustus Merriam, three-oh-three-oh Chateau Lafitte, Highway Three, Seabrook. You need the zip?"

Tod grunted. "The hell's the matter with you? You think I'm about to write Gus a letter?"

There was a pause so long that Cathy covered the mouthpiece and leaned back so she could see the door, wondering if she'd been discovered and it might be going to burst open. She had time to think how ridiculous it was to get so scared and guilty before Tod broke the silence. "Kind of hard to figure. Gus doesn't have any kids, does he? He marry again?"

"That old Buick," Cecil said. "Hell. Maybe he lost it in a game. Swapped it for a drink. Gave it to some little old gal served him coffee. You know Gus. Not like Gus to be chasin' around with some little old gal your kid's age, is it? He never did have your proclivities, did he?"

Tod snorted.

"Well, glad to be of help," Cecil said, all business. But then there was a short burst of laughter and he lapsed into the Louisiana accent: "I got me plenty of other 'tings I gone take care of, me, I guarontee."

"Yes. Yes," Tod said. "Help me out, here."

"You're lucky foh be gettin' dis much, my man," the man said.

"Cut that shit out," Tod said. "Here's what you do. Give Gus a call. Tell him that thing's parked across the street over here, and I'm gonna get it towed. No. No. You wanna buy it. That's it. Tell him you want to buy it. See if you can find out if he's still got the damned thing and, if he hasn't, who all's he letting drive it. Hell, shouldn't take more than a couple minutes of your valuable time, which I'm paying for."

"Only thing keeps me from killin' you, friend. But me, I don't know about this. How you arrive at I'm gone play snooper-poop with Gus, huh? I don't get in dis no deeper no way." He dropped the accent. "I decide what I do. I don't see pickin' on Gus."

"Oh, don't hand me that Cajun tribe pride crapola," Tod said. "All I'm asking is a little favor for all the bucks I throw your way and the bucks I figure I'll have to keep throwing your way down the line. That new lab is moving in on a couple of southeast dentists and we're gonna have to discourage all kinds of people. But you don't want my business, what the hell, I got people, Sees."

Cecil laughed again.

"What's funny?" Tod said. His voice changed. "You got somebody else on the phone over there? You keep fading in and out. You got one of those Radio Shack cheap phones or what? Maybe it's—just a minute."

Cathy hung up. She moved away from the phone. By the time Tod got to the head of the stairs she had a clothes basket full of clothes in her arms and what she hoped was an innocently blank face.

The next call, a few days later, was easier. Tod answered the upstairs phone just as Cathy picked up the one in the kitchen on the second ring and held it, trying not to breathe into it, expecting to hear Tod's peremptory, "I've got it." Evidently he didn't hear her.

"Tod?" It was the same voice. "Gus says he sold the Buick for three hundred big ones a hell of a long time ago. Don't remember who to. He can't believe it's still running."

"Myself."

"But you know who answers the phone over to Gus's? Dixie. Cut N' Shoot Dixie. My, my. Mercy me." A chuckle expanded into a cackle. "Looks like you gonna have to start fillin' your new family in on your past, my man. It be pilin' up."

"That's it, huh? That's it? Well. Got to let you go, I guess. Got to let you go, now."

Cathy hung up.

A couple of minutes later she found Tod standing at a window in the living room, running his fingers down one of the burglar bars. "The paint feels a little rough on some of these," he said. He turned to look deeply into her eyes and let the frown on his face dissolve into a sunny smile. "You don't need any paint on you, do you, my lady? You are one fine lookin' lady," he murmured. "Come over here and give an old man a hug. I've been standing here thinkin' about you. About all your good stuff."

No you haven't, Cathy thought. She stiffened and moved away.

"Now what?" He pulled a face and sighed, exasperated.

"You haven't been thinking about me. You've been thinking about a man named Gus and somebody named Cut N' Shoot something. I think it might be time for you to talk to me, Tod."

He backed away with his hands up. "Whoa." His chin tightened. "You have any idea how I feel about eavesdroppers?"

"Do you have any idea how I loathe being lied to?"

"What? What? What makes you think—"

"What's going on? And don't go into a lot of twaddle about how you've been thinking about me. Why can't you be honest?"

"What?" he said. "What?"

"Honest." Cathy started to shake but she didn't care. She stared at her trembling hands.

"Well now, well now," he sputtered. "You tell me what's so honest about listening in on a business call that has nothing to do with—ah, hell— I thought I might spare you, that's all. Wanted to try and spare my little wife, if I could. Anyway, you know who Gus Merriam is, if you think about it. I told you about Gus and Lynn and all that. Bored the hell out of you, as I recall. Cut N' Shoot is a place. A town. Look it up. Up there past the Gone and Lost River some place. And Dixie." He laughed angrily. "Why Dixie's a place, now, too. Thanks to me. Got her own place. Dixie's place. I set her up. A long time ago. Ancient history. Back in Seabrook, before I had any idea I was going to end up married. To anybody." His mouth twisted. He beginning to seethe, gathering himself up for a tirade.

She retreated and sat down. "What have these people to do with us?"

"Hell if I know. That's what I've been trying to figure out—but no, you have to know all about whatever crap I have to dig up to dope this thing out." He got rolling, stamping up and down, pounding his palm, sending flecks of spittle into the air, fuming about how nobody who gave a rat's ass about anyone would ever pull a crappy stunt like that, listen in on the phone like that, no defense for a man when he was up against a thing like that in his own home, supposed to be his castle, the lowest trick in the book, oh, he couldn't believe she had so little respect—

And somewhere in all that Cathy realized who Gus Merriam might be. "He married your Lynn, didn't he? Isn't Gus the man your Lynn was married to when she killed herself?"

"Yeah. Yeah. Gus," Tod said.

"And you're trying to find out just who that girl is?"

He nodded wearily. He made Cathy tired. "So you can help her?"

Tod snorted and walked out of the room.

The next day, when Gus Merriam called, Cathy was having a fight with the dishwasher. The people who'd installed the thing warned her it might be too much for the old house's plumbing. They'd had a terrible time hooking it up and then Tod didn't want her running it without a full load so it had to be fully loaded, both racks, when it overflowed into a spreading lake on the worn linoleum and that's when the telephone shrilled.

It was a nasal male voice wanting Tod.

Cathy identified herself hastily and said please, please couldn't he tell her what he wanted with Tod because she knew all about everything now, it was her house too, and her life, too.

The man sounded old, strained, with an East Texas twang. "Just tell him Augustus Merriam called," he said, and added, "You tell him for me that he comes poking around me asking a lot of questions about that old Buick or any other damned business and I'll take and shove it right up his ass, excuse my French, ma'am."

"I beg your pardon?" Cathy couldn't seem to turn off the dishwasher and the plug wouldn't come out of the wall. When she yanked at it her wet fingers slid against the metal prongs of the plug and shocked her all the way up her arm and down her ribs. The thing had a surprising kick. She got the plug out but then she slipped to the wet floor.

She must have gasped.

"I'm sorry, lady," the man on the phone said. "I'm just real sorry. But you sure are married to one lousy son of a bitch if you ain't noticed." After a minute he added, "I don't mean to take it out on you."

"I'll tell Tod you called." Cathy clambered up to lean, damply, against a chair and tipped over the phone. "I don't think he means to bother you, Mr. Merriam," she said, righting it. "It's just that he wants to know who might be driving your automobile, or one you once had? An old Buick? You may not know her. She might be someone who bought the car or a friend or, I don't know. But she sounds like someone who needs help."

"Can't imagine a grown man getting all het up over some little old gal," Gus said. "Especially a mean bastard like Tod. He's had a slew of women mad at him. Ought to be used to it by now."

The lake on the floor kept spreading, soaking into worn places of the linoleum. A corner of one of the dish towels she'd thrown into it was making a wet place on a wallpapered wall.

Cathy kicked at the towel. "I'm so sorry, Mr. Merriam. Truly."

It sounded as though the man sobbed. He might be simply breathing with some difficulty. He wheezed hoarsely. "Tod tell you about her?"

"No."

"Well, she's sick. And you tell Tod the only woman ever drives that car is Dixie, once in a while. He knows Dixie. Hell. Ever'body knows Dixie. Ask him if he's afraid of all his ladies. Maybe he ought to be, the son of a bitch, excuse me."

"I don't know Dixie," Cathy said. "But I would like to, I think. That might be the first step toward solving our problem."

"Dixie ain't got the inclination or the time to go fool around with Tod anymore. And little Dixie's not able. She's just real real poorly. So you tell him to leave Dixie and us out of whatever it is he's thinkin' to work up, you hear? You all just leave us out of it." His voice rose. "I got high blood pressure and the emphysema and none of this ain't doin' nobody no good. He wants to talk to me, you tell him all he has to do is come on by."

"Is little Dixie Dixie's daughter?"

"You didn't know that?"

"Well, no. But if—listen. I have a son, myself. A teenaged son, but a teenager is a teenager. They're never easy. If this girl is so sick, well. This whole thing is beginning to squeeze my heart. For her. Tell her that, please."

The man wheezed. "I just hope your boy is healthy. And lady, if I was you, I'd keep that boy away from Tod Benjamin. I tell you what. I hate to think of anybody married to that bastard and that's the truth." He wheezed some more. "You know how a spider does, to its catch? Makes it a nice cocoon, and then just makes mush out of its insides. Sucks it dry. Spider gets through, all's left is a little bitty dry husk."

The phone hummed for a minute.

"Not even admittin' up to that poor little old gal," the man said.

Cathy's grip was so tight on the receiver that it was beginning to quiver. Possibly she'd not understood. "Do you mean that Tod has refused to admit something to—to some little girl?"

"Anh, anh, you know better'n that, lady. Not admittin' to her. Ownin' up to how she's his. You know what I mean. You taken one look, anybody can see she's his, all right. But that's okay. Dixie don't want no part of him neither, not since he first started in messin' things up. Him givin' her that bait shack place, that wasn't none of her doin'. That was me, and I don't mind tellin' you that was about the onliest halfway right thang he ever done and it ain't all that much neither. It was that or own up to what he done or pay some bunch of lyin' bastards to say they was sleepin' with her, too, like what he done to poor little old Chloe, shit, and her just a little old girl not out of her child years."

He was scarcely coherent.

"I don't understand," Cathy said.

"Don't guess you do. I'm goin' to have to let you go now, ma'am. Have to let you go, now. I'm sure you got a lot of things to do, now."

The dial tone hummed in her ear.

Cathy ran and got some bigger towels to mop up the water, all the while thinking: Dixie. From Cut n' Shoot, Texas.

When she called the dishwasher people, she was put on hold, a long hold, with guitars being abused by several different people. She had plenty of time to remember Tod's casual description: "I'm the one set the little lady up in a place of her own. 'Dixie's' she calls it. 'Dixie's Place.' I told her she ought to call it 'Tod's' but what the hell."

Dixie. From Cut n' Shoot. In Dixie's Place. In Seabrook. How hard could it be to find one Dixie's Place in Seabrook, half an hour away over there where NASA One came to an end?

Somebody at the dishwasher place finally broke into the music only to say that they couldn't send anybody out to look at the thing for a couple of days. Cathy said that would be all right, thank you and hung up and picked the phone up again and dialed Chub's number.

Chub answered as if she might be in a hurry.

When she heard who it was, she sounded less hurried.

Cathy meant to be calm and pleasant, say it was such a pretty day, and why couldn't they drive down the coast, just the two of them, and have some shrimp or something for lunch, but all of a sudden she couldn't stand having Chub sound so preoccupied. "Are you teaching or painting or anything?" she asked. "Because if you're not, could you come here and go to Seabrook to lunch with me because I don't want to interrupt anything but oh, Chub, there's something I have to do and I don't know if I—I'm so—I'm just getting so—"

"Oh, my dear," Chub said.

"Dangerous," Cathy whispered.

"Dangerous? Is he—"

"No," Cathy said. "I am. I've been thinking of how—of the ways people murder their husbands."

"Ah," Chub said. "Let me count the ways." She laughed once, a quick bark, and stopped laughing, and said, quietly, sounding very much like the old Chub: "I'm on my way."

Less than an hour later, she was ringing the front door bell and banging on the door.

Cathy and Chub almost broke each others' ribs for minutes. Then Chub came in, looked around and said, "Why's it so dark in here? Let's sit in the kitchen." She looked wonderful, clear-eyed and slim in a blue linen shirt, a blue silk scarf holding back her springy hair.

"It's darker in the kitchen," Cathy said. "Some of the lights don't work. It's something to do with the wiring. Do you want coffee?"

Chub shook her head. "This place is like Transylvania. How long have you had bars all over all the windows? No wonder you have the jeebies." She walked over to the sofa and sat down. "No, thanks, no coffee. Sit. Tell me."

Cathy said, "Or a drink?"

"No, dear heart," Chub said. "Give." She patted the cushion beside her, her down-slanted eyes totally focused.

"I'm sorry if I sounded ridiculously dramatic," Cathy said. "It's just that I—" She looked at Chub and blurted, "Tod's not exactly sane. He keeps blaming me, if we go anywhere, he keeps having these jealous fits."

Chub, blessed healthy Chub, nodded, got an arm around her and leaned close enough to touch her brow to Cathy's, briefly. "Honey," she said.

Cathy twisted her hands. "I've been—I thought I ought to try to help him." She shook herself. "I don't know. Maybe I should. But now, it seems, Tod's a father. No. He isn't, not really, he isn't a father at all. But he has sired a daughter. Maybe he didn't even know about her, or he might have been trying to spare me, but now I think he knows and he's so awful."

Chub looked so sympathetic that Cathy blurted out the whole story. The minute she got through Chub wanted to find Gregory and take the two of them home with her.

"I've got to go to Seabrook, to talk to this Dixie," Cathy said.

"Are you sure?"

"I have to, Chub. I have to know."

"You do know, though. Don't you?"

"Not enough."

Chub opened her mouth and closed it. After a couple of seconds she relaxed and nodded. "Okay," she said. "Dixie's Place. In Seabrook."

When they were getting into her car Chub grinned and said, "Hey, a bar in Seabrook. Probably one of those astronaut hangouts. Might be fun."

"Sure," Cathy said, but when she tried to smile back, Chub reached over and touched her hand and said, so sadly, "Oh honey. Honey."

*****

32

Dixie's Place wasn't hard to find. A small, balding, wrinkled man knelt on the splintered gray steps, carefully fitting a clean board into place to replace a tread of the stair leading to the door. The man glanced up and flattened himself against the railing to let Cathy and Chub ease past. He smelled of stale sweat. When he smiled he pulled his lips back together, possibly because his eye teeth were missing.

Cathy edged by, trying not to inhale, following Chub as she moved carefully, murmuring, "Watch yourself." The man, hearing her, said defensively, "Hold onto the railing then."

"Are you Mr. Merriam?" Cathy asked but Chub was tugging open a door warped into layers of plywood and the man seemed not to have heard so she went on in.

The sudden lack of sunlight made her clumsy. Cathy stumbled and caught herself as a little freckled woman with unruly red hair looked up at them. She had on a peculiar get-up, an orange shirt under a mesh vest and canvas apron coverall but when she smiled she looked friendly; an Irish setter sort of person who'd gone overboard with the mascara and lip gloss. The woman opened a hinged door and came to the bar. "Y'all watch it. Gus is fixing them rotten steps. He ain't got around to the floor in here."

The bar was a converted cottage, one main room with a tiny kitchen behind a bar. A glowing neon Budweiser sign flickered above a mirror. A longer room had been added, somewhat haphazardly, to hold half a dozen small tables, three of them pulled together so several men could watch a couple of men playing dominoes.

"What'll it be?" The woman wiped her hands on a towel and indicated a table. Cathy licked perspiration from her upper lip and returned the woman's cheery smile. Chub said, briskly, "Two Buds, thanks. And could we buy you one and get you to sit with us for a minute?"

The woman's smile faded and her eyes went wary. "You got a summons or you sellin' somethin'? Because I'm not about to be a customer, I'll clue you." She served them and dragged a chair over and sat down. "So what'd you have in mind?"

"Are you Dixie?" Cathy asked.

"Like the sign says." Dixie put her head back. Gracious, Cathy thought, iridescent green eye shadow. She swallowed and found a Kleenex to dab at the perspiration trickling down her face. "I scarcely know where to begin. I'm Cathy. Benjamin. Tod Benjamin's wife?" Then, in a rush, she added, "I don't know why you should help me but I'm so miserable." The look on Dixie's face stopped her. "I've got to understand. About Tod."

"That so?" Dixie looked bored.

Cathy got to her feet, clumsily. "I'm sorry."

"For what?" Dixie said. "He been arrested again or what?"

"Oh no," Cathy said.

Dixie got up and walked over to the men across the room. When she came back and sat down again she said, "Tod send you around? We been halfway expecting that, from what Gus said. The Buick and all. Whatever the hell that's all about. I guess Gus's been letting little Dixie use that old clunk some but she's back in the hospital again now so...so that's that. Don't worry about it."

"Tod doesn't know we're here," Chub said.

Cathy poured her beer into a glass. It foamed and overflowed. Dixie tossed her a rag and as she wiped up the foam, she said, "I need to know some things. About Tod. Mr. Merriam called and I just thought, maybe, that you'd talk to me. Chub, my friend, came along for support."

Dixie shrugged, her face softening. "Gus called you?" She considered that. "Well, hell, I don't know why I should talk about Toddy, but I'm not real sensible, I guess. That's Gus, out in front. Why'd he call you?"

"He wanted Tod," Cathy said, fighting her tongue a little. "He said—I d-d-don't think he meant to, exactly—that you and Tod were quite in-in-intimate a very long t-time ago? And now he wants T-Tod to leave you alone. Has Tod been b-bothering you?"

"Hell, no. Gus knows better than that." Dixie stood up as if she meant to call out to the man or go outside and get him.

"Oh, wait," Cathy said. "It's you I want to talk with. I don't want to make trouble at all."

"You couldn't make any trouble for Gus far as I'm concerned," Dixie said, but she sat down. "That's one saintly man. I guess you could say Gus is pretty much on my side. Always has been, always will be." She had expressive eyebrows. "He might get a mite over protective. Ever since Lynn's passing, Gus's just kind of wandered around like a dog without a tail, hoping for folks to be a lot friendlier than they generally turn out. He's been nothin' but good to us, though." She squinted at Chub. Chub gazed back steadily and Dixie smiled a slow smile. "Shoot," she said. "You ask. I'll answer. You got to know, though: Gus said somebody's been calling up Tod and scaring shit out of him and I'll tell you up front, that's not me. Tod ought to know that, but he's kind of forgetful, isn't he? Tod can be kind of forgetful."

One of the men across the room called out, jovially, noisily, that he wanted a beer and a hamburger. Dixie shrugged and excused herself.

Chub and Cathy finished their beer. "You picked a fine time to leave me, Lucille," the juke box sang. Chub looked around. "Lucille rhymes with field," she said. "In Kemah and Seabrook, anyway. Why don't we have another of these while you tell me about this Gus what's-his-name."

"Merriam," Cathy said, "He's been lurking and stalking, I guess. Ever since I met Tod. Even back in Houston, in our old house, this Gus showed up. I looked out in front one night and there was this man out on the walk, just standing there. As if...I don't know. Greg came home, I think it was from church or somewhere, and there was this man standing out in front. He gave Greg a fit. Maybe we'd better talk about it on the way home."

She watched Dixie move around behind her tiny bar, unwrapping meat, lining up a bun, opening pickles, asking the customer about mustard and mayonnaise. "I think Tod has a daughter. She came to the house and she's sick. Very. Oh, Chub, is this unreal?"

"Tell you what, kiddo," Chub said. "People talk about little bastards in places like this all the time."

She called out to Dixie that they could use two more, when she got a minute. Dixie came back to serve them. She sat down with a beer of her own. She hadn't wanted to irritate that particular customer, she said, cheerfully, since he might be sensitive: "Gerry is fresh out of Huntsville."

"That so?" Chub said, as if she knew lots of people fresh out of prison.

"He's doin' okay," Dixie said, "but I bet his mama wishes he could get him some steady employment so he'd quit spending her money." She sat down and stuck her feet out in front of her. Both her tennis shoes were worn through over her little toes. "Say," she added, wiggling her feet, "you reckon Tod stomped on a few toes up at Huntsville?"

Chub stiffened, rummaged in her purse and came up with a packet of tissues. "Huntsville?" She handed the tissues to Cathy.

Cathy stared. "Huntsville? Tod?"

"T.D.C.J.," Dixie said. "Texas Department of Criminal Justice. Your husband didn't mention that? How come him to not mention that, do you suppose? Shit fire." She laughed. "He can be real forgetful, can't he? Never planted no peas while he was up at the pea patch, though. Where'd you think the man learned his trade?"

She looked into Cathy's eyes and her voice dropped. "Ah, hell, I'm sorry. Tod tends to forget. You know who had to tell me? Lynn. That's right. Lynn was the one had to let me in on that hot little item. Of course, I thought she was tryin' to break us up. That's what Tod said. So would I listen?" She rolled her eyes. "Didn't listen for shucks. Ran straight to the man to ask him about it and earned myself a split lip and a tooth that's just deader'n hell. He furnished the cap for it, though, I'll say that for the little prick." She grinned. "He still got a short fuse?"

Cathy's ears were ringing. "Prison?" she whispered.

"Five to ten and he got out three. Good behavior." She lifted an eyebrow. "Good behavior." She chuckled ruefully and looked around. "Lynn waited around for him all while he was up there. Went to see him every weekend. That's what Gus can't forget, the way Lynn kept on keeping on and him doing her like he done the minute he got out. Listen, y'all excuse me. I got to help that old boy over there. This isn't the best place in the world to talk, now, is it, ladies? You want another?"

"Why not?" Chub said. But after Dixie was out of earshot she said, "You look sort of greenish. You want to go?"

"Oh, Chub. What am I going to do?" Cathy swallowed salty tears.

"Let's go," Chub said. She stood up. But Dixie was back, wiping the table, plunking down two more bottles, sliding into a chair with a comfortable small groan.

Cathy cleared her throat and focused on the table. "Why did he go to prison?" she asked. She had to repeat herself before Dixie heard her.

"Ah, he—what's the word? Fondled. He fondled some little girl. You know where Bull Schneider's place is? In Galveston? The Brass Bull? I don't even know if it's there anymore. Tod got involved with Bull's little old girl. She was a lot too young. And her daddy come after him Tod and this other dude got Bull in a phone booth and stomped him. Landed him in the closed head injuries unit at the Medical Branch for I don't know how long. Say, there's somebody wants to see old Tod in the wringer. That old boy's wife. They almost killed that old boy. Schneider's been dragging his left side for years now. Stomped the fire out of him." Shee stood to demonstrate, stamping her feet. "In a phone booth. That's why they quit putting those booths in bars, know that? Arguments of that caliber aren't all that uncommon. We had us three shootings in this county over little pissant nothing quarrels lately and it's been against the law to carry a gun inside in how long, now? I don't know what it is with some men."

She sat down and leaned back in the chair. "You got Toddy figured? He's just broke down to the kind of fool only wants what belongs to somebody else. You get him relaxed, he'll tell you that, himself. Somebody else's wife or mother or even their kid—Don't look like that, now."

She went behind the bar and came back with a glass of water. "You're not going to pass out on me, are you?" she said.

"I'm fine," Cathy said. She took a sip of water. "Thank you. I guess I'm just not used to—somebody's *mother*?"

"Whatever. You look like you need to go on home and lie down."

"Why did you say 'somebody's mother'?" Cathy said.

"I dunno. I just meant, you know, the forbidden fruit." Dixie looked around. "Has to have somebody new all the time, somebody he knows he ought to leave alone, somebody belongs to somebody else." Realization dawned in her eyes. Her voice softened. "Who'd he take you away from?"

Cathy shook her head.

"He's a very troubled person," Chub said.

Dixie looked at her. "Oh, yeah," she said.

Cathy kept picking up her glass and putting it down in a new place, making a series of interlocking damp rings on the table top. When she saw the other two women watching her, she put her hands in her lap. "Prison."

Dixie shrugged. "Sorry if I bummed you out. You going to be okay? Gus tell you about Little Dixie?"

"Is she yours?" Cathy asked. She shook her head, willing herself to listen as Dixie went on.

"My baby. She's—we had to put her away." She wiped her eyes with the heels of her hands. "Never has been right. She's real sick, now." She inhaled and hesitated, seeking the right words. "She's the only one I got." She surveyed the room. "Tod, well, that's all done with. I always figured her to be none of his business. Only thing he ever gave her was toes like his. Lynn and me, we got to be real close, after I had Little Dixie. Lynn used to be like Little Dixie's mama, too. Better than me, sometimes. I had to work, and Lynn loved my girl like her own, long as she lived. It was real, real tough on my girl when Lynn done what she done."

She accepted a tissue from Chub and held it to the corners of her eyes. "I'm gonna do you one hell of a favor," she confided. "As soon as my baby's gone, I'm gonna take that bastard off your hands. I'm fighting big C, myself. Big C. Kind of puts a perspective on things. So as soon as my baby goes, I'm gonna kill that little son of a bitch. Let the state put me to sleep. Beats colon cancer, right? Colon cancer, you get to tear your guts out. I watched a friend go like that. No thanks."

Chub had her head in her hands. "Oh, Lord."

"Yeah," Dixie said. "Unless Gus beats me to it."

Later, in the car, Chub said, "That is one determined lady. A little crazy, maybe, but determined. I don't know how anybody stays sane."

"We don't. Oh, Chub." Cathy swallowed, hard. "I keep going in circles. The last fight we had, he looked at me with these hateful eyes and he said he'd get Greg if I ever tried to leave him."

"Get Greg?" Chub said. "How could he get Greg? That's crazy. But, like I said, I don't know how anybody stays sane around Tod."

Cathy had her fist against her teeth. "They d-d-don't," she said.

*****

33

Chub looked up at the house and pounded the steering wheel again. "I'm not letting you go back into that house by yourself," she yelled. "Look at this damned place 'The Haunting of Hill House.'"

The carved faces at the tops of the columns gleamed through pale washes of moonlight flickering through the swaying trees. The oleanders looked scraggly and strange, a chiascuro of jagged shapes. Poisonous, Cathy remembered, wearily bemused. All oleanders were poisonous. Beautiful, flamingly tropical and poisonous. "But I love my house," she said.

"You're coming home with me," Chub said, her voice croaky.

"Not without Greg," Cathy said. "Go home, okay? I have to be practical. I've got to get Greg. I'm not even sure where he and Shep are and Greg might take some persuading, though he'll be glad to get away from

Tod. And I've got to gather up our clothes and some things." She put her hand on top of Chub's hand. Chub hand turned over to grip hers, hard. "I'll be okay," Cathy said. "Don't make this any harder than it is. I love you. I'll call you in the morning."

"Cathy, you're dying, damn it. You can hardly hold your head up."

"Darling Chub. Let me out of this car and go. Just go. Please."

Chub didn't start the car until Cathy had walked up the steps and turned to wave her off so she could go through that heavy, creaking, front door and close it behind her.

Tod found her in the bedroom, huddled against the headboard, too tired to get up and run the hot tub she'd been promising herself. He came in calling for her but as soon as he got upstairs and close enough to look into her face he drew back with a blank pinched look. "All right," he growled. "Okay. What is it, now?"

Cathy said, "I met Dixie today. We had a long talk."

He put his hand up and turned away, shaking his head and broke in, "And you believe her, of course. She had the balls to come around here?"

"Chub drove me to Kemah."

He started pacing. "Same old thing, isn't it? You're all set to believe anybody, anybody but the chump, that it? What's Dixie want? Money? Like that crazy dame with the twins? Hell. You'll go out of your way to believe anybody but me."

He stamped out of the room, came back up the stairs with a drink, swallowed it and began pacing, ranting in a furious monotone, "Oh, yeah, supposed to be my wife, all set to believe anything anybody wants to pull, that right? I want an answer to that. You're the one who says every argument is so damned basic, that right? Well, kid, this is basic. You're so sure I'm—what do they call 'em?—some kind of a goddam psycho? Supposed to have a little piece of action on the side, well, Dixie is history, didn't I tell you about old Dixie? What's the big deal here? You trying to rake up something, see what you can get out of the chump?"

Cathy stook up. "You're very ill. I'm sorry. Don't touch me."

He kept getting in her way. "You've got to think about something, here, kid. You keep wanting to dump me, you might make it. But then what? You got some place to go? You and Greggy?"

She was beyond trying to frame a reply, until he started to plead. "If you're so damned sure I'm sick, what then, huh? What's the plan? Throw the old man out? Listen. If you got sick, you think I'd dump you? I'd do any damned thing in the world to help you. No matter what. My wife needs help, she gets help. She doesn't get thrown out on her ass."

Tears sparkled on his face, in his lashes, as he leaned close, breathing whiskey fumes into her face. "I happen to love you. You got any idea what that means?" He collapsed onto the bed, his face in his hands. "I guess not. All that love crap doesn't mean a rat's ass to you, does it? What if Greg's in trouble, eh? You gonna toss the kid out, too? You ever think about that? Somebody needs help, you toss 'em out?"

He jumped up and went stamping down the stairs. She could hear him in the living room, in the hall, back and forth in the kitchen, walking heavily, talking to himself. Possibly to her. Something about Greg, about Greg being in real trouble, about being over a barrel.

He came back up to the bedroom with a fresh drink. Cathy had taken a sheet and pillows to the window seat. She curled up on it and closed her eyes. What do you say to a sexual deviant? She was too sick to talk.

"What'd Dixie have to say?" He crossed the bedroom and tried to stroke her back.

She flinched away. "Don't. I'm too tired to talk."

"Oh, don't pull that" He swallowed a belch. "She charge you for the drinks? Dixie?" He touched her shoulder again and, when she shuddered, flipped his stiffened fingers against her arm, a stinging rebuke.

"I have to call Chub," Cathy said, sitting up. "She and Patrick want Greg and me to come and stay with them for a while."

"Well, I'll be a raving son of a bitch," Tod said. "You got money for a lawyer, babe? Chub and Pat in on this, too, now?"

I mustn't talk to him any more, she thought, but suddenly it took far too much effort to go on resisting telling him the rest of it. It all came out at once, in a garbled rush.

"Prison. Dixie told me about how you went to prison for almost murdering a man. And you have a daughter. She's sick. Little Dixie is sick. If Gus has been sitting in that car across the street, he has his reasons, hasn't he? Don't keep shouting and stamping. Greg might come home and walk in on this. I'm not listening to any more of this."

He gripped her shoulder. "What's that? What's that? Dixie leave anything out? I'd hate to think she left anything out."

Cathy closed her eyes. "Little Dixie has hair like yours. She's yours and she's sick and none of this matters to you, does it, Tod? But we're through. Leave me alone." She drew her legs up and gripped her toes to warm them and remembered. "She has toes like yours. Little Dixie."

"Toes like mine? What the fuck is that supposed to mean? You see her feet? I've never seen her feet, you know. It's nice to be invited, goddam, might be nice, I never get invited but that's beside the point, isn't it?"

There was more, but it didn't make sense. He ended up slumped in a chair, his head in his hands. He'd gotten a haircut. A small area of pale skin shone along the hairline on the back of his neck. He groaned. "Everything I touch turns to shit. What do you expect me to do? Erase all that crap? You want to go into all that, what am I supposed to do?"

He looked…sick. And frightened. A scared old man.

"I don't know," Cathy said. "But I can't help you. Not any more."

"You can't leave me, though," he said. "You can't do that, Cathy. You know you can't. Tear a hole in somebody and walk away and leave them to bleed to death? Plenty of women can do that but you can't. Can you." It wasn't a question.

Cathy's head was in her arms.

"I will give you brooches," he said softly, "and toys, for your delight, of birdsong at morning and star shine at night. That's all I want to do. Oh, darlin', don't you know how all I want is the chance to do that? To heal you, heal us? I married you for all the right reasons, I love you, you know that. Why did you marry me, baby? For love, right? Tell me it was for love." He sank to one knee, his eyes brimming. "Why did you marry me?"

The extent of the danger finally registered. Even his hard clutching hands hadn't been so frightening as this, his desperate tearful crooning. His terror and misery rode all through her veins. "Sickening," she said. She pushed his hands away. "Don't touch me."

He moved away, still breathing brokenly, exhaling an occasional sob but his voice deepened, sank into a snort. "I'm not the only one with a little crap to shove under the rug," he said, almost giggling. He straightened up and got out a cigar. "Wasn't going to tell you this, but maybe there's a little something you might want to take into consideration. Your Greg has a few problems. He's a goddam thief. What do you make of that? I figured I'd cover for him. Call it a loan. Let him work it off. Never even bother you with it, but what the hell. You and your kid don't give a rat's ass about the chump, maybe the chump plays hard ball. Let you and your boy find out about life in the real world. It's cold out there, baby. How're you gonna like visiting your boy in Huntsville? Because that's where he's headed, you walk out on me."

He sounded so dispassionate that she had trouble understanding what he was saying. "Nice tender white boy like Greggy," he said, his voice coldly sane, almost business like. "Unless you got somebody on retainer? Too bad he won't be able to take his fiddle with him."

You're babbling, Cathy thought. She couldn't get breath enough to say it aloud, but she didn't need to.

Tod watched her, his eyes glittering with tears and triumph. "Oh, yeah," he said, "you need me, lady. You're going to need Tod." He swallowed the rest of his drink and very nearly lost his balance coming across the room, dragging a chair up to the window seat. "Kid's in a shit load of trouble. And I'm the one with the shovel."

"What are you talking about?"

"Aw, I don't want to go into it. Take my word for it. Kid gets back, we're going to have to have a long talk. Then we might see what we can do. He's got a record, you know. He ever tell you about the pot party?"

Cathy closed her eyes.

"I didn't think so. Well, we got him off. Ask him about that. We got him off. But that makes two, Mama."

"Two?"

"Two," Tod said. He squinted through a wreathe of smoke. "And this is gonna make three." He inhaled and sat back and blew a smoke ring. "Remember what I said about money being such a great little deodorizer? Sure has cleaned up the air for our boy a couple of times, but we're talking felony, this go round. Felony." He wielded the word like a club.

"Got his hand in the till," Tod said. "The boy's a thief, Mama. I figured I'd keep it under wraps, for your sake, but what the hell, we're tossing crap around, we might as well talk about Greg's little deal, here. A couple of thousand, near as I can tell. That kind of money, what he's going to need, he's going to need somebody like Arnold. You want to walk out of here and find yourself a counselor? Cut Greggy off from the old life line? No more Tod to pick up the tab? I was going to get him off in a corner and try to figure the thing out, see what we could come up with. God, I hate a thief, now that's one thing I never have been, a goddam thief. I don't know anybody likes a thief." He couldn't stop talking.

"I don't believe you."

His face wavered before her, the skin drawn tight against the planes of his brow, his cheeks, the top of the bridge of his nose shone white, as white as the whites of his eyes that gleamed, showing all around the irises. Perspiration shone across his upper lip and on his brow, little droplets in the curling hair and his eyebrows. He said, softly, "Yeah, you do."

She yanked the quilt from her knees, climbed out of her window seat and went down the stairs. She paced, stumbling, all through the house. She ended up in the garage, looking at her boxes, telling herself to stop listening to him. She had to be practical. Some of the boxes were so dirty the labels were hard to read. She'd lived without whatever was in them for months. Maybe there wasn't anything there that she and Greg would need.

When Tod came out to the garage, she was sifting through a box of Greg's sheet music. "Some of these things we'll take with us. I ought to determine what we'll need before Chub gets here, in the morning, though."

He leaned in the doorway, swirling the ice in his drink. "And I take it you don't give a shit if your baby goes to Huntsville? Like I said, he's got to look pretty juicy to the home boys."

"I'm sorry," Cathy interrupted him. She looked around, her lips pursed, trying to think where her suitcases might be. If he wouldn't leave her alone, she might get down a suitcase. Start to pack. She might call a cab. Greg's suitcases had to be on top of one of the shelves, but hers didn't seem to be anywhere in sight. "Did we put my cases on the rafters out here or in the downstairs hall closet?" she said, trying to remember.

"You listening?" He moved toward her. "No, you're not. Don't say one more fucking word. You want to get out, go ahead. Walk. Either walk or get back upstairs, or goddam it, you're gonna get hurt." He loomed in front of her, his fists clenched, the muscles knotted along his jaw. He grabbed her shoulders and shook her hard, until she could break away. She shoved at him. He spun into the edge of the gray metal shelves along the wall behind him. The shelves were full of jangling metal boxes and tools. He righted himself, rubbing his head, moved his feet, jiggling, prancing in place, his breath whistling. The more he did that, the more he snorted those furious snorts and jiggled in front of her, the more calm Cathy felt, dizzy, and strange. Strangely calm. How very peculiar he sounded, this boozy, fuming, little person, with his bull doggy bloodshot eyes.

"I'm so sorry," she said. When she decided not to watch him anymore, she knocked his hands from her arms and turned to walk away.

The floor slammed against her face and he was on her back, clawing at her dress, his fingers caught in her hair. He grunted and panted, surprisingly heavy, a great weight all along her. Cathy writhed and shoved, bright flecks dancing in front of her eyes, the concrete swimming beneath her. She heard herself panting, scrabbling. She had to make him know he was hurting her. "My wrists," she cried, "my hair," caught, bound around and held down against the cold rough surface of the floor.

Tod gasped and let go. He tried, clumsily, to help her get to her feet, but Cathy pulled herself up, her mouth filling with the salty taste of blood. He drew away, panting. "Ah, baby," he said, his breath whistling, "what is this? What are we doing?"

Cathy's legs buckled. She sat down and pushed herself up. She drew her legs under her, got to her feet, went wobbling into the house. She started up the stairs, changed her mind, went to the kitchen to get a cloth to hold beneath the faucet. She had to break ice cubes out of a tray to make the cloth cold.

She could hear Tod walking around upstairs as she went out the front door, the cloth cold against her face, the ground tilting and righting itself. She was a block away, standing beneath a streetlight when a passing car slowed, and drew up alongside her. A woman rolled down a window. "Do you need help?" Someone in the car said, "She doesn't need help."

Cathy told the departing car that she was fine, thank you. She turned to go home and sat down on the sidewalk, thinking, I don't have my purse.

She walked back to the house, telling herself that Tod ought to be finished with all that blubbering and rolling around. He might be drunkenly asleep. Snoring.

There was blood in the kitchen sink. She wrung out the cloth, rinsed the blood out of the sink, got out a clean cloth and went to the refrigerator to get out a tray of ice cubes.

A note slid from under the smiley faced magnet that had been on the freezer door of the refrigerator. She knelt on the cracked linoleum and picked up the note. It was printed with a purple crayon. Cathy made herself focus on the scrawled purple letters. "Out of gin."

She giggled. When the giggle began to catch and slide into a whimper, she leaned against the refrigerator, cooling her brow, telling herself to snap out of it, to think. Tod hadn't been able to find another bottle of gin. They had run out. He had gone somewhere to buy some more. Of course.

*****

34

When a car pulled up out in front, Cathy thought, for a brief, delirious couple of seconds, that it might be the car that had stopped out in the street when she was leaning against a streetlight, frantically wondering what to do. She went to the door and opened it as Greg was coming up the walk, shouting a merry farewell over his shoulder to Shep, in a noisy jalopy. She batted back tears of relief.

Greg hugged her and drew back, saying, "What's with the cloth and ice? You got a toothache?"

He seemed determined to behave as though walking into the house at two a.m. after all he'd put her through, was a perfectly normal way to behave. Cathy didn't want to take the icy cloth away from her face. Her chin and the place under her eye were starting to look as bad as they felt.

He went to the kitchen and came back, deliberately nonchalant, chewing on an apple. "When did you start watching TV with the sound off?"

"Don't talk with your mouth full," Cathy said. She took the cloth from her face and Greg stared, shocked. He came over and collapsed to one knee in front of her.

"Holy shit. What happened?"

"I fell," she said.

"Under a train? Let me look."

"Out in the garage. On the cement. It d-d-doesn't matter."

"I'm going to kill that little bastard."

"Tod didn't do it. I fell. We both did," Cathy said, wearily. "Greg, we have to g-g-get out of here."

"No shize, Sherlock." Greg got up and dropped down beside her on the sofa. "Why don't I just kill him?"

Cathy could hear Dixie's nasal voice. A small hysterical laugh bubbled in her throat. The cloth had gotten warm. When she got up to refill it, Greg followed her into the kitchen and edged her away from the sink saying, "Here, let me do that. You're getting ice on the man's floor."

"Tomorrow," Cathy said. "We're g-g-going t-t-to go. To Chub's. I have to think straight." Certainly she didn't feel up to confronting Greg about Tod's accusations about him.

"You go on up to bed," Greg said. "I'm thinking straight."

"No. You're not."

Greg walked back into the living room and collapsed into the recliner. "Okay, so I don't kill him. I can't. I promised these guys I'd pay them out of my pay, every week and I'm supposed to be making deliveries for the lab. The man is my boss. Like he's all the time saying, I got my ducks in a row." He looked away. Twiddled with the lamp. "You go on to Chub's. I'll be okay here. For a while. What happened, anyway? I mean, you really have to get out but maybe he'll keep me on? I'm working for the man. I know the route now and...and like that."

"You can't be working for him," Cathy said. "There are other jobs." She had to tell him, then, about Dixie, about the man in the telephone booth, about how dangerous Tod was, how he'd been in prison. It all came out at once, all while she kept uneasily wondering if Tod might walk in on them. "So we can't stay. We can sleep here tonight, maybe, but that's it."

"Yeah," Greg bit his lip. "But I have to earn some dough, Mom, and I have what you might call a pretty good reason to stay with the lab."

"How much do you owe?" she asked and, when he wouldn't answer, she burst out, "It all started with some damned marijuana, d-didn't it? Listen to me. We'll face it. We'll figure out some way to pay it back."

"It's more like I owe the company, in a way." She could hardly hear him. "Okay, you want us to go now? You think your car can make it to Houston?" He sounded croaky with sarcasm and a kind of despairing bravado. "Or haven't you thought this thing all the way through?"

"We have to go," she said, wondering what had happened to the Jeep..

"Don't, Mom," Greg said. "We'll think of something." He got to his feet. He brought his shoulders up and let them drop; held a hand out toward her and let it drop. "You're not stuck. I am. Thing is, I sort of borrowed some money. The company's. To make a payment. These guys I owe —I've got to pay off some guys." He looked away, rubbing his hands, scrubbing at his scalp. "It's not that much. A couple thousand. A little less than that. Enough, though, I guess, huh?" He dashed tears from his eyes.

"Go to bed," Cathy said. "Let me think."

"No. You go on up. I've got to talk to the man."

"Oh, please," Cathy said. "He won't be in any condition to talk."

"Fine with me," Greg said. He slid down to stretch out on the carpet and closed his eyes. "Shep's in a lot deeper than I am." He grimaced and yawned hugely, his jaws cracking, and fell silent for so long that she thought he might be asleep but then he said, "I've got to pay 'em." He rolled over talking, the words muffled until he rolled face up and peered at the ceiling. "You wouldn't believe the mentality. It's like they get their jollies fooling around with people like us. They're all the time bored. I don't know, I guess I figured old Tod would have to be easier to deal with as far as the money goes." He yawned again. "Once, when we first got into this, Shep said, 'Man, this would just about kill our moms.'" His voice broke. "That's how you look. Half-killed. How'm I supposed to go to sleep?"

Cathy slid down to sit on the floor next to him. She wanted to hold him, just get as much of him as she could gather to her, to hold close. That was all she could think of to do. She was beyond thinking of any way to really help either of them. Her mind ran up and down and around, up and around and back and down again.

Caught. We're caught. Caught, she thought. He can make us stay with him for as long as he wants to. In this house. This house that I want, she thought, dully, touching the smooth patterned bits of wood inlaid in the floor beneath her hand, gazing around at the wainscoting, dark in the glow of the lamplight, the jeweled rubies and indigos and greens of the fanlight over the door, spangled in the pale light from the street light out in front.

One day he won't come home, she thought. One of them will catch up with him. He's caught, too. Trapped. Trapped and sliding around, clawing at anything that comes near.

They didn't hear the car in the drive. When the garage door lifted with its faint buzzing hum and rattled back down again, Greg broke free of her and went into the downstairs bathroom to wash his face. The garage door thumped shut. She could hear Tod's car thrumming away out there for what felt like a very long time. It was several long minutes, before he came in to lounge in the doorway to the kitchen and look at her, wobbly-headed. "You still up?" He said, thick-tongued with derision.

Greg came into the living room. "She's been putting ice on her face. What's the story on that?"

Tod tried to smile through a confused frown. He lifted his chin and gazed at Greg. "Why? You want to put some ice on your cheek too?"

Greg's mouth twisted. "That what you've got in mind?" He started to move toward Tod.

Cathy scrambled up and got between them. "If anything more happens I'm calling nine-one-one," she said.

"Go right ahead," Tod said, backing off. He lifted his chin and stared all around. "You really want the cops coming around here, Mama?" He didn't wait for a reply. He lurched into the wall of the hall and slid along it, shambling and mumbling. "Wanna see your boy in cuffs? Me, I got to grab a little shuteye. Got to get up in a couple or three hours. Blue water comin' in at the jetties. Gonna meet Cecil. My partner wants to go catch some speckled trout."

"Drunk as a bastard," Greg said, under his breath.

Tod called out from the stairs, "You want to come along and get some trout or you gonna sit around here whining to your mama for the rest of the night?"

Cathy crossed the room in three long strides and stood close to Greg. She put her fingers over his mouth. "Don't." When Greg backed away from her, she followed, whispering fiercely, "Be still. Let him go."

Tod bumbled around upstairs, bumping into things. When it sounded as though he might be coming back down the stairs, she grabbed Greg's arm and shook him. "If you'll just get out of here, he'll leave. Don't stand around and pick a fight. Go. I mean it."

"Leave you alone with that mean little prick? No way." Greg looked like he might start up the stairs.

"Oh, please." Cathy was so tired she couldn't breathe right. The living room swam and righted itself. "I'm begging you. Just go. Let Cecil handle him—"

"But what if he—"

"He won't. He's going out in a boat with Cecil. You heard him."

How could Greg be so maddeningly slow? The big kid looked down at her, slightly off balance, shifting from foot to foot, his face working.

"Get out of this room," Cathy hissed. "Now." She gave him a shove, trying to steer him to the kitchen stairway but he turned and went the other way, toward the front door.

Tod must not have heard the door close. He was sitting on the bed with an unfocused smile. When Cathy came into the bedroom, he went into the bathroom, urinated noisily and came back to sprawl, fully dressed, on the bed. "Got to grab some shuteye." He sat up, pulled off a shoe, squinted at it, put it down beside him on the coverlet, fell over on top of it, burrowed into the bedclothes and began gasping great rasping snores.

Cathy sat beside him, watching and listening, telling herself to be calm. It was important not to let herself look at his gaping mouth or his eyes that might open if he felt her staring. She didn't let herself look at his face at all. What she had to do was keep her mind still, keep her entire self as placid as the clean rippled sand at the bottom of a lake.

It took a very long time to get his foot worked back into his shoe. She tied both his shoes. She hoisted him up, slowly working her right shoulder around under his arm so they could stand. He leaned, muttering. She half lifted him, coaxing and cajoling, her heart squeezing each time he seemed to jerk awake, each time the snores stopped, forcing herself to be still, to wait patiently until he relaxed. The gasps and exhalations got noisier as they lurched along. By the time they were at the bottom of the stairs, he was snoring so hard his whole body vibrated. She had to keep breathing, too, murmuring, soothing both of them with the lulling sing-songing croon that mothers have always known: "It's all right, my darling, it's going to be all right. Everything's going to be all right," over and over. "Blue water coming in," she crooned, "you and Cecil can get go catch some lovely big trout, oh, yes, you can. Yes, you can. But you've got to keep moving, don't want to make Cecil wait, don't want to make Cecil wait." She walked him, step by dragging step, through the living room, into the kitchen.

He sagged against her, a thin thread of drool shining on his chin.

Oh, don't look, she told herself and told him, again, of the lovely big fish waiting to be caught in the clear blue water and of how everything would be all right and of how Cecil would be waiting—waiting—

—all the long way through the kitchen to the steep small steps that led to the garage. He seemed to hear her, to rouse for a minute, when they stepped on the cool concrete floor of the garage. He gasped and shook free of her, glared around, blinking, swinging in a clumsy circle. "What?" he demanded and she said, soothingly, not looking at him, "It's all right. We're going to go out get into the car now," the hair on the back of her neck prickling beneath his breath, her voice calm. "Here we go."

"Car?" But he was agreeing. He staggered, sliding against her, letting her help him fall forward the rest of the way out into the garage all the way up to the door of the Cadillac. He didn't want help with the door. He fumbled at it, cursing, grumbling protests. For a wild moment she thought it might be locked. It wasn't. He got it open and fell in.

She waited while he righted himself and collapsed behind the wheel and began snoring again, snorting and blowing as she opened the car door on the other side and eased herself in. She slid over next to him. "Let's start the car," Cathy said, gently. "Honey, love, let's start the car." When he didn't react, she realized he must have the key in his pocket. She reached across him and dug into his pocket. The key wasn't in any of his pockets.

She went back into the house. She found the key right where she knew it would be: in the copper bowl on the nightstand, right where he always dumped it, along with the change in his pocket, each night, his final act as he climbed into bed. When she came back down to the garage, his head had fallen forward against the wheel.

Good, Cathy thought. Hide your face.

She slid back in to the car. Found a Kleenex down next to the seat to wrap around the key. Got the key into the ignition. Turned it. And, when the engine turned over at once and hummed, she wadded up the tissue, dropped it back alongside the seat and got back out of the car.

She closed the garage door and walked into the house.

Stood listening to the car thrum in the garage.

She could hear the thrumming from the kitchen, where she stood for a long while with her head back, her hands spread along the wall, regaining her balance. After a while, she slid to the scabby linoleum next to the refrigerator. It was damp, in places, from the ice she'd dropped. She ought to get up and get out more ice. Such an ugly floor, she thought, shivering. We'll have to do something about this floor, right away.

She didn't get up to get out more ice for a long time. She sat on the torn linoleum, her hands covering her ears, too frightened to listen to the thrumming in the garage; too frightened to think, until she realized she was hurting her hand, squeezing it against her ring.

Look at your ring, she thought, you love your ring. She gazed at her emerald, turning it so it could catch the light, whispering about how pretty it looked, flaming green, the sharp little diamonds alongside the big stone so bright they brought tears to her eyes. She held her hand up to look at it, to go *into* it, as she crooned to herself, "There, there, now then, it's going to be all right. Everything's going to be all right, there, there."

She must not let herself hear an insistent cold tired whisper that kept demanding to know how long it would take.

*****

35

The body looked pink.

Greg couldn't see much from the doorway, just a glimpse of Tod's cheek and brow and the fingers of a hand when it fell down and had to be picked up and tucked into the bag thing that they had, out there, that they slid the zipper shut on and loaded onto a gurney.

"He doesn't look very...dead," Greg said.

"Nope. That's the thing with carbon monoxide," the cop said. "That's what makes it so...hard. They look so healthy." He shook his head.

Maybe that's why Greg kept feeling as though Tod would have to be waking up any minute now, mad as hell at all the commotion.

The body was all bagged up, though, just like the ones on the six o'clock news. They slid Tod into the hearse, closed the two black doors and went wheeling down the drive.

The guys in the garage didn't leave right away. The atmosphere changed out there; quickened, got busier. The worried looking big cop who stayed in the house kept stifling nervous yawns, pinching at his moustache, walking around, glancing at Cathy's bruised face.

Greg asked the cop if he wanted a Coke and, when he nodded, he went into the kitchen and popped open three Cokes. As he got the coasters out, he noticed an ashtray with a couple of cigar butts on the drain board of the sink. He dumped out the ashtray and brought the cop a Coke.

A car door slammed out in front. Somebody laughed. Don't laugh, Greg thought. Don't stand around laughing. Leave. Please. Because he had to do something about Cathy, right away. Her face looked like it had to be hurting like hell. It was swollen so tight the cartilage showed through the skin at the top of her nose. Her chin looked the way Greg's chin looked the time he hit a rock on his skateboard and rode all the way down that concrete ramp at the end of the seawall on one elbow and his chin.

He figured she needed to get to a doctor. Did doctors make house calls for somebody left behind after somebody died? Pat's a doctor. He ought to know. Maybe he ought to call Patrick and Chub, get them over.

He'd have to start concentrating. It didn't look like Cathy could.

He might even tell Pat and Chub about that damn money. How much did the bookkeeper and the accountant and the rest of them know about the money? Maybe he could talk the accountant into letting him have a little more time. Straighten things out.

Maybe Tod hadn't even told any of them about it.

Oh, if he let himself think that, that he could be out from under all that, God, jeez, Greg was afraid he might sink to his knees and start gibbering and bawling with relief.

Mom looked terrible.

Greg walked back out to the kitchen. The kitchen door was partly open. He could see one of the men who must be a detective out there, standing next to the Cadillac, silhouetted against the light. The guy had this sharp nose that made him look, his profile, like that hatchet-faced guy always had a hat on, in the funny papers. The detective in the comics. Dick Tracy. Except this detective didn't have the hat. He wasn't talking or moving, just standing there, like he was thinking, looking at the car, looking around the garage.

Greg wondered what that would be like, to be a detective in some garage looking at some body.

When he came back into the living room, Cathy wasn't on the sofa. He waited a couple of minutes before he tapped on the door of the downstairs bathroom. She wasn't in there. He started to get worried. Jeez, could she have made it all the way up the stairs, as wobbly as she looked?

He was on his way to the stairs when the noise started. It sounded like somebody using a skill saw somewhere out in back. No. It had to be inside, in the house somewhere. Upstairs? A hell of a noise. A metallic shriek. Man. Greg ran. The noise trembled, stopped, started up again. Upstairs.

The cop came up behind him fast as Greg passed the landing and he could hear more steps behind the cop, all of them running. They took the last of the stairs together, Greg falling up, banging his knees, clawing himself to his feet, taking a bunch of steps at a time, careening into the edge of his mom's bedroom doorway, the cop getting in his way, both of them trying to get into the bathroom.

The detective caught up, breathing hard. Cathy was hunched over, screaming, every breath ending in a gasp so she could scream again, cowering away from the tiled shelf in front of her. She was staring at a glass of water with some teeth in it. A gold band clamped around porcelain teeth.

Greg tried to get an arm around her to hold her up and lead her out of there, away from the realization dawning on the big cop's face and the other guy's face, the detective's, as he crowded in with them because, oh, God, the sharp-faced, sharp-eyed detective was coming in to stand there looking down at his screaming mother, gaping at the glass of water with Tod's partial plate in it, twinkling, reflected in the bathroom mirror.

When Cathy ran out of screams and sank down against him, Greg heard the man, low, like talking to himself, in the sudden silence. "Mr. Benjamin wasn't going anywhere, was he? Unless he didn't care whether he had his smile in right."

Greg said exactly the wrong thing then. "That's the only thing he did give a damn about," he said. "The little bastard."

The detective nodded.

That's all Greg could get out before he sank to the floor to sit holding his mother, both of them crying, swaying and crying and hanging on to each other, while the detective and the cop stood there glancing at each other and looking away, everybody sick as hell.

*****